Acclaim for Isla Dewar:

'Dewar writes with enjoyably sharp humour about the tribulations of family life, making some thoughtful points about what growing up means along the way'
Times Metro

'Crackling with wit, and shot through with sharp observations'
Woman & Home

'Dewar's gift is to pull you into the minutiae of her people's lives . . . few writers are so good at making the reader empathise'
Scotland on Sunday

'Breathless . . . appealingly spirited . . . sparkiness, freshness and verve'
Mail on Sunday

'Observant and needle-sharp . . . entertainment with energy and attack'
The Times

'Both explosively funny and chokingly poignant . . . [Dewar] makes the reader care about the eventual fate of every one of her characters'
Scotland on Sunday

'Remarkable . . . uplifting, sharp and funny'
Edinburgh Evening News

'Enchanting'
Options

'Frank, funny writing'
Big Issue in Scotland

'Acute observations . . . A wonderfully strong female character'
Tom Shields, *Herald*

Two Kinds
of
Wonderful

Isla Dewar

review

First published in 2000
by HEADLINE BOOK PUBLISHING

First published in paperback in 2001
by HEADLINE BOOK PUBLISHNG

A REVIEW paperback

10 9 8 7 6 5 4 3 2 1

ISBN 0 7472 6157 1

Printed and bound in Great Britain by
Clays Ltd, St Ives plc.

HEADLINE BOOK PUBLISHING
A division of Hodder Headline
338 Euston Road
London NW1 3BH

www.reviewbooks.co.uk
www.hodderheadline.com

For Sandra

CHAPTER ONE

On Tuesday Nan phoned Roz with details of her funeral.

'I've been to the undertaker's. Got a coffin. Plain pine. I don't know. Undertakers.' She breathed out frustration. She hated not getting what she wanted. 'Dour lot. Why can't they do a nice box in pink? Or red? Stripes, maybe. Or tartan? Such a price for a boring lump of wood you're going to burn anyway.'

Not really registering what she was hearing, Roz pointed out that such coffins *were* available these days.

'Where?' asked Nan, affronted. 'Not at my undertaker's. Anyway, I've chose my songs. I want a bit of Bob Marley. None of your "Oh Perfect Love". That stuff. I want a good tune. A bit of toe-tapping.'

Roz pulled the receiver from her ear, considered it. She didn't like the sound of this. But, Nan. You never knew what Nan was going to come up with next. A few weeks ago she'd spent a bit of time trying to get on to *Who Wants To Be a Millionaire*? But this? This time she'd gone too far. 'For God's sake, Nan. There's no need for all that. You're not going to die. Not for ages and ages. You've got years left in you.'

'Rubbish,' said Nan. 'I'm old.'

The times Nan had said that. For the past ten years, she'd phoned Roz, in London, Crouch End, at least twice weekly from her house in a long grey Edinburgh terrace. Every time she'd remarked on her great age. Roz, then, couldn't count the times Nan had said, 'I'm old.' This time it was different. For the first time, Roz realised, Nan hadn't been telling her about her ancientness. She'd been telling herself. Reminding herself. Coming to terms with it.

'I'm old,' Nan repeated firmly. 'Old. That's what happens. It sneaks up on you – age. You get born, you live, you do the things you do. Then you snuff it. I've done the things I've done. Death's the next thing. It's time to get things sorted. I've not got long.'

'You're not going to die,' Roz repeated desperately. And realised she wasn't telling Nan. Comforting Nan. She was telling herself. Reassuring herself. Nan couldn't die. Roz needed her. Nan was her lifeline. Her hope. The only one who understood the terrible thing she'd done. The only person from that distant life in Edinburgh who kept regularly in touch.

She stood by the window. Four floors up, a stiff climb, especially if she'd been to Sainsbury's and had a week's supply of pasta, sauces, bread and wine, but worth it. Though only from the front. She could see for miles over rooftops, spires and tower blocks. The docks, and, on a clear day, if she squinted, St Paul's.

The back was close-packed buildings, windows staring into windows, scrubby, tiny squirrel-infested yards. She squinted now. It took her mind off this conversation. The uncomfortable weirdness of discussing a funeral with the soon-to-be-deceased.

Chats with Nan were usually about what was on television. Or what was happening with the family. Or what some of her equally aged cronies were up to. Or the garden. Or the birds she fed. Not this.

'Am too going to die,' said Nan. 'I get funny turns. Dizzy. My left arm goes numb. It's my heart. It's fed up beating. Been beating day in day out for eighty-odd years. It's had enough.'

'Have you been to a doctor?' Roz asked, trying to sound as if this would stop the approaching heartache. Didn't succeed.

'Course. I watched him listen to my chest. He's young. Got no control of his face. "You're fine," he said. "You're a goner," his face said.'

Roz took a breath. No.

Nan was the only one who'd stood by her when she'd done the thing – become a wanton and disgraceful woman.

'So it's time to get things fixed,' said Nan. 'Now, I've ordered a car for the family. Black Merc. I wanted red but they only have

2

black at the undertaker's. Actually, I want a coach with black horses with plumes and a jazz band leading the way. You'd think they'd have something like that. There's not a wide selection for the dead. I don't like black. Gloomy. You'll have to make your own way there. Don't be late. You're late for everything. I've baked a nice fruit cake for after.'

Roz sobbed.

'Stop that,' Nan snapped. 'I don't want any boring funeral food. Egg and cress sandwiches, or tuna. Stuff you'd put in your man's lunchbox. I want fancy. Smoked salmon. I've bought in a case of that Australian Chardonnay they talk about on telly. Recommended. Might get in some champagne. I want a good do. You only die once. Oh, and I've left money for my gas and electricity in the biscuit tin in the kitchen cupboard.'

Roz could see Nan sitting in her pink velvet chair, fat ankles crossed on the matching footstool in front of her. Across the room the huge-screened telly would be beaming, sound down. Apart from her family, that television was now the core of Nan's life. She spent her days watching soaps, cookery and wildlife programmes and quizzes. Her conversations were littered with quick things to do with leftover mushrooms and a red pepper, the nomadic life of the male brown bear, and the backstabbing sexual chicaneries of the inhabitants of daytime soaps nobody who worked the nine-to-five had ever heard of, and judged, therefore, when they heard her chat about them, that they must be actual acquaintances of Nan. They decided she must have a set of very colourful friends.

'Also,' said Nan, 'I want you to scatter my ashes. On Mull. Had some lovely times there. Lovely, lovely times.'

'I didn't know you'd been to Mull.'

'There's lots about me you don't know. Mull's one of them. And that's where I want to spent my eternity. You can pick my ashes up after the funeral, and take them to Calgary Bay sometime after when it suits. It's a bit of a trek. The ferry and that. Calgary Bay's way the other side. The Atlantic. I want to float away on the Atlantic with whales singing in the distance and birds crying overhead. And we can have a last chat about what's been going on since I passed away. I expect you'll be needing that.'

'Nan,' Roz sang out her protest, 'I hate this. Stop talking like this. I'm not going to chat to your ashes. I prefer the chats we have now. When you're here. It's easier.'

'Right enough. But think on. When I'm dead, I'll not be answering you back. You can say what you like.'

Roz doubted she'd dare. Even then. Oh God, no, she thought. You can't die. Not you. Only you were there for me. I need you. Without you I'll be alone with my family. Without you I'll look at them and see myself through their eyes – a heartless, reckless loose woman. Which is what I am.

'But Nan,' she whined, 'I don't want to face everybody. Not on my own. Not all of them at the same time. You know what they think of me.'

'Quite right too,' said Nan. 'You're a wicked woman. It'll all have to be properly faced up to one day. These children of yours are messes. Both of them. Jamie. Well, Jamie. He's not so bad. But God knows what's going on in that head of his. And Zoe. Zoe's headed for no good. Then there's the boy. Sucks his thumb, stares, never speaks. Wets the bed. Mind you, with Zoe for a mother, what would you expect? She's worse than you. And that's saying something. I won't be around to sort things out. Make your peace. You won't be happy else.'

'I can't do anything about Toby. He's Zoe's problem. Nothing to do with me. I doubt she'd let me near him.'

'That's for you to sort out.'

'I can't.'

'You can and you will. You owe them.'

Those were her last words to Roz. On Thursday, Matthew, Roz's ex, father of Zoe and Jamie, phoned. 'Nan's dead,' he said, voice flat. No emotion. Well, none for Roz anyway. He hadn't forgiven her. Never would. 'I just thought you might like to know.'

'Of course I'd like to know. I loved Nan.'

'Are you coming to the funeral?'

'Yes. She wanted me to come. She wants me to scatter her ashes on Mull.'

'Mull? She's never been to Mull.'

'She said she has. She said she had lovely, lovely times there.'

'When?'

'I don't know. I'm just telling you what she told me.'

'Right.' Still no emotion. 'Monday, half ten at Warriston. See you there. There's drinks after at the house. If you want to come.'

She didn't. She didn't ever want to go to that Edinburgh bungalow again. Not since she'd walked out of it ten years ago, leaving Matthew, Jamie and Zoe. Just like that, she'd gone. No warning. She'd left a scant little note. *I've gone. I'm sorry. I'll be in London. I'll phone. Love Roz.* Ten words, excluding the *Love Roz* at the end, that had taken four hours to write. Four hours and the sixteen years she'd been married. They'd taken a while to come, those words.

Monday was hell. Roz knew it would be. Up before five. A bath of sorts since the water was barely tepid, and there was only a cracked sliver of soap, too small to work up a proper lather. The towels were damp. Then there was clothes. Nothing clean except her black crêpe pants and plum-coloured silk shirt. Perhaps it was a bit gaudy to wear to a funeral. Still, Nan wouldn't want funereal clothes. Quite right, too.

She found a cleanish cup in the sink, buried beneath the dirty dishes and the frying pan. Made tea. Found a high-heeled boot, looked hopelessly about for the other. Under the bed? It was there along with several pairs of tights, knickers and a tie. Whose? No matter, somebody's. She threw it back to rest for ever in the dust and debris. Then lay a moment, face flat to the floor, looking at the silhouetted shapes and mouldering things that had found their way to this darkened place below the mattress, and scolded herself. I'm too old to live like this. Alone. Unloved. A mess. And messy. She wallowed in a moment's gloom. Thought that if anyone were to look into her soul, something very like this heap of rubbish under the bed was what they'd see. Dark, fathomless shapes, dust, looming shaded shadows of neglected dreams, forgotten thoughts, memories and people she'd let go. Her children, for example.

An hour and a half on the tube, another fretful hour in the airport getting up from her seat every ten minutes or so to check her flight number and departure time on the screen. And, at last, she was ten miles high. Up there with the rising sun. On such a day it was the place to be. Moving through a paintbrush sky. Watching colours of daybreak shift across the clouds below, the sun lipping the horizon. Dazzling. It almost made Roz forget the dread ahead. Forehead on the window she sang, 'The sun has got his hat on.' How gross. Of all the songs about the sun, why did that one slide into her head?

Also, noting the way the suited man next to her squirmed stiffly in his seat, twisting away from her, rustling his sheaves of business papers, she realised she must have sung it out loud. Poor bloke. It was bad enough to be next to the nutter on the bus; at least then you could get off. But the nutter on the plane? He was stuck with her all the way to Edinburgh.

She could hear food trolleys trundling down the aisle. Smell the dubious airline breakfast. Watched the suit wave it away, a slight but assertive flap of the hand. Thought to do that, too. Wanted to be poised, sophisticated. But she knew she wouldn't. Well, it was always something to do – eat. Then again, refusing anything didn't seem to be something she ever did. 'No' didn't come easily to her lips.

So she took the tray. Ate the cornflakes. Then opened with dismay the lid on the funny moulded omelette thing and toyed with it, watching, from the isolation of her grief, the day beyond the window flourish from pale dawn into full-blown morning. And thought about Nan.

Was she alone when it happened? Was she afraid? No, not Nan. Nothing frightened her, especially not death. Roz's eyes filled with tears. She thought of Nan alone at home on her chair, feet up on the footstool, thick tights wrinkled at the ankles, watching an afternoon cooking programme when death seized her. Did she pop off just as some celebrity chef was flamboyantly tossing onions and garlic in a pan? Some tears, rebel tears, escaped down Roz's cheeks. She slipped her cuff over her hand, wiped her cheeks. The

6

suit turned, stared at her. She sniffed, glared back. Don't mess with me, I'm the nutter on the plane.

How dare Nan do this to her? How dare she die? Stupid woman. Lovely, comfortable, huge-hearted Nan, who had hardly turned a hair when Roz walked out on her family.

'I've gone, Nan,' Roz had phoned to say.

'I know that. Everyone's talking about you. You're a scandal. A shameful woman. A hussy.'

'Probably,' said Roz. 'Though I'm not a hussy. I didn't go with other men.'

'According to the rumour which is gathering speed, you did.'

'Well I didn't. I wouldn't.'

'Wouldn't you? Perhaps you'd still be here if you had found a little something on the side to cheer you up. Lots of people do.'

'I'm in London.'

'I know. Matthew told me.'

'I'd had enough. I just saw my life going on and on. Getting more and more mundane. Nothing happening. Jamie's got his life. He's fifteen, off to university in a couple of years. And Zoe hardly speaks to me. Especially since I lost my job. I've no money. Nothing. I don't feel like a person any more. Just a mum and a wife.'

'Nothing wrong with that.'

'Maybe not in your day. But now things are different.'

'Huh. You think women didn't get bored in my day? You think they didn't feel unwanted? Or useless? We just sorted things out in our own way.'

'What way?'

'Never you mind. Too late for any of that now.'

'Well. It was Matthew. I know he's your son, but . . .'

'But?' said Nan.

'But . . . you know . . . he's obsessive. And silent with it. He pulls all the plugs out at night. And sits in front of the telly with his arms folded. Never a word. And he counts. He counts, Nan. And he has these rages. Intense rages. He just stands glowing fury. I used to think he'd hit me. But he never did. Perhaps it'd have been better if he had. We'd have spoken about what was bothering him. And he might've stopped counting things.'

'What things?'

'The steps he takes from the front door to the kitchen. The number of times he wipes a fork dry. The buttons of his shirt as he does them up in the morning. Then again as he undoes them at night. As if there'd be more buttons at eleven o'clock than there were at half seven. I dunno. He just counts. It was driving me crazy.'

'I know,' said Nan. 'He's always been on the fussy side. But it's gone haywire. Maybe it's the strain.'

'What strain? He's an accountant. Not a very senior one. Hardly seems a strain to me.'

'Maybe it's the sums. Don't ask me. His father was the same.'

'It's not just that.' Roz did a small, frustrated knee-bend. 'It's me. It's my life. It was passing me by as I lived in that silent, immaculate house with clocks ticking and a man who counts. All the bloody time.' Roz gulped. Drew a breath. 'What do you think of me?' she asked, dreading the reply.

'Well, on the one hand I don't blame you. There've been times when I could happily have done what you've done. You're brave. Then again, I think you're daft. And more than a bit selfish.'

'I could agree with that.' Roz was always willing to indulge in a spot of self-deprecation.

'You'll have to make your peace one day,' Nan said.

'I know. I'm willing. But Matthew will never forgive me. Jamie will. He's like that. But Zoe. She'll hate me for ever.'

'Nonsense,' said Nan. 'You're her mother. A disgraceful, shameful, brazen bitch. But Mum nonetheless.'

Talks with Nan were always like that. A scolding, but a gentle one. Nan could say the truest, most hurtful things, mildly. People seemed to take her tickings-off to heart, and love her for them. She cared. Roz phoned her every week, and knew what was coming – a gentle, comforting, knowing rebuke. It eased the guilt. It saved her life.

'We are coming in to land at Edinburgh,' the pilot said, his voice cracking in Roz's popping ears. She looked out the window. Edinburgh, Fife beyond. The Forth. They swept low over the bridges and earth came looming up. They landed.

Quarter past nine. Roz wandered Princes Street. She went into Virgin, clicked through the CDs. Bought The Verve, though she thought herself too old for the young faces on the cover, and a Billie Holiday collection, though she already had all the songs on other CDs.

She looked at her watch. Nine thirty. What time had Matthew said? Ten? Half past? She couldn't remember. Ten, he'd said ten. She'd half an hour to get there. She took the bus. She was late. Felt sweaty with panic. She ran from the bus stop, heels clattering on the pavement, handbag banging against her thigh, till, reflected in a shop window, she caught a glimpse of a scurrying creature, hair on end, jacket flapping, face white and riven with panic. A fleeting moment of astonished thinking, who is that absurd creature? As the surprised absurd creature stared back at her, she realised it was herself. This won't do, she thought. So she sat in the crematorium grounds considering the graves, flowers and farewell messages, the late October wind pushing against her cheeks. She composed herself. 'Right,' she said. 'Go in. Do it. Do it.'

She was late. But then wasn't she always late for everything? The service was under way. She slipped into the back row. Looked round. Didn't recognise anyone.

A tearful, raddled middle-aged woman got up. 'We've come today to celebrate the life of Roberta Wise.' She sniffed. Wiped an unashamed tear from her watery eye. 'She was adored by everyone. And, oh God, we'll miss her,' she choked. There were nods and murmurs of agreement from the gathering.

Roz reddened. Who the hell was Roberta Wise? Jesus, no. Wrong funeral. My stupid life, she cursed.

As funerals went, Nan's was mundane and predictable compared to Roberta Wise's. Now that had been a stonker. Someone read the last passage from *Hiawatha*. Everyone cried. It was a Kleenex-fest. As the coffin, behind a dark blue velvet screen, lowered gently to the valley below – fleeting sounds of an inferno – someone started to sing 'Knockin' On Heaven's Door', a slow, mournful, spontaneous chant. Others joined in. Those who did not know the lyrics hummed, swayed in rhythm. A musical grieving filled the room. Even Roz cried, and she hadn't known the woman. Roberta Wise, loved in life, adored in death. Roz envied her.

Nan's parting was not so gloriously celebrated. Matthew made a mumbling dedication to his mother. A kindly woman, beloved grandmother of Jamie and Zoe, great-grandmother of Toby. The end of a generation. Nothing about Nan's knowing scoldings, her splendid brewings of tea, her knowledge of the mating habits of wildebeest, the tasty, swift, nutritious recipes that, of course, she never actually cooked, or the conversations cluttered with the doings of the Colbys or the convoluted plots of *Murder She Wrote*. Nothing about the real Nan. They sang the twenty-third psalm. Badly. There was no Bob Marley. Roz seethed. She would have words with Matthew later.

Was this the beginning of it? Of what Nan had told her to do? Sort out her family. They prayed with no conviction. Nan wouldn't have liked it, but would have accepted it as inevitable. What else would boring Matthew come up with?

Roz watched her children. Jamie, twenty-five now, tall, slouching, dark curly hair. He wore black cargo pants. Sat, booted foot on opposite knee, elbow draped over the end of the pew. He yawned. Looked round. Saw her, and smiled sheepishly. She smiled back.

Next to him sat Zoe, a year younger than her brother, dark hair cropped, but such a face. All lips. It had known too much emotion, that face. It fell naturally into crying mode. A face made for weeping. Beautiful, though. Zoe was in black, head to toe. High-collared black silk shirt, tight straight black skirt that stopped mid-calf, black patent high heels. Very high heels. Face pale. But those lips were at full pout, and painted scarlet. That's my girl, thought Roz. She's been the same since she was two – never be dramatic when you can be overdramatic. Go for it, kid.

Zoe was with her partner, Will. Roz knew about him, but had

never seen him. He was tall, almost as handsome as Zoe, though less ostentatiously dressed. All the way down the aisle, he had kept his hand on her shoulder, leading their son, Toby, by the hand. The child was placed between them. Every now and then, during the service, he'd lean across and touch Zoe. An are-you-OK? comforting stroke. She'd turn to him, smile a pale, pained, upward turn of her mouth.

They were a striking couple. Gorgeous together. Roz remembered an article she'd read about good-looking people attracting other good-looking people. Wondered what that said about her, since her lover, Fred, was hardly a crowd-stopper. He was comfortable. Wore clothes for comfort, complained about underpants that didn't give him room to move freely. He'd stand in his bedroom flapping a pair of oversize scarlet boxers declaring that this was what a chap needed: 'Air. Breathing space for the important bits.'

His car, a twenty-year-old Citroën that spent more time at the garage than at his front door, was bought for comfort. Huge seats for sinking into and a blaster of a heater. He had a comfortable face. Warm, friendly, usually unshaven. She loved him best in his thick, chunky navy jersey. She could cuddle up to him. She scolded herself for considering him half man, half teddy bear. Did this mean she was at a time of life when she sought solace rather than euphoria? Perhaps. Perhaps. She found herself nodding in agreement with herself, smiling slightly. 'Hot-water-bottle man,' she said. The woman next to her turned, glowered. Roz cringed. What a thing to say at a funeral. She was doing it again – talking to herself. Out loud. The curse of those who lived alone.

The boy, Toby, had Zoe's looks. Lips. That slightly demented way of glaring out at the world. A mop of dark hair that badly needed cutting and clothes that seemed too large for his skinny little body. He spent the entire service, thumb in mouth, looking at his knees. Every now and then Zoe would turn to him, pull the thumb out of her son's mouth, place the damp little hand on the child's knee, where it would remain for a few seconds. As soon as Zoe looked away, the thumb slowly slipped back up, mouthwards.

The child's eyes would close as he drifted into sucking and staring. Such comfort. Roz wished it was acceptable behaviour for a forty-five-year-old errant mother.

Trooping out, Zoe cast a scathing glance at Roz. Jamie grinned, again. And Matthew ignored her. But as he passed, he placed a careful and solicitous hand on his new wife Claire's shoulder. She winced. Roz was sure she winced. Yes, she thought, she winced. It wasn't just me.

There was the usual post-funeral milling at the door. People shaking hands, offering sympathy, and discussing who was going in whose car back to Matthew's for drinks.

Roz travelled with Zoe and Will. She sat in the back with Toby, who sucked his thumb and looked out of the window, jiggling occasionally as some unwanted disquieting thought ran through his fragile little mind. From time to time he turned to stare at her, thumb still wedged down his throat. She looked back, smiled. He ignored the gesture. In the front Zoe and Will chatted about a party they were going to tonight. And who was going to be there. Their friends all sounded deranged, or at least they had deranged names. Weasel, Zak, Mac, Denny, Ziggy and Zu-Zu. Their mothers surely couldn't have given them those names. 'Ooh, my baby, my darling child. I'll call him Weasel.'

Will would have to collect the baby-sitter. 'Early,' said Zoe. 'I want to go to The Vincent first for a drink.'

From time to time Zoe turned in her seat to ask Roz how her flight had been, and what the weather was like in London. It was done stiffly, without interest. She had to let Roz know she wasn't speaking to her. And not actually speaking didn't quite do the trick. Speaking with indifference was so much more hostile.

Roz found Zoe's malice formidable. It wasn't the malice, exactly. It was the constancy of it. It was an icy flow that ran deep and steady through Zoe's life. She would turn to Roz with those heartbreak eyes of hers, and speak in that light, almost petulant voice, and no matter what she said, the bitterness would show. She would always hate Roz. But Roz would never be able to accurately place it, never be able to confront it. Never soothe it.

Stop it. Zoe was determined that the malice would remain between them for the rest of their lives. Roz found it terrifying.

As they drove through the Edinburgh suburbs, through the edges of Corstorphine, and turned into the street where once she'd lived, run away from, Roz's heart shuddered, seemed suddenly too large for her ribcage. Nothing had changed. Same trimmed hedges. Same weeping cherry trees, leaves turning autumnal. Same neat little front gates. Same painted front doors.

She couldn't do this. She thought to jump from the car and run, top speed, away. Jump on the first bus and never come back. But she didn't. Well, that was what was expected of her. And surprise was her best attack. She climbed from the car, gathered her handbag, and went in.

The smell got her. That family smell. She couldn't define it. It wasn't like other houses, other families. There was nothing welcoming about it. It lay, an undertow odour, moving insidiously beneath the scents of Sparkle spray polish, lavender room freshener and the suffocating blast from the electric fire. Roz let it roll round her nostrils. What was it? Damp? Fear? Boredom? Instant microwave meals for two? She didn't know.

There was a ripple when she entered the room. A shudder. People stopped talking, drinking, to turn and look. Their congregated faces seemed to shrink into disapproval and curiosity. Nobody smiled.

A group of elderly busty ladies in tweed skirts and twin sets burst into semi-hysterical hissed gossiping. Nan's cronies. Roz noted with rage the egg and cress sandwiches and lack of smoked salmon. Took a glass of Rosemount Chardonnay and decided she could not touch the fruit cake. Moist though it obviously was, it would, somehow, be like eating Nan. No, she would not touch the cake.

People milled round her. She spoke only to those who were on the edges of the in-crowd. Her family cast occasional derisory glances in her direction. Except Jamie, who smiled apologetically whenever he caught her looking at him. He was ashamed of what he thought of her. He was a man, unsure of his past, enraptured with his possible future. A dreamer. She'd met, slept with such types in her time away from home. She recognised him. Feared for him. He wanted everyone to love him. He needed a mum, and she was all he had.

Zoe came across the room to talk to her. Waltzed past the sofa with the huge red-on-beige swirls, little mincing steps over the mushroom-coloured carpet. 'So you came to pay your respects to Nan.' She drew on a Marlboro Light, hissed smoke in Roz's face.

'Yes, of course,' said Roz. 'So how are you?'

'Oh, doing away.' Small, overdramatic pause. 'As one must.'

'One absolutely must,' said Roz. 'What are you up to these days, anyway?'

'A spot of this. A lot of that.'

'What exactly does that mean?' Roz wanted to know.

'I work in a design shop in the West End. You know, knick-knacky things, throws sort of stuff. And I deal. Well, Will deals. I hang out and help.' Zoe waved at Will, who smiled – well, leered – at Roz. She leered back. He was lovely, though. Such hands. Long, slender. A woman, she thought, could ache for hands like that to touch her, stroke her. Then she was ashamed of herself. But when was she not? A woman of doubtful reputation getting wet over her daughter's lover. Stop it, she told herself. You've damaged these people enough as it is.

'For God's sake, Zoe, do you have to? You've got brains. You know what you're getting into. Don't be an arse,' she said.

'Of course I'm an arse,' Zoe said. 'Runs in the family.'

'Well, maybe. But you've out-arsed me. I never did anything that would land me in prison.'

'Chicken,' mocked Zoe.

'No. Just sane.' Roz walked past her daughter. 'I'll talk to you later. I've a bone to pick with your father.'

Zoe watched her go. And grinned. Gotcha, she thought. There was nothing more satisfying than shocking people. But shocking her mother, this woman who had so suddenly disappeared from her life, was such a kick. She wondered what other terrible lies she could tell Roz. Anything just to watch the slow-spreading disapproval cross her face. And the way she fought it, worked at not showing it. Anything, her mother would do anything, just to try and make some peace between them. She never could, though. Zoe was adamant about that.

Clutching her glass, Roz walked through the small, unfriendly horde. Matthew was alone in the kitchen. And Roz wanted a fight.

'How dare you,' she said, pulling the door shut behind her.

'What d'you mean?' he huffed. He was filling the kettle.

'You know what I mean. Nan. She wanted Bob Marley.'

'We couldn't have Bob Marley at a funeral. What would people think?'

'Nothing,' said Roz, trying to keep her voice low. 'They'd think nothing. Christ, what are you like? Your mother's dying wishes you deny in favour of what a bunch of nothing, boring people think. Of course you can have Bob Marley. They had Bob Dylan at the funeral before Nan's.'

'How do you know that?'

'I went. I made a mistake about the time.'

He turned on her. Mocking. 'Still a mess. Going to the wrong funeral.'

'Yes. Absolutely a mess. Always will be. But an honest mess. You could've given her what she wanted. Smoked salmon. A bit of a flash do. You only die once, she said.'

He shrugged.

'Did she tell you about the money in the biscuit tin? For her bills?' Roz asked.

Matthew nodded. 'There was ten thousand pounds in rolled-up fivers and tenners.'

'My God.' Roz reeled. 'You could've hired a room at the Balmoral. Ten thousand pounds? How did she manage that?'

'She saved it. I dunno. Lived on baked potatoes. But there it was in rolls, held together with old elastic bands.'

'Ten thousand pounds! You could've at least bought smoked salmon. You're a pig, Matthew. No. You're not even that. You're boring. It's a sin how boring you are.'

The kitchen where they were hissing at each other was immaculate. Shiny floor. Gleaming units. There was nothing to it. Nothing. Roz realised that was what the smell was. It was the smell of nothing. These people who lived here had no scent. No perfumes. No hint of what they had for supper last night. Not even a whiff of the food that was laid out for the mumblingly polite guests in the living room. No nostril-arousing blasts of bath foam, cigarettes, garlic, booze, fabric conditioner, hair gel, old cheese trapped in the back of the fridge. Nothing. My God, it was frightening how empty these lives were.

'How dare you come in here and criticise me?' Matthew said. 'You, who buggered off. You bitch. I stayed here and did my bit for my family.'

'And a right mess you made of it, too. Jamie's so laid-back and confused he looks like he'll fall down any minute. And Zoe . . .'

'What about Zoe?' She was standing in the doorway, glass in hand. Looking amused. She always looked amused. A slight grin was a wonderful thing to hide behind. 'Glad to see you two are still bickering. It would so upset my emotional balance if your relationship changed. I just wouldn't know how to handle it.' She swept off, a waft of Calvin Klein's Escape trailing in her wake. A smell, at last, Roz thought. There's life out there.

'See what you've done now,' Matthew accused.

'Me?' said Roz. 'Oh, everything's my fault.'

'Glad you see that.'

'I was being sardonic,' Roz said. Then as she was doing her own dramatic sweep from the room, she turned. 'I still think you're an uptight arse.'

She returned to the gathering in the living room, refilled her glass and sidled out to sit on the stairs and brood.

It was the sucking noise that pulled her from her sulk. Toby was standing watching her.

'Hello,' she smiled. He didn't reply. They stared. She stuck her thumb into her mouth, watching him. He considered this. Then he smiled, a slow spreading of the mouth either side of the thumb, a small spill of drool escaping down his chin. He lifted his free hand

and stroked his ear lobe. She copied. He watched her. Disconcerted, he abandoned the lobe, put his hand between his legs to find further, deeper, mildly pleasurable comfort fiddling with himself.

'You got me there,' Roz said. 'Not even for you am I going to grope myself in public.'

He continued fiddling. He'd won. 'Do you do it when you're alone?'

She laughed. 'Good one. Yeah. I probably do. Who doesn't?'

'My grandad,' he told her.

'Matthew?' She laughed again. 'I'll bet he doesn't. You're an astute one.'

He continued fiddling till a drift of laughter from the living room distracted him. He took thumb from mouth, hand from between his legs and stared round at the door. 'Why are they laughing when my Granma Nan has gone to heaven?'

'Beats me,' Roz said. 'It's the way of things. I expect they don't want to think about going to heaven in case they're next. Ignore them. They're just a bunch of Beseleys.'

'What's a Beseley?'

'Just a bunch of folk I've got myself involved with.'

'Are they nice?'

'Their problem is they think they are. Makes you sort of sick.'

He looked at his thumb, relishing the next suck. 'I'm not a Beseley.'

'No,' Roz agreed. 'The way you grope your willy, I doubt they'd have you.'

He looked at her. Weighed up the delights of not being a Beseley, whoever they were. Grinned. Placed thumb in mouth, shoved his other hand between his legs. And smiled.

CHAPTER TWO

On a fine and mellow September day ten years ago, Roz had walked out of her family home. A pleasant Edinburgh bungalow, cherry trees drooping, turning slow gold, centre lawn. It wasn't an impulsive act. She'd thought about this, and thought about it. Wrestled with her conscience. Leaving Matthew wasn't a problem. Leaving Zoe and Jamie was. Her head was filled with chaos. Alone at her breakfast table after everyone had gone off to their day's doings, she sat. Let the turmoil roll.

Unhappiness. She had grown used to that. And cursed herself for it. Nobody, she told herself, should just mildly accept a life that had slipped well below mediocrity. Not when there were wonderful things out there in the world waiting for them. You just had to grab your moment.

A year before she'd lost her job when the company she worked for had gone bankrupt. From a tiny office in Stockbridge she'd helped produce alternative guides to Scotland. Mostly she'd answered the phone, chasing up meanly paid contributors and printers. But now and then she'd been let loose, allowed to explore her country – alternatively. She'd gone to St Andrews, played putting on the Himalayas – the ludicrously hilly putting green next to the Old Course – eaten fudge doughnuts from Fisher and Donaldson, vanilla cream oozing over her lips. She'd taken the West Highland Line, leaning out the window, watching mountains, giant, silent peaks. Breathing in peaty air, sipping whisky from the bar. She'd been more than happy. Ecstatic.

The trouble was, she knew why. These occasional trips gave her the chance to get out of the house overnight. No affairs. Just a chance to be somewhere where she was Roz. And far from

Matthew and his unbearable silence. In the past five years his silence, always bothering, had got louder and louder. It had become alarming. Roz didn't know why.

She asked. Enquired politely. 'Is there something troubling you?'

He'd draw his lips tight. 'No. Why do you ask?'

She'd shrug. 'You just seem troubled.'

He'd shrug back. Then leave the room. He'd go potter in his garden shed. Or he'd polish the car. They had the shiniest car in town. An eight-year-old Audi estate that rattled, whined and gleamed.

The day before she left, Matthew had surpassed himself. He'd taken eight cloths from the cupboard. Placed two at each wheel of the car. Moving round, he'd used one to put wax on each wheel. Removing the hub caps, carefully coating the insides. Then he'd started on his second round. The wiping-off trip.

Roz watched from the window. Then went to confront him. 'Don't you think you're taking your displacement activities too far? The time you've spent doing this needless thing you could've spent with me. Going for a walk. Or choosing a new lamp for the living room. Or talking. Talking would be good.'

Matthew flushed. Looked away. And for the first time, Roz realised that he knew what he was doing. Hiding from her. Hiding from his children. Hiding from himself. It was then she decided to go. She thought that if she did something drastic, Matthew would come back to her.

She missed work. Missed the company. The crack. Jokes. Banter. In the time since she'd been made unemployed, she'd tried for over one hundred and six jobs. *Dear Sir, I am writing in answer to your advertisement in the* Evening News *for a receptionist . . .*

Dear Sir, I am writing in answer to your advertisement in the Scotsman *for a telesales person . . .*

Dear Sir. Dear Sir. Dear Sir.

She'd had fifty replies. Forty telling her the situation was filled. Ten interviews. But all the jobs had gone to younger, cheaper people. Fifty-six people hadn't bothered to write back to her. She though herself inadequate. She thought them rude.

She missed her children. It seemed to her they no longer needed her. They came and they went, in and out of the house, living their own separate lives. Time was, long ago, it seemed, they had been her friends. Centre of her world. They'd held hands walking to the park. Chatting about what might lurk behind fences. About how bees flew. About how Jamie could jump higher than her. Zoe wanted to be an ice-skating star.

They'd watch television together. Make brownies together. Bedtime she'd read stories. Or make up her own. Sometimes, on starry nights, they'd stand in the garden beneath an icy sky, making wishes. Starlight. Starbright. First star I see tonight. Wish I may. Wish I might. Have the wish I wish tonight.

But they'd grown. People do, Roz thought. It's the way of things. No more wishing in the garden. No more chats about wild things lurking behind suburban fences. And bees just fly, it's what they do.

Zoe, after a disastrous trip to the ice rink, no longer wanted to be a skating star, skimming over pristine ice, spotlight on her, crowds awed. She'd fallen on her bum. Got embarrassingly soaked. Declared skating rubbish and tossed aside her new, expensive skates. She took solace in Duran Duran. Fell in love with Simon Le Bon.

These days Jamie came home from school, muttered, 'Hi.' Or 'Nymph.' And disappeared upstairs to his computer. Zoe, on the other hand, didn't come home after school. She disappeared into her own world of boys, make-up, music and more boys. She chatted with friends. Came home. Phoned the same friends. Chatted some more. A gigglish, thrilled gossip that stilled when Roz came into the room.

Roz felt abandoned. She suggested to Jamie they go for a walk.

'I can't go out with you. You're my mother. I'd lose my cred.'

Did Zoe want to catch a film together?

'No. I'm going with Ziggy and Zak.'

Even Roz had to admit Ziggy and Zak sounded more interesting than she did. She had lost her little friends. They'd grown up on her without her really noticing. She mourned them.

Roz cleaned the house till there was nothing more to clean. She filled the freezer with lasagnes, curries, stews. Apple crumbles. Carrot soup. Tomato soup. Potage Bonne Femme, from her Elizabeth David cookbook. 'Potage Bonne Femme,' she said proudly.

'It's just potato and leek,' said Matthew, poking at it. 'With a bit of carrot.'

'Well,' said Roz defensively. 'That's culinary wizardry for you. That's what bonne femmes do with potato, leek and carrot.'

Roz joined the library. Read five novels a week, and started pestering the librarian to get in more easily digestible books. The librarian suggested she read Virginia Woolf, or Thomas Mann. But Roz refused. She didn't want any heavy reading. She wanted escapism. The librarian tutted.

Roz washed clothes. She nagged Jamie about his socks. And Zoe to clean up her room. She took down all the curtains, washed and ironed them. Removed the loose covers. Washed and ironed them. She applied for more jobs. Got none of them. In the emptiness of the house, she started talking to herself. A habit she still had.

She visited Nan, who was always glad to see her. Matthew rarely visited now. He always had an excuse. He had to clean the car. He had to rearrange the tools in his garden shed. He had to dab a tiny dent in the plaster, that Jamie had knocked with his mountain bike, with a spot of Polyfilla. On and on, paltry excuses. Nan always asked tentatively after Matthew. 'How's he doing? Is he well?'

Roz would answer, fine. She was aware there was a certain coolness between Nan and Matthew but didn't really examine it. They'd never been close. Nan, meantime, was taken up with her old friends Mavis and Fran. Since her husband, Alec, died five years ago, she'd been seeing a lot of them.

'When can I meet them?' Roz asked.

'Oooh. Sometime,' Nan said. 'They're not really your type. A bit old, like me.'

Roz supposed Nan had a right to her own friends. Her own life. She didn't insist.

Matthew grew more intense. He hummed tunelessly. Whistled through his teeth. He counted. He did anything that would block Roz communicating with him.

'We don't talk,' she said.

'When did we ever?' he said.

'Well, we never did much. But it's worse now.'

'I don't like to speak,' said Matthew. 'That's what people do nowadays. And I can't be bothered with it. People talk. They communicate. Negotiate relationships. It's weird. It isn't right. I hate it.' He shuddered. The idea of probing his inner self was intolerable. Probing his inner self in the company of someone else was disgusting.

Roz picked fights. Evenings when, now that Jamie and Zoe were off somewhere living their own lives, they sat alone together in the living room.

'Talk to me!' Roz shouted.

'What about?'

'Goddammit. About anything. Car polishing. I don't know. Just say something. You're always lost in your own little world.'

Matthew shrugged and left the room, heading for the kitchen. 'Want a cup of tea?'

'NO!'

Roz fought. One night in the bedroom, after a particularly silent evening, she flew at him, beat him on the chest. Fists flailing ineffectively. 'Talk to me. Do something. Say something.'

Matthew stepped back. Holding his arms up. Eyes wide. 'Goodness,' he said. 'That's a bit much. No need for that. Conversation isn't that important.'

After that, Roz gave up. Humming tunelessly, whistling breathily, counting mindlessly, whatever it was Matthew did, was simply some sort of displacement activity. A personal therapy to escape from something that was troubling him. Whatever it was, he was not going to discuss it with her. He locked himself away, dealt with it in his head. By himself.

Thing was, in his own way, he seemed happy. Roz decided that whatever it was that had been troubling him was troubling him no longer. But he'd found such comfort in the displacement activities, he'd kept them up. Now they had taken over from the problem. The little activities were more important than dealing with life. His habits were there for ever. He would always hum, whistle, count. And shut her out.

So Roz filled the freezer, cleaned things that were already clean, listened to the radio, applied for jobs, got none. And felt inadequate. She started speaking quietly. Avoiding eye contact with shop assistants, neighbours, anyone who spoke to her. She dressed badly. She rarely bought new clothes. Never bought the CDs or books she longed for. She didn't deserve them. At the few parties she went to, when people asked what she did, she flushed, looked away. Said sheepishly she was between jobs at the moment. She cooked what Zoe and Jamie liked to eat. Watched what Matthew wanted to see on television. And she forgot about herself. Who she was.

Every now and then, out shopping at the supermarket, in the library, in the street, Roz would brush up against some confident, stroppy woman. Some female person, head up, barging ahead, shouting the odds, demanding her rights. How does she do that? Roz would stop and watch from a distance. Staring out at the assertive one from beneath her unstyled hair. What's going on in her head that she is so sure of her rightness? Roz would wonder. Is it upbringing? Arrogance? Confidence? Why can't I be like that? Why can't I just let go and shout out loud? It was what she longed to do. Daydreamed about. She thought she had become dowdy. If not in the way she dressed, then in the way she presented herself to the world. She was emotionally dowdy. And she hated that in herself.

Once a week, Wednesdays, she went to her writing group. It gave her heart. She read out her pieces, and people laughed. She could discuss books they'd read. Afterwards, she went to the pub with Janey. Janey was bold. Confident. Opinionated. Janey drank black Russians. Janey was cool. And Janey was headed for London.

'You should come,' she said.

'I can't,' said Roz.

'Why not?'

'I have a family. I can't leave Zoe and Jamie.'

'Why not?' Janey knew nothing of motherly love. She'd no children. Didn't want any. Her own mother had declared her impossible and given up on her when she'd come home and found Janey in bed with the window cleaner.

'They need me,' said Roz.

'Do they? Doesn't sound like it to me. The way you talk. The things you write about.'

Roz exposed her soul to her writing class.

'I'll put you up till you find a job. And you'll get one.'

Roz said, 'Hmmm.' She didn't quite believe this.

'Do you ever think about you?' Janey asked. 'I mean, Jamie and Zoe are sorted now. Made. You've done all you can for them.' Janey knew little of the needs of teenagers. She'd declared herself a grown-up, responsible for her own needs, when she'd left home at sixteen. 'And Matthew's impossible, according to you. Isn't it time for you? Like I said, don't you ever think about you? You matter.'

They got up. Headed for the door.

Roz thought about this. She didn't think she did think about herself. She thought she used to. She'd lost the knack.

They walked across the car park. Janey offered Roz a lift. Roz refused. She'd take the bus.

She rarely drove. Had passed her test, but was never comfortable behind the wheel of a car. The constant pressures put on her by other road-users upset her. They got up too close behind her. Or beside her at junctions. Then there was the decision thing. In a car, you had to know where you were going.

'You can't just set off and decide where to go on the way,' Roz had complained to Nan only this morning after a serious contretemps at a junction.

She had signalled left, to head for Nan's house. Changed her mind, thought to go to the library instead. Signalled right.

Thought, no. Too early for the library. The good books come in after four. Signalled left again. Thought, no, the library, perhaps I'll get to the good books first. Right indicator on. No, Nan. Left indicator on. She swithered. Mind racing. Right or left? The driver behind her banged his hand on his horn. The rasp of sound made Roz jump. She glared in her rear mirror. Not enough. This man was rude. She got out, ran along the road to the car behind. Tapped on the window. 'Do you *mind*. Will you please stop tooting at me whilst I choose which way to turn.'

Roz had told Nan all this matter-of-factly. As if she was in the right. As if chronic indecision was normal. Nan had thought, 'This one still needs sorting out.'

Now Janey's words spun round Roz's head as she stood waiting for the bus. Embedded themselves deep inside her. 'What about me? I matter,' she told herself. 'I matter.' Nobody had ever mentioned this to her before. The bus came. She got on, climbed upstairs. 'I matter,' she said.

Roz loved upstairs on the bus. Especially at night. She could look into windows. Spot people in their living rooms, living their lives. It was her hobby. Tonight, she did not indulge in it. She sat, rattling through the Edinburgh suburbs. I matter. I matter. I matter. What *about* me? This was a new and interesting concept.

Three days later came the day of the cloths, as Roz called it. She'd stood at the kitchen window watching Matthew, absorbed as he cleaned the already immaculate insides of his hub caps, and realised that her life was slipping away. As was Matthew's. But if he wouldn't do something about it, she would. She mattered, Janey had told her. A shot at redemption. A chance to discard her dowdiness.

Next day she wrote her note. Packed her bags and left. She had wanted to take Zoe and Jamie with her. She had asked them.

'How do you feel about going to London, Jamie?'

'London? Yeah. Might go when I've done my exams.'

'Now,' said Roz.

'Not now. I've got school. Besides, what about Chrissy? She'd go off with someone else.' Chrissy was the current love of his life.

His first steady girlfriend. She'd gone off with someone else anyway. Three weeks after Roz left.

'How'd you like to come to London, Zoe?'

'No way. I'd have to make new friends. I've got Ziggy and Zak and Weasel here.' Zoe was horrified at the thought of moving.

'Well,' Roz had asked them both, 'what if I go? Would you come and see me?'

'Cool,' they'd agreed. 'Great.'

Jamie thought he and Chrissy could do some clubs. Zoe thought she and Ziggy could hang out at Harvey Nicks. Neither of them really thought Roz meant she was actually going to London. It was a fantasy.

Roz decided they'd both probably be happier here in Edinburgh. Besides, there was no room in Janey's flat. Plus Roz couldn't afford to keep them. She had no money of her own. She'd taken a thousand pounds from her and Matthew's savings. There was still plenty left. Matthew was a great saver. She thought this money was her due. All the cleaning and wiping. The pristine loose covers. The Potage Bonne Femme.

Her trip to London was hell. Hours in the bus. Head pressed against the window, feeling the thrum of wheels on tarmac taking her further and further from Zoe and Jamie. Landscapes whooshed by. She wanted to cry, 'Stop the bus. I have to get off!' She'd wept most of the way. Would Zoe keep up her studies? Would she and Jamie clean their teeth without her reminding them every night as they went to bed? Who would wash their socks? Would they heat up the frozen lasagne in the freezer? Would they miss her? Even notice she was not there?

She arrived in London, foot-swollen, stiff-boned and heavy-hearted. It was always in her mind to go home. It never occurred to her that Matthew would have nothing more to do with her. She'd always intended to go back. Once she had some money. Proved to herself she was not inadequate. Learned to stick up for herself, shout out loud in public. Then her children would come to her. Come running.

But something awful had happened. Every time she phoned

home Matthew replied. And no, he'd tell her, she couldn't speak to Jamie or Zoe. They were out. Always out. Neither of them ever replied to her letters. And they never acknowledged the many, many presents she sent them.

In time Matthew married again. Claire. To ease his new relationship he at last allowed Jamie and Zoe to visit Roz. By now they were both in their late teens. Roz took them for meals and to the cinema. She talked about her work, tried to get them to talk about their lives back in Edinburgh. But they were uncomfortable with her. Jamie smiled, swept his hair from his head, said little, and went clubbing.

Zoe never came to visit without bringing support – usually Ziggy. They'd disappear mornings, to cruise the shops. Return late, usually drunk. When Roz spoke to Zoe, she would look away, or answer with short, sharp, curt replies. She had no intention of ever forgivng Roz for leaving her. She made that clear.

Time passed, Roz hardly saw her children. She'd visited Zoe once, when Toby was born, and had her usual cool reception. Then nothing. She'd written. Sent gifts for birthdays and Christmas but received no reply. As she'd had so little communication she did not know where either Jamie or Zoe now lived and had sent everything to Matthew to pass on. She'd heard nothing.

She considered the damage she'd done to her relationship with them beyond repair. It more than bothered her. When she thought about it, for the first time she understood Matthew's behaviour. She wanted to cast it from her mind, whistling mindlessly, humming tunelessly. It was awful.

CHAPTER THREE

Zoe enfolded Toby's head in her arms, pulled it to her breasts, stroking his face. Kissed his brow. 'So what did you think of my mother? Your gran?' She grinned. Roz was a grandma. Ha. Ha.

'She's nice,' Toby said.

Zoe frowned. 'You think?'

'She said I wasn't a Beseley.'

'Is she still doing them? Of course you're not a Beseley. The one good thing I'll say about my family, none of them are Beseleys. Well, maybe Jamie. If he's not one, he'd like to be.'

'Who are the Beseleys?'

'Your gran.' Zoe grinned again, relishing that last word. 'Your gran.' She said it again. Grinned again. 'Writes them. They're noxious. Always smiling and laughing and waving. Makes you sick.'

Toby pulled away from the cuddle. His mother was always cuddling him. He looked at her, puzzled. Why did a family that was always smiling and laughing and waving make you sick? They sounded nice to him. A cheery mum and dad who took you to the seaside, like the ones in his school storybook, were what he wanted. Somehow he knew better than to mention it. Zoe started to button his pyjamas. He shoved her hands away. 'I can do it.'

'Of course you can. You're a big boy now. I keep forgetting.' She took his favourite video, *Toy Story*, from the pile and shoved it on. 'There. Bed right after.'

Toby curled on the sofa. Took up his favourite comfort activities.

Zoe watched. 'I wish you wouldn't do that. You being big and all.'

He looked back at her wide-eyed. But the thumb stayed in the

29

mouth and the other hand was down his pyjama trousers gently twiddling. He pursued pleasantness, and couldn't understand why it bothered his mother.

Zoe went upstairs to the bedroom, flopped on top of the bed. Looked with gushing love at Will as he dressed. 'What do you think of my mother?'

'She seems nice.' He shrugged.

'Nice!' Zoe flounced. Not many people could flounce whilst lying down. But Zoe could – a horizontal flounce. 'That woman walked out on me whilst I was at a tender and crucial point in my young development.'

'Christ, Zoe,' said Will. 'Forget it. Leave it behind you.'

'I will not,' she cried. 'I'm scarred. Emotionally scarred.'

Will did up his shirt. Eight buttons. Recently he'd noticed he'd started counting. He wished he wouldn't do that. Matthew counted. Will wondered if it was the effect Zoe had on people. They found safety from her constant verbal barrage in numbers.

'You don't understand,' Zoe sulked. 'Nobody understands.'

'Of course I understand,' said Will, pulling on his chinos, trying not to count. One leg. Two legs. 'Everybody understands. It must've been very traumatic for you. Suddenly losing a parent. Your mother. A real rejection. All I'm saying is, try to get over it. Don't let it ruin your life.'

'It *has* ruined my life. My life is in ruins. I'll never recover.'

He buttoned his fly. Three buttons. Oh God, stop it. This was the third outburst of the day. And she was still sober. He dreaded the tantrums when half a dozen gins took their toll.

The first scene had been this morning, nine o'clock, when she was getting dressed for the funeral. Zoe had wanted to wear a black hat with a veil.

'You can't wear that,' Will had protested. 'You look like a Greek widow.'

'That's the look I'm after. My gran is dead. She cared for me when my mother walked out. I'm motherless. I want the world to see my grief.'

'Why can't you cry like normal folk?'

'Can't cry. Won't cry. My mother'll be there. I will not let her see my tears.'

'Do you have to be so dramatic?'

'I'm not dramatic. I express myself is all. It's everybody else that's repressed.'

'No they're not. You're overdramatic. Pack it in. Wear that veil and I won't go with you. I'll take Toby to the zoo instead. He shouldn't be going to a funeral, anyway. He's too young.'

'Nobody is too young to encounter death.'

'Yes they are. How old were you when you first encountered death?'

'This age. Now. This is my first death. And I want to experience the whole upset totally. I want to be in touch with my grief.'

'Grow up.'

'Will not grow up. Growing up's for . . .' She couldn't imagine who growing up might be for. 'Bores,' she decided.

Will took the hat, opened the window. 'It's it or me.'

Zoe swithered. She did not want to let go of this mood. Till Will opened the window she'd felt she had the upper hand. She sulked. Turned her back on him. He threw the hat into the street. Sent it skimming out into the traffic below. A mud-splattered van with *Lawson's Meats* in swirling red lettering on the side flattened it.

Zoe crossed the room and hung glumly, scarcely clad, out the window, looking down at the wounded lump of felt. 'My hat. My poor hat. You've murdered it.'

'It was a hat.'

'Was, indeed. Now it's dead. It's a sign. It's a sign on this funereal day.'

'Shut up. Stop flashing your tits. Get dressed.'

'That hat cost a fortune,' Zoe mourned. It hadn't. She'd spotted it in a charity shop window only the day before and known immediately the dramatic impact it would add to her entrance at the crematorium. Fifty pee it had cost.

Tantrum number two came after the service, when Zoe had kicked up a fuss about taking her mother back to Matthew's house.

'She's not getting in our car. I do not want her touching anything

31

of mine. Her bum will be on our back seat. I'd have to scrub it tomorrow.'

'For God's sake, Zoe. She can't walk.'

'Can't she? Well let her take the bus.'

'Zoe.'

'Let her go with Matthew and Claire.'

'They're taking Jamie and Aunty something-or-other.'

'I refuse to travel with that woman. And I refuse to let her presence pollute my journey. I'm grieving for Nan.'

Toby silently watched this exchange. And watched whilst Will went smiling to Roz and offered her a lift.

Now here was tantrum number three. Will rubbed the bridge of his nose. This woman was killing him. If she wasn't so exquisite, if she wasn't so good in bed, he'd go. Except it was his flat; she should go. Then again, when she wasn't at home, he missed her. Rooms without her were more than empty. The house seemed soulless. And at work, in the bookshop, he thought about her. He wondered what she was up to. Smiled to think of her working in the design shop, arranging displays, chatting to customers. Worried about her walking home alone. What if she got run over, or mugged? Sometimes when he caught a glimpse of her standing in the kitchen, or idly flicking through a magazine, he wanted to cross the room and hug her. That moment when she was off guard, had stopped being dramatic, and her vulnerability showed. He loved that. He loved her. But, and this worried him, he sometimes thought he loved her more when he was not with her than when he was.

The doorbell rang.

'The baby-sitter's here,' he said, leaving the room.

Zoe stripped off her dramatic black outfit. Reached under the bed for the morning's post. She had a few minutes to thumb through the secret mail before he came stomping back. He didn't know about the credit card bills, and he didn't know about the regular rejections he got from record companies and DJs.

Will was a musician. He worked days in a bookshop. Nights, he played piano in a restaurant to bring in extra money. Money,

money, money, he'd say, where does it all go? Why are we always broke?

Zoe was convinced, Zoe just *knew*, he had an amazing talent. When Will played the piano at home, softly singing his own compositions, and when Will played boogie at the restaurant, Zoe recorded him. She made umpteen duplicates of each tape and, weekly, sent them off to anybody she considered might be interested. She'd set herself up as an agent. Calling herself Vincent Enterprises, after the pub where they drank. She'd had headed notepaper printed, and a set of business cards. Will knew nothing of all this. Meantime, Zoe sent off letter after letter, *Dear Sir, As one of Edinburgh's leading management agencies I'd like to draw your attention to the latest addition to our extensive and celebrated list, Will Abrahams. The very name sounds magic. His music is at once gentle, lyrical yet incisive, cutting and excitingly modern. His humour is both bitingly satirical and genially self-deprecating. One look at the enclosed photographs will affirm that the man's looks have brought him a large female following. He has already established a huge fan base in this country and we are seeking to spread the word about Will south of the border and beyond and beyond and beyond . . . blah blah glowing blah*, wrote Zoe.

Nothing happened. The tapes came back. Or, more often, they didn't.

So Zoe would wake each morning, say, 'Fuck. I'm awake.' She'd lie spread-eagled, forcing Will to the edge of their mattress. Then, 'I'm awake and I need a pee.' A few luxuriating moments more, before forcing herself from bed. It was a drag getting up early to beat Will to the mail. However, when he was famous, rich, respected – no, adored – when the world adored him as she did, it would all be worth while. Will naively enjoyed the few moments alone in bed every morning, unaware of the magnificent career Zoe was planning for him.

Today's post was not as disappointing as usual. There was a dire letter from her credit card company threatening court proceedings if she did not put some funds into her account. She stuffed it under the pillow, would send off a cheque, a smallish cheque, in the morning.

There was another letter, from a small recording company, saying that whilst they recognised the talent of Will Abrahams they didn't feel his music fitted into any current trend. But they were always interested in what was happening outside London and if she had any other, younger bands on her list they'd be glad to hear about them.

Zoe reread the letter. And reread it. Implications, opportunities skimmed through her mind. She could trawl the pubs and local halls, find a few bands, pack their demos off to London. One of them might hit. One of them might make the big time. And she'd be in for a whack. A wad, she thought. A fat wad. Money. That's for me. It would help put Toby through Oxford when the time came. Unless, of course, he'd inherited Will's gift and was musical. Hard to tell when he sucked his thumb and fiddled with his willy so much. Unless, the revelation struck her, it was a sign of deep sensitivity. He could not cope with reality. She gasped. Why had this not occurred to her sooner? That was it. The child had an emotional depth neither she nor Will had noticed before. They'd been too preoccupied with themselves. She thought about Toby's young hands, his long fingers. Like Will's fingers. Musicians' fingers. The violin probably.

She imagined Toby twenty years hence playing with the London Philharmonic. He'd be incredible. A sensuous, tortured face. Exquisite music. And a rebellious streak. He'd refuse to comply with the required dress code, turn out before the throng in jeans and T-shirt. There'd be gasps of dismay, disapproval. Then he'd tuck the violin under his chin, his steely, manly chin, gently stroke the strings with his bow. Women would swoon. The sensuousness of it, the unabashed sexuality. The horror would turn to awe. And the music, the music, would pour over them all. Yes, she had to somehow take advantage of this new offer. She had to find a band, for Toby. For the future of a brilliant musician.

She got up from the bed, stood in front of the mirror. Pouted. Lowered her lips, sucked in her cheeks. Smiled, a slight alluring upturn of the lips. Then turned. Ran her hands over her bum. 'Yes, kid, face it, you've got a great arse.' She gave each armpit a spray of Escape. Put the black outfit back on. Gave her lips a fresh coating of scarlet, blusher on her cheeks and mascara on her lashes. Ruffled her hair and declared herself ravishing and ready for the night.

Downstairs Will, Sonia – the baby-sitter – and Toby were ensconced in front of *Toy Story*. Will looked up in dismay when she entered. 'You're not going out like that, are you?'

'I certainly am. What's wrong with this.' She raised her arms, displaying herself.

'It's sort of . . .' He searched for something diplomatic. 'Widowish.'

'I'm dressed like this in respect for the dead. For Nan. I'm in mourning.'

'How long will it last?' Will dreaded the reply.

'I don't know. How long is mourning expected to last?'

'In your case twenty minutes. But obviously you're planning a bit longer than that.'

'I certainly am,' said Zoe. She picked up her handbag – bright red – smothered Toby in kisses, told Sonia to help herself to anything in the kitchen (though she hoped she wouldn't) and left, a thick drift of Escape trailing in her wake. Will followed.

The air outside was sharp. That shrill tang of autumn, cold coming soon. Zoe shivered and pulled her coat round her. 'Have you noticed Toby's hands?'

'Why?'

'Musicians' hands,' she said. 'I think Toby has potential.'

'Oh God, Zoe. Leave the boy alone. Let him be. You fuss round him. He's spoilt.'

'He is not.'

'He never stops sucking his thumb.'

'I know.' Zoe had noticed. In fact, recently it had started to worry her. At first she'd told herself the child would grow out of it. But now she wondered if he would. She had this nightmare vision of Toby at twenty-five, sucking a man-size thumb, great hand wedged down the front of his trousers. Now, it was an innocent, comfort, childish thing. And she worried about how, exactly, to stop him doing it without making him feel guilty. If he kept up the habit into adulthood, well, by that time his genitals would be less . . . less endearing, she thought. Such behaviour, she had to admit, would be a drawback socially.

'He's sensitive,' she declared. 'The world is too harsh for him. I bet Paganini was the same when he was a boy.'

'Paganini? He'd have been too busy practising to do anything like that.'

'Well,' said Zoe. 'We must get him a violin.'

'What?' Will stopped in his tracks.

'You heard,' Zoe continued. 'He's obviously musical. How much do they cost?'

'Violins? A great deal more than we've got. For a good one.'

Nonsense, Zoe thought. The man plainly did not know that a girl with a pocketful of credit cards could get anything. Anything in the world she wanted.

'We should play him music. Great concertos. Expose him to wonderful sounds. Get him in the mood.'

Will sighed. It was going to be one of those nights. Three gins in, Zoe would light up a Marlboro and start to expound and everybody would cringe. The women more than the men. But then none of the women had slept with her. At least, he stopped to think about this, he didn't think they had. You never knew with Zoe. But the blokes, every bloke there tonight, had known the delights of Zoe's mouth. She'd had affairs with them all before she took up with Will.

The crowd she knew was the same group of people she'd been running around with since school days. They had moved in and out of affairs with one another. But Zoe was the only one who'd slept with every bloke. Before she met Will, she'd hooked men, reeled them in. Loved them till they declared undying passion for her. Then she'd let them go. She never allowed herself to love anyone. Love was too painful. Love broke your heart.

Sometimes at get-togethers, odd nights in the pub Will would catch Zoe's exes looking at those painted lips. Salivating. Remembering.

He could not bear to think of his Zoe with anyone else. He had moments of shuddering jealousy. Though Zoe swore that she took her men one at a time. 'I'm always faithful,' she declared. 'Though not for long. You are my longest-lasting love. I've moved in with you. Had your child. Nobody else has got this far with me.'

It seemed when she said it like a compliment. In fact, every time she said this – and she repeated it often – he'd flushed with pride. But later it seemed like nothing at all. People everywhere moved in together, had babies together. He wanted more. He wanted Zoe to swear undying, everlasting love to him. As he did, often, to her.

He told himself that Zoe's past sexual shenanigans were a kind of morale boost. She needed to make people want her. She needed to fire their desires. Then she could reject them. Cast them from her, before they cast her from them. But, having comforted himself with that, he waited in unspoken dread for the day she would cast him away, too. Whilst telling himself he could love her so much, she would not need to seek reassurance elsewhere. He could make her love, as much as he loved, the frail, vulnerable person inside.

Except for now, when his jealousy welled up within him. 'Is there a cock in Edinburgh you haven't sucked?' he asked. Suddenly. Cruelly.

'Of course there is.' Zoe did not respond to the jibe. In fact, this was the kind of jibe she liked. She rose to the challenge. Looked round. There was a small man wearing a cap and raincoat across the road.

'That man over there,' Zoe pointed.

The man turned.

'I haven't given him a blow job.'

She whirled full circle. Men walking on the pavement. Men in cars. Looked up at all the windows, light against the chilled October night. Men in there. 'Hundreds of them.'

She sensed this remark had given her the advantage in this little spat, so chose not to mention that none of them interested her.

CHAPTER FOUR

How Nan had laughed when Roz landed the Beseleys. 'Serves you right. You walk out on your own family and land up with that lot. They're worse.'

Roz had pointed out that she hadn't left her family. It had always been her intention to return. 'But Matthew wouldn't have me.'

'Don't blame him,' joked Nan.

Time and umpteen phone calls to Nan had eased Roz's pain. Nan figured that if Roz had reached a point of taking a bit of teasing, she'd survive. She hadn't the same hope for herself. Roz's sudden departure had broken her heart. And she always wondered if in some way she was partly to blame.

The Beseleys were the brainchildren of Ronnie Cardew. They were his pride and joy, all five of them. Mr and Mrs Beseley, Pam and Frank, and the three little Beseleys, Simon, thirteen, Susan, eleven, and the impish but lovable four-year-old Sammy. They appeared weekly on the back page of *Let's Chat* magazine. One of those eternal publications that appeared week in, week out without anyone really noticing. It was the sort of magazine people would come across on newsagents' shelves and exclaim, 'That thing. Is that still on the go? My gran used to get that.' Roz worked for it. Two years as part of the staff, working with Ronnie, seven freelance. For most of that time she'd written the Beseleys.

Like death, like trauma, there were three stages with the Beseleys. Denial. Rage. And acceptance. At first Roz had avoided telling people what she did. At parties, in pubs, she told new people in her life she was a nurse, or she was in insurance. Invariably, though, she met people who were in the same field and they'd want to talk shop. So she said she played the flute in an orchestra, thinking she'd never, absolutely never, meet an actual flautist. But she did. To her embarrassment, she'd had to confess that she'd never even been to an orchestral concert. Rock'n'roll was more her thing. After that she told the truth. She wrote a silly soap opera for a somewhat tepid and old-fashioned magazine. Nobody turned a hair. Denial over. She moved into rage. She hated the Beseleys. It took her months to persuade Ronnie Cardew that children in the late twentieth century did not say 'Gosh, Mummy . . .' She dreamed up hideous deaths, malforming illnesses for them. She imagined Daddy Beseley losing his job, ending up living in a box somewhere in Soho. Mummy Beseley on the streets, cat-calling kerb-crawlers. Susan and Simon on drugs and little Sammy taken into care, fostered out to a malevolent couple who'd feed him boiled cabbage every second day. She knew viler things happened to children, but couldn't bring herself to let her imagination rip on poor Sammy.

After that came acceptance. She became almost fond of them. Sent them on sunny holidays, allowed them friendly family meals. And for a while all the Beseleys' mishaps were minor ones. Then Roz went beyond acceptance. She wanted to sort them. She wanted to make them real. She wanted them to suffer. To drag them kicking and screaming into the world. Then they'd know joy, maybe, she thought. Mostly, though, Roz wanted to set the horribly zany and desperately dithery Mrs Beseley, Pam, free.

The Beseleys had first appeared in 1963, when Roz was eight and reading *Bunty*. People were singing about the times being a-changin'. There were suspicious new pills to stop women having babies. That wasn't right, Ronnie Cardew had thought. Why, they'd be out without their husbands, doing God knows what. And in no time at all there'd be anarchy in the land. 'Anarchy,' he'd said, thumping his fist on his desk. 'Utter anarchy.' He was twenty-five at the time. And considering all that was going on for other people his age, missing out on a lot. He resented that, but never admitted it. He wore a tweed jacket with patches on the elbows. He was on the make. He'd be managing editor before he was thirty. He still had hair. 'We must do our bit to maintain family values.' Cue the Beseleys.

For the first thirty years of their life, the Beseleys had been written by Willa Morris. Ah, Willa. Ronnie loved her. Sang her praises. 'She's a woman of worth. A woman who knows the real importance of the family in society's structure.'

He fantasised about her. She'd be tall. She sounded tall. Dark, probably, he thought. Perhaps, slightly, very slightly, flecked with grey. Long hands, manicured nails, painted perfect pale pink. The room where she worked would be white. Walls, carpet, everything, except the long desk she sat before. That would be some sort of silken highly polished wood. It would have on it a single notepad, a pen – a proper fountain pen – the very latest in word processors and a single white orchid. White curtains would billow in the soft breeze that wafted in through the slightly open window. When Willa mused – and such a woman would often muse – she would look through that window at the countryside surrounding her grand, but not overly grand, ivy-clad house. She would gaze out on a rolling landscape, lush. Hills and distant trees. Sometimes Ronnie dreamed about making love to Willa. It would be passionate, in a way love with his wife never was. In fact, love with his wife had stopped. Willa would stroke his hair, whisper his name. In the morning they would sit at her breakfast table. He'd be dressed, but not overly so. He'd leave his jacket and tie in the bedroom. She'd be in a long wafty sort of thing. They'd eat eggs, lightly poached. Drink freshly brewed coffee. Vow lasting love. But he was a family man, he had duties. Responsibilities. It was never to be. When they parted they'd kiss, one long, final meeting of lips. Her tongue would brush the inside of his mouth. 'Goodbye, Ronnie,' she'd breathe.

Many an afternoon, when he should have been busy with other things, Ronnie would sit at his desk and dream. He made regular trips to meet his contributors. Every time he arranged to meet Willa, she would put him off. She'd sprained her ankle. She had to take her cat to the vet. She'd be away visiting her son. She was going on holiday. She was waiting for the plumber, 'And you

41

know how it is with plumbers. When you've got one, you don't let them go.' Once she phoned to say she had to go into hospital.

'Nothing serious, I hope,' he said.

'Oh no, just a wee op.'

'Goodness, what's wrong?'

'Oh, nothing you'd want to know about. I'll be back at my desk in no time.' She had a husky voice. It never occurred to him that it was caused by a serious nicotine habit. He just loved the way she demurred about telling him what sort of operation she was about to undergo. That was what he loved in a woman – no messiness.

Willa worked for many publications throughout the building. In time Ronnie discovered that nobody had met her, and he was not the only one who fantasised. Though his fantasies were the only flattering ones. Others fancied she was hideously disfigured and wanted nobody to see her. Or she was ancient and wrinkled and a hermit. Or she wrote so much she'd forgotten how to communicate by actually talking.

Willa was amazing. Among other things, she wrote children's comic strips. 'Patsy's Secret Pony' – *Oh, Poppy, you're my very own secret pony. And I love you more than anything*. 'Bea of the Ballet' – *Oh, Daddy, I may be in a wheelchair. But I swear I will dance again*. 'Mike the Boy Magician' – *With one wave of my magic marble I can make mountains disappear*. And she wrote the Beseleys – *Gosh, Mummy, we didn't know you could juggle*. (When Mummy slipped on a wet patch and tossed three eggs in the air.) *Mummy's such a clown*.

At last, after writing the Beseleys for fifteen years in obscurity, Willa Morris phoned Ronnie to tell him that she was coming to London and could she pop in to see him?

'Of course. Of course,' Ronnie crooned. 'We'll roll out the red carpet.'

She arrived a week later. Ronnie waited by the lift as it hurtled her to the fifth floor. He'd bought a new suit. The doors slid open. A tall woman stepped out. Ronnie moved forward, hand extended. He did not notice the tiny woman who was shuffling in front of him. She stopped a considerable distance from his chin. Wrestled with a selection of carrier bags. She was at least seventy.

'Willa,' Ronnie gushed to the tall woman.

'That's me,' said the dwarf. 'You must be Ronnie. Glad to meet you.' Digging deep into one of her bags, she produced a battered Tupperware box. 'I've baked you a fruit cake.' She was more than small. She was minuscule. Her face was crumpled with time, hair thinning. As was his. But that was OK, he was a bloke. Blokes could have thinning hair. It was allowed. She wore a miserable green anorak, rumpled skirt, flat shoes. Her nails were rimmed with grime. She caught him looking at them. 'Had to do the hens before I left.'

'Hens?' he said. Did not think to conceal the horror in his voice. 'Hens?'

'Oh yes. Take the eggs to market every Saturday. Every little helps.'

Ronnie let this roll round his mind. He realised slowly that Willa, not having asked for a raise in rates, had never had one since she started writing for him. It was now 1978. She was on 1963 rates. No wonder she kept hens.

Time passed. Eased his shock. Slowly, slowly Willa stopped being Willa and became again the sophisticated creature of his imaginings.

Then she died. Died and left the Beseleys orphans. Ronnie got a letter from her lawyer telling him she'd left him something in her will. Would he come to collect it? Or would he like it sent? He'd collect it. He wanted to stand in the white room, see the ivy-clad house.

Leaving his wife at home, he drove on a rainy Saturday to Yorkshire. After meandering down a maze of tiny lanes, he found the house where Willa had lived down a muddy bog of a path. The word that sprang to mind when he saw it was hovel. It could well have housed a couple of Dickensian ne'er-do-wells.

Damp glistened on the outside walls. The roof sagged. Hens ran amok on the scrubby lawn. Untended Brussels sprouts and cabbages lurked in a sodden vegetable patch. Six of her fourteen dogs rushed to greet him, howling. Three of her sixteen cats sat scrunged against the bitter November afternoon on the doorstep.

The lawyer, a paunchy, ruddy-cheeked fellow in checked trousers – sort of Dickensian, Ronnie thought; I've stepped back a century – greeted him. 'Terrible place,' he said, waving his arm at the small, cold kitchen. A single-bar electric fire, a wobbly Formica-topped table, a kettle poised on a stained unit, beside a plug with a couple of adaptors jutting from it, and jutting from the adaptors umpteen plugs with frayed wires leading to the fire, a becrumbed toaster, a spin drier *circa* 1940, a rumbling fridge and God knew what else.

'I have a gift for you,' said the lawyer. He produced Willa's typewriter – a prewar Imperial portable with two broken keys. So that was why she always carefully lettered in her a's and e's.

It was only then, standing in that chilled, loveless, filthy kitchen, that Ronnie's fantasies were finally crushed. The magical, gracious, sophisticated, perfumed Willa disappeared. He at last acknowledged what he'd been denying for years. The woman had been a wrinkled, careworn, impoverished and somewhat grubby dwarf. Who, God bless her, had actually believed the ludicrous sentimental – go on, he said to himself, admit it, admit it, you po-faced, humourless, snotty bastard, admit it – crap, yes crap, that she'd written.

Ronnie never dreamed again. He turned inwards. Worried. He stroked his thinning hair and told himself that he had reached the heart attack time of life. He'd spend glum hours at his desk worrying that even as he sat his arteries were hardening. He'd wait by the lift knowing that at any moment the Big Pain could strike. Every moment of every day the big clot was moving closer and closer to his heart. He was going to die.

The only person he knew capable of taking over the Beseleys was Roz Rutherford. Roz who had sat at the desk across from his for the past two years. He hated the idea. She had walked out on her own family. What would such a person know of family values? She was one of those feminist people. He spat the word, even when it only flitted through his head. This woman was not a Beseley person at all. But he'd no option. Neither did Roz. She needed the money. She agreed to take them on. She'd leave the office and go freelance. At proper rates, she insisted. With them and the other jobs she could pick up, she'd have enough to pay a small mortgage, and some left over to send home to help feed and clothe that other family in her life, the one she'd abandoned.

Roz had drifted into writing. Whilst other writers she met had fretted and worried, chasing their dreams, she hadn't dreamed at all. She did what she did. Wrote what she was asked to. She paid the bills.

Before she left her family, Roz had written a little. It had started with poems when she was thirteen. She fancied herself a poetess of note. It wasn't so much what she'd put down on the page. It was the image. She'd wear dark velvet clothes, swathe her neck in eccentric jewellery, have lovers, smoke French cigarettes, drink red wine and appear in public only after dark. And, at that, with her sensitive emotions concealed behind sunglasses. It took several years and a deal of mockery before she came to the painful conclusion that her poems weren't bad. They were worse than that – mediocre. She abandoned the poet dream and turned to short stories. These she kept in a drawer. Nobody was going to see them. Nobody would be given the opportunity to mock. Time and life made her stop. She grew up a little. Started dating. Going out. Pubbing. Meeting boys. Met Matthew. One day she realised she hadn't written or even thought about writing for years.

After she married, when the silence began, when Matthew sat, arms folded, in front of the telly, and Jamie and Zoe were sleeping, she started to write again. She submitted odd jokey outpourings to magazines' letters pages. Then she wrote short, self-deprecating articles. In time some got accepted. Acceptance, publication was enough. The money a bonus. Icing on the cake. She did not really take it seriously.

When she arrived in London, tired, guilty and swollen of foot from hours in the bus from Edinburgh, she had limped to Janey's flat. Janey had given her gin and sympathy and a sofa to sleep on. She had helped find Roz a job as receptionist in the publishing firm that produced *Let's Chat* along with dozens and dozens of other titles. Over the years, Janey was the only person from her past with whom Roz kept in touch. They saw each other every week to drink, chat and exchange mutual moans about work, men, life.

Every week Roz had scanned the noticeboard that advertised in-house jobs. Eventually she was interviewed by Ronnie, who took her on. He had not known at the time about her murky past. He thought her amenable, and amenable was what he liked in colleagues. Amenable was what he liked in women; in everybody, in fact.

Roz found she had a knack for quirky, whimsical articles about dieting, fat days and thin days, waiting for the phone to ring (hers rarely did), looking for the perfect lipstick, the uncomfortableness of sexy underwear, daydreaming, and the elusiveness of the perfect new man. She wrote quizzes, filled in for the agony aunt when she had her appendix out, and did the occasional episode of the Beseleys when Willa Morris was having one of her many operations.

After a year she found she could knock out a thousand words in an afternoon without needing to eat biscuits and chocolate or drink fourteen cups of tea. She was what Ronnie called a pro. Though by the time he called her that, she'd fallen from grace in his eyes. He'd found out about her leaving her children, considered her a loose woman with a secret, sordid private life. 'I wish,' Roz sighed.

When she was offered the opportunity to write the Beseleys, Roz jumped at it. Then doubted herself. She hated them. But the chance to work in a room that didn't have Ronnie in it was too good to miss.

She phoned Nan. She always phoned Nan, whatever turns her life took.

'You've what?' said Nan. 'Given up a good job? To go off on your own? Is that a good idea?' She worried for Roz. Fretted for Roz.

'Yes. It's an opportunity.'

'What sort of opportunity? No pension. No regular pay. You'll sit alone at home. Nobody to talk to. No security. Your feet'll get cold.'

'I'll make a lot more money,' said Roz. 'I'll save some for my old age. I'll be fine. I'll wear cosy socks.'

When Nan had first met Roz, Roz had been nineteen. Young, vulnerable and pregnant with Jamie. They had looked at one another with suspicion. So, thought Nan, this is the girl who is taking my son from me. So, thought Roz, this is the woman who'll be watching me, criticising how I make Matthew's tea, iron his shirts, bring up his child.

Time passed. Roz got bigger. Nan watched her. Here was the daughter she'd always wished for. She'd dreamed of having a large family, living in a converted farmhouse, children wriggling, squabbling, playing, breathing life around her. But one son was all she'd managed to produce.

Roz found in Nan the mother she'd never had. Her own had died earlier that year, and had been a self-contained, uncommunicative woman who lectured in business studies. She'd been given to making monthly inventories of her pantry and freezer. And had been horror-struck when her daughter announced she was pregnant, going to drop out of university, keep the baby and marry Matthew. 'That boy,' she'd cried. 'He's not for you. He's too quiet.'

But here in Roz's life was Nan, a woman who would talk about the secret uncomfortableness of pregnancy. Offer advice on heartburn and put cushions at the small of her back when she sat on the sofa. There was something about Nan. A worldliness. An understanding of the business of being a female human being, alone, insecure in a vast and busy world.

It did not take either of them long to bond. Every time Nan saw Roz, or thought about Roz, she smiled. On their first meeting, Roz had reminded Nan of a wounded sparrow, trembling in cupped hands. She was six months pregnant, skinny with it, with huge eyes that looked round her living room, taking it in, judging if it was a safe place to be. She was motherless and scared. When she got to know her, Nan found Roz to be a lot tougher than that. A sparrow with a steely core, she thought. So when Roz eventually fled to London, she was not surprised. The sparrow's flown at last, she thought. Knew it would.

When Roz thought about Nan, she felt comforted by the presence of this older, wiser, saner, understanding woman in her life.

'You're so lucky to have a mum like Nan,' Roz would say to Matthew.

'You think?' Matthew would reply, stiffly. Not looking at her.

In time, both Roz and Matthew knew that Roz had become a lot closer to Nan than Nan had ever been to him. Roz phoned Nan daily. Roz dropped in on Nan. Roz made herself at home in Nan's house. Knew where everything was. Would knock on the door, open it, yell, 'Hello, it's me.' Come in. Put on the kettle and settle down for a chat. And how they would chat. Endless, endless, never-ending chat. It puzzled Matthew. What could two people who had seen each other on Tuesday find to avidly talk about on Wednesday? Their lives weren't that busy. He felt ousted. Not that he'd been close to Nan. He just didn't want anyone else to be, especially someone he'd introduced to her. The relationship irritated him. But there was nothing he could do about it. It was some sort of rollercoaster that swept him aside. He withdrew further and further into himself. The more Roz talked to, confided in Nan, the less she communicated with Matthew. And the closer she grew to Nan, the less he wanted her to communicate with him. If it was Nan or him, Roz, as far as he was concerned, had chosen Nan.

CHAPTER FIVE

Zoe had a hangover. And was foul with it. She refused to get out of bed. Lay in a swoon, insisting that Will bring her large quantities of iced orange juice, complaining about being forced to mix her drinks. 'If I'd stuck to gin, I'd've been fine. But, oh no, people insisted on filling me up with brandy. Then wine. And now I'm incapable of functioning. I'm going to lose twenty-four hours out of my life.'

'You didn't have to drink three white Russians. Or the tequila,' Will pointed out.

'I was being sociable.'

'I noticed,' said Will.

From his spot across the room he'd watched Zoe party. She'd danced, snogged and schmoozed, laughed too loud and stilled the room into silent amazement when she'd put her arms round Ruth Williams and kissed her long on the mouth. 'There, darling. Haven't you been longing for that?'

'No,' protested Ruth. Hands to lips.

'Of course you have. I know all about you. I've watched you watching the girls.'

'Oh for God's sake. How could you do this to me?' Ruth, a newcomer to Zoe's crowd, was scarlet and flustered.

'Easy. I think you ought to be in touch with your true self. I like you, Ruth. I like you very much.'

'Oh,' Ruth simpered.

'Not that kind of very much,' Zoe corrected her.

She turned in bed, pulling the pillow over her face. Remembering. Why did she do it? Why did she so avidly seek disapproval from everyone she met? It gave her such glee when she saw that look of shock, horror and utter helplessness cross people's faces. As it had done when she'd lied to her mother about being a drug-dealer. Nobody knew what to do with her. She turned back to Will, came out from behind the pillow.

'What did I do last night?' she asked. 'You know, after Ruth?'

'Do you really want to know?' Will said.

'No. Not really. Not at all. Was I awful?'

'You surpassed yourself.'

'Oh well.'

Will threw back the duvet. Sat on the edge of the bed, scratching himself. Zoe reached over, touched his back. 'Don't get up.'

She'd already been up. Collected the post. 'Stay. Cuddle me. I need a cuddle.'

'Toby's up,' Will told her. 'I can hear him crashing about downstairs.'

'He'll be OK. Please.'

'No. Toby won't be OK. He's got school. God knows what he's doing.' He walked round the bed. Stopped beside her.

She eased back the duvet. Revealed herself naked, slightly sweaty. 'Please.'

'No. You're a dreadful woman. You're horrible.'

'I know.'

'Well cut it out.'

'I'll try.' But she wouldn't. She knew she wouldn't. She watched Will cross the room, put his hand on the doorknob. 'I hate being me.'

He tried not to respond. But couldn't help it. He always thought one day he'd save her from herself and her remorseless morning-after scourging. 'I know you do. But I don't hate you being you. Neither does Toby. We love you.' He returned to the bed, kissed her cheek. He closed his eyes a moment, breathed the scent of her. Toothpaste, nicotine, a faint booziness, make-up remover, moisturiser and underneath it all – Zoe. Her skin. He told her again that he loved her. She said, 'I know you do.' Then he went downstairs to see to Toby.

Zoe reached under the bed for her mail. It was a good day

today. Nothing nasty from any of her credit card companies, and no rejections for Will.

Toby was wandering the kitchen in his underpants eating cornflakes straight from the packet. He looked up at Will. 'Hello,' he said, mouth spewing crumbs.

'Could you not put these in a bowl with milk? Like normal folk?' asked Will, taking the packet.

'I like them like that,' said Toby. He watched Will fill a bowl with cornflakes, cover them with milk and sugar and set it on the table.

'Do you want to do anything today?' asked Will. 'After school. I worked late the other night. I get off at four.'

'Play football in the park. With you. Not Mummy.'

'Don't let her hear you saying that. Why not Mummy?'

'She can't play football. She just walks and talks. She talks all the time.'

'It's what she does,' sighed Will. He filled a glass with orange juice, cold from the fridge, dropped in several ice cubes. Handed it to Toby. 'Here, take this to her.'

The child took it, shuffled slowly from the kitchen, glass clutched in both hands, clinking all the way up the stairs.

Zoe took the drink and downed it in one. 'You are a good boy, bringing me that.' Toby watched, said nothing. Waited for the empty glass. She handed it to him. 'Any chance of some coffee?'

Ten minutes later Toby returned with two paracetamol and a cup of coffee, shuffling ever more cautiously to stop the tiny wavelets in the cup splashing over into the saucer. She took them shakily. 'Oh, perfect.' Gingerly raised the steaming cup to her lips. 'Just what I needed.' She gazed fondly after Toby as he went to the door. Pouring love on him. 'How would you like to learn to play the violin?'

This was a new thought to Toby. His current ambitions fluctuated between becoming a footballer, a vet or a waiter. A footballer because he fancied scoring goals and doing somersaults to wild cheers from the assembled thousands. A vet because you got to play with kittens and puppies. And a waiter because the few restaurants he'd been to all had a fine selection of puddings – something Zoe never served. Playing the violin flummoxed him. He had an instant vision of himself turning up at school with a fiddle in a battered case and being taunted by the big boys. No, he didn't want to learn to play the violin. However, he knew better than to say. So he stared. The thumb started towards his mouth.

'I think you have a great musical gift,' his mother told him.

Toby continued to stare.

'And we mustn't let it go to waste,' Zoe continued. 'That would be a sin.'

Toby stared. Sin? He knew about sins. There was a chap who came to school on Fridays and spoke about love and sinning and Jesus. As far as he could tell, and he didn't pay much attention to the man, love was good, sinning wasn't so good, but, strangely, Jesus loved you anyway. But the man never mentioned playing the violin. Toby was confused. Went downstairs, sucking his thumb, and stood vacantly in front of Will.

'I wish you'd stop that,' Will said. 'It isn't good for your teeth. Also it's what babies do. You're too old for that sort of thing.'

Toby took his thumb from his mouth. Said nothing. Silently he finished his cornflakes, soggy now that he'd left them to take Zoe her coffee. Just the way he liked them. Silently he went to his room, pulled on his school clothes. Then he returned to the kitchen and without a word held up his shoes for Will to tie his laces. He sat in the back of the car on the ten-minute journey to school, still silent. At last, as he was clambering out at the gates, he turned to Will and said, 'Why do I have to learn the violin? I don't like violins. They're girlie.'

'Christ, Zoe,' said Will. Then, to Toby, 'It's OK. You don't have to if you don't want to.' He drove off. Saw Toby standing in the middle of the pavement by the school gates forlornly looking after him. Stopped. Rolled down the window and shouted to him, 'Don't worry.'

But Toby was already worried.

At home Zoe stumbled into the living room. Naked. She clutched her head. Oh God. Oh God. Why did she do it? Drink.

Say the things she did. Tell Ruth wotsit she was a dyke when she plainly wasn't. As if it mattered, anyway. And the other things she did, that she couldn't remember. It was a power trip. That moment of looking round and seeing that everyone was appalled by her. So empowering. She loved it. She slumped on the sofa. It would all have to stop. She knew that. Before it went too far. If it hadn't already. She always pushed people too far. Wondered how much it would take to shove them over the edge and abandon her. Only Will so far had hung on. At first his tolerance amazed her. Now it was starting to get to her. It was as if he was winning. And it bothered her that she liked that he was winning.

The room was silent. She hated that. She switched on the telly. Surfed the morning channels. Then, finding nothing, read her horoscope for the day on Teletext. Quarter to nine; she had to be at work by ten. She should move. She sat. Stared. This was not the room she'd planned. The trouble was, people came into it, rumpled the rugs, left things lying – cups, newspapers. They sat down, left bum indentations on the sofa cushions. Never thought to plump them. There were gatherings and rolls of dust on the wooden floor. Nobody thought to vacuum them up. The huge fig tree in the corner was drooping and thirsty, a shower of fallen leaves round the dark red ceramic pot she'd lugged home to put it in. And furthermore, that pot was chipped. 'Nobody does anything round here,' she complained, out loud. It never occurred to her that she might be the one to sometimes do something round here. That wasn't on.

She looked glumly at the scattering of CDs on the floor, on the shelf by the television. Empty cases, left open. And discs lying abandoned, getting scratched, gathering dust. She sighed. Supposed she would have to do it. Tidying up a few CDs wasn't too demeaning for a woman of her legendary skills. Dusting was.

She heaved herself stiffly from her slump and moved across the room to kneel beside the musical debris. She considered the pile. Her whole life was in these songs. The tracks she was playing when her mother left. The soundtrack to her rebel years when she skipped school, started to smoke, took E, came home late, had a screaming match with her father, then climbed out the bedroom window after he thought she'd gone to bed, to party and booze till morning, when, at seven, she'd climb back in again. Appear dishevelled and baggy-eyed and foul-tempered at the breakfast table, force down some cornflakes, run upstairs to the loo, throw them up again, and go back to bed to sleep till four in the afternoon. Zoe smiled. Those were the days. Sex and drugs and rock'n'roll. Vomit and tantrums. Why hadn't she thought to enjoy them more when she was going through them? By God, if Toby ever behaved like that – 'I'll kill him,' she said. But then Toby wouldn't behave in any such nonsensical way. No sex and drugs for him. He'd be too busy with his music, his violin practice, to misbehave. Teenage crap was beyond genius. And by now Zoe had decided she was mother to a profound and disturbingly sensitive creative talent. Why else would Toby behave the way he did?

She fondly turned over Marvin Gaye, *Let's Get It On*. They'd played it over and over when she'd discovered she was pregnant. Nineteen, and in her first year at university. How they'd got it on, and on, once they figured Zoe was pregnant anyway so there was nothing more to worry about.

Except, of course, her father. She was four months gone, and starting to show, slightly, when they told him. Matthew had received the news silently. Lips tight. Oh dear, Zoe thought. I've never seen him like this.

Like mother, like daughter, he was thinking. This is what Roz did. Pregnant at nineteen. She threw her life, and mine, away. I wanted more than this. He never blamed himself for his part in Roz's early pregnancy. He thought that she was the one who should have taken precautions.

He'd stared at the kitchen wall for a full five minutes before the rage started. And then his fury was so intense, so implosively violent, Zoe had thought he was going to have a heart attack. She wondered if the doctor's number was in the little book by the phone.

He'd clutched a spoon that was lying, quite innocently, on the kitchen table. He'd gone a worrying shade of red, eyes bulging,

'You bloody pair of ignorant arses,' he'd said. 'You . . . you . . . half-witted, sex-crazed . . . fucking . . .' Zoe had never heard her father say 'fucking'. She idly let his polite pronunciation of the word roll round her brain. Fucking. Fucking. And then Matthew had run out of words. He glared at them. Threw the spoon. It hit the drying crockery on the draining board, smashing a plate. He stood up. Punched the table. 'Haven't you heard of condoms?'

'Oh yes,' Zoe had said mildly. 'We've heard of them. We just didn't ever use one.' She looked at her father. A woman now. She could talk frankly to him. 'It's just not the same, is it? You don't feel as much.'

Matthew had gone silent. Terrifyingly silent. Will cringed. Matthew seemed to go pale and get smaller simultaneously. Then he started to tremble. At first the body movement was only slight. He held on to the table. The veins in his temples started to throb. And the trembling engulfed him. 'You. Filthy. Little. Cow.' The words splattered from him. Zoe had thought to say that he shouldn't be so uptight. Then again, perhaps not. Well, not now. Matthew stamped from the room. Thundered up the stairs. Zoe well remembered it was one of the few occasions he went up them without counting. Thrilled, she'd turned to Will. 'Brilliant, isn't it? It's like being in one of those crap old films on telly on Sunday afternoon. Folks with deep northern accents in black and white.' She'd smiled wildly. Wasn't melodrama lovely.

Will's face was contorted. He was trying not to laugh at Zoe's enthusiastic reaction to Matthew's rage, whilst being a little shocked at her himself. He'd crossed the room and hugged her. He wanted this woman more than he'd ever wanted anything, anybody.

Remembering all this, Zoe smirked. Continued putting CDs into their cases. Slotting them back into their places on the shelf. Will liked to keep them alphabetised, so that he could easily find what he had a notion to hear. He always had a notion of what he wanted to hear. You could judge his mood, the day he'd had, by what was pouring from the living room. Robert Jonstone – gritty, hard-working. Early Beatles – amiable. Thelonious Monk –

confused, tiring. His cracked vinyl recording of *Carmen*, full blast – hellish, keep away from him till after supper.

Ah Will, she smiled softly. She loved him. She found his tape, an old recording from his acned days, long ago. He'd played with an ever-changing line-up of local musicians. Kinetic, they called themselves, sometimes. The Bruisers, sometimes. And sometimes Gauche. They did not want to commit to anything as labelling as a name. A bunch of cheerful we'll-never-give-up-the-day-job boys who wanted to boogie. And revel in the plentiful perks. Sex, and there was lots of that, and free pints. Neither fame nor wealth interested them.

Zoe clutched the tape to her. She would change all that. Nothing interested her more than fame and wealth. And since she considered she had no talents that would bring them to her, she was looking to Will. There he was on the cover, pictured in London. Two hundred miles and fifteen years ago. Young, skinny, enthusiastic. Grinning and blind drunk.

The notion came to her slowly. It seeped into her mind. Once there, it refused to go away. Why not send this tape to those record people in London? She could tell them they were her newest signing and were the hottest ticket in town. Who would know? It was a well-documented fact that those sort of folks never went north. They certainly wouldn't consider coming to Scotland. Once interest was shown, it would be easy to persuade Will to return to his old rocking days. She was convinced she could persuade Will to do anything. She had *ways*. Once famous, he could declare his yen to move on, to explore new sounds. Go solo. All big stars did that. You read it in the tabloids all the time. He'd release his first album, songs all written by himself. Wild acclaim. They'd be made. Rich. Famous. What more could anyone want?

She took the tape to work where she kept her secret headed notepaper. At lunchtime she sat at her boss's computer and flew. Zoe at her most flamboyant. This band was exuberant. Their hottest signing for years. Huge following. They had a cheek and musical enthusiasm not seen in this country since John, Paul,

George and Ringo got *that* haircut and emerged to be embraced globally. And yes, the music was raw, unformed. But that was what was really thrilling about them. With the right producer the possibilities were endless. Blah. Blah. Completely over the top, bullshitting blah. Zoe put the glowing, lying letter and tape into a Jiffy bag, and posted it on her way home, after she'd been to the music shop to price violins.

'They start at around three thousand pounds,' the assistant told her.

Zoe smiled. Hiding her shock. 'Ah,' she said. 'That's about right. My son needs an instrument that reflects his talents.'

'Absolutely,' the assistant agreed. 'I'm so glad you feel that way. The number of people we get in who think that some inferior instrument will do. But it does not do. Talent needs to be expressed. An inferior instrument only leads to frustration.'

'Exactly,' said Zoe. Her Mastercard was past its limit; her Visa bringing in foul letters. What to do? Three thousand pounds. And a fiddle was so little. Who'd have thought it. Where did they get that price? A small amount of wood, a few strings of catgut. She'd reckoned a couple of hundred, top whack. She smiled again. 'Thing to do is bring him in. See what suits. What fits. Under his chin sort of thing.'

The assistant smiled back. 'I'd advise that.'

Zoe nodded. 'Wonderful. He'll be so excited. He has such a gift. I'd love to surprise him. But in the circumstances, perhaps it's best he selects his own . . .' She paused, stopped herself, was about to say 'fiddle'. But these people did not sell fiddles. They sold violins. Instruments. Wonderfully crafted things that produced exquisite music. 'Meantime,' she smiled again, worn down by all this smiling, nodding, lying, 'I'll buy a couple of CDs.'

She went through to the record section, flipped through the CDs. Now here was a mystery. She knew nothing about classical music. Was drawn to the more intricate names Stockhausen, Stravinsky. 'Who's the best composer?' she asked the assistant.

'Christ. How do I know? I only listen to hip-hop and dance. Folks buy a lot of Mozart.'

'Did he do a violin concerto?'

'Yes. It's in there. Under M.'

'Is it popular?'

'Not as much as the Bruch.'

'Bruch,' said Zoe. 'Is that good?' She'd have preferred someone with a longer, flashier name.

The assistant shrugged. 'Number one, G minor,' he said. 'Sells.'

Zoe flicked through the Bs. Beethoven, Berlioz, Bizet, Bruckner. These guys had names. You wouldn't find a John Smith here. Maybe she should get Will to change his to something grander. Bouvier? Wainwright-Jones? Maybe they should start calling Toby Tobias. Whatever it took. She found the Bruch. 'Right,' she said. 'What else?'

'If it's violins you're after, the Vivaldi, *Four Seasons*, has a lot of violin in it.'

'Oh, right,' said Zoe. She moved to the Vs, found the Vivaldi. Took them to the counter. Eyed the assistant. A moment's flirting. She couldn't stop herself. Grinned. 'It's for my mother. Can't abide the stuff myself. Hip-hop's more my thing. Like you.'

She emerged from the shop, and cursed herself. Why did she do that? Seek approval, friendship wherever she went? She should stop. Perhaps analysis? An assertiveness course? She should take Will's advice and grow up.

At home, she put on the Bruch. What was it about this piece of music that sold? A roll on the drums, a slow violin that slowly soared, alone, no orchestra. She looked round the room. It was not used to music like this. Will's bad-day *Carmen* and the odd bit of Mozart was all the classical music it got. The orchestra caught up with the solo. She could hear it in the background. A rhythm. A drama.

She was fourteen when Roz left. First home from school, she had moved through the house, opening and shutting doors, calling for her mother. Nobody home. She'd made herself a cup of coffee. Put on the television. Nobody about, she could rummage through her mother's drawers. Look at her secret things. Roz's mother's wedding ring. Removed by the undertaker from her dead body, handed over and kept in a small brown envelope underneath a pile of knickers. Roz's contraceptive pills. A fresh hole pricked out in the foil every time Roz took one out. Zoe was always tempted to steal one, but never did. Sex fascinated her. Did her mum and dad do it? In this house? When she was here? Did they stick their tongues down each other's throats, as she had done only this afternoon with Stephen Dundas? She'd hated it.

'You're meant to suck,' he'd instructed.

'I'm not doing that,' she'd protested.

There was always a special silence in Roz and Matthew's bedroom. It smelled of essential oils, lavender and geranium, that her mother sprinkled on the pillows, swearing that it soothed her insomnia. There had been a note on her father's pillow. Zoe opened it. Read. *I've gone. I'm sorry. I'll be in London. I'll phone. Love Roz.* She read it again. And again. What did it mean? She'll be in London. She should be here making the tea. Was she coming home? When? There was something final about the note. It didn't read like Roz was coming back.

In the room, now, the Bruch played. The whole orchestra quivered and sighed.

But Zoe was fourteen again. Remembering. Who did her mother know in London? She was Mum. She stayed here. Made toast for folks coming home in the afternoon. Shopped on Saturday morning. On Sundays made the only full breakfast the family ate, bacon, eggs, sausages, tomatoes. Oxford marmalade on the table. Papers laid out. Fresh coffee. This lonely woman watched soaps. Had one or two friends with whom she went to the theatre once a month, writing group once a week. She wouldn't go.

The second movement started. A throb, it was. A repeating throb. It hummed through her. Zoe had put the note back on her father's pillow. She'd gone downstairs, nursing her first ever tremor of real fear. Sat clutching her coffee watching cartoons till Matthew came home.

'Where's your mother?'

Zoe shrugged. 'Dunno.'

Matthew had gone upstairs, counting. Zoe listened. Nothing.

Twenty minutes later (she timed it) he appeared at the door with the note. 'She's left us. Gone to London.'

Zoe had looked at him. Said nothing. Her mother. Gone. She couldn't understand her confusion. She wanted her mother here to help her through this moment that her mother had caused. That woman. That body she so rarely touched now. The comfort of it. Warmth that came from somewhere beneath her breasts. She had shrugged at her father. 'Suppose London's better than here.'

Now, she stood surrounded by music. The violin took off on its own. Building up to some sort of climax. The orchestra followed. It roared a huge sigh. Tears flowed down her cheeks. And she didn't know they were there.

It had started then. The pain she felt in Matthew's house. She rarely went there now, but every time she did, she was reminded of that longing. The anxious child waiting for the loved one to return.

'Mummy.' Toby was tugging at her sleeve. Pulling her from her memories. She hadn't heard him and Will come in. 'Daddy and me have been playing football in the park. I'm starving.'

Zoe could hardly see him for tears. 'Toby, I want you to know I will never leave you.'

'Are there any biscuits?' asked Toby, moving out of the room. His mother at full throb was always too much to bear. 'Did you finish the KitKats? If there's not any KitKats could I have a plate of Coco-Pops?'

As he left the room he heard his mother call, 'This is real music. This is the violin. I want you to listen to this.'

Will came in. Turned down the music. 'What's going on?'

'I just bought this CD,' Zoe explained. 'And when I put it on I started to remember the day my mother left.'

Will put his arms round her.

'It wasn't me,' Zoe said. 'I keep telling myself it wasn't me. I know it wasn't. But somehow I can't make myself believe it. I always think I did something wrong.'

CHAPTER SIX

More or less daily, Roz spent time wondering how to shake the Beseley family up. No group of individuals went through life without being hit by some major nonsense, some drama, some tragedy. They were a family who rejoiced in their mundaneness. Blithely trudging through life. That was how Roz thought of them, blithe trudgers.

'It's no way to be,' she said.

'What?' said Fred. He turned to face her. Head on pillow, eyes glued from sleep.

'Nothing,' she said. Three in the morning. He'd been snoring. Not that she minded. It was good to have a body in bed beside her. Someone familiar breathing in the night. Reminded her she was not alone.

'You said something.' He hated it when she did that. Said, 'Nothing,' when it plainly was something. She was always doing that. Finding cursed things in her head and crying out for pain of them. Or alternatively she discovered jokes, funny lines, juicy things to write down, and would laugh out loud at them. And never tell him what it was. If there wasn't some desolation he couldn't soothe, there was a party going on in her head. Either way he wasn't allowed in. Life with Roz could be lonely.

'I went to the wrong funeral the other day,' she told him. 'Then I had to hang about and go to the right one. I felt like a funeral groupie.'

They lay side by side, looking at the ceiling. Words moving slowly from them, into the dark above them. This was Roz's confessional position. How she spoke her sins and follies out loud, as if hearing them made them forgivable. As if she hadn't been trying to forgive herself for the past ten years. As if she was anywhere near succeeding.

'Nan's service was a dull old affair. What else would you expect from Matthew? But the other one was wonderful. Singing and clapping. Folks weeping with abandon. I want that, what Roberta Wise had. Promise me when I go you'll fix up a funeral like that for me.'

'What makes you think we'll still be together? What makes you think you'll go first?'

'Well, if we are. And if I do. Promise me.'

'OK. I promise.' Though the thought of organising a hearty funeral filled him with dread. Then again, these days, since his marriage had fallen apart, most things filled him with dread. Forty-six years old and he didn't know what had happened to him. His wife had announced there was someone else. She was seeking a divorce. It had happened so suddenly. A marriage, children, a life. Then, suddenly, nothing. For two years his wife had been having an affair and he'd hadn't known. Hadn't the smallest inkling.

He worked from home, as an illustrator. She was a lawyer, went out every morning at eight. Came home most nights sometime after six. He'd usually prepared the evening meal, kissed her when she came to the kitchen, bearing news of her busy day, the people she met, the life she led when she was not with him. All that time, all those kisses, she'd been seeing someone else. He took it hard. He'd met Roz two years ago. Cared for her. Thought about her when he was not with her. But commit? That was hard. He wasn't ready for that.

'Maybe this Roberta Wise person was some great benefactor. Maybe she donated thousands to charity. Maybe she helped people. Took old folk to the park in their wheelchairs. Took in underfed, matted stray puppies. Threw parties with balloons and big cakes for orphans type thing. You just don't know,' he said.

'I do, I do,' insisted Roz. 'I was there. This woman was loved for who she was. That's all there is to it.'

'Um . . .' said Fred. He wasn't sure he should say this. But, shit, he was going to anyway. 'Don't you think that to be loved, you have to love first? I mean, sort of give it to get it.'

Roz turned on her side to face the wall. That was the truth. 'You think?'

Fred said, 'I know.' And turned to face the other wall. He was peeved she hadn't said she loved him. Then again, if she had, he might have to say he loved her. He didn't know if he could do that. Though, and this was a big part of his mental wrestlings, he didn't know if he wanted her to say she loved him. Even in a jokey way. Love was such a responsibility.

Roz thought that she loved Fred. But she hadn't ever told him. She was waiting till he told her. She sensed his fear of commitment, and never, ever admitted to her own. She reached over to touch him. She wanted him.

'Nah,' said Fred. 'Not now you haven't said you love me. Obviously you just want me for my body.'

'Obviously,' agreed Roz. She thought a bit of physical activity might be comforting. 'That and your cuddly jumper. And I like going out in your car.'

'Knew it.' Fred reached out, stroked her hair. 'You are a woman of loose morals.'

'Yep,' said Roz. She turned from him. Pulled her pillow round her shoulders, settling in for a serious bit of sleeping. Fred curled into her back, spooning.

It hadn't always been like this. Once there had been passion, delight. That constant anticipation that come evening they would see one another. Once they hadn't been able to wait. They'd phone on the slightest excuse. Linger, not wanting to ring off. Exchanging trivialities. 'See you tonight.' 'OK.' 'Bye, then.' 'OK.' 'Well, ring off then.' 'You ring off.' 'No, you.' And on, till their phone bills became a worry. They both supported estranged families.

Fred remembered their first date. Two years ago. Both just past forty and behaving like love-shy teenagers. Looking at each other, and smiling at each other. Then looking away. Smiling away. He had taken her hand. She'd thrilled at that. How long since someone had so tenderly linked his fingers in hers? He'd lifted it to examine it, like some precious jewel. Squeezed it, softly. 'I love your hand,' he told her. 'It's resilient. Squeezeable.'

She had looked down at their entwined flesh. Resilient. That was nice.

They'd gone to the cinema. Left early because they wanted to talk. She disagreed with almost everything he said. He loved that. Recently he'd been dating younger women, much younger women. It wasn't that they lacked opinions. If anything, he thought, they had too many opinions. But they seemed to opine about things he either hadn't thought about, or didn't really care about.

Fred had started as an illustrator at eighteen years old, fresh from school. No art school training for him. His father wanted him to be a plumber, like he was. But he'd been saved from a life of welding pipes and installing baths and lavatories by his teacher, who'd submitted his portfolio of school drawings to R. M. Harrower and Son, publishers of children's comic books and strip love stories. He'd been taken on and put in the art department. 'In those days, they had art departments,' he'd reminisce. 'Not like now, when everybody's freelance.'

There had been fifteen artists sitting at desks, three rows of five, side by side. It was just like school. Fred fitted in. He loved it. Not a lot of work. And the crack was good. All he really wanted from life was the odd pint, some sex and lots of good crack.

'Good tea, plenty of crack and no genitals,' he said, rapping his knuckles on the table of the bar they were in at the time.

'What, no genitals? None at all?' asked Roz.

'Well,' said Fred, 'some. But not at work. They interfere with the crack.'

For three years Fred had sat at his rickety drawing board modernising old strips. Whitening out flared trousers, inking in straight legs. Taking white gauche to fifties bobs, turning them into Farrah Fawcett layered tumbles.

'There were characters then. All dead. None left. There was Jimmy the crotch-watcher.'

'The what?'

'The crotch-watcher. He'd whiten out wrinkles in the groin area of trousers. So's people wouldn't get the impression naughty bits in there. No tell-tale protuberances, male or female. Our characters were clean-cut guys. Like I said, no genitals. I used to do a bit of crotch-watching myself.'

For several years Fred had sat at his drawing board updating old illustrations, doing the odd bit of crotch-whitening. Till one day, when nobody else was available, Gemma, from one of the women's magazines, stuck for someone to illustrate a cookery page, had invited Fred to do a small drawing of a fish, some parsley, an onion and perhaps a plate or a knife. 'To make it kitcheny,' she said.

The result had changed Fred's young life. His drawing had been perfect. A beautiful fish, a half-chopped onion with the layers of finely veined skin sketched immaculately. Fronds of curly parsley. It had led to more and more cookery illustrations. Till someone wondered if he could do gardens. He could. He drew delicate flowers. Shrubs, cross-hatched, deep shady corners, ivy-covered tree trunks. Slow snails sliding over moss. Fred spent two years doing kitchens and gardens before his talent for people was discovered.

And it was people that he still drew. Fred's characters were wonderful. His children were filled with mischief, glee or woe; his adults beset with dilemmas. They were drawn with quick, fine lines.

But the two characters that had made his name were a man and a woman. Both going through life wrestling with love, divorce, bills, tangled relationships. Both completely naked. Though the woman sometimes wore a huge ornate hat, and the man occasionally carried a briefcase. The nakedness, however, seemed incidental. The people they encountered were all too polite to mention it. They were both slightly porky, going to seed. Living in their own world. It was their expressions, the way Fred captured their mood with a movement of his pen, that people loved. The way their shoulders slumped, or the way they leapt in the air, clicking their heels. The nudity was nothing. Besides, neither of them had any genitals. They did, however, talk an awful lot.

...that clouded Roz and Fred's ... ...he past stopped it developing into ...g-term love. They were both afraid of ...onsidered themselves lacking in dedication, ... marriage had ended badly. His wife had the ...rarely saw them. Neither he nor Roz wanted to fall c... ...y in love, scared of the pain of falling out of love again. Stil... they kept seeing one another. They allowed themselves to be lovers and mates. They liked the same books, movies. Laughed at the same jokes. They agreed about everything. They even shared an uneasiness about commitment. Neither realised that this like-mindedness, and their laughter and good sex, was the best grounding any relationship could have.

In the morning, they woke still curled together. Sweat-drenched from pressing into one another under Roz's thirteen-tog duvet. In the hallway, the post rattled through the letterbox. Roz heaved herself into a sitting position, flapped some air into the overheated bed. 'I can do without feeling like this in the morning. I'm boiled. It's you. You radiate heat.'

'It's your age. You've reached the sweaty time of life. You're not as young as you used to be,' said Fred. He wasn't ready to move yet.

'I'm exactly as young as I've ever been. My body's got older, is all. I can't do anything about it.' She got out of bed. Shivering, wrapped her robe round her. 'It's freezing in here.'

'Doesn't your heating come on?'

'The timer's gone. I don't want to know how much it'll cost to get it fixed.' She went through to the kitchen. A cup of tea first before she faced the mail. Bills were all she ever got. 'Do you want some tea?' she called through to Fred.

'Coffee,' said Fred. 'You make crap tea. Tea-making's an art.'

She brought two steaming mugs back to the bedroom, climbed into bed again. 'I'll keep cosy in here till the heating comes through.' She tried to sip her tea. 'It's too hot.' She put the mug on the dresser beside the bed to cool.

She saw him move uncomfortably. Lifted the duvet. Saw the

state of him. 'Pity you didn't have that last night.'

'You were whining about the Beseleys.'

She took his mug, put it on the dresser with hers. Turned to him. Kissed him. 'It's a pity to waste it.'

'Lay off. What's going on with my body under the duvet's my business.'

'Rubbish,' said Roz. 'You're mine. Well, your body is. Well, for the next little while. Then you can have it back.'

Later, Fred got up, showered. Dressed, he came to kiss Roz goodbye. She was still in bed.

'What sort of day have you got ahead?' she asked.

'Naked people wrestling with life. You?'

'I'm Beseleying. I have to go for a meeting with Ronnie. He likes to have a hand in what's going to happen in the next half-dozen episodes. He doesn't trust me.'

'Wise chap,' said Fred. 'Look how you've just taken advantage of me.' He kissed her.

When he'd gone, leaving her in bed, she waited, sleepily, a full twenty minutes luxuriating, before she went to fetch the mail that had landed on the mat in the hall over a couple of hours ago. She thumbed through it. Bills. An offer of a personal loan. An insurance company flier. And a letter postmarked Edinburgh. She turned it over. Held it to her ear, listening to the contents rattle, before opening it.

It was a letter from Nan's solicitor.

Dear Ms Rutherford,

I am enclosing herewith a cassette tape made by my client, Nancy Rutherford, the day before her death. She specifically requested this be sent to you after her funeral.

Yours sincerely

Thomas J. Anderson.

Roz turned the tape over in her hand. Nan had touched this. She stroked it. Nan. Missed already, and barely cold in her grave.

'Hello, Roz,' Nan said. 'You'll be back in London now. You'll have been to my funeral. No doubt Matthew didn't play Bob Marley. No doubt it was the usual boring service. Rubbish about me being the last of a generation. Sorely missed. Beloved grandmother and great-grandmother.' She sighed.

Roz sniffed. She should have done something. Phoned Matthew, insisted he do as Nan wanted. How awful to die knowing your last wishes would be ignored.

'I knew it,' Nan continued. 'No matter. I've sent Matthew a tape telling him how disappointed I am. There's nothing like a voice from the grave to send shivers down the spine. I'm hoping the guilt shakes him up a bit. But I'm not counting on it.

'No. I'm counting on you. I've gone and died and there's things to be done. I'm presuming you've got my ashes. Remember I want them scattered on Mull.'

Roz had the ashes. After the small farewell do at Matthew's, she'd returned to the crematorium and picked them up. A large jar, not unlike a giant-size jar of instant coffee, with *Nan Rutherford* scrawled on a sticky label on the side. Roz had felt awkward carrying it home on the plane. What if someone asked what was in it? What if they hit some turbulence and she dropped the jar, and it broke, spilling the contents? She hadn't put it in the overhead rack, kept it wedged safely between her feet.

Once home, she'd put the jar on the living room coffee table. Stared at it. Then, feeling unable to function with Nan in the room, had put it, apologising as she did so, in the cupboard in the hall. As soon as she shut the door, she felt guilty. A dark cupboard was no place for Nan to rest. She opened it again. Then took some gold Christmas paper and wrapped it round the jar, put a silk ribbon bow on top, made a wreath of sorts from tinsel and put it back. 'That's the best I can do,' she apologised again. 'It's just ashes, in the living room. It might, you know, upset folk.' She nodded. She thought Nan knew.

She had no idea when she'd be able to travel to Mull to scatter them. 'One day,' she said. 'One day, soon.' She wanted rid of them. Then again, she dreaded the actual scattering. White, grey ashes, which were Nan. Flying off into the wind. She didn't want to finally say goodbye to Nan. At least with the ashes here with her, it wasn't quite over.

'Second of all,' Nan went on, 'I want you to know you should dedicate your life to doing what you want to do. And some of what you want to do should be silly. Comes to this – if you don't, what's the point?

'I always think you spend the first half of your life getting yourself sorted. Then you sit about for years thinking, Now what? You come and you go and you take up hobbies to pass the time. Passing time is no way to pass time. I think you should spend the second half of your life getting yourself unsorted. There ought to be a law. I've sat here in this chair for the past few years thinking this. And you should take notice. I mean, what's the point of all my thinking if nobody's going to get the benefit.'

Roz could hear Bob Marley in the background. 'No Woman No Cry'. She loved that track, too.

'So,' Nan went on, 'there's a little something for you. M. and N. Thomson's not far from you. I know you'll like it. Like it? You'll love it. I wish to hell I could have had it. It's one of the things I thought about. Have a fine time. I want it for you. I'm an old lady. But in my heart, I want all sorts of things. I want to whisk along country roads, loud music roaring. I want to be chums with my child. But Matthew? Does he have chums? I fear for him. I mean, he's so enclosed, isn't he? What's going on in that mind of his? All that counting. What did you two ever find to talk about? Did you talk? Or laugh? Or argue? Did you two ever have a really good fight? That's the problem, I think. You should have had more fights, cleared the air. Your marriage was like an old person's room that had the windows shut tight all year round, only stagnant air to breathe and the musty smell of unaired things, if you ask me.

'I sit in my room. I get my life experience second hand now. From telly. Such rubbish I see. I wonder about it. It hurtles at me, flows into me. Rubbish. And, the mood of me, that's all I want. Is that how you feel? Do you think the human race is predisposed to rubbish? Stuff to make you forget? I wonder, if *Family Fortunes* had been available at the time of the great Chinese philosophers, would we have gathered any important information at all?

'All the things I want. They grow daily. And they're so little. I want to walk to the shops. I want to weed my garden. Make huge pots of soup for my family. I used to love waking in the morning and seeing a man's face on the pillow next to mine. Hear his breathing in the night. Then if it was the weekend we could stay in bed all day if we wanted. Listen to the radio, take cups of tea. Make love again and again.'

Roz's eyes widened. Nan? Nan did that? When?

'But me, I'm just an old screwed-up lady, and you're just a young screwed-up lady. Do you suppose life would be better if we could choose the ways in which we are screwed up? Me, I wish and I wish and I wish. Here's us with our messed-up lives, and the clock ticking. Me, waiting for death. And you staring into your future with your brows knit.

'I want to smile to strangers,' said Nan. 'I want to make love again. I long for that. I think about that.'

Alone in her living room, Roz didn't know where to look. Nan? Men? Sex? She had never thought of Nan in that sort of way.

'Anyway,' Nan went on, 'enjoy the thing. Love it. For me. I always wanted one. But the day dawns that you're too old to be silly. When you're young, silliness becomes you. You'll be hearing from me again. It's not over. It's far from over. I may be dead, but I'm not dead yet.'

CHAPTER SEVEN

'Do you have to lie there like that?' Zoe came through from the kitchen where she'd been preparing a nutritious, brain-developing, balanced meal for Toby, saw Jamie lying sprawled on her sofa, felt jealous that it was not she who was lying sprawled, pulled a cushion from under Jamie's head and hit him with it. 'It's all you do, lie about.'

Jamie looked at her. Moved his shoulders up and down. He even shrugged lazily.

'What have you done today?' Zoe asked. 'Anything?'

'Got up,' said Jamie. 'That's something.'

'It's nothing. Everybody gets up.'

'No they don't. I don't. Not always.'

'Christ, Jamie. You've got to sort yourself out. Get a job. Do something.'

'Why?'

'Why! Because this is your life. You're wasting it.'

'Why is lying about wasting your life? I like lying about. It's fun. It just pisses you off to see someone lying about when you're so driven.'

'Driven? What do you mean, driven?'

'All this stuff about Toby playing the violin. And sending Will's tapes off to some London company. It's as well nothing'll come of it. What'd Will say if he found out?'

'He'd be overjoyed. Success. Recognition of his talent.'

'He's not talented. He's competent. Not enough.'

'Rubbish.' Zoe dismissed this. 'He's sensitive. A human attribute you'd know nothing about. You're a waster and a layabout.'

'Wasters and layabouts are sensitive. Often they're the most

71

sensitive of all. It hurts to face the world.'

Zoe sighed. There was no arguing with Jamie. She had almost given up on him. But not quite. He just needed a shove. But what exactly that shove should be escaped her.

'Anyway,' said Jamie, 'it may look to you like I'm lying about. But it's all going on up here.' He tapped his forehead. 'I'm thinking. Making plans.'

Zoe knew all about Jamie's plans. Jamie was waiting for the Big Idea to come to him. He believed in big ideas. 'All you need is one and you're made. For example, the cat's-eye man. One corking idea and he never had to work again.' Jamie often cited the cat's-eye man as the sort of entrepreneur he admired. One idea, putting cat's-eye reflectors up the middle of roads, and he'd conquered the world. That was what a young and ambitious chap wanted. One spurt of work, then sit back for the rest of your life drinking beer, swimming in your pool, watching videos, and polishing your fleet of Aston Martins.

'What ideas are you toying with this week?' asked Zoe.

'Right,' said Jamie, sitting up to reach for one of Zoe's cigarettes. Lighting it. Lying back. 'There's electronic kites.'

'How would they work?'

'Dunno yet. It's just in embryo form. But they'd light up at night.'

'Wouldn't that distract aircraft?'

'Nah. They're way higher than your average kite. Then there's talking vibrators.'

'What would they say?'

' "Uh-uh-ooh. You're fantastic." It's for women who don't have partners. Or they could say something dirty. Haven't decided yet. Or romantic. They could recite love poems.'

'Before, after, or during use?' Zoe wanted to know.

'One of those.'

Zoe's face went intent with concentration. The talk of vibrators reminded her she hadn't done her pelvic-floor exercises today. She started doing them. She was fanatical about her pelvic-floor exercises. Her feminine maintenance she called them.

' 'S'up with you?' asked Jamie. 'You've gone all constipated and cross-eyed-looking.'

'Nothing.' She went back to the kitchen to check on Toby's cod soaked in lemon juice and herbs with lentils. He'd whine about it now, but come his twenty-first birthday, when with clean skin, strong bones and fertile mind he faced the world, he'd be grateful.

Jamie surfed the channels on the television, then gave up. Afternoon chat shows could be a bore. He followed Zoe into the kitchen. 'Maybe the vibrators could give women a score, like computer games. Wow, you got three thousand. Sorry, you're a two. Have you done this before? It'd make women try harder. Get the hang of sex.'

'Like they haven't already.'

'Well, they'd use it more trying to up their points.'

'Get a job, Jamie.'

'No. Absolutely never. I'll come up with the right scam. See if I don't.'

Zoe mixed olive oil and lemon juice, poured it over the fish.

'What's that?' Jamie wanted to know.

'Food for Toby. Fish. Good for the brain.'

'Poor kid. He'll grow up and only ever eat burgers. Childhood deprivation.'

'Rubbish. He'll thank me. This is more than our mother ever did for us.'

'She fed us OK.'

'Like you remember.'

'Yes. She made great pancakes. Apple crumbles. That Potage Bonne Femme thing. She did a mean chicken curry. She wasn't all bad.'

'She was.'

'Wasn't.'

'She walked out on us.'

'Can you blame her? I mean, Dad. Christ. I don't know how she stood it for as long as she did. He's so uptight. D'you suppose they ever actually shagged?'

'Well, we're here, aren't we?'

'Yeah, but after we were born?'

'I can't imagine it.' She shivered. 'Gives me the creeps. Oh yuck.'

'I was thinking of going to see her.'

'You weren't. How could you?' She turned, waved the knife she was using to chop herbs at him. 'It'd be a betrayal. After all we've been through.'

'I think it was tough on her too. Anyway, at the funeral she looked cool. I want to know her.'

'Cool! It wasn't very cool to walk out on us. Her children. She didn't care. She could've taken us with her.'

'How? She'd no money. No job. Nowhere to live. We went to see her soon after Dad and Claire got together. She told us any time we wanted to go, the door was open. What more could she do?'

'Lots,' said Zoe. Though she couldn't think what. 'If you go I'll never speak to you again. Never. I absolutely forbid you to do it.'

Jamie laughed. When did anybody forbid him to do anything? His father had given up years ago. After he'd been brought home by the police, caught truanting in a games arcade. Matthew had raged. Jamie had shrugged his mild, lazy shrug. He was suspended from school for two weeks, which he'd enjoyed enormously.

When he returned to his classes, the teachers who knew him took him aside and either spoke to him kindly about how he was wasting his life, his brains; or berated him, fists clenched lest they shook him or throttled him. He had that effect on people. Too clever by half, people said. He had an easy wit, a lazy intelligence. It came naturally. He rarely studied. Opened his books the night before an exam. Next day, he'd stroll in, hands in pockets, sit at his desk, yawning, writing as little as possible, and always, always got A's. It more than irritated people. It drove them wild. What could he achieve if he tried? Nobody would ever know. Jamie had no intention of trying. Especially when not trying had such an effect on the people he seriously did not want to impress.

Two weeks after returning to school, Jamie had set fire to the English class. He hadn't meant to do it. He'd been idly flicking his

Zippo on and off. Flame was fascinating. Watched it flicker. Snapped it off. On again. Watched it again. Set it to his copy of *King Lear*, watched the heat spread, char the edges of the page, stubbed it out. After that he held the lighter against a poster of the Edinburgh Festival performance of *Faust*. Tinder dry, it had been pinned to the wall for the past twenty years. It erupted. The flames caught the curtains. Jamie looked at them with mild interest as they disintegrated. Flames billowed. Spread to a pile of papers on the teacher's desk. The smoke alarm sounded. It was amazing, Jamie thought, how things happened. So suddenly. So out of control. The class was evacuated as the English teacher grappled, yelling abuse, with the extinguisher, which didn't work. Fire alarms sirened through the building. Pupils trooped, in twos, into the playground. Amazed, and mostly pleased to be free for the rest of the afternoon. The fire brigade were called, but by the time they arrived the fire was out.

Jamie noticed something. The worse your crime, the less anybody could do about it. He was yelled at. Expelled from school. Who cared? He didn't like school anyway. He was grounded by his father for six weeks. He didn't mind. Where was he going to go nights? He'd no money and most of his friends were forbidden by their parents to speak to him.

He was charged with wilful damage and arson and appeared in court. His lawyer claimed Jamie had been traumatised at an early age by the departure of his mother. Jamie adamantly denied any such thing. Said he didn't blame his mother for going. It was his father drove him to it. The court thought him disturbed and he was let off with a warning.

The school claimed fire damage from their insurance company and received several thousand pounds, enough to refurbish the classroom. All that, and they were finally rid of Jamie. The headmaster thought it an excellent outcome.

Jamie settled into staying home, watching daytime television, drinking too much coffee and running up huge telephone bills calling chat-lines. He never admitted to the isolation he felt. His delinquencies were never intentional. He just got notions, and acted on them. Or started off on some naughty scheme and took it too far. He had once climbed on to the school roof to retrieve a ball, and when up there climbed higher and higher till he was on its highest peak, with the flagpole, waving his arms and shouting with joy at being so far off the ground. Six weeks picking up litter in the playground after school for that.

Then again, he thought it'd be cool to take Matthew's car for a spin one winter evening when there wasn't a lot to do. Enjoying the speed at which he was covering the ground, he drove further and further, till he was miles down the motorway. He might have got away with this mischief except that he ran out of petrol and had to leave the car on the hard shoulder whilst he walked four miles to the nearest garage, filled up the can Matthew kept in the boot, then trudged four miles back again. By which time it was dawn. Rather than drive to the next turn-off, he did a U-turn on the motorway, bumping over into the lanes going in the opposite direction. He was spotted by the police and, after a short, siren-wailing chase, pulled over. He gave his name as Matthew Rutherford, said he hadn't his licence with him and explained that he'd had to turn back as his mother was seriously ill and he'd got vibes that he should go to her. 'She's mystic,' he said. 'She has powers.' He could tell the police doubted him. But they let him go after breathalysing him.

For a week he thought he'd got away with it. Then the summons came.

'What's this?' Matthew said. 'I haven't been down the motorway in months.'

'It was me,' Jamie told him. 'I got caught doing a U-turn on the motorway in your car.'

'My car? You stole my car?'

Jamie shrugged.

'Where the hell were you going?'

'Dunno,' said Jamie.

Matthew looked at him. Words failed him. He stood, opening and shutting his mouth, fists clenched. Anger coursed through him. He turned to storm up the stairs. Changed his mind. Stormed back up to Jamie and punched him. Jamie reeled, fell back on to the sink, knocking the breakfast bowls to the floor. Shattering them.

'Clear that mess up,' Matthew yelled.

'OK, OK. Don't lose the head,' Jamie said. As he bent to pick up the shattered china, drops of blood from his split lip dripped on to the vinyl tiles. 'Christ,' he said, hand to swollen face. 'There was no need for that.'

'There was every need for that,' Matthew shouted. 'You're a waste of space.'

Jamie unravelled a huge chunk of patterned kitchen roll and nursed his face. 'Fuck you,' he said. 'I don't do nothing anybody else doesn't do. I just always get caught.'

'You're a waste of space,' Matthew repeated. 'And it's *anything*.'

Matthew took the blame, got fined two hundred pounds and had a couple of points taken off his licence. And didn't speak to Jamie for weeks. He found forgiveness hard.

After that Jamie drifted into the wastrel life. Drugs. Cannabis mainly, some speed, spot of E when he could afford it. Then there was women. He'd loved how he could shock Matthew with the people he brought home. Girls who looked spaced out, the wilder the better. He never chose anybody who looked remotely normal. He loved to watch Matthew politely trying to cope with the misfits he introduced into the living room. Girls plastered with eye make-up, purple hair, leather gear, everything pierced, who had long lost the knack of communicating in formal English. 'Would you like a cup of tea, Tanya? Coffee? Cocoa?'

'Uh-huh.'

The girls were just an adornment to his wild-boy image. He thought that in the business of shocking Matthew, he had peaked with the U-turn on the motorway. And the summons. He hadn't bothered after that. In fact he hadn't bothered with anything after that.

Now Zoe chopped violently. 'Our mother is a woman of no substance. She hadn't the strength to see us through our childhoods.'

'Nan wanted me to go see her,' Jamie said. 'Couple of days before she died, she made me promise I'd visit her.'

'Nan?' said Zoe. 'She was an old romantic. What did she know? Why should you make up with our mother for her? Our mother felt nothing for us. Why else would she walk out? What interest did she show in us? Where was she when my periods started? Where was she when Michael Leslie left me for Julia Harrington? My heart was broken. I do believe I haven't fully recovered. My confidence took such a knock.'

'You were sixteen.'

'A teenage trauma can affect your whole life. Where was she when my child was born? She should have been there.'

'She came next day. Brought flowers and all sorts of baby junk.'

'If she'd been about when we were growing up, you wouldn't have turned into the aimless layabout you are, and I . . . I . . .' Zoe raked through her brain for some dramatic yet glamorous way to describe herself.

'Wouldn't be the hysterical promiscuous neurotic you are?' Jamie offered.

'Exactly,' said Zoe. 'It's all her fault.'

Realising what she'd just admitted to, Zoe stopped chopping.

The front door slammed. They heard Toby's feet running down the hall into the living room, Will behind him.

Zoe and Jamie stared at each other. Started to giggle at her passionate absurdity. Will stuck his head round the door. 'What's going on?'

'Nothing,' said Zoe. 'Just preparing supper.'

Will looked at them. They were snickering. Huddled and snickering. Private jokes. They had a closeness he could never infiltrate. They were involved in a little world of smiles. He wanted to be more than Zoe's lover; he wanted to be her mentor, adviser and confidant. Her partner proper. But she had Jamie to confide in, lean on. There was a time, then, when Will had resented Jamie. Whilst liking him. Everyone liked Jamie. Now he was glad of Jamie, someone to share the load. Someone else to soak up Zoe's woes, insecurities.

'Hi, Jamie,' he said. 'How're you doing?'

'Great,' said Jamie. Jamie, according to Jamie, was always doing great.

Will went through to the living room. Thumbed through his CDs, put on The Band, 'The Weight'. Zoe looked up, listening. This was a new after-work tune. What did it mean?

Jamie said he was going.

'Aren't you staying to eat?' asked Zoe.

'Nah. Things to do. Plans to make.'

'I'm warning you,' said Zoe. 'You go chasing after that woman and I'll never speak to you again.

Jamie left. On his way up the hall he met Toby heading for the kitchen. 'Hi, Tobes.' As he left the house, he heard the child wail, 'Fish and lentils. I'm not eating that. Why can't we have pizza like real people?'

He paused before shutting the door, waiting for Zoe's reply. Mouthed along with her: 'Pizza's all fat. You'll be grateful when you're twenty-one. Wait and see.'

He did not reckon on the impact Zoe's overactive mothering would have on Toby.

'Will not wait till I'm twenty-one. I'll *never* be twenty-one. I want pizza. I *want* it.' Then Toby started to scream. Jamie heard a wild hammering on the floor. The child was having a tantrum. A full-blown howler of a tantrum. He was lying drumming his heels on the kitchen floor yelling for pizza. He rose a good ten points in his uncle's estimation. 'Good on ya, kid,' Jamie said. As he shut the door he wondered if there was money to be made in selling secret junk food to kids with nutritionally zealous mothers. A pizza-pusher. Furtive Fries. Nah, he thought, imagining the wrath of women in espadrilles descending upon him.

CHAPTER EIGHT

Roz had never believed in love at first sight. But chemistry at first sight, yes, that could happen. It happened now. She clapped eyes on the red Triumph convertible and her heart turned over. 'For me?' she asked the sales assistant.

After receiving Nan's tape, and a swift breakfast of coffee and a couple of chocolate biscuits, because she had nothing else to eat in her flat, she'd gone to find M. and N. Thomson's. It was a garage.

'Yes,' shrugged the salesman. 'Old dear phoned and asked what was the silliest car we had. We told her this. "Is it a soft top?" she asks. She insisted it be a soft top. "I'll take it," she says. We told her she should see it. Drive it about a bit. "How the hell can I do that? I'm in Edinburgh," she says. "Besides, I'm eighty years old and haven't even got a driving licence." Said it was for her daughter-in-law. Is that you?'

'Nan bought this for me?' Roz couldn't believe it. 'It's beautiful. It's so beautiful.'

'If that's the sort of thing you like,' said the salesman. 'Only half a car if you ask me. I've never liked convertibles. No protection.'

Roz shot him a glance. This man had no soul.

'But it's lovely.' She ran a slow hand over the bonnet. If the salesman had not been standing beside her, she thought she might have kissed it.

'It's got rust. It'll need new sills this time next year. And these spoked wheels are a bugger to clean.'

Clean? thought Roz. Clean? How typical of a bloke to look at a lovely, sexy car and think about cleaning it. 'I'm not going to clean it,' she almost said. But thought better of it.

'We'll need your insurance and driving licence. Can't hand a car over these days without them.'

Roz hadn't thought to bring her licence. 'I don't have insurance for a car. And my licence is at home.' She wanted to jump up and down with frustration, the desire to drive off was so overwhelming. But she trailed home, found her licence, which took some time as she hadn't used it for over ten years.

For a while she wondered if she'd left it behind when she left home all those years ago, and sat down and cried at the thought. She'd have to apply for another, and that would take ages and ages. She'd *never* get to drive that car. To swish about town looking grand. She'd get a new pair of sunglasses. Ray Bans. Cost a fortune, but who gave a damn? A car like that deserved the best. She was blowing her nose on her third Kleenex when she remembered the brown envelope she'd stuffed in the lower drawer of the chest in the bedroom. It had all her life's paperwork in it. Her divorce papers. Her birth certificate. All the stuff she didn't want to look at. Or run into accidentally when searching for something else. That was the thing about looking for something: you always found something you'd been looking for weeks before and had given up on. To guard against running into her past and the flood of painful memories it brought, she'd rammed the envelope underneath her old sweaters in that drawer. She was sure she'd put her driving licence in there, thinking she'd never need it again.

She had. Feeling foolish for snivelling – well, more outright howling – she shoved it into her handbag and hurried back to the garage. She had to have that car. Now. Like a child with a new bike, she wanted to drive it round and round and round and never stop. As she ran from her flat the phone rang. She stopped, looked at it. 'Oh, stuff it. Let the answering machine cope.' She ran on, slammed the door. Today was hers. Nothing could be more important than that car.

She sipped indigestibly weak scalding coffee in the salesman's claustrophobic cubicle whilst he filled in forms arranging her insurance and registering the car in her name. She jiggled. Fondled the car keys. 'These are mine.' The salesman looked at her. Wincing under his gaze, she apologised. 'I've never had my own car before.'

When at last she inched her way from the garage and out into the traffic, first gear, hood down despite the weather, which was inhospitable, threatening rain, she could not see the way ahead for tears. She was wearing two jumpers, taken from the flat when she'd returned to search for the licence. and a thick alpaca scarf, wrapped several times round her neck. Sunglasses perched on her nose, she felt ostentatiously pretentious. But what the hell. In this car ostentatiously pretentious was what was demanded of you. Anything less would be letting it down. New standards were required. This wasn't a car. It was a lifestyle.

She drove down the road, gingerly. Crunching gears. It had been years since she'd been behind the wheel. By the time she'd jerked along to the end of the next street she was beginning to doubt her new outrageous image.

A little boy with a freckle-smattered face and cheek in his heart, hurtling precariously along the pavement on a tiny bike, stopped to watch her go. 'Wanker,' he shouted.

He's right, she thought. Someone crouched over the wheel, peering anxiously at the road ahead, moving this slowly, this badly, ought to have the modesty to keep the hood up. Hiding. At least then they wouldn't hear the abuse shouted by passers-by.

She crept along till she found a parking space large enough for her to go into forwards. She wasn't up to anything as bold as reverse parking yet. In fact she was already planning a circuitous route home that avoided anything tricky like holding the car on the clutch at junctions, or fancy turns against the flow of traffic coming in the opposite direction. That was, if she had her bearings right. She realised that after living in London for years she did not really know how to navigate the city above ground. She took the tube everywhere. A mole's existence. She still envied those people who knew how to navigate from Chiswick to Crouch End without disappearing into the bowels of the earth.

She put the hood up. Switched off the engine and sat. Stroked the steering wheel, fondled the gear stick. Was it right that a person should love a thing? A car? Still, it was a start. She had long suspected she hadn't ever loved in her life. Not properly. Fully. Wholly. With that unquestioning commitment she'd seen in her friends.

They had all been, at first, consumed with desire. Touching one another, holding on to each other in public. Then slipped into something quieter, more settled, when passion quelled a little. In crowded rooms, she would watch couples she knew. How they arrived together, moved away from one another, yet one always knew where the other was. And sometimes their eyes would meet, and they'd say silent things to each other with the raising of an eyebrow, a slip of a smile, a pout, anything. She'd wonder what they did when they got home. Did they talk about who they'd met? And what was said? Did they make love? Did they mind the bedtime routine? One making tea, the other hogging the bathroom? What was it like to live with someone you loved? She would wonder about it because her relationship with Matthew had never been like that. They'd married too young and for the wrong reason. It had seemed the right thing to do. Nobody, she thought, should do something as drastic as marrying because they thought they ought.

Roz ran her hands round the steering wheel. Thanking Nan over and over, she flicked the lights off and on, played with the windscreen wipers. But this was a car to go places in. If only she could think of somewhere to go.

Fred. She could show it off to him. She started the engine. Before she'd driven a hundred yards, she started to worry about parking when she got there. Then there were lanes; which to choose? She crawled along, clutching the wheel, leaning forward. Switched off the radio. Mindless disc jockey banterings were offputting.

The journey, which on foot usually took twenty minutes, took Roz three-quarters of an hour. She chose the wrong lane; instead of turning left had to turn right, carry on till she found a safe place to get her car pointing in the correct direction again. She stalled at a set of traffic lights, sat wrestling with the ignition, tears in her eyes, whilst a driver behind leaned out of his window and yelled, 'Get that effing pushbike off the road.' She hadn't noticed that the street where Fred lived, that she walked up and down often, was one-way to traffic. It was hell out here on the Queen's highway.

It was past three when she parked at Fred's door, behind his comforting Citroën. She shivered. Her two jumpers and alpaca scarf were not nearly enough protection for the chill late-October day. The whole business of going to the garage to get the car, returning home to find her licence, getting insured, and driving to Fred's had taken five hours. She cursed herself for her idiocy. She'd wasted a day. Was sure she had something she ought to have been doing, but couldn't quite remember what. She felt her memory had disappeared into a black hole in her brain.

When Fred found her on his doorstep, she was trembling with cold, chilled through. Barely able to move. Especially her hands, which were curled numb from gripping the steering wheel. And she was in tears.

'For God's sake, Roz,' he said, ushering her in. He thought something dreadful had happened to her. A fire. A death. She'd been told she had a terminal disease. 'What's wrong?'

'It's my car,' she wailed. 'It hates me.'

He held her to him. Rubbed some warmth into her. She stuck her frozen hands into his armpits. He did not wince. 'When did you get a car?'

'Today. Nan left it to me. She bought it over the phone. I just heard after you left.'

'Where is it?'

'At the door. You never told me you lived in a one-way street.' Accusingly.

Still gently rubbing her back, 'Sorry. I didn't think to mention it.'

'How long has it been one-way?'

'About fifteen years. Long before I moved here.'

'Oh.'

He went to the window, looked out. 'It's lovely. It's a car all right.'

'How do you know which one's mine?'

'It's facing the wrong way.' It was Roz's, it had to be. He went back to hug her, warm her. Dry her crying eyes with the sleeve of his shirt.

Fred amused himself often thinking of Roz. In gym class at school, Roz would be the one who turned left when the teacher shouted, 'Right!' He'd taken her to her first classical concert. She'd started clapping enthusiastically at the end of the second movement of Beethoven's seventh. Looked round, embarrassed, turned to him, said, 'There's more? When these guys wrote a tune, they wrote a tune.' Loudly. People nearby hissed, 'Sssh . . .' Roz at a dinner party he'd taken her to recently had gone to the loo, lost her bearings – and she regularly lost her bearings, her sense of direction was nonexistent – walked into a cupboard, found the loo. Lost her bearings again on emerging and walked out the back door. Roz sang Nina Simone to assistants in record shops when she didn't know the name of the song she wanted to buy. Providing the orchestration and piano accompaniment. She had regular fits of the giggles. Her coat pockets were filled with treasures – an oak apple, a tiny golden stone crisscrossed with white lines so that it looked like a Christmas parcel, a lipstick she loved. She phoned him at least once a week with crossword clues she could not get. 'What's the pointer thing on a sundial called? Something n, something m, something, something.' No 'Hello, it's me.' Just straight in with the question. 'A gnomon,' he told her. Thanks, and she rang off. Nothing more to say. Till she was stuck at the next clue. Roz took ages to select what she wanted from a menu. Took a bite of a chocolate, decided she didn't like the centre, gave it to him to finish whilst she selected something else. She dithered. Walked into rooms, stood staring, trying to remember why she was there. Said, 'No, can't think.' Walked out again. Roz was the innocent naked lady he drew, stumbling through life with her doubts, fears and insecurities hanging out for all the world to see.

All his friends knew it was her. Everyone at the magazine she worked for recognised her. The only person who did not know that it was her was Roz. Fred's fans adored her. So did Fred.

Holding her to him, stroking her, cheek resting on the top of her head, he thought, Mental note, tell her. That'd be the thing to do.

He led her to the gas fire. Switched it on. Sat her down. He'd make her coffee. 'I don't expect you've eaten today.'

'I had some chocolate biscuits for breakfast. After you left.'

'Right,' he said. And went off to his kitchen. Returned with coffee and a sandwich. Chicken and salad and fine slices of Gruyere cheese. Watched her eat.

'You're a good cook, Fred.' She sipped her coffee. 'This tastes funny.'

'I put a splash of whisky in. To heat you up.'

She nodded. Mayonnaise oozed out of the sides of the bread on to her lips. He handed her a napkin.

'You didn't realise how cold it was today?' he asked.

'There was nothing about cold on the radio.'

'Roz, you only had to step outside to know it was cold.'

'I just thought it was me. I didn't think it was the day.' She drank her coffee. He thought: Only Roz.

'Why,' he asked, 'do you think Nan gave you a car?' He didn't have to ask, though. He knew.

'I don't know. She loved me.'

Fred was about to say he loved her, and the last thing he would give her was a car. She was so indecisive. She had no sense of direction.

'Nan was lovely,' Roz enthused. 'Lovely.'

'I'm sure,' he said.

Nan had given Roz a car. It would make her mobile. It would free her to make decisions, small decisions. But regular small decisions. That might lead to bigger decisions. Roz was a drifter and a ditherer. The only big decision she had made in her life had been to leave Matthew. And at that, she'd convinced herself she'd go back to him. Fred suspected that in her heart she'd known she wouldn't.

'Don't you have work to do?' he asked.

She nodded.

'So have I,' he said. 'I'll drive you home.'

'What about my car?'

'We'll go in your car. I'll leave it at your door.'

'And walk back?'

'It'll do me good.'

Fred parked the precious new car in Roz's street. Refused the offer of coffee. 'Some of us have to work instead of playing with our new toys.'

'Piss off,' she told him.

He smiled, patted her cheek. 'Never mind. Next time you want to go out in it, call me. I'll walk in front waving a red flag.'

'Sarcasm,' she told him, quoting her old English teacher, who had been quoting someone else, she couldn't remember who, 'is the lowest form of wit, and the highest form of vulgarity.'

'I know.' He gently punched her arm. 'That's why I love it.'

Once inside, she decided to take a bath. Put on her robe. That way, she'd not be tempted to nip downstairs to check the beloved, gleaming at the door of her building, to make sure she was safe. Unvandalised. She, she thought. It's a goddamn thing. It hasn't got a personality. She went through to the bathroom, started to fill the bath. Poured Yling-ylang and sandalwood oil into the swirl of waters under the tap.

She would not allow herself to fall in love with this car. It'd only end in grief. All her relationships did. She'd end up neglecting it. Or resenting the responsibilities it brought her; taxing it, MOTing it, insuring it. She'd berate it if it let her down. And it surely would. But in the end, she knew, she would be the one to fail it. She always failed everybody. She'd fill it with rubbish, sweet wrappers, soft drink tins. She'd never clean it, have it serviced, put water in the little tank thing that squished the windscreen. It'd end badly. Like all her relationships. It hating her because it'd wind up in some breaker's yard stripped of its important bits facing the great crusher. Her weeping because it'd all be her fault. Best be honest with the thing now. Let it know right at the start that she was an unreliable lover, never willing to commit.

Once bathed, Roz went to work at her desk in the corner of her living room. She left her answering machine blinking. She'd get her messages tomorrow. There couldn't be anything important. There never was.

Fred walked home. Once there, he sat at his board. He drew his naked lady, standing at a bus stop in a blizzard, wearing only her fabulous hat. 'Chilly today,' she said to the warmly wrapped man standing next to her. *To Roz*, he wrote, *who I adore*. He put the drawing in an envelope. Wrote her name and address on the front. Put the envelope in the pocket of his jacket.

He made lists. To-do lists. Next day's list included phoning the electrician about a new light fitting, finishing an illustration, and posting Roz's drawing. Having made a list, Fred thought, Things sorted. Dealt with. He always lost his lists.

That evening his ex-wife phoned to tell him that his eighteen-year-old daughter needed a lift from London to Manchester where she was at university. She couldn't take the train as she was taking her stereo system with her. Next day, eight o'clock, Fred set off. Deciding that driving with his jacket on was too uncomfortable, he threw it on to the back seat. And when he got home, left it there. The weather turned chillier and he took to wearing his coat. The jacket stayed in the back of the car, Roz's drawing still in the pocket. Fred forgot about it. It had been on another day's to-do list. He never did post it.

CHAPTER NINE

Six messages on Roz's machine. She finally got round to listening to them, the day after picking up her car. The first was Connie, Ronnie's deputy. 'Hi, Roz.' Cheerily. 'You're not there. I guess you're on your way here. We'll see you soon. Ronnie's keen to get on with the meeting. He's got some ideas for the Beseleys.'

The second was Connie. Again. 'Hi, Roz.' Slightly less cheery. 'It's past twelve. You were due here at nine. Perhaps there's some sort of hold-up on the tube. Give us a ring if you can't manage it.'

The third was Connie. Not cheery at all. 'Roz. Are you there? Please pick up. I don't know why, but Ronnie's getting agitated.' A breathy pause. The sound of a hand cupping over the receiver. 'He's getting into a state. For heaven's sake, it's only the Beseleys. I mean, really. I don't think anybody even reads them.'

Roz's stomach heaved. It was all very well for her to hate the Beseleys. But other people? That wasn't on. She felt strangely protective towards them. How dare Connie speak about them like that.

She looked round. A creeping panic. What if Connie took over? What if the Beseleys were dumped? Fifteen hundred words four times a month, five some months, paid for most of this. What would she do? She couldn't afford the mortgage. Then, horror, hand to alarmed mouth. 'I couldn't afford the car.'

The fourth message, Connie – yet again. Sounding crazed. 'Roz, where are you? Ronnie's in a strop. He's stamping about, swearing and shouting. I've never seen him like this. It's so unmanly. I didn't know he was like this. He's usually so quiet, staring out the window. Dreaming. I said to him, "Roz is a creative person," I said. "People like that are never completely reliable. Some muse might have come over her. Who knows what intricate things she's thinking?" "Thinking?" he says. "I don't pay her to think. I'm the editor. I think. She writes." It's quite perturbing.'

Connie was twenty-five. Looked forty. Not forty now, but forty from forty years ago. She shrouded her body in tweed skirts, baggy jumpers and pearls. When she spoke, she circumnavigated the language. Never coming to the point. Dealing with Connie made Roz wish she worked for the more modern magazines in the building, where people kissed your cheek, said 'Hello, how are you?' and came to the point. It seemed simpler.

Once she had taken Connie out for a drink and over a gin and tonic – well, she had gin, Connie had a white wine – had asked her right out why she spoke that way.

'I feel safe,' Connie told her. 'If I use as many words as possible it stops me saying what I think. It gives me time.'

Roz said, 'Ah' and 'Hmm.' She thought she knew what Connie meant. It gave her her first inkling that there might be a normal human being in there, somewhere beneath the bundles of clothes.

The fifth message was from Jamie. 'Hi, Ma. Well, Roz, I don't call you Ma, do I? It's Jamie. I'm coming to London in a couple of days, thought I'd look you up.' Pause, slightly nervous pause, Roz thought. 'Um, can I stay with you? Only for a while till I get myself sorted. Won't be long.' Then – knowing this would pave the way for a reasonable welcome – 'Nan said I should come see you. Well, catch up with you soon. Tomorrow, actually. If you don't mind.'

Tomorrow, thought Roz. That's today now. She looked, once again, round the room. Saw it as others might see it. Three pairs of shoes lying where they'd landed when she'd kicked them off. The remains of last night's supper on the coffee table – a plate of Optima bran flakes and a banana. The blackening skin lying limp beside the becrumbed bowl. There was a selection of jumpers on the sofa. She hadn't vacuumed for weeks. She slipped the sleeve of her robe over her hand and swiftly dusted round the answering machine. The windows were past seeing through. Newspapers and magazines were taking over the area round the sofa. There were abandoned cups – well – everywhere. Oh God. She was a slut.

The last call was Connie. Again. Resigned this time. 'No point coming in now. Ronnie's gone home. Actually he's been taken home. He came over very peculiar. Started throwing papers off his desk saying what was the point. Nobody paid any attention to him. Then he went into the cupboard and wouldn't come out. He just sat in there telling everyone to leave him alone.'

Roz switched off the machine. Whilst she had been playing with her new toy, driving the wrong way down one-way streets, her phone had gone haywire.

She phoned at quarter to ten, not wanting to appear overly anxious by calling at nine. Ronnie wasn't there. She got Connie.

'I don't know what got into him,' she said. 'He got all upset.'

'But he's out of the cupboard now?' asked Roz.

'Oh yes. He was in there most of the afternoon. We kept an eye on him. Through the keyhole sort of thing. Then someone brought him a cup of tea.'

'Then what?'

'He drank it.'

'No,' said Roz. 'How did you get him out of the cupboard?'

'Oh, Mary who does the letters page and the crossword and the knitting patterns went in and took his hand and led him out. She got his coat. Helped him into it and took him home. He's not in today.'

'Well, I'm terribly sorry,' said Roz. 'I . . .' She what? 'My son turned up unexpectedly,' she lied. 'I got caught up.'

'Oh, really?' said Connie. 'Well, that's nice.'

'Yes,' said Roz. 'It's lovely to have him here. Did Ronnie have a tantrum just because I didn't turn up?'

'No,' said Connie. 'It's been coming for a while.' A tight silence. 'He got passed over again. Someone got the job he was after. A woman. A younger woman. A much younger woman. He can't stand that. And his wife has gone all stroppy. Bossing him about. Complaining about the amount he earns. Going out every night. He said he's a shell. A shell of the man he was.'

'When did he say that?'

'In the cupboard. He said he wanted Willa.'

'Willa? Willa Morris? But she's dead.'

'Not to Ronnie. I think he was in love with her.'

'Weird,' said Roz. 'Should I come in today, then?'

'Yes,' said Connie. 'In case he turns up. But I don't think he will.'

Roz put the phone down and panicked. Things to do. Check car. Clean up before Jamie arrives. She did a slow, vacuous twirl, deciding. The spare room. She went to look at it. Opened the door, gazed round. There were piles of boxes, a rail of clothes she hadn't worn in years but wasn't going to throw out. Just in case. Just in case what? They might come into fashion again. She looked at them. She didn't think so. And even if they did, she wasn't going to wear them. There was an old rowing machine and an exercise bike, a guitar, rolled-up posters, shoes. In the corner was an old double bed with a thin threadbare mattress. 'My God,' she said. Shut the door again. Closed her eyes and cursed the slut she was. The only people who came here were Fred and a few of her friends – mostly Janey – and they knew her well enough to tell her how disgusting the place was. So they didn't matter.

She stopped mid-panic. Thought of Nan. Here I go, Nan. A chance to make friends with my son.

She shoved on the first clothes she found. Ran down the stairs to the car. It was there. Gleaming, she thought, in the sun. She patted it. Looked round, checking nobody was watching this foolishness.

She sat in the tube. Leaned back. Tried to plan her coming conversation with Connie. But couldn't. Recently, since Nan's funeral, her life with Matthew had kept sneaking up on her. She just had to shut her eyes, and there she was back in that kitchen of her young married life. The smell of bleach. The absurd sparkle of sterility. Their life. She thought her life was divided into two phases. The clean years and the dirty years. She had squeezed a lifetime's cleaning into her time with Matthew. Now she had no intention of doing any more. The clean years: there was nothing to them. Only the grim pursuit of a certain unquestioned respectability. What were we thinking of? she asked herself. We were so young. All the things we could have been doing instead of following soaps and keeping the garden perfect.

Fifteen years ago, when the silence started to become unbearable. The kettle was on, the kitchen cleaned a stage beyond gleaming. In the living room the television chattered unattended. And Matthew was counting. Polishing the cutlery. Counting. Four wipes to every fork, four prongs to a fork. Then the spoons. They had thirty-nine spoons. How come? Roz wondered. Four wipes to a spoon. He whispered his counting hoarsely under his breath. One. Two. Three. Four. When he'd done, he'd go to the living room to sit in front of the telly. Twelve steps. A person, Roz knew, shouldn't be aware of such things. It led to craziness. It stopped you thinking.

She watched Matthew. What had happened to him? Perhaps he'd always been this way and she hadn't noticed. Years ago they were students together. They'd go Friday nights to the pub, then back to his flat, stopping off at the off-licence for a bottle of wine. Blue Nun, she remembered. Winced. Ah, but back then it had made her heady, and horny. So eager to get her knickers off. To clamber into his bed. Had he been counting then? If he had, she hadn't noticed. Too keen to get under the sheets with him. His skin on hers. The sweetness of it. Then she'd phone home, tell her mother she was staying over with her then best friend Susan.

She'd wake. Eight in the morning. Love with the postman rattling past, the landlady's radio playing upstairs. She'd got pregnant. Silly bugger, me, she thought. As if she hadn't heard of condoms. As if half her friends weren't on the pill. Could've had an abortion. Except that that had been Jamie, and it didn't seem right aborting a foetus that now had a personality, a face that loomed before her. 'Who, me? Abort me? But I'd have missed *Star Wars*.'

Jamie would be with her soon. She did a swift mental inventory of her fridge. One carton of yoghurt, Greek with honey, half-eaten. Two tomatoes, one gone wrinkly. Small piece of cucumber, bitten into, tooth-marked. One dubious lettuce. One slice of ham, dried at edges. 'Shop,' she instructed herself. Out loud. The woman next to her looked round. Roz turned to the window, went back to her memories.

Matthew finished his wiping. He walked across the kitchen. Picked up the newspaper, one. Folded it shut, two. Folded it over, three. And over, four. Put it down, five. Oh God, what was he thinking in there? What was he hiding from? Roz had remembered something from her book of modern quotations, Thoreau, 'The mass of men lead lives of quiet desperation.'

'Do you lead a life of quiet desperation, Matthew?'

'What?'

'Do you lead a life of quiet desperation?' She said it again. Louder.

'No,' he'd said. And walked from the room. Six steps. The pipes gurgled. Three gurgles. Roz had known then that if there was something troubling Matthew, he was never going to tell her.

The train stopped. She looked in dismay, realising she was two stations past her stop. She rose, heaved her coat and bag over her shoulder. Gathered her briefcase. Why she carried it, she did not know. She rarely opened it. It held a notepad, a couple of pens, dried up, a lipstick she never used, a book she'd never read, a scarf she never wore, an empty cellophane pack that had once held a prawn sandwich, and several crumpled chocolate wrappers. A nonsensical collection of things, she realised, she took to every meeting she went to.

By the time she got to the office, Ronnie's wife had phoned to say he wouldn't be in today, or for many a day to come.

'He's had a bit of a breakdown,' whispered Connie. As if having a bit of a breakdown was more acceptable than having a full-blown one.

'So there's no point in me being here,' said Roz. Then, realising that that was not the required reaction, 'Oh dear, poor Ronnie. Send him my regards.'

They looked at one another. Shrugged.

'The Beseleys,' said Connie. 'What are we to do? I don't know when Ronnie will be back. A complete sort of breakdown.' With Connie everything was sort of, and kind of, and you know, in the way of. Roz wondered if it was an attempt to soften the truth. Connie was a person who eased her way through life. Roz thought she hid from the reality of things. If Connie could pass her days with a bag over her head and a T-shirt that read *This Isn't Really Me*, she would.

'Yes,' said Connie. 'Poor Ronnie's been taken to a sort of institution. You know, sort of place you go when you've, well, broken down, I suppose. Life,' she sighed, 'got the better of him.'

'Well, there you go,' said Roz. 'Life, eh. Can't live with it . . . et cetera, et cetera.'

'Exactly,' said Connie. 'That says it all.' She leaned back, drifting, musing. Then, coming to, 'So, the Beseleys. I have no idea what was in Ronnie's mind.'

'Who does?' said Roz. 'But I should think, what with him being after promotion and all, he was going to modernise them. You know, bring them up to date. Issues of the moment, sort of thing.' This sort-of business was catching.

Connie thought this very likely.

'Of course,' said Roz, admiring her own cunning, 'we'd have to do it gently. Ease the reader in. We don't want to alienate our established readership.'

Connie agreed. 'Absolutely. I'm sure that's what Ronnie wanted.'

'Well,' Roz heaved herself from her seat, 'I'd better go get on with it. When Ronnie comes back, we'll have set the Beseleys on course for the next couple of decades. The thoroughly modern Beseleys.' She smiled, pleased with herself. With Ronnie out of the way, she could do what she liked with the Beseleys. Connie was so, sort of, well, easy to manipulate.

'Yes,' said Connie. 'Yes. That would sort of do it. Well, look forward to reading your efforts.'

She walked Roz to the lift. Came back, sat at her desk. That woman was manipulating her. She picked up a pile of papers, tapped them into a perfect sheaf. Ronnie had no intention of changing the Beseleys. Roz had spotted an opportunity and was taking it as far as she could.

Connie snorted indignantly. She wished she could do that. Opportunities came and just, well, kind of went without her realising it was happening. Forever a deputy. Forever second best. Still, she could change that now. For once, here was an opportunity she'd spotted in time.

It had always been the same for her. At home her pretty younger sister had got all the boys, all the dates, whilst she stayed home with her mother. Saying it was where she'd rather be. Really. Really. Really. She had books to read. Studying to get on with. Programmes on telly she didn't want to miss. Oh yes, she was in control of her life.

Then there was her mother. A fussy woman who, to this day, tidied Connie before she went out to face the world. 'Collar, Connie,' smoothing her rumpled shirt. 'Make-up, Connie,' rubbing the line on her face where foundation ended and neck began. It was so irritating.

Connie had passion, though. She knew that. She just didn't know how to show it, or deal with it. Did she not regularly conduct the Berlin Symphony Orchestra when she put Beethoven's third on her CD player. Then, in other moods, she was Tina Turner. Shimmying up and down the room, music roaring. Shaking her shoulders, snaking her hips, doing that Tina dance. *Oooh, steamy windows*. All, of course, when her mother was out.

Then there were men. Afterwards they all said the same thing. 'Christ, Connie, I didn't know you were like that. My God.' Oh yes. She had passion all right. What about *the* man? Her secret shame. Secret glee.

On a long train journey from London to Aberdeen, years ago. Bored, she had played eye games with a young man, an oil worker, she thought, good-looking in a rougher way than her usual flings (and she'd had plenty). She looked at him. He at her. She looked away, smiling slightly. Then she'd got up, walked slowly down the corridor to the loo. He followed. Followed her inside. What they did had been wild, frantic. Her up on the sink. His breath hot on her neck, unshaven cheek hurting hers. Then it was over. They adjusted themselves silently. He left. She washed. Fixed her lipstick. When she got back to her seat he was gone. She never saw him again. Knew nothing about him. It had been fabulous. She'd smirked, gloated, feeling wild and sexy. And cheap. A swirling mix of emotions. But there it was. She'd done it. Couldn't undo it.

Still, this Beseley thing was good. Ronnie's breakdown was good. At last she could do the things she wanted to do. Fill the magazine with pinks and lavenders. Put in some sexier copy than Ronnie would allow. And if it all went wrong, she could shrug and say they needed to experiment, telling Ronnie he was right and they needed his strong guiding hand. And if this Beseley business came off, she could take the credit. If it didn't, Roz could take the blame. Connie smiled, looked round. Who was manipulating who?

After her meeting, Roz went to the supermarket, heaped a trolley. Filled five carrier bags. Took a taxi back to her flat. Sitting back, she thought herself absurd. It had been such a while since she'd catered for Jamie, she'd bought him things he used to like all those years ago: Coco-Pops, alphabetti spaghetti and chocolate fingers for a grown man.

'I'm a fool, Nan,' she said to the ghost that haunted her.

Jamie was waiting for her when she came up the stairs. He was sitting on the top of the flight leading to her door, smiling as she staggered towards him, laden with goodies. He got up, came to her to take some of her load.

'Hi,' he said.

She apologised for not being in to welcome him. 'I'd nothing in.'

He shrugged. 'It's OK. No problem. I like sitting on doorsteps.' The bags looked light in his hands. He was so tall now.

'It's so lovely to see you,' she said. Stopping herself from telling him he'd grown. She had tears in her eyes, and was smiling more than she thought she ought. Couldn't help it. It was as if her face had a life of its own. Her son had come to her. Unasked. Of his own will. She thought this might be the happiest day of her life.

CHAPTER TEN

The restaurant was crowded. The clunk of cutlery. A fug of smoke, babble of voices. Occasionally a howl of laughter would escape from some gathering and peal across the room. Bottles dwindled. Waiters skimmed to and fro carrying plates. The breeze from the kitchen door every time it swung open sent thick wafts of frenetic cooking over Will.

He sat watching his hands move across the piano keyboard. He felt removed from the sound he was making. It was just a thing he did. Meant nothing any more. He'd played a selection of Scott Joplin rags. Had done some variations on a theme from *Sergeant Pepper*. Tinkled around with his favourite Brubeck pieces. Nobody was listening. Which he thought a pity. Tonight, he congratulated himself, he was playing rather well.

Across the room in a corner sat a slightly demented couple. The sort of customer that made the waiters nervous. They drank. Were on their fourth or fifth whisky, which they were having instead of wine with their julienne of pigeon with Madeira reduction. The woman chain-smoked. Tapping the end of her cigarette into her cupped hand, emptying her ash-filled palm into an ashtray. She played with her food. When she wasn't leaning back, letting smoke drift from her mouth, she was stretched over the table, her face close to the man's, talking with passion. She'd been crying. Even from where he was, yards away, Will could see that.

The man was gaunt. Wore a suit that had a patina of constant wear. A dull gleam about the shoulders and elbows. His hair clung greasily to the collar. His tie was knotted slightly to the left of centre.

She wore a long grey cardigan, red silk scarf knotted at the neck, a brown velvet skirt that had seen happier days. Her hair spread, grey and unwashed, past her shoulders. Every now and then she looked across at Will. Hungrily. He shifted uncomfortably in his seat. Sometimes a woman would take a shine to the piano player. He found it embarrassing. Started on a Mozart piece. The hungry gaze turned cold when she heard him.

The man got up, made his way past the hovering waiters to the lavatory. She rose. Crossed the room to Will. Close up, Will could see the life she'd had etched on her face. Deep grooves from eye to lip. A pallor about her. This was a well-thumbed lady. 'You're fairly murderin' the Mozart,' she said.

He agreed. 'I know.' He looked at her. He never could do justice to Wolfgang Amadeus. She had an interesting face. An intelligence. It struck him, now, that it hadn't been him she'd been eyeing; it was the piano.

'Shove over,' she told him.

The room quietened. The head waiter moved to stop her. Too late. She took one long heave on her cigarette. Balanced it on the edge of the piano. Rolled up her sleeves. And played the twenty-first.

'Famous one,' she said. Gravelled, nicotined voice. 'Of course there should be an orchestra.'

Her touch was light. A soft, delicate melody rolled out. And for the first time since he was ten years old, Will wanted to cry. Oh God, if he could play like that. Only in his head. Only in his dreams.

'You get the whole tune when you've got the fiddles and the horns.'

Stained fingers flew.

The head waiter looked at Will. Should he stop this? Will motioned him away.

'Nice piano,' she said. 'Lovely action. Do you know Mozart?'

'Not personally,' said Will.

'Now there's a man I'd like to have met.' Note-perfect, she barely looked at the keys. 'Bet he was a great shag.'

'He did his fair share of that.'

She agreed with a wistful intake of breath. Took another long puff and rolled into the second movement. '*Andante*. Love this. Mother taught me. Now *she* could play. Died a couple of weeks ago. Great lady.'

Will was dying. The ache. That moment when the truth hits. No matter how hard he practised, he would never play like this. He went to the bar to listen. Drink and listen.

'*Allegro vivace assai*,' the gravelled voice announced.

Her partner returned to his table, sat smiling for the first time since they'd entered the restaurant.

She finished. Stood up. Nodded to the ripple of applause. Will had never been applauded. It hurt. He went back to his stool. Gravel-voice moved to let him sit. 'I needed that.' She nodded to her shiny-suited friend, who was waiting by the door.

Will could not hide his envy. 'Who are you?'

'Marianne,' she said. Walked off.

Will sat. Spread his fingers on the keys, let out a long breath. Shut the piano lid. He got up. Headed for the door, the head waiter rushing after him.

'You can't go. You've got another two hours.'

'Enough,' said Will. 'Enough.' Hand on the door handle. 'Enough.'

'What d'you mean, enough?'

'I mean enough. It's over. I'm through. I quit. Enough. Nobody's listening. Nobody ever listened to me like they listened to her.'

'They're not meant to listen. They're here to eat. You're here to add ambience.'

'I just got so much ambience in me, I'm going home.'

'You can't give up just because some old bag can outplay you.'

'I can. And I will. I just discovered something. I don't want to do this any more. Enough. Enough to coming here to play to eaters and drinkers, smokers and laughers who don't listen.'

'Don't expect us to pay you.'

'I don't expect anything. I've long stopped expecting anything. That's another thing I just discovered.'

'Maybe that's why nobody listens.'

Too painful. Too near the knuckle. Will glared at him. 'Fuck off.'

He left. A blast of city air. He filled his lungs, shut his eyes. Wonderful. Started walking at a pace along the street. How long had he hated playing the piano in that place? Years. The dread he had felt every piano day, knowing come eight o'clock he'd be sitting before that Yamaha, wearing the black suit the manager insisted upon, tinkling delicately and blandly through a selection of tunes that deserved a better player than him whilst all around people ate, drank, giggled and ignored him. Or complained about the noise he was making. There were occasional tips. Free drinks. And drunken people requesting songs. Singing them loudly if he didn't know them. ' "Slow Boat to China", do ye know that?' He'd nod. But somehow it'd have flown his brain. 'I said "Slow Boat to China".' And the requester would start singing.' A slow, drunken, tuneless riff.

Will shuddered. 'Enough,' he said. Started walking quicker. A ruinous, relentless drizzle rained on him. He turned his face up to it, mouth open, drinking it. 'Enough.' He turned up his collar, pulled his jacket round him and headed home.

Three weeks ago, on one of his last visits to Nan, she'd taken his hand and said, 'You should give up that piano-playing.'

'I need the money,' he told her.

'No you don't. You don't need it that much. Money isn't worth putting up with something that makes you miserable. Well, not that miserable.' Then she'd turned to check the roads on Teletext. 'There's a lorry broke on the Forth Bridge. And a pile-up on the M4.' Keeping in touch with road conditions made her feel part of the world she'd left behind. She rarely went out. 'Second time this week. That's a road and a half, that M4.'

Will shook his head. 'How do you know playing in the restaurant makes me miserable?'

'How do I know it's ten past six on a Friday evening and I'm sitting in my living room and God's not in his heaven? Well, not for me, he's not. He can't be letting me feel like this. Miserable's coming off you in waves.' She dialled up the weather for the next three days. 'Rain again.'

'I suppose you know about misery.'

She looked away. 'I do that. More than any of you know. And you've not got misery. Misery's when your children die. Or you have to go out scrubbing floors to put food on the table 'cos your man drinks all the money. Misery's when a typhoon wrecks your home, when war makes a refugee of you, when everyone round you is starving . . .'

'OK, OK.' Will was shamed.

'You're just miserable because when you play the piano, no matter how hard you try, you can't make it sound out loud like it does in your head. That's middle-class miserable. It's fixable. Just stop playing out loud in public.'

Will shrugged. He supposed she was right.

'Then again,' said Nan, 'there was Liberace. He was never that good. And he had a fine time with it. Maybe you should just get yourself a sequined suit and start enjoying not being as good as you want to be.' She grinned at this. Will in a sequined suit. Ha, ha, ha. She reached out, took his hand. 'Nice hand,' she told him, stroking it. 'Another thing you could do is tell that lovely woman of yours to stop spending.'

'Zoe?' he asked.

'Who else,' she said. Nodding.

Will started to run down the street, away, away from the piano-playing. 'Enough. Enough. Enough.' Tanking along the pavement. Ducking through the crowds. He reached Princes Street, still celebrating the joys of release from his piano bondage. He was soaked. He turned down his collar. Giving in to the rain, he half walked, half ran to Frederick Street. Reached Queen's Street. Tore down Dundas Street. Home. Burst in. Stood red-faced, gasping, dripping in front of Zoe. The folly of his outburst hit him. He bent double, clutching his sides. 'Christ, shouldn't've done that.' He heaved and coughed. 'I'm going to die.'

Zoe watched him blandly. 'What the hell are you doing? And why are you here anyway? You're soaking the carpet.'

He looked at her, too agonised to speak. Slumped on a chair, legs splayed in front of him, shaking his head. His trousers clung to his legs. At last he had air in his lungs. He could speak. 'I quit,' he told her. 'No more piano bashing for me. It's over.'

Zoe looked at him, then at her credit card accounts spread on the coffee table. She didn't know what to do. Snatch them up and he'd demand to know what they were. She leaned back, put her feet on the table on top of them. 'Do you think that's wise? I mean, the money's handy.'

Will shivered.

'Go dry yourself. Have a bath. You'll catch a chill,' Zoe told him.

'In a minute. I need a drink first.' He got up, crossed the room to the whisky bottle. Zoe watched him. A silence. A wary, electric silence. She was sitting, looking cool, shoulders tense, eyes wide. Smiling stiffly.

Will watched her. He knew her. This was Zoe being guilty and trying to hide it. He put down the bottle, walked to the table, picked up one of the credit card statements. Read it. Took another and read that. Then another. Now he didn't bother to read; just looked at the money owed at the bottom of Zoe's long list of spending. 'I seriously do need a drink.' He poured whisky into a glass, did not offer Zoe any. He remembered Nan's words, 'Tell that lovely woman of yours to stop spending.' Asked Zoe, 'So how much?'

She shrugged. 'A few thousand. Nothing too drastic.'

'A few thousand? Ten? Twelve?'

'Nearer twelve than ten. About fifteen.'

'Christ.'

'We can cope. It isn't too bad. You'll have to get your piano thing back.'

'No way.'

'Two nights a week. We could put the money aside.'

'Two nights a week till I'm fifty. I don't think so. Why don't you get a job? Serving in a bar two nights a week for the next twenty years?'

'That's not very nice.'

'Nice,' he said quietly. 'Nice. What's nice anyway?'

She didn't answer.

He got up. 'I'm going to have a bath.'

'Why did you give up your job?'

'I'm no good at it.'

'But you are,' she protested.

'No I'm not. I wanted to be good. But I'm not. I'll never be able to play the way I want to. I'll never make it sound the way it does in my head. I don't want to talk about it. And I don't want to talk about your debts either.' He was soaked, shaking.

'Aren't you angry?'

He turned on her. Reached out, gripped her throat. The strength of his fingers, years of thumping keys. She could hardly swallow.

'I'm so angry, I'm scared of how angry I am.' He let go. 'Don't speak to me. Don't come near me.' He was white. 'What the hell did you do with all that money?' He looked round. 'Where has it gone?'

'On things.'

'What things?'

'Things. Stuff I wanted.'

'What?'

'I don't know. Just stuff.'

Zoe had a problem with just stuff. She was smitten with a lust for things. She couldn't go into a shop and come out with a CD; she'd buy six or ten at a time. Why shouldn't she have them? She deserved them. That she couldn't afford them wasn't an issue. So it was with expensive throws for her sofa. Irish linen for her bed. Make-up, moisturisers, oils for the bath – she was Zoe, she should have the very best. Wine by the case. A selection of single malts on the dresser by the window. A selection of single-estate olive oils in the kitchen. Mail-order designer clothes that arrived when Will was out. It went on and on. And on Zoe's credit cards. Had done for years. It was all so subtle it passed Will by. He'd got used to a standard of living without ever questioning how they afforded it.

He lay soaking in the bath, relishing his twenty-year-old

ISLA DEWAR

Speyside malt, knowing it would be his last for years, wondering how he could have been so stupid. He slid under the water, held his breath. He was a blind, bumbling fool. His lungs ached. He released small gasps of air. Life with Zoe was fabulous, and it was painful. It was a whirl and it was a worry. Sometimes he didn't know why he did it. Her affairs. Her dramatics. Her fluctuating moods. He could walk from a room, leaving Zoe laughing, high and wild. Come back three minutes later, she'd be curled on the sofa, face crumpled, eyes smeared with tears. With Zoe, you never knew what was coming next. What she'd say. What she'd do. Life with Zoe was never boring.

Sometimes he thought a bit of boredom would be a relief. He had quiet moments when he indulged in placid little daydreams. A mumsy woman who'd wear an apron, bake scones, hold his head to her warm breasts and say soothing things to him. 'I will pay the electric bill and the mortgage, William.' Or, 'Hard day? There, there. I've baked you a pie.' It'd never happen. If it did, he thought, he'd leave her. In truth, he'd be smothered. Still, he could dream, couldn't he?

He realised that for years, he'd been nursing a silent angst. A gnawing thing he'd become used to.

When he surfaced, Zoe was sitting on the edge of the bath, waiting for him. Hands cupped round a cup of coffee freshly made with mail-order beans from a shop in Soho. The cup was from the Conran shop. There was nothing in the house they could actually afford.

'What are you doing?' she asked.

'Diving. Slipping underwater. Drowning.'

She reached under the surface for him.

'Piss off. That doesn't solve anything.'

'It does. When you're fucking you have a moment when you think of nothing but coming. It's good for you.'

'Then what? You finish and it's all still there.'

'But we have each other. That's all we need.'

'Grow up, Zoe.'

'I am grown up. You don't understand. Buying things helps. It

108

stops the pain. Bringing them home. Unwrapping them. It's sort of soothing.'

'You're going to have to find a cheaper kind of solace.' He leaned back. 'Do you know, I was happy tonight. I just had fifteen minutes of utter, mindless joy. Walking out of that place. Getting soaked. First time in years I've been at peace. I'd forgotten how it felt.'

'Sorry,' she said.

'Don't say sorry. Sorry sucks.'

She pouted. It usually worked.

Will finished his drink. 'When I was a boy we used to go to the seaside every year.'

'I know, you told me.'

'Well I'm telling you again. Little place on the West Coast. We rented a house. Me and my brother used to play on the beach. And there was this old woman who walked her dog every day. Mangy little thing. Ran in front of her, slipping on the rocks. She was ancient, I realise that now. But she was fit. All wiry. One day she comes up to me and points to a rock. Just a rock sticking up alone. You know, an ordinary lump of stone in the middle of the shore, and she says, "See that rock. I've been watching it. Thirty years I've been walking here and I've been looking at it every day. And it's changed." '

Zoe sniggered.

'No, don't laugh. It's interesting. *We* laughed at her, my brother and me. We called her the rock lady. We used to go to the rock and say, "Yes, it's changed. It's changed." We thought she was mad. But now I think about her. And I envy her. Imagine having that much peace of mind you've got time to watch a rock and notice the slight changes the sea and storms make as they wash over it.'

'No, I won't' said Zoe. Horrified at the thought of slowing her life to such a pace.

'The peace of it. The state of her mind. Tranquillity.'

'Well you can go off to some godforsaken place and watch rocks. But I'm not coming with you. I'm too young for that. I'd go insane.'

'Jesus, Zoe. I'm not suggesting we live in some godforsaken place and sit side by side in the sunset watching stones. I'm saying she had peace of mind. And I envy her.'

'Well I don't. Stupid old bag. Looking at stones. What good does that do? What does she know. She wouldn't know a Chablis from a Sancerre. Or a Versace from a . . .' She was too infuriated to think. 'A whatever.'

'You don't need to know a Versace from a whatever to be happy.'

'Yes you do.' She was starting to shout. She knew she was wrong. Was damned if she was going to admit it. 'You do. You do. You do.'

Will got out of the bath, started to dry himself. 'You don't.'

'Do.'

'Don't.'

They were both shouting.

'You half-witted, money-grubbing, acquisitive bitch. I had fifteen minutes of happiness. Fifteen fucking minutes. You ruined it.'

'Did not.'

'Did. Did. Did.'

They were yelling. Realising how childish they sounded, they were on the verge of laughing, mouths trembling with mirth they couldn't restrain. Then they stopped. Someone was there, watching. Toby was standing in the hall just beyond the open bathroom door. The trousers of his Spiderman pyjamas were soaked. 'I've wet the bed.' He held himself, apologetic, and jiggling. The laughter moment slipped away.

'Toby,' Will sighed. Wrapped his towel round his waist. How much had this thick fluffy towel cost?

'I'll do it,' said Zoe, stepping in front of him.

Will pushed her aside. 'I'll do it. Me.' He reached out for Toby's hand. 'OK, Tobes. Let's get you sorted.' He looked back at Zoe standing alone, unneeded. This small triumph was his. If there was any martyrdom going, he would have it.

He got two paces down the hall. Zoe's torn and lonely face lingered in his mind. He couldn't bear it. He backed up, still leading Toby. Peeped round the door. She pouted at him. Looked woeful, huge-eyed. He stuck out his tongue. 'Hold that thought. The one from before the bicker. I'll catch you later.'

She grinned. She'd got him. Again. She'd known she would.

CHAPTER ELEVEN

Nine o'clock at night. Jamie lay stretched on the sofa downing the last bottle of Chilean white, eating his chocolate fingers. Roz sat at the table, tapping at her keyboard, headphones on to drown the screams of a woman being murdered on the telly, her favourite old Al Green tracks roasting her eardrums as she wrote: 'Take me to the River . . .'

'Well,' said Pam Beseley. 'Simon, you just can't do your paper round if you've got chicken pox. You're not well. Besides, think of other people. You could spread your germs.'

'I want to spread my germs,' said Simon. 'Why should I be the only one with them?'

Roz looked across at Jamie. Removed the headphones. 'You might've left me some.'

'Sorry,' he said. 'Didn't think. Didn't not think. Just sort of drank it.'

'Hmm.' Roz disappeared back into her noise. Typed on.

'Don't be mean,' said Pam. 'So, have you arranged for someone else to do it?'

'No,' sulked Simon.

'Why not?' pestered Pam.

'Couldn't find anybody.'

'Have you told Mr Williams at the newsagent's?'

'No,' said Simon. 'Forgot.'

Pam looked at him. Sometimes she could shake the boy. She really, really could.

❀   ❀   ❀

Roz sipped her tea. That was good. Sulked Simon. Pestered Pam. A little alliteration there. Ronnie liked his alliteration. He really, really did, did Ronnie. She sighed. Clicked on word count. Ninety-seven words. One thousand four hundred and three to go. She'd never do it. Also, she hated Simon. Spoilt brat. A smack in the mouth would do him a lot of good. But Ronnie would have no such thing happen in the Beseley household. 'It's all about love,' he'd say. 'Love and understanding.'

'Stuff love,' said Roz.

'What's that?' said Jamie.

Lead me . . . Al Green sang.

Roz took off her headphones. 'What?'

'I said *what*. You said something.'

'Did I?'

'Yes.' Jamie turned to look at her. 'You mumble all the time when you're working. Did you know that? And you make faces. Right now you're looking irritated. A moment ago you were looking sort of long-suffering.'

'Was I?' Oh well, she was doing Pam Beseley. She would be long-suffering, wouldn't she? 'Must remember not to mumble,' she mumbled.

'There you go again.'

'Sorry.'

Six days Jamie had been living with her, and already Roz was feeling the strain. She mumbled when she worked. She couldn't suddenly shout out, 'Bastards!' when she remembered some vile slight or insult of years ago. She had to lock the bathroom door. There was nothing in the house to eat. No change there, then. Except that now she had a mouth to feed; she'd have to shop tomorrow. And she'd shopped yesterday. The boy could eat. He left pools of water on the floor after every bath, soaked all the towels. She'd have to have a word there. He was constantly on the phone. Or occupying the sofa. Or watching things on telly she didn't want to see. Or playing strange CDs in her machine. Or sleeping till well after noon. That was all right. At least he was out of the way. Then there was the mess. She knew she was messy, too. But that was her own mess. She knew it well, where everything in it was. Didn't trip over it. Was this motherhood? An extra mess. When on the tube home the other day she had thought about Jamie coming to stay, she had anticipated a little gentle bonding. Not this. She remembered an old Paul Simon song from *Graceland*, *You are the burden* . . . something, something . . . She looked up. Had she sung that out loud? Jamie looked round. 'Sorry,' she said. 'Just working. Working and thinking.'

Pam Beseley sighed. 'Well, you're going to have to do something.'

Simon looked sorry for himself.

'OK, OK,' said Pam. 'I'll phone Mr Williams. But really it should be you. It's your job. Your responsibility.'

'Thanks, Mum,' said Simon, snuggling down in bed, pulling the duvet over his head.

Pam went downstairs to the phone. 'Hello, Mr Williams. Pam Beseley here. You know, Simon's mum? I'm afraid Simon won't be in today. He's got chicken pox.'

'Well, has he got someone to do his round?' asked Mr Williams gruffly.

'I'm afraid not. He's been rather under the weather all day. He hasn't been up to getting in touch with anyone.'

'Rules here are he should get someone to stand in for him if he can't manage. What about his sister?'

'Susan! She's far too young. Besides, she's got homework. And it's pouring rain.'

'Exactly. And where am I going to get someone in weather like this?'

'I don't know.'

'Well, that's it. If young Simon can't get someone to do his round, it's quits for him. It's over. There's plenty would want that job. I've got a waiting list.'

'Can't you get someone from that to do it?'

'Anyone from the waiting list who comes in to do the round gets the job.'

Pam was vexed. Simon needed that job. He was saving for a new computer. Hadn't she and Frank told him that if he could get half the money, they'd give him the rest? Now this. Oh dear. What was she to do?

'Oh, all right, Mr Williams.' Pam sounded cross. 'I'll do it. Just wait till I get there and I'll deliver the papers.'

'Doormat!' shouted Roz. 'Doormat, doormat. Stupid woman.'

Jamie sat up. 'For God's sake. Can't you work quietly?'

'No,' said Roz. 'Never. If you don't like it you know what you can do.' Damned if she was any sort of doormat.

'So who's a doormat?' Jamie asked.

'Pam bloody Beseley. Isn't she just going out in the pouring rain to do Simon's paper round? The fool.'

'You're writing it. Stop her. Poor soul.' Jamie was indignant.

'I can't. It's beyond my control. Out into the teeming weather she goes. Leaky shoes. Old raincoat. And she delivers the wrong papers to the wrong houses. Hundreds of complaints. She has to go back out again into the cruel storm to sort it out. Then make the tea when she comes home. The meal's late. The family isn't happy. Complaints and jibes for Mrs B.'

'The woman's a prat. Fix her.'

'I will. I will.' Roz took off her headphones. 'I have plans for Mrs B. Her cosy world is about to crumble. Life's cruelties are about to catch up with her.' She narrowed her eyes as she spoke.

'Oh dear,' said Jamie. 'Poor Mrs B.'

'Ha, ha,' cried Roz. 'They are doomed. Now that Ronnie is entombed in the loony bin for the next few months, the Beseleys are doomed.'

'Christ, Ma. You sound like some clapped-out old thespian overplaying panto in the provinces.'

She threw her pen at him. Missed. He grinned. He called her Ma. She'd thrown her pen in jest. Was this a piece of gentle bonding? Was this a glow inside? All the mess was worth it after all.

'So,' said Jamie, 'have you gone into this Beseley business

properly? You're planning their doom. If they end, what are you going to do? How are you going to make a living? Pay for all this?'

Roz looked round. That was just the sort of irritating, sensible remark his father would make. 'I'll manage,' she said.

Jamie shrugged. It wasn't his worry.

'How are *you* going to manage?' Roz asked Jamie. 'Have you thought what you're going to do?'

'I'm thinking,' said Jamie.

'I thought you were lying on the sofa watching telly, drinking the last of my wine.'

'It only appears like that on the surface. To the casual observer. But in here,' tapping his brain, 'it's all going on. Believe me.'

She didn't.

Pam Beseley dried the last of the cutlery and put it away. It had been a dreadful day. Truly, truly dreadful. She watched the late-night rain run down the window. Too tired to make sense of her feelings. The family had laughed at her. 'Mum can't even deliver papers. Never mind, Mum. We love you just the way you are.' How dare they? She was only trying to help. Twice she'd got a soaking today. Once delivering the papers. Once again redelivering them when she'd got it all wrong.

Yet she had quietly enjoyed being out alone in the teeming weather. There was a peace out there she hadn't felt in years.

Frank came in. Switched off the lights. 'Time for bed for the delivery lady, I think.'

'Oh, you go on up.' Switching the lights on again. 'I'll just have a quiet cup of tea and a think. I'll come up in a bit.'

Frank looked surprised. 'OK.' He went out of the room. As he mounted the stairs, Pam heard him count the steps. 'Silly habit,' she told herself. 'At least I don't do that.'

CHAPTER TWELVE

Thing was, having encountered Marianne once, in the restaurant, where she'd played the piano so exquisitely, Will kept on seeing her. He wondered if she'd always been there on the edge of his life and he'd never noticed her. She was not, after all, a particularly noticeable woman. Yet there she was in the bookshop buying a second-hand copy of *Madame Bovary*. He imagined her saying, 'I like a bit of Flaubert.' But she didn't; she barely acknowledged him. A slight nod was all he got.

Three days later he saw her coming out of a pub in the West End. Then again, walking swiftly along George Street. He started to fantasise about her. Imagined her home to be old, high-ceilinged, dusty, filled with neglected treasures and antiques, and a piano. A beloved thing, covered on top with cup rings and cigarette burns and mountains of sheet music.

On the walls would be sombre oil paintings in thick gilt frames. She'd drink strong tea constantly throughout the day. He wondered what she did. A music teacher? Reluctant children would come to her parlour to sit, legs dangling from her piano stool, and thump their scales. A writer? Sitting day upon day in a small smoke-fugged study, looking mildly insane as she tapped at an early Amstrad computer. A drama coach? A painter? Some sort of obscure professorish thing, specialising in something nobody else in the world knew anything about – the mating habits of manatees, the molecular construction of malarial bacteria. She'd have nobody to talk to, except at seminars or on the Internet. He wondered if the man she'd been with had been a colleague, perhaps from some remote university; or maybe her brother. They hadn't seemed intimate enough to be lovers, even long-term ones in a neglected relationship.

It surprised Will that his fantasy woman should be someone like Marianne. He'd never really thought about it before. But now that he did, he knew that he'd always supposed that a fantasy woman should be gorgeous. Marianne was far from that. She wasn't even striking. She was the sort of person he would pass in the street without registering her presence. Her clothes were worn and shabby, her hair unkempt. She wore little make-up. Her shoes were scuffed. She was thin, scraggy. Time, and life's tragedies and absurdities, had been unkind to her face. Their ravages showed. She was no dream woman. But she could play the piano. And when she played, all the pain, all the joy was there to see, to hear. She was not afraid of what she had inside. Unlike Will.

Recently he'd been doing some soul-searching. He didn't like it. Hated the things about himself he came across when he delved within. He wondered why he hadn't noticed Zoe's extravagances. Decided he was the sort of person who didn't really take in the day-to-day things around him. He was too accepting. He was unassuming. God, how awful. A gentle, unassuming man. Sounded like some sort of mark con men sought out. Unassuming, in the nineties, he felt meant a fool. Naive. A twit with a shy smile and retiring body language who would willingly hand over his life savings to someone trying to sell him the Leaning Tower of Pisa. He never really noticed how women smiled at him. He didn't know how good-looking he was.

Then there was the piano-playing. As a lad, young, energetic, bragging, he'd thought he was good. Some days, when the sun was shining and his bloodstream swimming with beer, he even thought great. Later, disappointments soothed, he came to terms with himself. He wasn't good. But he was OK. He could live with that.

He went daily to the bookshop. Drove if it was raining. Walked when it wasn't. He wiped second-hand tomes with a soft clean yellow duster, that he washed himself in the little hand basin at the back. He quietly read the stock. He did the *Scotsman* crossword. He smoked the odd cigarette outside, leaning on the doorpost, when the weather was fine. He sold books. Sometimes he was even busy. Then again, sometimes he wasn't. On slow days he thought he stood stock still, patient and uncomplaining, like a heron standing ankle-deep in icy water waiting for a fish to come by. He decided he was *too* unassuming. He'd have to change. Then again, he thought, wiping a dusty copy of *Zorba the Greek*, why should he? He enjoyed working in the bookshop. Sometimes, sitting by the counter, reading a long-loved tome, he experienced complete and utter content. 'And what's wrong with that?' he asked, out loud.

The big fight with Zoe hadn't been resolved. It had been, like all their problems, shoved to one side, smoothed over. They did not discuss it. They ate meals together, watched television in the evenings together, took Toby to the park or the cinema together. They drank wine. Went out with friends. They came home. Made love. But they did not talk about the fight or the mounting debt that had caused it. Indeed, they hid from the debt.

Zoe continued to spend. Will's drink in the bath had not been his last twenty-year-old Speyside. The whisky bottles emptied and got replaced. New clothes appeared on Zoe's back. New shoes on her feet. A choice of three Aveda moods for the bath. Clarins for her skin. The more she secretly worried, the more stuff appeared. The more Will secretly worried, the more stuff he ate and drank.

It was raining. The wipers squeaked against the windscreen as Will drove home. The traffic was merciless. Everyone keen to make it to their firesides and out of the weather. Will sat in a queue of cars at the traffic lights. He drummed his fingers on the wheel in time to a song on the radio. U2, 'Where the Streets Have No Name', a blast from his personal past. He remembered going to see them live. It seemed everyone he knew was there. If you weren't there, you were nobody. It had been important not to be nobody. Women gathered about him in a ring and did an Irish jig. The night was balmy. He shared spliffs with strangers. He'd been happy then.

The song finished. The traffic moved up a yard or two. Stopped.

'Something new,' said the DJ. 'We like it. "My Beloved's Tooth-brush".' Will smiled. Christ, he'd written a thing called 'My Beloved's Toothbrush' when he was young and stupid. Now that he was old and stupid he wouldn't think about doing such a thing. He'd written all sorts of songs. He wondered if all young people thought the same things. Taking vaguely outrageous or ridiculous words and sticking them in front of slightly sacred ones. 'Consti-pated Angel' was a fairly innocuous example. 'My Beloved's Toothbrush' was about a man alone, bereft, after his love had gone, leaving only her soggy toothbrush on the bathroom sink.

The music started. It seemed familiar. A certain rhythm to it. But it was a novelty number. A slow, brassy oom-pa-pa. A kneebend tempo. Oom-pa-pa, oom-pa-pa. And a squeaky, girlie *ooooh* backing. A boy started to sing. Will stared at the radio. That was him. That was his voice, distorted maybe, but it was him. And that was his song. His band. His embarrassing youth. Playing loudly for the world to hear. He looked out at the people passing in the street. Turned down the volume, lest they hear. *I pull the flush, and in the hush, I turn, see my beloved's toothbrush*. Yes, he wrote that. That was him flexing his vowels so *gone* rhymed with *alone*. As only singers can. He cringed. 'How?' he said out loud.

The car in front moved forward and through the lights. He stayed still. Transfixed. The night filled with outraged blasts from cars behind him. He didn't hear. Or see their flashing headlights. 'Zoe,' he said. Put the car into gear. Ignored the gestures from fellow motorists, vowed to murder Zoe when he got home. She had gone too far. Oom-pa-pa, oom-pa-pa, girlie *ooooh*, the song went embarrassingly on. And on. The longest two and a half minutes of his life.

It was the usual supper-time scene when he got in. Toby wailing at the table, refusing to eat his grilled mackerel and alfalfa bean salad. Demanding spaghetti hoops and chips, 'Like proper boys eat.'

Zoe was looking sweaty and fraught. 'This is what you need to make you tall and strong. When you're a man . . .'

'Don't want to be a man. Won't be a man. I'm a boy. Boys eat burgers and little sausages with no skin on.' He was choking. Tears pouring down his cheeks. Little fingers rummaging in his mouth, pulling and spitting out the forkfuls Zoe had shoved in.

Zoe turned to Will for help. Saw his face. And knew he knew. 'I did it for you,' she pleaded.

'Who asked you?'

'Nobody. But I thought you'd be pleased. Someone out there likes what you do. They think you have potential.'

'Have you heard what they did?'

'I thought it was . . . interesting.'

'Interesting? It was awful. It was cringe-making.'

'That's what goes down these days.'

'Not for me. How much did you get?'

'Nothing yet.'

Toby saw his chance. He scraped the contents of his plate into the bin. Will watched him in silence. 'What do you mean, nothing yet?' He was terrifyingly controlled.

'Once sales have covered the studio costs and such, then we'll get something.'

'Right. More debt.'

'I want everyone to know about you. How good you are. You're so talented. You're wasted in that shop, Will. Wasted.'

'Zoe, this is me. This is who I am. I work in a bookshop. I like it. I don't want anything more. Leave me alone.'

'You can't just do that. You're too good for that.'

'I want to do that.'

'I won't let you.'

Toby was up on a chair behind Zoe. Hand in the biscuit tin. Cheeks pouched with the couple of animal biscuits he'd already stuffed into his mouth. He watched them silently. He was used to scenes.

'It's not up to you,' Will said. 'You can do whatever you like with your own life. Just leave me alone.'

'What will become of us if you work in a bookshop? You won't earn enough money. We'll be . . .' she howled the word out, '. . . poor.'

'No we won't be. We just won't be rich. There's a difference. We might even be happy.'

'I don't want to be happy. Not like that.' She turned on him. Glared. 'You don't understand. I want *things*. I need things. You're nothing without things.'

Will looked at her softly. 'Yes you are. You're whatever you want to be, with or without things. Things aren't what it's about.'

'Is,' said Zoe.

'Isn't,' said Will.

'Is,' said Zoe.

'Fuck off. I'm not getting into that is-isn't shite.'

'You don't understand. I need things. What am I without them? I'm . . . nothing. Nobody.' She wept the words.

'You're never that.'

'I am. I am. I don't have talent like you. How can you say you want to work in a bookshop, when there's so much more? I don't want you to do that. I want to be proud of you.'

'Like you're not now?'

She looked away. 'It's not that I'm not proud of you.' This conversation was out of control. She hated that. She thought she controlled everything, everyone. 'It's just . . . I want to be *more* proud of you.'

'Nice try.' Will stalked out of the room. 'OK, OK. I get the picture.'

Zoe heard him punch the wall. The room shuddered. She rubbed her temples. Normally she could talk her way out of anything. But not today. Things were slipping away from her. She turned, saw Toby standing on the kitchen chair so that he could reach the chocolate she kept on the upper shelf of the dresser. He'd stopped crying, but stains from his tantrum were still on his face, as was drool from the huge slab of Lindt he'd rammed into his mouth. His GAP sweatshirt and jeans were streaked and smudged where he'd wiped his hands. 'Oh, Toby.'

He shoved the chocolate bar up his sweatshirt. She wasn't getting it.

'Oh, Toby.' Zoe felt she was always saying 'Oh, Toby.' She

could hear Will upstairs crashing about. Slamming doors. What was he doing? She did not dare go up to find out. It sounded like he was packing. He was leaving her.

She left Toby to his chocolate. Went into the living room, to fret and drink.

Will appeared when she was halfway through her second whisky. He had a suitcase in each hand. 'Oh God. You're going.'

'Me?' he said. She noticed his hand was bruised and swollen where he'd taken out his wrath on the wall. 'Me? No, Zoe. I'm not going anywhere. You're going.'

'Me? You're throwing me out.'

'Yeah. Yeah. If you want to put it like that. I'm politely telling you to leave. I love you, and I want you. But I only want you if you want me, the way I am. You can come back when you accept me. Me, Will the bookseller. And Toby the boy who likes burgers and doesn't want to play the violin.' He handed her a case. Took her by the elbow and led her from the room. Took her coat from the hook in the hall. Draped it over her shoulders.

'But . . . you can't do this. I live here.'

'Not any more.' He opened the door.

'This is my home,' Zoe insisted.

'Actually, it's mine. You moved in with me, remember? I can tell you to leave whenever I want. Like now. Go away, Zoe. Come back when you've learned to stop manipulating people. When you've grown up.'

'But . . .' She was starting to panic. He meant this. He was going to do this. 'Wait. Where'll I go?'

'Right now I really don't care, as long as it's far away from me. And Toby. You'll find someone to take you in. Besides, you've got your old crowd. And with your special talents you'll find someone to take you in.'

'What do you mean by that?'

He put her case on the doorstep. 'You know what I mean. I'm tired of mixing with all those blokes who've slept with you. Tired of them smirking at me.'

'For God's sake, Will.'

Down the hall, Toby bit into his chocolate bar, played with himself, and watched.

Will pushed Zoe outside. 'Goodbye. Come back when you've sorted yourself out. We'll be here. Waiting.' He shut the door.

Zoe rang the bell. 'Let me in.'

'Go away.'

'I'm sorted. I'll change. Please let me in.'

Will opened the letter box. 'Go away, Zoe.'

'Please, Will.' Her anguished cry filled the street. 'Please.'

Will slid to the floor. Put his face in his hands. He was crying. 'Go away.'

Silence.

Toby moved slowly up to Will. Put a chocolatey hand on his head. Squeezed on to his lap. Will held him. Buried his head in the stained GAP sweatshirt. A lungful of chocolate and rejected mackerel. Toby pulled up his sweatshirt and dabbed Will's eyes. It was how he coped with tears. Nobody in this house ever had a tissue. 'I don't want Mummy to go.'

'Neither do I.' Will buried his head in the child again.

Toby looked round. His mummy and daddy were always holding him too close. Hiding their faces in him. He wished they wouldn't. It was upsetting. Already the house, without Zoe, was unfamiliarly silent. He could hear the clock in the living room tick. Zoe was always fussing round him, stroking him. Ruffling his hair. Lavishing kisses on him. 'Who'll look after me when I come home from school?'

'We'll think of something. You can come to the shop if you want.'

He nodded. He wanted. Sort of. 'I can go to Edward's house.'

'Is he your best friend?' asked Will.

'He's my friend. Not my best friend. I don't have a best friend. Who's your best friend?'

It was Zoe. Despite everything. Her debts. Those wild drunken nights that now only came back to him in a series of glisteningly real fragments. Her tears. Tantrums. Demands. Expectations. It was Zoe. 'I don't think I have one either,' said Will. He got up.

'C'mon, we better find you something to eat.'

'Does this mean I can have fish fingers and beans?' Toby wanted to know. There was always a bright side. If you looked for it.

Will kissed the top of his head, told him, 'Maybe.'

CHAPTER THIRTEEN

Thinking, Roz thought, had become an elusive occupation. She remembered lost thoughts, distant daydreams with fondness. Recently, her brain hummed a hack's routine. She woke. She worried. She worked. And in secret moments she communicated with the ghost of Nan.

She fretted about the Beseleys. She felt her mind to be filled with things she ought to have left behind long ago. If indeed these things should ever have been in her head at all. Mrs Beseley's new diet – grilled fish or chicken, low-cal everything, plenty of greens. The family were complaining. Mrs Beseley's morning exercise plan – a workout with weights after a jog round the park. Her night classes – French and word-processing.

Then, when she was not fretting about the Beseleys, she was fretting about Jamie. Jamie lay on her sofa, dreaming of the Big Idea. She shopped for him. Cleared up after him. Bantered with him. She loved him. What if he disappeared from her life once more? It would break her heart.

But she felt that all she ever said to him was 'Get a job, Jamie.' He'd been lying on her sofa for three weeks now. Drinking her wine. Every so often he would heave himself to his feet. Lumber to the kitchen, messily make a sandwich. Lumber back. Flop down. Eat horizontally. All day the television glimmered.

Roz became aware of a whole underworld of people she'd never heard of before. Folk confessed on chat shows. They looked only slightly repentant as their sins slid across the bottom of the screen for the world to read: *Her husband found her in bed with his mother; She put on forty-two pounds in a fortnight; Her husband makes her sleep in the dog's basket.* Roz, cocooned in her world of computer screen with

Al Green or Van Morrison humming through her earphones, would look up. 'Surely not,' she'd say.

Jamie would swear it was true.

Roz would wonder if there was material here for the downfall of the Beseleys. But then thought no. True-life drama went too far. So she just fretted.

'What month is this?'

'November now,' Jamie told her.

'I have to take Nan's ashes to Mull. I could do it over Christmas.'

'Sounds cool.'

One thing Roz liked about Jamie. He approved. He encouraged. He urged her on. He read the Beseleys. Contributed ideas, things young Simon might say. It pushed her to greater heights than she ever pushed herself to. If only he would push himself. She'd look at him, sprawled on her sofa. Dreaming. Long lashes. Dimples when he smiled. God, she loved him. It almost made her weep the way she loved him. She wanted everything for him. He could be so happy. There wouldn't be a person in the world, she thought, wouldn't appreciate how lovely he was. If only he'd get up off the sofa. She wondered what Nan would say to him.

'Get a job, Jamie,' Roz said.

'That's all you ever say to me.'

'I wonder why?'

'I don't know. I may not be actually employed, but I'm working on it. I'm thinking.'

Well, thought Roz. The boy's got a thick hide, it'll serve him well should he ever get his act together and actually work.

'It's not easy coming up with the right scheme. I've got to make my pile before I'm thirty.'

'Get a job, Jamie,' sighed Roz.

'No. Won't. You just see me lying here. You don't realise what's going on in my brain. I'm planning. Scheming. It's tiring.'

'Good job you're sprawled on the sofa, then. I wouldn't want you to overdo it.'

'You'll be sorry you were sarcastic when I've made it.'

'Get a job, Jamie.'

'Stop it. Stop saying that to me. If I got a job it'd cramp my style. I wouldn't have time to dream.'

'You'd have money. You could pay me some rent. Cover the cost of keeping you in coffee, toilet rolls, baths and telephone bills. Not to mention the food you go through.'

'When I've got my scheme in place I'll have money. I'm not giving you any.'

'What's today's plan?' she asked.

'Dirty Monopoly.'

'What?'

'You heard. You know Monopoly. You make your fortune buying properties. Well, this is about sleeping your way to the top. The pros and cons of it. Ups and downs. Caught sleeping with the boss, go back six places sort of thing.'

'You'd have to get someone to draw a board.'

'No problem. I've got a mate who . . .' Jamie seemed to have a thousand mates who . . . 'Instead of the boot and the iron, I'll have little plastic knickers and boxers and condoms. I've got it all worked out.'

Roz went back into her cocoon to stare and secretly fret. What was going to become of the boy? He was a waster. And it was all her fault. She'd abandoned him at a vulnerable age.

She adored his affable confidence. His apparently unshakeable belief that one day the Big Idea would come to him. Out of the blue it would drift into his mind, and with little or no effort he'd be absurdly rich. But sometimes, from beneath the bluff, a glimmer of fear would show. She knew what he was scared of. The Big Idea. What if it actually did strike? What if he actually had to get up off the sofa, go out into the world and sell it? And sell himself? And what if nobody wanted it? Or him?

But he had such aplomb. She loved it. Last week, going to the supermarket, he'd tired of her timorous driving. Insisted she pull in to the kerb and let him take over. 'A car like this needs to be driven. Foot to the floor, Ma. Give it hell.'

They'd rushed through streets. Squeezed between cars, moving from lane to lane. Shot full throttle away from traffic lights. For the first time since acquiring the car, Roz had felt the wind shift through her hair, glowed under the envious glances from other, lesser vehicles. This was how it ought to be. When they got home, Jamie had reverse-parked at a lick. Jumped from the driver's seat, slammed the door shut, spread his arms, shouted, 'See, I said I could do it. I could easily pass my test.'

'What? You've not got a licence?'

'Nah. Bastards kept failing me. They didn't like me.'

'It was nothing to do with your driving, then?'

'I only went up a one-way street the wrong way.'

That was test one. Test two, he had done some seriously aggressive overtaking. Test three, he had *only* backed into another car at the testing centre before he even got on to the road. How was he to have known it was the examiner's? Test four, he had turned right up the wrong road and, upon being told, done a U-turn in the road without checking his mirror or signalling. Test five, he had been told that perhaps his concentration would be more effective if he didn't eat so many chocolate bars whilst driving. Test six . . . Roz didn't want to hear any more.

'They've got it in for me,' pleaded Jamie. 'I tell you, they have.'

Three times a week now, Roz and Jamie went driving, L-plates on. Doing three-point turns. Reverse-parking. Roz spent her time in the passenger seat, stamping her foot on the floor, as if her pretend braking would do any good. She covered her eyes, put her hands on her head when they veered too close to lorries. And had stopped looking when he swung flamboyantly into parking spaces.

'You'll never pass if you keep driving like this.'

Chewing gum, looking away from her, hands in pockets. 'I'll never pass anyway. I tell you, they've got it in for me.'

'Nobody's got it in for you. They just want to see that you can competently manoeuvre a car. That's all.'

'They hate me.'

'Rubbish. Look. Just do it properly for one hour of your life.

Then drive yourself to hell if you want. As long as it's not in my car.'

'You don't understand,' he said.

Unfortunately, she thought she did. But knew this was not the moment to say so.

Meantime she and Jamie moved round one another. Discovering each other. She said nothing about the damp towels in the bathroom, nothing about the pools of water and wet footprints across the carpet he left after every bath. She picked up his dirty clothes. Washed his dishes, shopped for the food he liked. She encouraged his fantasies.

'I know,' suddenly one morning after the toast burned, 'see-thru toasters.'

'What?'

'See-thru toasters. Where you can see what the toast's doing. I mean, doesn't it drive you daft? You never know what's happening in there. If you could see . . . perfect toast every time.'

'That's a great idea. That'd work.'

'All I have to do is get a mate to draw up a plan. And send it to Philips. Or whoever makes toasters.'

'What if they pinch your plan?'

'I'll patent it.'

'Right. How do you do that?'

'Dunno. I've got a mate who . . .'

'Right,' she said.

'I've got to think about this. This is great. This is the one.'

He disappeared to the living room to lie on the sofa. Ten minutes later, Roz went through to see how the thinking was going. He was lying, eyes shut. She could have sworn he was sleeping, but didn't want to disturb him. He'd only complain she'd disrupted his thoughts.

There were areas where they could not go. Subjects that loomed up that they backed away from.

'Do you want a cheese sandwich?' Roz asked.

'Nah. I hate cheese.'

'Since when? You used to love cheese.'

'I always hated it.'

'I remember I used to make you cheese sandwiches. With chutney.'

'When was that?'

'When you were little. Before I . . . left.' She shrugged. Guilty.

'Before you did a runner on Dad?'

She nodded. They never mentioned cheese again. Stick with see-thru toasters, Roz thought. It's safer. So she picked up after him, she washed his clothes, she shopped for him and decided they were, at last, forming a relationship.

Wednesday evening. Roz was working. She felt these days she was always working. It was all the interruptions. Kept her at her desk till late in the evenings. There were endless phone calls from Fred. He missed her. Longed for her. She'd never known him like this. Perhaps she should have stayed away from him before. Absence makes the heart grow fonder. He wanted her. He ached, he told her, to touch her. Be with her. Sleep with her. Maybe, with Fred, it was just abstinence made the heart grow fonder.

'When can I see you? Can I come round?'

'No. Not yet. It's my son. He's come to stay.'

'He won't mind.'

'No. But I mind. I don't want him to meet you yet. I'm just getting to know him. And I don't want to, you know,' she turned to the wall, whispered, 'do it when he's in the house. It doesn't seem right.'

'He's a grown-up. You're a grown-up. What's the problem? He must know you behave like a grown-up.'

'He doesn't know about *that* yet.'

'Well come round here. To my place.'

'No. I don't want to leave him alone. Not yet.'

Fred had hung up. But he phoned the next day. Every day. Same conversation. More guilt for Roz. It always took two cups of tea and a chocolate digestive biscuit to recover.

Then there was Connie, whose concern for the Beseleys was growing daily.

'I'm sort of, you know, worried about Mrs B. Her diet. Her workouts. She doesn't seem like our lovable Pam any more. Her new attitude. Is it right?'

'Of course it's right. Trust me,' said Roz.

'Oh, all right,' Connie agreed. But she didn't. She didn't trust anybody. It was the only way to get by.

And if it wasn't Fred or Connie, it was Jamie. At least three times a day he'd come, sit opposite her and unload his worries. Which mainly centred round the Big Idea. What if he never had it, now that see-thru toasters might prove to be too much trouble?

'I mean, what if I don't sell the idea? What if nobody wants it? Then I'd have to go it alone. Design them. Manufacture them. Advertise them. All that. I could lose a fortune. Debt. Bankruptcy. I don't know.'

'You'll just have to get a job,' Roz advised.

'Don't say that.'

'OK. I'll just think it.'

'You don't understand. I'm not a job person. I couldn't get up every morning at the same time. And come home nights at the same time. It'd kill me.'

'It kills us all. But we get over it.'

He looked at her. That look. It's all your fault. She didn't need it. She knew everything was her fault. His failings. His unwilling-ness to commit. This present guilt was a two-cup-of-tea, four-biscuit job. She'd never get over it. Soon she'd be guilty and fat with it.

She was sitting tapping furiously at a magazine quiz about managing money. Not that she could manage money. She could only write quizzes about it. Quizzes she'd fail spectacularly. Jamie was lying reading a book on Zen teaching of Hui Hai. Something about sudden illumination. One thing about Jamie. He read. He read furiously. In between bouts of trash telly, he read. All sorts of books. Mostly ones from her shelf that she'd only managed to get quarter of the way through. But he got to the end. Then he'd toss the book aside, for her to pick up, and start another. It was sudden illumination at the moment. 'Yeah, right,' he was saying. Maybe it was coming to him.

'Illumination?' Roz asked.

'Yeah,' he said. Uncertainly. 'I have to awaken to the Way in front of me to attain deliverance in my bodily form.'

'Right,' said Roz. She typed. *A maiden aunt dies and leaves you £5,000. Do you: a) Invest it? b) Squander it on clothes and make-up? c) Buy something of lasting value, that you will love for years to come? d)* – duh, she thought, what else could someone do with a windfall?

'It is just by not allowing my mind to dwell upon anything whatsoever that I will perceive my own nature. Says here. In other words, if I stop thinking I'll find out who I am,' he enthused.

'Well, you seem to be getting there,' said Roz. 'If you don't mind my saying so.' *d) Give it to someone you love, who may need it more than you*? 'Actually, with the way of Zen, there is no I. No self. A oneness with everything. The universe.'

'Really?' asked Jamie. 'How do you know that?'

'I know lots of things you don't know I know. You think I'm just sitting here, working away at my keyboard. But it's all going on up here.' Roz tapped her head.

'You taking the piss?' asked Jamie.

'Absolutely,' said Roz.

The doorbell rang.

Jamie and Roz looked at one another.

'Who's that?' she asked.

Jamie shrugged. 'Somebody of yours?'

'I don't have anybody who'd come at this time of night. Unless something awful's happened.'

The bell rang again. And again.

For a moment, before going to find out who was making the din, they amiably discussed possibilities.

'The police?' asked Jamie. 'You been doing drugs?'

'No. Good heavens, no.' Then, horrible thought, 'Have you?'

'Gave up years ago.'

'Right. Well, that's something anyway. Sudden illumination?'

'Yeah. Sort of. No money also.'

The ringing continued.

'Aren't you going to answer it?' Jamie didn't move.

'Aren't you?' Roz didn't move. They eyed one another. A small battle. Roz lost. Sighed. Clicked on Save and got up.

It was the sort of night Zoe would have had laid on, if she had control of such things, for her arrival. Dramatic. Wind shivered round the building. Panes rattled, battered by storming rain. She brought the weather in with her. Dripping from her long velvet coat. Her hair was plastered to her head. Mascara streaming down her cheeks. She still looked exquisite. The room smelled of rain and wind and the night outside.

'Don't you answer your door?' she said, pulling off the coat. Handing it to Roz.

Roz said, 'Zoe. My God. How lovely to see you.'

Zoe nodded.

'I never expected you to come here.'

Zoe nodded again. Had she not been cold and wet, she'd have said *she'd* never expected she would come here. 'I know,' she said quietly.

She'd had a dreadful journey. Six hours on the train. Sniffing and sobbing and looking indignantly at the man across the aisle, who stared. She hadn't thought to buy anything to read, so thumbed through a wrinkled copy of the *Sun* someone had left behind, or studied the chirpy in-train magazine. She gazed at the tea-cup ring on the table in front of her. Or looked miserably at her tear-stained face reflected in the darkened window. She was starving. She vowed she would arrive at her mother's house with dignity. She would just say she'd come for a couple of days to see Jamie. She would not tell them she was alone, homeless.

But now she was here in the warmth, her mother fussing round her – 'Tea, Zoe? Coffee? A drink? Sit by the fire, you're freezing. Pour soul. Jamie, make room for your sister. Something to eat? You must be hungry...' – Zoe broke down. She blamed the sympathy. She never could resist it.

'Will threw me out. He tossed my clothes out into the street, and me after them.' She sank on to the sofa, weeping.

'Will?' Jamie couldn't believe this.

'Ye-ee-es.' Zoe howled. Curled, head on knees, shoulders shaking.

Jamie put his arm round her, looked up at Roz. Made a goodness-me face. Roz stood holding Zoe's dripping coat, not knowing quite what to do. She wanted to do what Jamie was doing. Hold her daughter. But knew they weren't that well acquainted – yet.

'I'll fetch you tea,' she said.

'Yes,' sniffed Zoe.

'Or a drink?'

'Yes,' sniffed Zoe. Again. 'Both. And I'd rather have coffee.' She looked up, woebegone, tragic, tear-smeared. 'And a sandwich. Do you have, maybe, fresh crab with slices of cherry tomato, avocado and just a hint of mayo. Just to hold it together.'

'I'll see what I can do,' said Roz. 'But I wouldn't hold out too much hope. Chicken and bacon?'

Zoe nodded. Her full dramatic nod. That would do.

Roz took the sodden coat out into the hall. Went into the kitchen thinking that in moments of crisis, tragedy, childbirth and death, bystanders were always glad of a kettle. It gave them something to do. She heard Zoe pour out her tale to Jamie.

'I had to come here. There was nowhere else for me to go. He was awful to me. He said terrible things.'

She heard Jamie say lovely things like 'Never mind.' And 'It'll be all right.'

She held a piece of sliced white bread in her hand. Looked misty. Zoe was here. Heartbroken, shivering and hungry. The girl had come to her. They might even become friends. 'Look at you,' she heard Jamie say. 'You've soaked my collar.' He was such a nice man. Roz wondered how come she and Matthew had produced such a nice son and beautiful daughter. There must be rogue genes somewhere.

She returned to the living room with coffee, whisky and a sandwich for Zoe. Put them in front of her. Zoe caught Roz's scent as she leaned over. Same scent Roz had always worn, rive gauche. Zoe breathed it, and something within her stirred. Food, and a certain smell. Instant comfort. She resisted the emotions. Put down her sandwich. Sipped her whisky. A less childish thing to do, drink.

'It's wonderful to have you here,' Roz said. She thought she might be gushing. Told herself to stop. She'd put the girl off. Chase her away.

Zoe thought to say it was wonderful to be here. Thought that might be a bit too friendly. She'd decided on the train that yes, she would stay with her mother, but she wasn't going to speak to her, be friends with her. She would just exchange the occasional polite word with her, frostily. She took up her sandwich, bit into it. Looked round. Between bread wedged in her mouth and black fringe – huge eyes.

Roz's heart went out to her. As Zoe intended it to.

'It's just so lovely to see you,' she gushed again.

'Thank you,' said Zoe. Then – the food, the scent, the comfort, the sympathy – she lost control. 'Nobody would have me. I mean, they'd have me for a day or two, then you could see they wanted me to go. I'm too much for them. And also . . .' Also, she had slept with every one of her friends' partners at some time or other. None of her friends trusted her alone with their blokes. No, she thought, don't tell her that. 'Also, also . . . I wanted to see Jamie.'

'Well, stay as long as you want,' said Roz.

Jamie looked at her. Didn't like this. He was enjoying having Roz to himself. 'But you'll have to go home sometime. There's Toby.'

Zoe nodded. Toby. She caught her mother's eye. Was this how Roz had felt? All those years ago? Alone. Cold. Hungry. Frightened. And missing her children. Roz smiled. She knew.

'Yes,' said Zoe. 'There's Toby. I will have Toby.'

'A bath,' said Roz, changing the subject. 'Warm you up.'

She went through to the bathroom, Zoe at her heels, looking round as she went. Her mother's stuff – cheap, but tasteful. She thought she could do things with this flat. Then told herself to stop it. And told herself to stop it again when she noticed the supermarket-brand apple-scented bath foam her mother was pouring into the water.

'You don't believe all that stuff?' said Jamie when Roz got back to the living room.

'I suppose,' said Roz.

'It's bollocks. Zoe's being extravagant with the truth. Will, throw her out? Will? I don't think so.'

'Oh well,' Roz shrugged. 'It's good to see her anyway. I never thought she'd ever turn to me, no matter what happened to her.'

'I'll check on that thought in a week,' said Jamie. 'And this "I will have Toby" . . .' Jamie waved his arms in alarm. 'Don't get involved. Really. You'll find yourself all tangled up in intense conversations and backstabbing. I mean, Zoe pours love on people, then abandons them. She hurts people . . .'

Roz cut him short. 'I can't help it if Zoe uses me. Or hurts me. I'm here to be hurt and used. It's better than her hating me.'

He shrugged. 'Don't say you weren't warned.'

He was protesting too much, she thought. 'I love you,' she told him. 'I don't expect it's a conversation topic you go in for much. But I just thought I'd mention it. I thought you might like to know.'

He grinned at her. 'I do know that.' Then, 'This is mushy. Piss off, will you?'

'No problem. Off I am pissing to bed.'

'Yeah, well. Zoe'll pout at you and you'll find yourself running around doing insane things.'

Roz went to switch off her computer, which had been humming in the corner of the room, neglected since Zoe's arrival. She thought maybe she shouldn't get involved in Zoe's traumatic affairs. But how did she stay uninvolved? There was something about Zoe. Those eyes. Full and pouting lips. Her face, all emotion, not a rational thought ever crossed it. Roz had a horrible feeling that deep entangled involvement was on the way. You could tell that was how life with Zoe would be. Just one glance into those troubled eyes, one glimpse of that beautiful, emotion-racked face.

'How can I deny the pout,' she said to Jamie, 'when I suspect it's me put it on her face?'

She went to bed. Lay in the dark and spoke to Nan. 'What do you think of all this? You knew something like this was about to happen, didn't you? Or did you engineer it? It'd be the sort of thing you'd do.'

CHAPTER FOURTEEN

Life without Zoe was empty. During the day, Will was too busy organising Toby's life – feeding him, getting him to bed, taking him to school, picking him up from school, arranging baby-sitters – to notice. But late at night, whilst Toby slept, the emptiness surrounded him. Filled him. The silence seemed to hound him. There was nothing he could do about it. Put on some music and it moved through the room just above the silence. It did not steal through it, banish it. It was just there alongside it.

Will missed Zoe more than he'd thought he would. The home he returned to in the evenings was cold, noiseless. He wanted her there, her chatter, banter. The muffled clatter from other rooms. The scent of her. Her drama, her wild, instant opinions about what she heard on the radio. The rock station he turned on sounded like irritating babble without her disagreeing with today's disc jockey. Standing centre of the kitchen, hands on hips, saying, 'What a moron. He gets paid for talking drivel.' He wanted to see her, feel her in bed beside him. He wanted to enfold her. Pull her on top of him. Make her laugh. He loved her face when she slept. Then she ceased to be a butterfly. Wrapped against the dark, she became a happy caterpillar. Nights, he roamed from room to room, drinking tea, hoping the phone would ring. And he'd hear her voice. Trying not to think. Thinking was to be avoided. It only got you down.

He and Toby had established a set of routines. Their morning routine, evening routine, washing routine, Sunday routine. Mornings, they would shower. Pick fresh underwear from the tumble-drier. Will would put on the kettle. Toby filled bowls with cereal, fetched milk from the fridge. They waltzed round each other. A pleasant choreography. They didn't speak much. Toby filled glasses with orange juice. Will made coffee. Toby fetched the papers and mail from the front door. They'd breakfast, Will thumbing through the paper, Toby looking at a comic. They'd dress. Toby would struggle with his laces, refusing to let Will do them for him. He'd kneel on the floor, one foot before him, tongue out, wheezing with effort. It made them late every morning. No matter how Will tried to time it, the laces made them late.

It added to the uselessness Will felt. The sympathetic look from Toby's teacher, when he apologised. 'Sorry. We're having trouble doing up our shoes.' She'd smile, wanly. He could see her thinking, Men. What else do you expect?

He didn't know what to say. The accusation – his uselessness, his unforgivable maleness – was unspoken. He felt dull. Huge hands, badly shaven, slightly grubby jeans. Trailing behind him a thin, pale, troubled and, dammit, slightly incontinent child. He knew this was not strictly true. His hands were in perfect proportion to his body. His jeans were always clean. He shaved. His child, though pale and troubled, was looking better now that he ate regularly. There were no longer any food tantrums. Will fed Toby the food the child thought to be proper children's food, burgers, beans, fish fingers and chips. Toby looked, for the first time in years, nourished.

Still, Will felt he had lost his fabulousness. He never fooled himself that he had been fabulous. It had all come from Zoe. He missed her. He thought now he had overreacted when he threw her out. It had been his fury. The sudden sighting of himself years ago. The person he had long left behind, and didn't want to become again. He should have taken a deep breath, forgiven her. Laughed.

He had adored her. Fancied she had adored him. At least, her great talent was that she made him feel adored. He wanted to feel adored again. Sometimes the silence was unbearable. If he could have, he would have wept.

Sightings of Marianne continued. So regularly now that they

had gone beyond nodding terms. They said hello. Will had no desire to take the relationship any further. He preferred to keep Marianne in his fantasies. She was happy, happyish there. He didn't want to discover the truth about her. That she was a drunk? Miserable? Or, God forbid, ordinary.

Marianne had other ideas. She wanted to talk. Next time she came into the bookshop, she cornered him. He'd tried to avoid her. Pretending to do something important to a display of new paperbacks on the table by the door.

'You don't play at the restaurant any more.' She didn't really ask. She told him.

'No.' He readjusted a pile of books.

'Why not?'

'Too busy.'

'Oh, right. It'd be nothing to do with me, then?'

She was blunt. He had to hand her that.

'No.' He could not hide his lie.

'Thought so. You don't want to be put off every time someone comes along who can play better than you.'

'I'm not. I just discovered something. I'm mediocre.'

'Rubbish. You're just scared.'

He put down his book. 'What do you mean by that?' Offended.

'If you want to be good, really good, you've got to let go. Expose yourself. Stand naked before the crowd. Your critics. Your mother. Everybody.'

This was horrifying. My mother? thought Will. Fuck me, I don't think so.

Marianne saw the look. Guessed the thought. ''Fraid so.'

Will shook his head. 'I couldn't. I mean, I can't. It's painful.'

'Well,' Marianne shrugged, 'there you go. Pain's all you get. Really.'

'Anyway,' said Will, 'I can't now. I have my little boy. I have to look after him. My partner left me.'

'Why?' She had no notion of tact.

'She said I wasn't good enough. She wanted more than I could give her.' He weighed this up. 'Well, actually she wanted more than I wanted, more like.' He looked at her. 'She was fabulous. I'm not.'

'Oh well. If that's what you want to think, I can't stop you. I'll take these.' She handed him a bundle of books. Fished a couple of wrinkled twenty-pound notes from her purse, unfolded them and handed them to him. Watched his face as he counted the change into her hand. She made him feel nervous. 'Just because someone played a tune better than you is no excuse for letting your whole life fall apart.'

'I haven't done that,' he protested. Too loudly, he thought.

'Excuse me, but it sounds like you have.' She put her face closer to his. Her breath smelled of tobacco. 'It wouldn't be anything to do with me being a woman. Quite an old woman. Who's a wee bit nicotine-stained. A bit pickled. A face that's all the worse for alcohol. Would it? I'm fifty-eight. I've got the face I deserve. But it doesn't stop me playing the piano. It wouldn't be something to do with all that, would it?'

'No,' Will near as dammit shouted.

'Thought so,' she said. 'Well, there you go. But if you ask me, there's no tune in the world worth dying for.' She rammed her change loose into her handbag. Zipped it shut. Made for the door. Turned. 'Well, maybe the clarinet. Mozart. Maybe that.' She swung her bag over her shoulder. 'Which would you rather? To have written the clarinet concerto, or to make love to this fabulous person. You have one night, one night. Outside by some lonely lake with the water whispering near by and the sound of a nightjar in the trees overhead. 'Choose,' she ordered him.

'Oh, I . . .' He was flummoxed. He didn't know which daydream to pick. To have written Mozart's clarinet concerto – God, he'd be proud of that. He'd never have to do anything again. That would be the making of him. But Zoe, the lake, love and the nightjar. God, that would be fantastic. He wanted it. Her. Now. And the bloody thing about that wish was he could have fulfilled it. Again. And again. He wished he'd thought of it when he had her. His face contorted in indecisive agony.

'Thought so,' said Marianne. 'You're confused.' She opened the shop door. 'Well, no doubt I'll be seeing you again. I'm always seeing you these days.'

So she'd noticed, too. Will leaned to watch her leave and walk down the street. Who exactly was she? An angel, he thought. If he had a guardian angel that was just the sort of person she'd be. A bit weathered by life. An angel, he scoffed. That was the sort of notion Zoe came up with. She believed in external forces shoving through her life. She'd believe in guardian angels. She was always looking for signs, omens.

They used to go nights, late, up Arthur's Seat, when she was pregnant, climbing to the top to stand and stare at the sky, looking for shooting stars. Necks craned, they'd watch the heavens. Will would wonder at it all. 'God, all those planets, and I know nothing of them. Which one's Venus? Where's Pluto? Neptune? Orion?' He didn't know.

The only thing he knew for sure was that there was more he didn't know than he did. The names of flowers? Didn't know. Trees? Birds? Stones? Didn't know. Didn't know. Didn't know. Books he hadn't read. *Great Expectations. Jude the Obscure. Remembrance of Times Past. Billy Budd.* Hadn't read. Hadn't read. Hadn't read. Hadn't read. Though, even worse, he pretended he had. There was so much he didn't know, sometimes he wanted to fall to the ground, grovelling, apologising to the universe for his ignorance.

'We're not here to know the heavens,' Zoe told him. 'We're looking for shooting stars.'

'For God's sake, Zoe, we can't stand here with our necks cricked hoping a star will come by.'

'Why not? They're up there shooting for us. It'd be rude not to be watching when they pass.'

So they stared up. But never saw their star. Maybe that was what went wrong. Maybe they should have looked harder. Longer.

Marcia, who worked Thursday and Friday afternoons after school and Saturdays, came in. Blue lips today, black nails. Skirt up to her arse. But then, Will thought, she had the arse for it. She was seventeen and as cynical as only seventeen can be. She'd read Proust and all of Herman Melville.

'Do you believe in guardian angels?' Will asked her.

'Huh?' She didn't flinch at the question. 'Yeah. Why not?'

'Really?' Will was amazed. She was the last person he'd thought would believe in anything not proven.

'Oh yeah. Could be anyone. I always give money to beggars and buy the *Big Issue*. You never know who's watching you.'

'But you can't believe you've got a guardian angel?'

'Yes. They walk among us. Taking care of us. They brush against you. Or they just give you a little smile on the bus to let you know everything's going to be all right. All sorts of folk. Unlikely folk.'

It could be Zoe talking.

'Zoe and I used to go up Arthur's Seat late at night looking for shooting stars,' he told her. 'She believed they were up there shooting for her. Or at least one of them was, and it was up to her to be looking when it passed.'

'That's nice,' said Marcia. 'That's lovely.'

'We could've been mugged,' said Will. It was all he could think.

'But you weren't mugged,' said Marcia. She smiled, spread her palms. Life was easy. 'See. Your guardian angel was watching.'

CHAPTER FIFTEEN

Mrs Beseley had lost a stone. Her face glowed with health. She was getting stroppy. Everyone in the family said so. On evening class nights she'd slap a frozen pizza on the kitchen counter and tell them to get on with it. On sunny mornings she'd leave the dishes, leave the vacuuming and take Simon's bike round the park, singing to herself. Favourite songs. Old Abba and Bee Gees hits, 'Super Trouper', 'Jive Talkin'', listening to the hum of tyres on tarmac. She was happy. This was new to her. After night school she went to the pub with her new friends. She came home late.

Roz was starting to like her. This was new to *her*. She was starting to escape into Beseleyland. It was less crowded, messy and noisy than real life. Zoe was complaining nightly about sleeping on the sofa bed in the living room. Mornings she'd lie, moaning about being awake, duvet pulled over her head, refusing to move.

Roz would tiptoe to the kitchen, make coffee. Listen to the news on the radio, volume down. She'd wash, dress. Then hang about. She wanted to work, but thought the sound of clacking keyboard would be irritating. And she didn't want to annoy Zoe. It was so amazing to have her here in the flat, after all those unforgiving years. There she was, beautiful and fragile, spoilt, almost impossible to live with. But she was here. It was a chance, Roz thought, to get to know her. To make up for all the wrong she'd done her. She wanted to be friends. Roz so desperately wanted a relationship, she was treading softly through these early days.

If there was no sign of life before half past ten, Roz would shop. She'd trail the supermarket aisles, dumping food for Jamie into her trolley. Loaves of bread and ham slices for his sandwich habit. Giant packs of cereal. Pizzas. All Zoe seemed to eat was alfalfa beans. She fussed about her diet. 'If it's not organic, I'm not eating it. Eat junk. Become junk.' Roz and Jamie would wince under her furious gaze. E numbers coursed through their veins. They were junk.

Usually when Roz got home from the supermarket, heaving bags through the living room to the kitchen, Zoe would still be in bed. But by now she'd be awake enough to chat.

'You've been busy whilst I've been lying here,' she sighed, a contented exhalation. 'Oh, lying down. My favourite thing to do. Every night when I get to bed, I think, why didn't I come here earlier? Bed's lovely. And the good thing about it is, I start here every day. And end up here every night again. It's the bit in between I've got to get sorted.'

Roz nodded. 'That'd be good.' Then she doubted herself. Perhaps she shouldn't have suggested it would be good if Zoe sorted herself out. Was that pushy? Did it sound like she wanted rid of her? She apologised. 'Well, you know. It'd be nice to see you happy.'

Zoe smiled. Returned to her snooze position, whilst Roz emptied her shopping bags. But the noise and the bustle had wakened Zoe. She rose. Got on with her morning routine. Though it was nearly lunch time. She made coffee. Sat at the kitchen table, smoking, reading the paper. That done, she'd disappear into the bathroom for hours. She'd appear, glowing and dressed. After a light breakfast of fresh coffee, toasted organic bread spread thinly with organic butter, she'd go off to shop.

That she didn't have any money and her credit cards were all past their limit didn't stop Zoe shopping. It was what she did. She'd try on clothes she couldn't afford, had no intention of buying. She'd while away happy hours at make-up counters, rubbing lotions and foundation creams into her wrists. She'd spray herself with tester perfumes. She'd sit on outrageously priced sofas, ask if they were available in perhaps a more subtle shade. She'd finger cups, glasses, cutlery. There were sunglasses, rings, bracelets to play with. London was heaven for the enthusiastic penniless shopper. That done, Zoe would return to Roz's flat for an evening's bickering with Jamie. They'd sit on the sofa battling for possession of the TV remote. If they weren't fighting about that, they were battling for possession of the bath or the phone. There were also fights about the bath foam and the cheese. Roz agreed about the cheese, something very odd was happening in the cheese department. It kept disappearing. She knew better than to interfere in the fights. Whenever she did, they took sides against her.

'It's a no-win situation,' she complained to her friend Janey over the phone. 'If I try to sort them out, they take against me. One thing they're agreed upon is that I'm a dreadful mother.'

'They're right,' said Janey. 'Leave them to it. Move out.'

'I can't do that. Where would I go?' She raked her mind.

There was Will. There was only him and Toby in that house. And they'd be out all day. She thought longingly of empty rooms. Silences. She lived an electronic life. Cocooned behind her screen, headphones on, listening to Madonna on the computer CD deck. Removed from the world. No sounds save the din battering in her ears. Only words flicking up before her. It was lonely. Terrifying, if she stopped to think about it. So she tried not to. She worried vaguely about Zoe's eating habits instead. Zoe seemed to eat nothing. Organic toast in the morning. Then nothing, save alfalfa sprouts.

She should go scatter Nan's ashes. She should find a hotel in Mull. Book for sometime over Christmas. Christmas was a fine time to go away. Everything shut down for a couple of weeks. She'd do that. Definitely.

Then there was Fred. She hadn't heard from him for a couple of weeks now. She wondered if she'd done something wrong. She phoned him.

'How are you?'

'Fine,' he said. 'I thought you'd forgotten about me.'

'No. Of course not. I thought you weren't speaking to me,' she said.

'Why would you think that?'

'I don't know. You've just gone all sort of silent. You haven't phoned.'

'I was waiting for you to phone me.' He was wondering why she hadn't responded to his note telling her he adored her. Maybe she didn't want to be adored. Maybe he was pushing her into a commitment she didn't want to make. He decided not to mention it. He didn't know he hadn't posted the note. It was still in his jacket pocket. His jacket was still in the car. 'Can I come round?' he asked.

'Um,' she said. 'It's a bit awkward. Zoe . . . my daughter's here now. Can I come to you?'

'Any time,' he said.

'The door's always open?' she asked.

'More than the door,' he said.

They hung up. No final arrangements made. Roz thought that despite the open-door welcome, he sounded strange. Unsure. Maybe he'd gone off her. Found someone else. She looked across the room, feeling hopelessly jealous. She didn't want Fred to find someone else. She wondered what the someone else was like. Young, probably. Younger than her, definitely. Better looking. Better dressed. Witty. Sexy. Having decided what she looked like, Roz was convinced she existed. And she hated her. Stealing her man. 'The bitch,' she said.

Seven o'clock. Jamie was on a sandwich trip to the kitchen. His quest for enlightenment was hungry work. Roz pulled off her headphones. Time to cook supper. She walked across the room. Fred's new girlfriend moved from assumption to reality. She probably wore high heels. Absurdly high heels, in bed, definitely. She'd be called something like Sophy, or Mel. Yes, Mel, women like that were often called Mel.

'Bloody Mel,' she said, filling a huge pan with water. 'I hate her.'

'Who's Mel?' Zoe came into the room.

'Fred's girlfriend,' said Roz.

'Who's Fred?' Zoe was irritable. She didn't like the thought of her mother having friends she didn't know about.

This penniless shopping business was getting to her. There were all those lovely things waiting to be bought. And she'd no money. It wasn't fair. She missed Toby. Will had thrown her cruelly into the night. She could've been mugged. Murdered. He didn't care. He certainly wouldn't be making sure Toby got plenty of fish for his brain. That wasn't fair either. Now here she was in this filthy flat, with this woman who worked all the time, talked to herself and used cheap bath foam. Who was also her mother. Not the woman she'd have chosen if you could choose such things. It wasn't fair. Absolutely nothing, as far as Zoe could tell, was fair.

'Mel's boyfriend,' said Roz. She slipped a fistful of pasta into the pot of boiling water. Furiously shoved some lettuce into a colander, took it to the sink to wash it. 'Bugger the pair of them.'

She turned on the tap full blast. The cascade of water hit the pile of dishes left from breakfast time and Jamie's sandwich trips, and spewed out over the room. Drenching Zoe.

'Jesus Christ. Thanks a lot. My best dress.' She flounced off.

'Sorry,' Roz mumbled. Though she wasn't.

Ten minutes later, Roz laid three plates of pasta on the kitchen table. A bowl of salad and a warmed ciabatta. Jamie came through. Started to eat. Roz poured three glasses of Sainsbury's Chilean white. Called Zoe.

Zoe flounced back into the room, changed into jeans and a T-shirt. She sat, glared at her plate. And at Roz.

'I'm not eating that.'

'Why not?' asked Roz. 'It's vegetarian. Pasta. Low fat. What's wrong with it?'

'How many calories do you suppose you've presented me with? Two thousand? Three?'

'You don't have to eat it all,' Roz told her.

Jamie ate.

'Look at it. It's swimming in olive oil. It should be lightly drizzled. And what's this?' Flicking the Parmesan.

'You know what it is,' said Roz.

Jamie ate.

'This isn't Parmesan. It's sawdust. Parmesan should be freshly grated. Or served in delicate slivers. Not heaped mountainously on top. I refuse to eat this.'

'Well don't, then. But that's all there is till I shop tomorrow.'

'I'm not eating it. I'm not. What will become of me? I'll get fat. I'll get all wrinkled. I'll look like you. It's not fair.' She meant to sweep her plate aside. Overdid the arm movement, knocked it to the floor. Looked down at it. Refused to be repentant.

It was a fortunate arm sweep, Roz thought. The plate didn't go far. Landed in the middle of the floor, smashed. A splattering of sauce hit the units. That was all the damage. Apart, of course, from her pride. But then who cared about that?

Zoe was aching inside. She wanted Will. She wanted Toby. And nobody here in this flat seemed to know or care about her pain. She buried her head in her hands. 'I'm in turmoil. You don't understand. Nobody understands. All you do is feed me junk food and sit working at that damn computer all day, you stupid cunt,' she flared at Roz.

A thick hush. Jamie ate. Watched.

'What did you say?' Roz's voice was abnormally quiet. 'What did you call me?'

'A cunt.' Zoe was defiant. Roz was shocked. Zoe loved to shock.

'Don't you dare speak like that to me,' said Roz, lips tight. 'Don't you dare use a word like that in my kitchen.'

'Cunt,' said Zoe. Almost stamping her foot. 'Cunt. Cunt. Cunt.'

If Zoe had been ten years younger, Roz would have sent her to her room. If Zoe had had a room.

'You ungrateful little bitch. You lie about all morning. You hog the bathroom. Run up huge phone bills. I feed you, make your meals. And all you do is flounce. Flounce and criticise.'

'Cunt,' said Zoe. Though with less certainty this time.

'I will not have that word in my house,' snapped Roz. 'I hate it.' She flashed her eyes. Straightened her back. A woman with morals. 'I was fifteen before I heard that word. Eighteen before I knew what it meant. And at least thirty-six before I used it.'

'So you've used it,' Zoe triumphantly pointed out.

Jamie ate his pasta. This was a good confrontation. He was enjoying it.

'Maybe,' huffed Roz. 'But not often. And I certainly haven't ever called anybody it.' Little pause. 'Not anybody I'm related to, anyway.'

Zoe flounced out of the room. Paused and returned for her wine. Flounced out again.

Roz got an empty carrier bag from the drawer and started to clean up. Jamie ate. She looked up at him. He shrugged. 'You're not wrinkled,' he said. 'Or a cunt, come to that.' He swigged his wine. Refilled his glass.

'Well, thanks for that,' said Roz. 'That's something.'

He shrugged again. Nothing to him. 'As her tantrums go, that's a three. Maybe a four. Baby, you ain't seen nuthin' yet.'

'I can hardly wait,' said Roz.

After supper, Zoe sat where she'd been sitting since her outburst, and her scolding – on the sofa. Legs drawn up, chin on knees. She was sulking. Roz came through, unplugged her computer and carried it into her bedroom. She came back. Lifted her pile of papers and notebooks, carried them through. Several trips later, printer, keyboard and work table were transported too.

'You don't have to move on account of me,' Zoe said without looking at her. She might be saying words to Roz, but she certainly wasn't speaking to her.

I think I do, Roz thought. 'I'm not moving on account of you. I think I'll get more done if I'm tucked away. Should've gone through there ages ago.'

Roz slept fitfully. She'd heard Jamie go to bed sometime around one. Then Zoe on a long call to Will, demanding to know how he was feeding Toby. And wanting to speak to Toby. 'I know it's late. But I need him. A mother needs her babies as much as her babies need her.'

Roz had turned over at this, pulled a pillow over her head and slept. She woke again at three. A noise. A movement. She listened. Who would burgle her? There was nothing worth taking.

She got up to check. Wrapped herself in her robe and tiptoed down the hall. The whole long area was lined with books, because there was nowhere else to put them. Books and odd objects, found, adored momentarily, then forgotten. A jug. A shell. A candle in the shape of a rocking horse. Coats hung, bulking by the door. Weird shapes. A hallway, beloved and familiar by day, rendered scary. Mostly by the fears that cowered in the dark of Roz's mind. A light glowed under the kitchen door. Roz slid it open.

Zoe stood, naked, eating a packet of crisps. Cream cheese and chive flavour. The fridge was open. The cheese removed, on the unit, and diminished by about half. Zoe had made a pile of cheese and crackers. Crisps downed, she started on them. Crumbs tumbled on to her tits. She made an umming noise as she ate. Ramming as much as possible into her mouth. Jiggling as she chewed.

'Cheese mystery solved,' said Roz.

Zoe whirled and glared. And chewed. Hand to mouth to keep the food in.

'If you'd eaten your supper, there'd be no need for this cheese-fest,' Roz said, sounding, she thought, like a mother.

Zoe couldn't answer on account of the bulging cheeks, so glared harder.

'I must say,' Roz continued, leaning casually yet assertively, she thought, against the doorpost, 'that the *hugely calorific* pasta I cooked was probably a lot less damaging to the arteries than what you're stuffing down you now.'

Zoe swallowed. 'I was hungry.'

'I'll bet. Tantrums do that to you.'

Zoe took another bite and glared. 'You don't understand.' She sat at the table.

Roz had to admire the woman. Stark naked and unapologetic. If it had been her, she'd have rushed to cover herself. Still, if she'd a body like Zoe's, maybe not.

'Will's got Toby. And I want him.'

'Well go home,' said Roz. 'I'm sure he'll have you.'

'Never.' Then, seeking reassurance wherever she could get it, 'What makes you say that?'

'When I saw him at Nan's funeral, he couldn't keep his eyes off you. He thinks you're wonderful.'

'Well I don't think he's wonderful. He threw me out.'

'I wish I could believe that.'

'I did something,' Zoe confessed. Took another mouthful. 'I'm not telling you what. Don't ask.'

'Wasn't going to,' said Roz. She had been. 'I wish,' she said, 'you'd go and put something on. I find it difficult to talk seriously to you when you're naked.'

'What's wrong with naked?' Zoe demanded. 'It's natural. You must have seen me naked before.'

Of course she had. But not for years and years. She looked at the body she'd long lost touch with. Still thin; it always had been. Once she had been wholly intimate with that body. Knew, washed, tended every inch of it. No more. Once her body had been that body's world, its environment. No more. Right now she'd be rebuffed, cruelly, if she even reached out to touch it. Right now she could not even reach out to soothe the aching mind it contained.

'Not since you were about ten,' she said. 'You stopped letting me see you unclothed about then. Insisted on locking the bathroom door.'

'Like you cared,' said Zoe.

'I cared,' said Roz. 'I cared enough to let you. You were growing up.'

The couple in the flat below started to argue. Their voices came grumbling through the floor. Sounds of dissent. Muffled. Roz could not make out what they were saying. They seemed to bawl at each other all day, all night. They must, Roz thought, go out sometime – to work, to shop. They must sleep sometime. Didn't seem like it. The buzz of their fractured relationship rattled up to her flat all times of the day or night. She wondered what her flat sounded like to the people above. Had they heard Zoe's tea-time outburst? Maybe they were too busy seeking sudden illumination and fighting to notice. If the front wall of the building should fall off, would it reveal sets of people, families, couples, bickering, arguing, who all came out into the world every morning smiling and saying, 'Nice day'? Like the Beseleys.

Zoe glared at her. She'd never give this woman credit for any kind of thoughtful mothering. 'You have to help me,' she said. Flakes of cracker flew from her lips. Spewed before her, on to the table. 'You have to come with me whilst I get Toby back.'

'I can't do that. You can't do that. It's wrong.'

'You càn. You must. You owe me. I won't abandon my child. I know the pain. We must drive to Edinburgh. Take Toby and bring him here. Then I'll find a job, move out, and you'll never see us again.'

'Maybe I'd want to see you again.'

Zoe stopped chewing. Looked at her. 'You must help me. You must. I miss Toby. I want him. He's mine.'

'You can't just take the child. You'd upset him. He's settled where he is. Why don't you get custody? You're his mum.'

Zoe looked away. 'I don't think I'd get it. I've no money. No proper home. No work.' She stopped. Looked at Roz. 'That's why you didn't take us with you, isn't it?'

Roz nodded. 'You guessed it. By the time I got my act together, you'd grown up. Matthew wouldn't let me near you anyway. Not at first. Later, when he wanted to be with Claire, he let you come see me.'

'I'm sorry,' Zoe said. 'I never realised.'

Roz shrugged. 'I always missed you. I always wanted you.'

'Then you know how I feel.' Zoe seized the chance of a little sympathy. 'I know what it's like to suddenly lose your mother. I won't do it to my child. I want Toby. I want him. I want him.' She reached out. Pulled an imaginary Toby to her. Held him. Rocked him. Rocked back and forth.

Roz let out a slow breath. 'We'll go see him. And Will. Work something out. I'm sure Will will be reasonable. He's lovely.' The words hung before her. They seemed to linger in the air.

Zoe looked at her. 'You don't know that.'

'He seemed it to me,' said Roz. Yes, so he had. He had long fingers. Brown eyes, soulful and deep. His hair was cropped short, and when he smiled a dimple appeared on the edge of his cheek. She realised for the first time that she'd noticed more about Will than she'd thought she had. And she thought he was lovely.

Roz was suddenly too tired to speak. Her legs were no longer reliable. The blood seemed to have stopped circulating through them.

'When can we go, then?' Zoe wanted to know. 'Tomorrow?'

'No,' said Roz. 'I've got work. I can't just go. And I'm not driving.'

Roz shook her head. The thought horrified her. Drive? All the way to Edinburgh? In a car? She didn't think so. It was traumatic enough driving to the end of the street. She found driving disconcerting. The routes she had to plan ahead. Jostling into traffic lanes, moving in amongst other cars. They came too close. God, she hated it. And knew if she was ever going to fulfil her dream of breezing around in her flashy little car, she would have to master it. Not yet, she told herself. But soon.

Zoe pouted. Roz marvelled. What a pouter her daughter was. If only she could pout like that, the world would be hers. 'I'll go with you the day after. Wednesday. On the train,' she said.

Zoe smiled. Pouting worked. 'Great.'

'You'd better call Will tomorrow. Tell him you're coming.'

Zoe shook her head. 'No. I want it to be a surprise.' She wanted to arrive, dramatically, unexpectedly at the school gates. Half past three when Toby was set free. She'd be there, looking fabulous. Toby would rush into her arms. Zoe had the whole scene planned. Letting people know in advance that she was coming was not part of her scheme. She took another bite of cracker. Mumbled, 'Sorry I called you a cunt.' She looked away.

Roz looked at her. Nodded. 'Good.'

She went back to bed. Normally she'd have a swift chat with Nan. But right now she felt like talking to someone who would actually speak back to her.

It was late. Too late to phone anybody. Phoning somebody now would be downright uncivil.

She lifted the receiver. Dialled Fred's number.

'Hello.'

'Hello, Fred?'

'Yes. My God, Roz. Are you all right?'

'I'm fine.'

'You woke me. What time is it?'

'I'm sorry,' Roz said. 'It's after one.' It was a lot later than that.

'Really? It feels later.'

'Sorry,' Roz apologised. 'Look, can I see you? Can I come round?'

'Of course you can. Open door, remember?' His voice softened.

'Now?' said Roz.

'Roz, it's late.'

'I know, but . . . It's my daughter. She takes tantrums. I'm tired. I need a cuddle.'

'I'll cuddle you tomorrow. I don't want you getting a cab this time of night.'

'I can drive. I need a cuddle now.'

Thinking of her, his lovely Roz, careening through the darkened streets, forgetting to switch on her car lights, going the wrong way, ending up in Luton, or halfway to Oxford, he said, 'No, stay where you are. Keep safe.'

They hung up.

Roz turned her back on the phone. Punched her pillow. He didn't want her. He was probably with that other woman. The young, sexy one, whoever she was. Mel. Right now, turning to her, laughing. Kissing her. Holding her. 'Damn him,' she said. 'And damn her, too.'

Fred lay in his bed, smiling. Thinking of Roz.

CHAPTER SIXTEEN

Matthew whistled through his teeth. Not a tune, just an irritating rasping breathing that escaped without him realising it. He drummed in time with his whistle on the side of his chair, staring into the distance. 'You mean she's gone?' he said.

'Yes.' Will nodded.

'How long?'

'A couple of weeks.'

'And you only just told me? Why didn't you get in touch before?'

Because, thought Will, you'd whistle through your teeth and drum. 'I don't know. I was busy.'

'And she's gone to her mother?' Matthew couldn't believe this. Also, he tried to avoid at all times saying Roz's name. 'Why didn't she go to one of her friends?'

She did. But she was too much for them. They all phoned him after Zoe had been with them for a couple of days. 'How do you put up with her? She's impossible,' they sympathised. In fact, that he'd lived with her for years earned him their admiration.

He got vibes. A word placed discreetly here, another discreetly missed out there. Some of Zoe's friends would sleep with him. He only had to respond in an equally discreet way. Words, nods, smiles. He got invitations. 'I expect you're missing Zoe in all sorts of ways,' Suzie had said to him. As had Joanna, and Sophy and Ziggy and Ruth. He wanted none of it. Zoe's friends, he decided, weren't very nice. But then, when it came to friends, neither was Zoe.

It was, he thought, a revenge thing. Zoe had presumably slept with their husbands or partners. Zoe didn't have any friends. She just knew people. She was a fabulous acquaintance. An abominable friend.

'I think she fancied London,' Will said. 'The allure of the big city. Lots of shops. Zoe would love that.'

'I thought she'd never go to her mother,' said Matthew. He straightened his fork, though it was regimentally straight already. Turned his attention to his knife. Laid his palms flat on the table, considered the whole arrangement in front of him. Knife, fork, spoon, plate and wine glass. It seemed in order. The perfect order of things soothed him. He was sure if he kept everything about him in place perfectly, he'd have control of himself, of his life. He held himself in. He never let go.

'So,' Matthew said, 'why did she go, anyway?'

'I asked her to leave,' Will told him.

'You did?' Keep control. Realign the wine glass. 'Why?' Do not say more, you might explode.

'She more or less told me I wasn't good enough.'

'I see.' Slight smile. He agreed with that. Nobody was good enough for Zoe. Light of his life, who always danced for her daddy. When Jamie brought all that heartache, pain and worry, she would take his hand and smile at him. Zoe was beautiful. A wonder to behold, he thought. But then he did not know of her reputation as fellatrix extraordinaire.

'I told her to come back when she found out I *was* good enough. But I couldn't live with her thinking I could be better than I am. Always pushing me on. Always scheming on my behalf behind my back.'

'A good woman should always be egging her man on,' Matthew said. He looked at his hands. Hands were a problem. He never quite knew what to do with them. Sometimes he placed them neatly entwined in his lap. But that was too feminine. He could fold his arms, he did on occasion, but found it a bit authoritarian. Putting them in his pockets was scruffy. He clasped them together in a tidy bundle and placed them on the table in front of him. He wished he could detach them and put one on either side of his place-setting. One beside his knife. One beside his fork.

'A good man should be left to find his way without anyone egging him on to do things he doesn't want to do,' said Will. 'And a good woman should be too busy egging herself on to bother hustling her partner. I think Zoe's afraid of the world. I think that's why she shoves other people forward. She gets them to do the things she wishes she could do herself. She hides behind them. She makes a huge show. But inside she's cowering and very frightened.'

'My Zoe?' Matthew leaned back, folded his arms. Someone speaking out of turn about his Zoe. This called for a show of strength.

Will recognised the signal. 'I know she's lovely. But she's got a lot of growing up to do.'

Matthew snorted. Looked in derision at Will's thumb ring. Changed the subject. Asked, since they were talking about growing up, how Toby was doing.

He was fine, Will told him, tucking the offending bejewelled digit out of sight. Perhaps he was too old to wear such a thing. He told Matthew that Toby was still sucking his thumb, but no longer wetting the bed. Some progress there. They did not mention the genital-twiddling. Matthew found such things hard to discuss. There had been little improvement there.

But Toby was socialising better. He'd had to, with a selection of baby-sitters and mothers of school pals who looked after him in the gap between school finishing and Will coming home from work.

Yet there was still something isolated and lonely about the boy. He seemed to hum a constant sad tune in his little head. It sometimes escaped, a tuneless dirge sweetened by his childish voice. Every time he heard it, Will felt guilty. He thought Toby's tuneless hum could only be something he used to hide from some ache in his head. A worry. A painful memory. A niggling sadness that he could not sort out. Something. And whatever it was, it was Will's fault. He and Zoe had caused it with their flighty lives. Their partying. Their long looks, private jokes. Shutting Toby out. Then suddenly pulling him to them. Hugs and kisses. Their impassioned fights and even more impassioned making up again. The child had no belief in himself. They had not blessed him with confidence.

Now, Toby faced a painful few years. He'd be the last to be chosen on the football field when sides were picked. He'd stumble and trip about the gym hall. He'd never climb the rope or vault effortlessly over the horse thing. He'd be the geek.

Will stared at his table setting. Noticed he was straightening his knife, sorting his wine glass. He stopped. Put his hands on his lap. Hated that. Folded his arms across his chest. Looked at Matthew, sitting opposite, arms folded. They both unfolded their arms. Will stuck his hands in his pockets. Matthew placed one on top of the other on the table. Tapped a tuneless dirge with his fingers. Counted the taps. The clock ticked. They'd discussed, with as little arm-waving as possible, the route Will had taken to get here. The weather. And Zoe. There was nothing left. They didn't speak.

Outside, the sounds of the late-autumn gardeners. Voices from happier lawns than the one beyond the window. Will was reminded of the weather. It was sunny outside, he'd forgotten. In the polished mirror opposite the window he could see a weeping willow, drooping, and a hedge cruelly trimmed. There was a row of chrysanthemums beside the front path. They bloomed almost apologetically. The smell of roasting chicken seeped through from the kitchen.

He could hear Toby speaking to Claire. Telling her how much he hated Brussels sprouts. His voice sounded hollow. There was so little noise here. The Sunday paper, read, was neatly folded on the shelf by Matthew's armchair. Will looked round and at last realised why he hated coming here. This house was filled with regret.

'I was wondering,' said Will, 'if you would look after Toby for a couple of days. I want to go to London.'

'Zoe?' asked Matthew.

Will nodded.

'You're going to persuade her to come back.' Matthew didn't ask. He assumed.

164

'Either that, or . . . I don't know. Work something out. She'll want to see Toby.'

'No problem,' said Matthew. 'Claire can do the fetching from school. I can drop him off on the way to work.' He was going to say that Toby was no trouble. But he didn't think that was true. Toby *was* trouble. But not the sort of trouble you spoke about. 'You'll be phoning Zoe to let her know you're coming?' he asked.

'Um. No. If she knows I'm coming, she'll make a point of being out. Zoe is very good at avoiding issues. I'll just arrive. Then she'll have to face me. And we can come to an arrangement about Toby.'

Will and Toby left soon after five. Toby was wrestling with a loose tooth. Mouth agape. Busy fingers wedged inside. He was drooling.

'The nights are drawing in,' said Will.

'What does that mean?' asked Toby.

'It means it's getting dark earlier,' Will told him.

'Then why don't we say that?'

'It's just an expression. Like keeping an eye out for something. It doesn't mean we'll take our eye out. It just means we'll look for it.'

'What?'

'Whatever it is we're keeping our eye out for.'

'Why does it get dark earlier?'

'Because in the winter we're further away from the sun.'

'Why doesn't the sun go away altogether, then?'

Will sighed. 'Because it doesn't. I don't know.'

Toby worked on the tooth. 'If it comes out, will I get a pound?'

'A pound? I think fifty pence is the going rate with the tooth fairy.'

'Is the tooth fairy all muscly?'

'I don't think so.'

'Then how does she carry all that money about every night? Bags and bags of it to put under all the pillows?'

'She must be muscly, now you mention it.' Will sighed. He didn't want to answer questions. He wanted to think about Zoe, and to sulk. He hated visiting Matthew. It depressed him.

They stopped at traffic lights.

'Why are traffic lights red?'

'Because red means danger. Watch out. Stop. Cars crossing your path.'

'They'd be prettier if they were blue. I like blue.'

'Suppose,' said Will.

The lights changed.

'What does she do with the teeth?' asked Toby.

'Who?'

'The tooth fairy.'

'I don't know.' Will white-knuckled the steering wheel.

Toby sensed his questions were having an effect on Will. He knew that when Will answered his questions, he was not wholly with him. But the questions were having an effect. So he kept asking them. Didn't care what the answers were. He wanted Will's attention. He only had Will now, and he wanted all of him. 'She must have thousands of teeth,' he said. 'Millions. Millions and trillions. And zillions.'

'Hmm,' said Will. Abstracted.

'Does she give extra for a good tooth? Say a tooth has a filling, will she only give twenty pence for that?' Toby asked.

'I don't know, Toby.' Will desperately wanted to disappear into himself. 'Probably.'

'Where do we go when we go further from the sun? Or is it the sun that goes? And where does it go?'

'It goes to the other side of the world.'

'Why? Why doesn't it stay here? Why isn't it hot all the time? If it stayed, the nights wouldn't draw in.'

'It goes to give the people on the other side of the world a shot at having summer.'

'Why don't they just come here?'

'TOBY!' Will yelled. 'I don't know. Who do you think I am? God? I don't know. I don't know. Don't ask. Stop asking.' He was yelling louder than he meant. He wanted to be alone. He wanted to think. He couldn't answer all those questions. He was a bloke with a silly thumb ring. What did he know about the tooth fairy and the movements of the planets?

Toby's eyes brimmed. He looked at Will. Then turned away. Put his head on the car window. 'Mummy never shouted at me,' he mumbled.

But Will heard. And he hated himself.

CHAPTER SEVENTEEN

If there had not been an almost constant layer of haze in the sky, from her window Roz could have seen the stars. She kept her bed by the window, curtains open, and lay staring up. On the ledge outside, a couple of pigeons roosted nightly, their cooings and bickerings keeping her awake. But she didn't mind. Sometimes, in the early dawn, she heard the shrill shriek of some bird of prey, skimming overhead. There would be pickings out there, she thought.

Simon Beseley locked up his bike so his mother couldn't take it, sunny mornings, cycling round the park. He said it was embarrassing his mum using his bike. He was losing his playground cred.

Jamie was learning to drive and doing, Roz suspected, nasty things to her clutch. They argued. The rest of the time Jamie watched television, complained about Zoe and searched Roz's books for sudden illumination. When he was spotted staring blankly at the ceiling, he said he wasn't staring, or snoozing. He was plotting his future. Waiting for the Big Idea to come to him. He'd dismissed Dirty Monopoly and see-thru toasters and was working on pagers for dogs. 'You could fit a vibrating thing in the collar. Train the dog to respond to it. And there you go, no more yelling hopelessly in the park.'

In the sky above, Uranus was moving. Sideways. A brilliant blue-green. Roz followed the movements of the heavens. She read about them. In the night, listening to the pigeons, she imagined them spinning up there. Shifting. She was overdrawn at the bank. There were letters about the Beseleys. A surprise for Roz; she'd imagined nobody read them.

Susan Beseley had recently demanded she be allowed to wear lipstick to a party. And on being refused permission, had not spoken to her mother for three days. They'd had forty letters from distraught mothers saying that this had happened to them. Eight of them were addressed to Pam Beseley. Roz had replied, as Pam, saying it was a phase and not to worry. Now she thought it wasn't a phase. Or if it was, worry, because it would soon be replaced by the next phase. And that would be as surprising and unwelcome as the last. Or, even worse, it wasn't a phase. It was the start of the non-communication.

In the night, Roz thought about her life. She came to the conclusion that if she'd been asked if she wanted to be born, if someone had shown her a list of her life's moments, its traumas, occasional highs, regular lows, laid out like a menu, she'd have turned it down. She'd have waved her hands like she did in a restaurant when offered pudding. 'No,' she'd have said, 'I'll pass on that. It'll only make me fat and cynical.'

The evening after her late-night call to Fred, she had gone to see him. When he was out of the room, fetching ice for their drinks, she had looked for signs of the other woman. Hadn't found any. But that doesn't mean she doesn't exist, she thought. It just means she's tidy. Unlike me.

She went over to Fred's drawing board. Sketches of his naked lady lay spread over the surface. In one, the lady, innocently nude, was in a bar. Someone had spilled wine over her. 'It's OK,' she was saying, wiping her skin down. 'This is waterproof.' In another she was standing, unclothed amidst the clothed, at a meeting of Cuddlers Anonymous – 'I am a cuddleaholic.' 'A day at a time,' some besuited man was comforting her. Roz smiled. Of all the people Fred drew, she loved this character most. She wished she knew her.

Fred came back with a bowl of ice cubes, dropped a couple into her gin and tonic. 'Spying?' he asked.

'No. Just looking.'

He took her glass. Headed off for the bedroom. 'I'm claiming my cuddle.'

She lay in his arms. Felt him against her, buried her face in his neck. Moved against him. 'Oh, Fred, everything's going wrong.'

This wasn't what he wanted. Fuck first, confess later.

'In what way?' he asked.

'There's Jamie sitting about waiting for the great idea.'

'It'll come to him. It's out there waiting for him. The great idea is to get a job. He'll figure it out.'

'Then there's Zoe. What will become of her? I worry.'

'She'll turn into an out-of-step-with-the-world dreamer like her mum.'

'Oh, piss off.' Kissing him. 'You're a nice man, Fred.'

'In what way am I nice?' he said, stroking her. 'Tell me. List six way in which I am nice. Starting now.'

She laughed. Punched his shoulder, ineffectually.

'If you're not going to cuddle me, and more, I want praise. Adulation,' he said.

'Oh shut up,' she said. 'You're just after my golden tongue when I'm offering you my body.'

'That'll do,' he said, pulling her to him. 'Especially if you do naughty things with your golden tongue.'

She froze. She wasn't ready to enjoy herself. Not just yet. There was a little bit more remorse to unburden. 'I left them behind. And now they're here with me again. It seems like they haven't grown up. They're still teenagers at heart.'

'Aren't we all?' said Fred. 'They're just behaving the way they remember they behaved when you were the old stay-at-home mum. Anyway, it's part of the new childhood thing. People are saying childhood is shorter. What they're not adding is that adolescence has got longer. A lot longer. You can be adolescent right into your fifties nowadays.'

'True. I've sunk back into adolescence and forgotten how to be a mum. I've lost the art of parenting.'

'It'll come back. It's like sex. Like riding a bike. You never forget.'

A long silence. They lay in the dark, holding hands. Then Roz said, 'I can't ride a bike.'

171

She kissed him. Slid under him. 'But the other thing. I remember how to do that.'

In the morning, home again, feeling restored, she stood at her bedroom window, forehead resting on the pane. Looked down at the tiny scrubby garden far below. First grey squirrels of the morning scuttled amongst the broken, abandoned toys. Planes heading for Heathrow skimmed overhead. Traffic on the roads nearby. The early vibrancy of the city she had come to, nursing her ailing heart. She had not been able to stay in Edinburgh. There she would always have been, amongst their circle of friends, the woman who abandoned her kids. Here she was just another face. It was what she wanted. Anonymity.

In less than an hour the cab she'd ordered would arrive to take them to King's Cross. She wanted to see Will. He seemed so kind, caring. She thought of him more than kindly. It was not lust. It was a longing, an ache she felt. She had only recently acknowledged it. She told herself, in her logical moments, that if she saw him just once more, she would cure herself of this absurd yearning. But somewhere in the depth of her, she knew this wasn't true.

It was a childish thing. And she was too old for childish things. She used to dream about what she would do when she was finally grown up. If that state really exists, she thought. She'd had a thousand notions about what she'd do, how it would be. The freedom she'd have. I started all those years and dreams ago waiting for the moment. As if it were a moment, she thought. I was sure there was such a thing as a grown-up. And now I'm here. I won't get any taller. I'm as wise as I'll ever be. Which, when I think about it, is pretty stupid. And I still feel confused, uncertain. I still don't know what I really want to be when I'm big. I don't think there's any such thing as a grown-up. I'm quivering inside, waiting. Hoping the real person will come take me by the hand, guide me home.

In other rooms of her flat two people were trying to grow up. Without realising that was what they were doing. She, on the other hand, felt to her horror that she was growing down. Touching another base. 'What do you think of that, Nan? Fuck this. I've got to stop talking to a dead person.'

Seven hours later, two o'clock in the afternoon, Roz and Zoe arrived in Edinburgh. Their journey had been nervy. Getting nervier the nearer they got to Waverly station.

Zoe fidgeted. 'What if he doesn't want me?'

'He'll want you,' said Roz. 'You're his mum. Don't worry.'

'Will says I smother him,' said Zoe.

'Do you?' asked Roz.

'Probably,' she confessed. She stared out of the window, watching the whoosh of passing fields. 'I want him to love me.'

'He'll love you. Children love their mums. It's later, when they discover their mothers are only human beings, that the trouble starts.'

'Hmm,' said Zoe. 'I have problems with love. I have affairs,' she said. 'All the time. I don't care who with. I just do it. So's people will like me. I wait till I have people hooked, declaring their passion. Then I reject them. Why do I do that?'

'You're insecure?' suggested Roz. 'Because you think I rejected you.'

Zoe nodded. 'That'll be it. So it's all your fault then?'

'I should think so. Blame me, why don't you?'

'I will,' said Zoe, eagerly embracing this notion. 'I do. Also, I get a real kick out of shocking people.'

'Like me, now?' asked Roz. 'When you told me you had affairs.'

Zoe nodded enthusiastically. They smiled.

'Were you happy? After you left?' asked Zoe.

Roz shrugged. 'I had my moments. But I missed you. I always sent presents. Money for your upkeep. Trainers. Lipsticks. CDs.'

'Did you? I never knew.'

Roz let out a slow breath. Matthew, she sighed.

'You're not going to go all soppy and say you love me,' said Zoe.

'But I do,' said Roz.

'Huh, just because you say you love me doesn't give you the right to say that you do.'

'But I do,' Roz told her. 'No matter how many affairs you have.'

'What if I don't want you to love me?'

'Nothing you can do about it. That's the burden you have to bear.'

'Bummer,' Zoe said. Fell into another long silence. When Roz looked over at her daughter, she was sleeping.

Edinburgh was cold. A watery sun in a pale sky. Roz shivered. They took a taxi down the hill into Stockbridge to Zoe's house. This Roz wanted to see. The home her daughter had made for herself and Will.

It was stuffed with an organised, tasteful confusion. Books, videos carefully arranged on shelves. Plants, things – a row of glass vases, ceramics – dark-grey, ochre and burnt-orange chenille and velvet throws over the sofa. Roz went to the loo. Observed the array of bath oils, shampoos and aroma therapy potions. Nothing cheap here. Her daughter had class clutter. God knows what she makes of my scruffy . . . Roz searched for a suitable word. *Hovel* was all she could come up with. She peed. Noticed the selection of glossy art books by the loo. Washed her hands, noticed the quality of the soap. You couldn't buy that in a supermarket. Dried them, noticed the thickness of the towel. Hers were got with points on her supermarket loyalty card.

Zoe phoned the bookshop where Will worked. 'He isn't there,' she said, putting down the receiver. 'Probably on his way to collect Toby. I want to do that. I want to see him. I want to be there when he comes out of school. We'll take the car. You drive.' She threw Roz the keys.

'Won't Will mind? Me driving his car? I mean, my driving isn't exactly expert,' said Roz.

Zoe shook her head. 'No. It's just a car. Not like your car, which is more than a car. It's something you could love, a lifestyle statement. Anyway, the school's only down the road. It'll be cold standing at the gates.'

They parked outside the school at three. Arriving early, at Zoe's insistence. She wanted to see Toby the instant he came out. They hardly spoke. Zoe smoked.

By three thirty there was a group chattering on the pavement, mothers waiting, and a row of cars lined up behind them. Roz remembered waiting at the school gates for Jamie and Zoe. 'The jury at the school gates,' she murmured.

'What?' asked Zoe.

'The mothers at the gate. I used to be one. There were scruff mums and neat mums. And we judged each other, and our children as they came out. I hated it. All that stuff you go through, you know nothing about when you get pregnant. Playgroup committees. The judging of the packed lunch. Marks out of ten for the way your child emerges, buttoned, unbuttoned, laces tied. It's hell.'

The bell rang. Zoe scanned the waiting groups for Will. She did not see Claire arriving, parking several cars behind them. The children spilled through the school door, rushed across the playground, like eager puppies. Toby appeared in amongst the hurtling infants. Nothing out of ten for his owner. His laces were undone, shirt open and hanging out of his trousers. His blazer was off his shoulders, halfway down his arms. He had a huge chocolate stain on his tie. His bag flapped; a stray pencil flew from his pocket.

'Look at him.' Zoe was dewy-eyed. 'He's lovely.'

'Toby,' Claire called. He turned towards her.

'Toby,' Zoe shrilled, jumping up and down. Waving.

Toby stalled. Looked between the two, hurtled for Zoe. Threw himself into her arms.

'Toby,' Claire called again, shoving through the milling mass of escapee infants and fussing mothers towards Zoe.

Zoe scooped Toby up and moved back to the car. She still did not see Claire.

'Coo-ee,' called Claire, jumping up and down, waving.

'Where's Will?' Zoe asked Toby. 'There's nobody here to fetch you.'

Toby did not mention Claire. He wanted to be with Zoe.

'That's dreadful.' Zoe was shocked. 'I can't believe Will would just leave you.'

Claire pushed through the small throng of mums. Waving, beaming. 'Yoo-hoo, Zoeeeee.'

Zoe turned. Saw Claire. Pretended she didn't see Claire. Claire's dutiful presence, picking up Toby from school, would scupper the master plan forming in her scheming mind.

Toby climbed into the back of the car. Zoe got into the passenger seat. Slammed and locked the door. Roz started the engine, drove off. Claire stood in the midst of the mass of squirming children and fussing mothers, watching them go. Feeling foolish. Had she shouted 'coo-ee'? How embarrassing.

Watching the car containing Toby slowly slip away, she was thinking, mouth moving. If Will was in London, what was Zoe doing here? And why had Zoe pretended not to see her? She rushed back to her car. Took off, behind Roz, lights flashing. She didn't like to toot. Tooting was vulgar.

Toby kneeled on the back seat, looking at Claire. He waved to her. Zoe saw him. Leaned over to grip the busy, hailing hand. She glanced back at the following car.

'Can't you go any faster?' she demanded.

'No,' said Roz. 'There are children about.'

Roz crawled on, clutching the wheel. Twenty-five miles an hour. She did not look in her rear mirror. Concentrating on the road ahead was enough. She reached the end of the street, turned right. Claire followed. A group of tourists moved out in front of them.

'Toot,' said Zoe. 'Toot your pissing horn.'

'Won't. I hate tooting. It draws attention to yourself. Why are you so agitated, anyway?' She was still unaware of Claire behind.

Zoe leaned over, pressed hard on the horn. The tourists scattered. Roz drove through. The tourists re-formed in front of Claire, who knocked on the windscreen and pleaded with them to move. She got out of the car, beseeched the group of bemused Japanese to stand aside. 'It's my step-daughter, she's got Toby. And I have an awful feeling . . . I mean . . . the way she deliberately ignored me . . .' The tourists gathered round her, cameras dangling, spread their hands, talked amongst themselves. They hadn't a clue what she was saying. They took her photograph. Claire wept.

Roz, still unaware that Claire had been following her, drove back to Zoe's flat. 'What now?' she said.

'Now we take Toby with us. Back to London,' said Zoe firmly. She'd made up her mind. Here was an excuse to have her son. She could say she was shocked to find nobody at the gates to collect Toby from school. It was her duty to take him. Of course Claire had been there, but Zoe hadn't seen her. Had she? 'There was nobody there to collect him from school. That's abominable. Just terrible. I'll take him with us. And phone Will when I get there to tell him what I think of him.'

She got out of the car, strode up and down. 'Terrible. Terrible. Terrible. Anything could have happened to him. He could've been abducted. I can't believe this.' She worked herself up. Such a fury. She almost believed herself.

Toby sucked his thumb. Moved his steady stare from Zoe to Roz. The thumb came out, he was about to say that Claire had been there. Hadn't they seen her? Zoe caught the moment. Oh no, he wasn't going to tell. She shoved the thumb back in. Ranted some more. 'You just don't know who's lurking around playgrounds these days. You can't be too careful.'

A taxi passed the end of the street. Zoe ran towards it, yelling, waving her arms. It stopped. She took the car keys, shoved them through the letter box. Bundled Roz and Toby into the cab, climbed in after them. 'Waverly,' she shouted. It was imperative they go before Claire caught up with them. They sped off. By the time Claire arrived, they were gone.

They were on the train before Roz said, 'Do you think all that was wise? I mean, I don't believe there wouldn't have been someone to pick Toby up. We hardly gave them a chance.'

'Claire was there,' said Toby.

'Was she?' Zoe faked surprise.

'Was she?' Roz was horrified. 'And we stole you away. My God, we should phone. They'll be frantic.'

Zoe put her arm round Toby. 'We'll let them know when we get there.' She hugged him. She had him and she was never going to part with him. She was high. Drama always made her high.

Toby was confused. He'd been in a car. Then a taxi. Now a train, and he still didn't know where he was going. He reached down. There it was between his legs, as always. It was to be relied on in this weird world he found himself moving through. He twiddled his penis through his trousers. Small comfort.

Roz looked at Zoe. 'Didn't you see Claire?'

Zoe looked out of the window. Didn't answer.

'You did, didn't you? Oh my God, you did. Oh, Jesus Christ. I should look in my rear mirror.'

It was nine o'clock and they were headed south. Nothing to be done about it. The table between Roz and Toby and Zoe was spread with Toby's burger cartons and Zoe's sandwich wrappers. Coffee cups. Roz had resorted to alcohol. What was she going to do with Zoe?

She watched her daughter open her coat and pull Toby in, wrap it round him. 'Soon be there, Toby. Isn't this fun?'

He nodded slowly. The thumb slipped between his lips. He thought his mother had a strange idea of fun. He sucked and looked across at Roz, sizing her up. Then he remembered something. He removed the thumb. 'I'm still not a Beseley,' he told her.

'So I see,' she agreed. 'I'm very glad of that.'

Half an hour later, both he and Zoe were asleep. Roz looked at her sleeping daughter, arm crooked round Toby. Could someone actually sleep and glow at the same time? It was the first time she'd seen the girl peaceful. Slumber removed all that pent-up passion she carried whilst awake.

Roz remembered her, the child she was, years ago, standing on the lawn, hands by her sides, staring up at the sky, waiting for snow. When it didn't come, she cried. Well, wept. Zoe never just cried. 'But he said it would,' rapping the television screen. 'That man who does the weather said it would snow.' Roz had known that if that weatherman was available to be confronted face-to-face by Zoe, he too, would have apologised profusely. All she'd have had to do was pout.

Memories of Zoe. Twelve years old, coming home with her brand-new shiny blue mountain bike. Soaked to the skin. Her good anorak draped over the bike. 'Zoe, what are you doing? Why haven't you got your jacket on?'

'The bike needed it. To keep dry.'

'But it's a bike. A mountain bike. It's meant to get wet. It's specially built for rough roads, foul weather.'

'This bike doesn't like the rain. It told me. It said, "I don't want to get wet." So I wrapped it up to keep it warm. Nice and cosy.'

Roz, remembering, shook her head fondly. Zoe. Nobody ever knew what to do with her.

CHAPTER EIGHTEEN

Will arrived at Roz's flat at midday. Jamie opened the door to him. 'What are you doing here?'

'I came to see Zoe.' He looked tired. Rumpled after his train journey.

'You've missed her, mate. She's gone to see you. Well, Toby.'

'What? Christ.' He ran his fingers through his hair. Looked back down the stairs, wondering if he should turn and head home.

'Better come in,' said Jamie, opening the door wider.

They went into the living room. Will looked round. God, this place was messy. Cups, abandoned where whoever had been drinking from them had left them. Newspapers. Clothes. A lustrous plant, looking superior. Smug. She feeds me. She loves me. Take that, all you absurd, screwed-up, abandoned ones.

'Have a seat,' said Jamie.

Will looked round, wondering where. He chose the empty space at the end of the sofa. The television prattled. Midday nonsense. A quiz show. The Chemical Brothers thumped from the hi-fi. The place smelled of recent deep bath, coffee and a fry-up. With Roz out of the way, Jamie was having a good time.

Will took in the room. At second glance, he caught a glimpse of the person who lived with all this mess. The pictures on the wall – mostly black-and-white prints, old photographs: a couple of tweenies sitting playing dominoes at a table covered with a crisp linen cloth; some tubby, top-hatted men milling about in front of a town hall, avidly discussing local events; a woman in ludicrously uncomfortable clothing holding a camel's reins; a pair of balloonists looming out of their wicker basket. This person had whimsy. He liked her. He noted the videos – *Casablanca, Fitzcarraldo, Trop Belle*

Pour Toi, My Life as a Dog, Diva, Il Postino, Moonstruck. Yes, he liked this woman. There were books. Shelves of them along the hall leading into the living room. And lying on the coffee table, on top of the telly, on the windowsill, everywhere.

'She's a reader, your mum,' Will said.

'Well, she's a book-buyer,' said Jamie. 'She'd keep you going.'

Will smiled. 'She doesn't read them?'

'Yeah, some of them. Paperbacks mostly. She browses a lot. Knows all sorts of things she'll never use. Comes out with stuff. Like Attila the Hun founded Venice. Or did you know female curlews have longer beaks than male curlews. And you always say, "I didn't know that." She's got a litter-bin brain. Full of throwaway fragments.'

'Hmm.' Will scratched his chin. He knew the sort. He was the same. Couldn't concentrate on reading for all the thoughts it conjured up. He picked up Jamie's book. 'What's this you're into now? Sudden illumination?'

'Yeah.' Jamie shrugged, mildly embarrassed. 'Seeking the inner me.' He cringed as he said it.

'Given up on the Big Idea, then?'

Jamie shook his head. 'I've decided against Dirty Monopoly and see-thru toasters. Though that's a beauty. It's a morning thing. Watching bread cook, slightly. Seeing the brown spread. It'd be soothing. Too much trouble to get it off the ground, though. Dog pagers. That's the latest thing.'

'Jamie,' Will scolded, a small, affectionate reproof.

Jamie shrugged again. 'I know. Don't.'

'Don't what?'

'Say anything. I know. My mother's been on at me. "Get a job, Jamie." "Grow up, Jamie." ' He made a face. 'Do you want coffee?'

Will nodded. 'Wouldn't say no.'

Jamie disappeared into the kitchen. Will leaned back, closed his eyes. This was a nightmare. Zoe gone to Edinburgh, and him coming to London. They must have crossed paths. Why hadn't he phoned to say he was coming? It seemed such a sane thing to do now he thought about it. Jamie came back with two steaming mugs.

'How's Zoe getting to Edinburgh?'

'She and Roz went on the train. Roz refused to drive.'

'She's got a car?'

'Nan bought her it. Great thing. Soft-top. Cool.'

Will was impressed. A woman with hundreds of books, assorted prints on the wall – pictures of *outré* people from distant times – and a cool car. It seemed so civilised after Zoe's absurdness, her tantrums, her raging insecurity. Pity Roz was Zoe's mum.

They leaned back, watching telly. Didn't feel any need to speak. Till, after a comfortable half-hour, Jamie suggested they go for a pint.

They found a corner in the pub. Chatted quietly about everything, anything, as long as they avoided the problem of Zoe and Zoe's trip north. They both felt it was trouble enough having her in their lives without talking about her.

Jamie was sipping silently whilst noticing the girl behind the bar. She spoke in clipped, upper-class tones. Blonde hair to her shoulders, a Nietzsche T-shirt. She was standing, hands on hips, saying to her boss, 'No, I will not go to the bank with your takings. That is not part of my contractual remit.' The boss was backing off. 'OK, OK. I only asked.' Cool, thought Jamie.

Three pints down, they thought it best to leave. Will walked Jamie to the end of his road, said goodbye. 'I've got to get back. Catch Zoe.'

'Right,' said Jamie.

'She'll be staying at the house overnight, I'd imagine. Fussing over Toby. Cheers, mate.' He started off down the road, thinking what a pleasant afternoon he'd had. He'd thought it would be spent bickering with Zoe about who should get custody of Toby. But instead it had been relaxing. Very relaxing.

'Cheers,' Jamie called after him. Then went back to sudden illumination, the Chemical Brothers and *Countdown* on telly. A fine afternoon. After that he returned to the pub. He fancied getting to know the bossy barmaid.

It was after nine when he got in and received the hysterical call from Claire. 'Where the hell have you been all day? I have to speak to Will. Zoe's taken Toby,' she said.

Jamie could almost smell the brewing tea in Claire's house, the angst. He could feel the chaos at the other end of the line. He was glad he wasn't there. Matthew would be whistling tuneless melodies and counting up a storm. 'Will's gone,' he said. 'Long gone. He'll be on the train back now.'

'What?' screamed Claire.

'He thought he'd missed Zoe, so he went home.'

'What are we going to do?' shrilled Claire.

Jamie shrugged. Third or maybe fourth shrug of the day. He felt he was shrugging a lot these days. He'd have to cut it out. 'Dunno,' he said. 'Will'll just have to come back down here. Suppose.'

At half past eleven Roz, Zoe and Toby arrived at the flat.

'We're back,' Roz announced before Zoe could make a dramatic statement. 'And Toby's with us.'

'Will was here,' Jamie told them. Roz's heart sank.

'Will?' Zoe said.

'He wanted to speak to you.'

'Shit. What a mess.'

'He'll be back,' said Jamie.

Roz's heart leapt. Though she told it not to.

Toby was ashen, bleary-eyed. Clutching Roz's hand, he stared blinking at the room, strewn with books, papers, cups, discarded shoes, life's rubbish. 'Don't you ever clean up?'

'No,' Roz told him.

He looked up at her. Gripped her palm. 'I want to be like you when I grow up.' Adoration.

'Marry me,' said Roz.

Will arrived in Edinburgh. Got the message on his machine that Zoe had snatched Toby. He drank several huge whiskies. It was Wednesday night. He'd taken a few days' holiday, was due back at work next Tuesday morning. He went to bed, slept fitfully. Got up at five. Caught the early train back to London, and arrived at the flat mid-morning, looking stunned.

CHAPTER NINETEEN

The sleeping arrangements reached a new crisis. Will refused to go back to Edinburgh without Toby. Zoe refused to let Toby go. Roz, rather too gladly, she thought, invited Will to stay whilst they sorted themselves out. Zoe would not allow Will into her bed. Jamie wasn't keen on giving up his room. Roz would gladly have had Will in her bed, but thought better of mentioning it. Will stood looking helpless. In the end they all shifted around. Jamie moved to the sofa bed. He'd been persuaded after Roz pointed out that he'd have late-night access to the television. Roz moved into the spare room, computer with her. Zoe moved, gleefully, to Roz's room, Toby with her. And Will would share the sofa with Jamie.

It had been a hell of a day. Will and Zoe had done a deal of glaring. Jamie had disappeared inside his Walkman. Toby had flagrantly fiddled with himself, sucked his thumb. He had a drool rash down the side of his chin. Roz had made tea. Huge amounts of tea. Nothing had been settled. They'd politely bumped into one another. Waited for the loo to be vacated. The television had played throughout the whole scenario. Zoe had smoked a pack of Marboros. They had opened the living room window to let smoke out, air in. Shut it again when everyone got too cold. Streaky bluish billows hung over Zoe's head as she ground out one cigarette, lit another, glaring at Will. They opened the window again.

Lunch time Roz emptied three tins of lentil and bacon soup into a pot and made some toasted cheese. Zoe refused to eat it. As did Toby. Roz made him one of her tuna sandwiches with little bits of celery.

Zoe looked enviously at him eating it. 'You might've made one for me. I like tuna sarnies.'

'You didn't say,' Roz defended the making of a single sandwich.

'You know I like them,' Zoe sulked.

The telly blared. The news. Then an Australian soap with fraught full-lipped women and tanned men.

Will took Toby on to his knee to read him a story. Zoe pulled him off, assumed control of the story-telling. Jamie read about sudden illumination in between checking the football news on Teletext.

Roz stood by the window. Across the street at the front of the house a man sat in a conservatory reading a newspaper. It seemed tranquil. Roz envied him. She was weary of the tension, the televised babble. She moved to stare out the window at the back. Squirrels darted over the dampened broken toys. In the flat opposite, fridgeless students put a row of milk cartons and yoghurts on their windowsill to keep cool. They joked and bantered. Roz envied them more.

Will came through to join her. He made her a cup of tea. 'What are you looking at out here?' he asked.

'Other people's lives. I've always loved watching other people's lives.'

'Glimpses from the bus? Or walking down streets sneaking glances through uncurtained windows?'

'Yes.' She nodded.

'I like doing that.' He smiled. 'Do you feel invaded? Suddenly four other people in your flat?'

'No, no, really.' Roz thought she protested too much. 'I love having you all here. I never thought the day would come. Have you and Zoe sorted anything out?'

'No,' said Will. 'Not yet. Zoe won't let go of Toby. When she loves, she loves with all of her.'

'I know,' said Roz. 'And when she loathes . . .'

'I know,' said Will. 'But she doesn't loathe you any more. She's mellowing.' He grinned. 'There's hope.'

Roz went to her new room, ignored the boxes and her own

neglected toys – the rowing machine, the sandwich toaster – and switched on her computer.

The Beseleys were arguing. Mr Beseley was making a fuss because Mrs Beseley had used the car without filling the tank, and he'd run out on the way to work.

'We agreed. Whoever uses the car should replace the petrol they've used. It's a house rule.'

'Oh, shut up about rules,' said Pam. 'Rules, rules, rules. I'm sick of them.'

'They're just guidelines for the smooth running of the household.'

'Oh, stop being so pompous.'

She stormed from the kitchen, not fast enough to miss Frank saying, 'Me? Pompous? It's you that's scatterbrained.'

Marching down the hall, she tripped over one of young Sammy's toy cars. Enraged, she kicked it into the door. Sammy started to howl. Pam barged into the living room where Simon was watching telly. Pam switched it off. 'Why aren't you outside on a nice day like this?'

'Nothing to do.'

Pam took her coat, stumped out of the house.

Roz sighed. Saved and shut down. She went into the living room. Jamie had gone to the pub. Will and Zoe were sitting on opposite ends of the sofa, saying nothing. Toby was in bed. Beth Orton sang on the hi-fi.

'You two need to talk,' Roz said. She left the room. I need to talk, she thought. Phone Nan. She had the receiver in her hand before she remembered. Nan's dead. 'Oh my God,' she said, 'I forgot.' Phoning Nan in moments of despair, crisis, indecision, happiness, glee had been so automatic Roz had simply reached out, without remembering the old lady was no longer there to listen. Right now, she needed somebody. She got her coat. Put her head round the living room door. 'I'm going out.'

'Where,' said Zoe, 'are you going this time of night?' It was half
past eight.

'I'm going to see Fred,' Roz told her.

'Fred and Mel?' asked Zoe.

Roz had a moment – who was Mel?

'Ah, yes.' Mel, the other woman she wasn't sure existed. 'Them,'
she said.

She drove to Fred's. Remembered when she was halfway there
to switch on her headlights. Found, great relief, a parking place
she could manoeuvre into forwards.

He opened the door to her. 'Roz.' Delighted to see her, he led
her down the hall to his sitting room. It was a good room. A bit
masculine, but Roz liked it. A beat-up grey corduroy sofa. Charcoal
sisal on the floor. Several huge piles of books beside the far wall
where Fred had been promising for the past five years that he'd
build shelves. A matt-black fan. Dark blue card-shaded lamps.
Picasso prints on the walls. The curtains – an old Liberty print
chosen by his wife, years ago, that he'd taken from their home –
were drawn. The room was dim. He'd been sitting in the dark
listening to Mahler, drinking gin.

'What are you doing?' said Roz.

'I'm drinking and thinking,' Fred confessed.

'Oh dear, sounds grim. I hope you're not depressed. Because
I've come to dump on you.'

'Dump on,' said Fred. 'I don't mind. Especially if you do it with
your clothes off. Lying down. Preferably with me on top of you.'

'That'd do the trick,' said Roz. 'I've reached the age of lying
down. It suits me better than standing up. Actually, I look a lot
better when I'm horizontal. Have you noticed that?'

'Yes, I have,' he agreed. Enthusiastically.

She went across to his drawing board. 'Can I look? Do you
mind?'

He shook his head.

There was another drawing of his naked lady. A woman,
definitely. Not a lady, this person. She was standing stroking her
rounded, slightly dimpled, exposed-to-the-world arse, asking her

naked man friend – lover? Roz never could tell – 'Does my bum look big in this?'

Roz grinned. 'I love this woman. I wish I knew her. We'd get along.'

'She's lovely,' said Fred, taking Roz to him.

'Oh, do that,' said Roz. 'Hold me. Touch me.'

He held her. Stroked her back.

Roz unbuttoned his shirt. Then her shirt. 'I want to feel you.'

'I'll agree to that,' said Fred.

She went to the bedroom, stripped off, letting her clothes fall to the floor in a heap. She crawled into his bed. It was a lovely bed. A large sled bed. It smelled of lavender polish and fresh sheets. Fred changed the bed linen every two days. His house was tidy. Unlike hers.

'It's lovely here,' she said. 'I could move in.' She yawned. Stretched. 'What are we doing, Fred? What will become of us? We'll become a pair of randy old pensioners moving from one orgasm to the next. All those *petits morts*. One day there will be no *petits* and we'll both be *morts*.' She rolled over, pulled the duvet over her head. 'It doesn't bear thinking about.'

Fred smiled. Went to the bathroom. Undressed. Cleaned his teeth. Slapped on some Paco Rabanne. Padded through to the bedroom. 'Why don't you, then? Move in? Before we're both *morts*. We could go for making a *petits morts* record. We don't have to marry. Well, not if you don't want to. I don't mind. I'd quite like to.' He looked at her. Climbed into bed beside her. Leaned over, kissed her shoulder. No response. He shook her gently. Nothing. He whispered her name. He said it louder. Nothing. Roz was sleeping.

At three in the morning, Roz woke. Instant guilt. She'd invited Fred to his bed and fallen asleep on him. The shame of it. She turned to him. 'Are you sleeping?'

'Yes.'

'So am I, then. Sorry.'

'What for?'

'Falling asleep on you. Sorry.'

'Doesn't matter,' he said. 'You looked so peaceful, I didn't like to disturb you.'

'You should have.' She ran her hands over him.

He turned to her.

'Anyway,' she said, 'it's always better when you've had a bit of a kip. You're not so tired. More energy.'

He smiled. Pulled her to him. Kissed her. She held him. Kissed his neck. Moved her hands down his back.

He was on her. Kissing. She licked his shoulder, gently. Hands cupped over his bum. 'Will,' she said.

Will? Had she said that? Oh God. Maybe Fred hadn't heard.

He had. 'Who?'

'Nobody.'

'Who's Will?'

'Nobody.'

'Doesn't sound like nobody.' He was tumbling out of bed. 'Your lover? Someone you've been seeing?'

She squirmed with horror at her gaffe. 'Will's my daughter's partner. They've both been on my mind. Sorry. And no, I haven't been seeing him. I've only met him a couple of times.'

Fred looked dubious.

'Really,' said Roz. 'Really, really. I'm distracted. I shouldn't have come here to dump on you.'

'I don't mind the dumping.' said Fred. 'It's the Will bit I mind.'

'So you should,' agreed Roz. 'I'd mind too.'

She curled into him. He lay, arm round her, looking up into the dark. He didn't think he'd mention the moving-in thing again. Not now. Not with this Will chap looming.

CHAPTER TWENTY

Friday morning, when Roz got home, Zoe, Will and Jamie were gathered round the table eating breakfast. Toby was on the floor, wrestling with a large jigsaw. He was punching a piece that didn't fit into place with the side of his fist.

'Where the hell have you been?' said Zoe.

'Out,' said Roz.

'All night?' said Zoe.

'All night,' Roz replied. She looked round. Someone had cleared up. She acknowledged the new cleanness with a small sweep of her arm. 'Thank you.'

'What for?' asked Jamie.

'Cleaning the kitchen. I've never seen it so tidy. I'd forgotten it could look like this. It's quite nice.'

It *was* nice. Roz had an eye. The kitchen was painted pale blue-grey, plants along the windowsill, pots hanging from ceiling hooks. On the wall a large pastel print of raspberries and strawberries in an ornate bowl beside a loaf of bread. The sun streamed in. She'd forgotten how pleasant her kitchen was.

'Will did it,' Jamie told her. Lest she thought it was him and expected him to do it again.

'Didn't think it was you,' said Roz. 'Thank you, Will.' She thought she was lavishing her gaze on him. Cursed herself. Stop this. You're being a fool. 'So did you two talk?'

Will give a wild shrug behind Zoe's back. No use talking to Zoe, the gesture said.

'Nothing to talk about,' Zoe said. 'I'm keeping Toby.'

Toby punched his jigsaw into shape. And Roz went off to see how the Beseleys were doing.

193

By four o'clock she'd had enough of the Beseleys. Their small-time arguing. No voices raised. No nasty words. Nothing thrown in rage. She had the sinking feeling that she was turning into a Beseley, desperately trying to keep some sort of harmony. Never saying what she really thought. She remembered soulfully the old days, only weeks ago, when she came home to an empty house. When she lived on whatever she wanted to eat. Even if it was only chocolate. A pear and a stare out of the window for lunch. When she could walk naked to the kitchen each morning if she wished. When she could bathe any time of day. When there was actual hot water all the time. When she could play her old Van Morrison tapes without facing ridicule for her musical taste. When she only had to pay for a takeaway for one. When she was her own person. Oh yes, those were the days. Come back, messiness and loneliness. I miss you. In no time she'd be Mrs Beseley, who raised her hands and had nothing more demanding to say than 'Yes, dear.' And that only to keep the peace. Peace she didn't really want.

Roz clicked on to Save, switched off and went through to the living room. Only Will was there. Zoe had taken Toby to the park and Jamie had gone out to wander the streets and grapple with his inner psyche, the hunt for sudden illumination. And after all that to go to the pub.

'I have to go to the supermarket,' Roz told Will. 'We're out of food again. And everything else, now I think about it. Though I'd rather not.'

He offered to come with her. She could not refuse. A couple of hours alone with Will, she liked that. As long as she remembered not to stare at him too long. Watching his lips. Or his hands.

They trundled their trolley up and down the aisles, choosing family-sized packs of everything. A long-forgotten experience for Roz.

'So where were you last night?' asked Will, taking a hefty pack of Alpen from the shelf. 'With your boyfriend?'

'Fred,' she said. 'Though I don't know if he's my boyfriend. We've never defined our relationship. Also . . .'

'Big row?'

'No. I just said something awful at the wrong time.'

He looked at her. She was shoving tins of tuna into the trolley, deliberately not looking at him. He knew not to ask. He offered to take over the trolley-pushing. In the changeover their hands brushed. Roz felt a tremor in her stomach. Stop it, she told herself.

'I don't know how you do it,' she said.

'What?'

'Put up with my daughter.'

'She's addictive. You never know what's coming next.'

'I know.'

'She wants too much,' Will said. 'She's hungry and she doesn't really know what for. Life,' he sighed. 'Something like that.'

'Right,' said Roz. 'I don't know how to help her.'

'Who does? She's a wastrel. Spends all the time. Some sort of comfort.'

'Can you afford her? If you don't mind my asking.'

'No,' Will said mildly. 'I can't afford her. She's got in serious bother with her credit cards. Not that we haven't been up shit creek many a time.'

'You cope?'

'We've always managed to get through. But not this time. Other times we've scraped the barrel but managed. Paid a little here and a little there, written recalcitrant letters to the bank manager. Zoe's a whizz at the recalcitrant letter. She has ways of coping.'

'Oh tell me. I need to know how she does it. So I can do it too.'

Will looked away. Here was something he couldn't tell her. Zoe's way of dealing with her chronic overspending was to shag. She had some idea that sex sorted everything. At dire times they'd lie in bed discussing their problems. At least Will would discuss them. Zoe would pull the duvet over her head and pretend it wasn't happening. Eventually, when she felt he had been droning on too long, and his voice, the seriousness of it, the edge it had, was stopping her from sleeping, she'd put her hand on him. 'Stop,' she'd say. 'Let's not talk about this. Not now. Not here. Let's shag.'

'No,' Will would say. 'That isn't going to help. Sex doesn't solve everything.'

'Yes it does.' She'd stroke him. 'Really it does.'

He'd give in to her. Always did. They'd make love. Fall asleep after. In the morning Zoe would get up feeling she had her problems under control. She'd faced them, discussed them – after a fashion. Everything was all right. She could go out shopping again. And she did.

Roz caught the look. 'She's spoilt,' she said. 'She always danced for her daddy. He gave her anything she wanted. She could twist him round her little finger.' She stopped, a revelation. Till she said this out loud, right now, she hadn't realised it.

'He must've loved her.'

'Yes. He never showed it. Except for the giving in to her.' Then, another dawning. An unwelcome one. 'It was me he didn't love.' She dropped a jar of mayonnaise into the trolley. 'God.' She turned to him, thunderstruck. 'I'm sorry. I never realised that till now.'

'I'm sure he did,' said Will. 'He just isn't a touchy-feely guy. He's undemonstrative.'

'He didn't love me.' Roz nodded. 'That was it. That was definitely it.' She took a deep breath, adjusting to this new knowledge. 'That was absolutely it.' She pulled herself together. She'd think about this later. Tonight. In bed. In the dark. It would stop her dwelling on her nonsensical hankering for Will. Though it would be nice to talk to Nan about it. Damn Nan for dying. It was the only inconsiderate thing she'd ever done in her life.

'Did you love him?' Will asked. Piercing stare.

She didn't meet it. Paused. 'No.' This was not a revelation. She'd known for years. Long before she left him. 'No, I didn't.' I loved Zoe and Jamie and Nan. And if it hadn't been for Matthew there would be no Zoe or Jamie. And I'd never have met Nan. But I've got a stupid crush on you, Will. I'll get over it. I must get over it. Soon, I hope. 'There you go,' she said to Will. 'I didn't love Matthew. Shameful, isn't it? Still, Zoe,' she said, heading for the biscuits. 'Spoilt rotten, cosseted, our Zoe is. Too protected. She hasn't been there.'

196

'Where?' Will didn't know what she was talking about.

'The depths. She's chicken. Afraid of the depths. You need to smack her about a bit and put her out into the rain.'

A woman dumping three packs of Viennese dark chocolate wafers into her trolley stared at her, horrified. Roz made a face. Crossed her eyes, stuck out her tongue.

Will looked embarrassed. 'Me? Smack Zoe? I don't think so. I've never hit anybody in my life. Especially a woman. I couldn't.'

'I don't mean literally. A metaphorical smacking-about.' Roz threw two packs of digestives into the trolley, envying the Viennese wafer woman. They were her favourites. She denied herself, reached for some crackers. 'I'm not advocating physical violence.' She hesitated over a pack of chocolate chip cookies. They'd only get eaten. Top speed. She'd never get one. 'I mean she needs toughening up. She's never gulped. You know, a life gulp. That horrified throaty swallow you do when you know you're for it.'

'What?'

'It.' She opted for the cookies after all. She'd have a couple with coffee soon as she got back. 'The dread *it*. The *it* you know is coming to you when you realise at last that you are on your own. You know the huge gulp Coyote does when Roadrunner tricks him into hurtling off the top of a cliff. He stands a moment looking into the abyss, legs pumping like pistons. The knowing swallow he does when he knows that's where he's going. To the bottom. And the only things down there are boulders. That *it*. That gulp. She's never been there, never gulped.'

'That's right.' Will's eyes widened. 'That's it.' He stood clutching a sixteen-pack of KitKats. It was his turn to have a sudden revelation. 'She's the one that *causes* the gulp.'

'Exactly,' said Roz. She headed for the checkout before she spent any more money.

'So,' Will came after her before *he* spent any more money, 'you don't think I should remortgage to pay off her debts.'

'No.' Roz turned to him. 'Never. Or at least you must never let her know you'll remortgage. Let her fret. You must make her gulp.'

'I've already arranged to pay them off at so much a month. But I was thinking to remortgage. Get it over with. Pay back the building society.'

'Don't ever tell her.' She gripped his arm. A tremor. She wished she hadn't done that. 'Let her think she has to pay her debts. Get a job. See her hard-earned money going back to the people she owes. Years of slog ahead. The gulp.' Roz gave a gulp. A demonstration life-gulp. Clutching her throat.

They reached the checkout girl. Watched their shopping, their lifestyle, flash before them. Anxiously waited for the total. 'Ninety-eight pounds ninety-five,' said the girl.

Roz blanched. Will took out his wallet and handed over his Visa card. 'We must be costing you a fortune. All the eating that's going on. It's frightening.'

They gathered their collection of bags and made for the car park.

'If I refuse to bail her out, Zoe will pout and sigh,' said Will. 'I can't stand that. I'd do anything to stop it.'

'You mustn't. Think about her. Her future. Right now Zoe could pout for Britain. But believe me, pouting when you're gone fifty is unseemly. And fifty is coming. For me sooner than anybody.' She stroked her neck, checking for wrinkles. Nothing so far. There was hope.

'You're not that old, surely,' said Will. 'You look great.'

Roz glowed. There really was hope.

'I think about Zoe all the time,' said Will. 'I've come to the conclusion I don't understand her.' He looked around at the other females packing their cars, shepherding children, dumping empty trolleys in the bay, walking to and fro, bored expressions, made-up faces. 'Actually, I don't understand women.'

'Don't worry about it,' said Roz. 'Let's face it, men will never understand women. It's impossible for them. They're baffled. They'll never master it. Unless . . .' She paused. Watched a man in beige sitting alone in his car, the *Sun* propped against his steering wheel, cigarette wedged between his lips. 'Unless that's why those men sit outside supermarkets in their cars waiting for their wives to shop. They wear putty-coloured clothes and read vacuous tabloids. It's all they can do now. They understand women, and the weight of it has bent them double. The Great Chakra has been revealed to them and blown their minds. All they are good for is waiting for the mighty ones to come with the cornflakes and instant coffee and chocolate chip cookies.'

Will smiled. He watched Roz open the boot and start dumping her carrier bags. He liked her. She was lovely. Made him laugh. Pity Zoe had felt too embittered about her to keep in touch. She had missed a lot.

There was nobody home when they arrived back at the flat. Roz put the shopping away and made them both a sandwich, nibbling a promised chocolate chip cookie as she did so. They sat side by side on the sofa, eating. The television wasn't on. Roz put her feet up on the coffee table. 'Peace. I'd forgotten what it was like.'

'Wonderful,' Will agreed.

A little silence. Then, 'What are you going to do?' asked Roz.

Will shrugged. 'Go home, I suppose. I have to get back to work.'

'What about Toby? He has to go to school.'

'I know. I know. I want to take him. But Zoe . . . well, Zoe in full flight is awesome.'

'Can't you leave him here?'

'I don't want to.'

'You can't persuade Zoe to go with you? Maybe live somewhere in Edinburgh? You could make some sort of arrangement. Like normal couples.'

'I don't want to leave him with Zoe.' Will was adamant.

'Why? She dotes on him.'

'She dotes on him. Spoils him. Shoves him into doing things he doesn't want. She won't just let him be a boy.'

Roz said nothing.

'And she . . .' Will looked pained. 'She's insecure. She sleeps around. Well, not quite that.'

'What?' Roz wanted to know.

'She . . . she . . .' He gave up skirting round the subject. 'She's got herself a bit of a reputation . . . you know . . .'

'She said she had affairs,' said Roz. 'The reputation I didn't know about. She didn't mention it. Well, she wouldn't. I'm her mother.'

'She wants men to like her.'

'That's no way to go about getting people to like her.'

'I know. Try telling her that. She says she's doing it for me. To help me.' He took a deep breath. Should he say this? He went for it. 'She's looking for the right cock to suck. For me. For Toby.'

'God's sake. I wish you hadn't told me that. Ignorance is bliss when it comes to Zoe.'

'I didn't mean to worry you.'

'I always worried. Now I'll fret.' Roz looked at him. 'Zoe's a mess. Jamie's not much better. And, secretly, Matthew's a mess too. It's all my fault.'

'No. No.' Will shook his head.

'It is. Thanks for saying it isn't. That's very kind of you. But it is.'

'No, I mean it.'

'It *is* my fault. I walked out on them. I should've stayed. They'd be OK if I had.'

'You think?' said Will. 'If you don't mind my saying so, from the way Zoe speaks about her family life, I think they were all a mess before you left. Matthew counting and being silent. Zoe taking tantrums – which, incidentally, she still does. Jamie disappearing into his room to do computery things.'

'You think?' She wrestled with this. 'I was a terrible mother even before I went.'

'I didn't say that. After you left, Matthew still whistled and counted. Zoe took tantrums. Jamie did computery things. I don't think things changed.'

'Oh God. They didn't even miss me.' Roz started to cry.

Will leaned towards her, touched her shoulder. 'No. No. They didn't address it. Didn't talk about it. Of course they missed you. Who wouldn't?'

'That's nice of you to say.' Tears flooded down Roz's cheeks. 'I'd miss you, too. I don't know why Zoe treats you the way she does. I'm sorry.'

'It's not your fault.'

'It is. Everything's my fault.'

He was sitting sideways on the sofa next to her. Hand on her. He was like that, touched people when he spoke to them. 'Stop beating yourself up.'

She wiped her nose on her sleeve. 'Won't. Been beating myself up for years. It's my hobby.'

He hugged her. She put her head on his chest. Breathed the scent on his sweatshirt. Lemon fabric conditioner, and that smell that was his smell. A lungful of Will. She clung on tight. Then pulled away, sniffing. Breathing.

'Well, pack it in,' he said. 'No more beating yourself up. And stop crying.' He punched her shoulder. A blokey thing. 'Us chaps don't cry.'

'I'm not a chap,' she said. 'And I'm not crying.'

He looked intently at her face. Puffy eyes. Red-rimmed.

'I'm just letting go a little,' she told him.

'Right. Zoe does that. Except she doesn't let go a little. She lets go a lot.'

She smiled. 'Thanks for that.'

'What?'

'Bit of comfort.' She kissed his cheek. 'I'm better now.'

They heard the front door open. Zoe and Toby came in. Toby ran down the hall ahead of her. Burst into the room. The child could tell an atmosphere when he encountered one. He was good at it. He stopped smiling. Looked from Roz to Will, stuck his thumb into his mouth.

'I wish you wouldn't do that,' said Will.

Toby didn't reply. He was too busy sucking.

Zoe came in, dumped her coat and handbag. Flopped down beside Will. 'I'm knackered.' She noticed the sandwiches. Picked one up. Accused Roz. 'You make your tuna sarnies for Will and Toby, but never for me.'

'I'll make you one now.' Roz couldn't wait to get out of the room.

'What's going on?' Zoe finally became aware of the frisson.

'Nothing,' said Will.

'You haven't been arguing with my mother, have you?'

'Far from it,' sighed Will. 'Nothing's going on.' He followed Roz into the kitchen.

Roz mashed tuna and mayonnaise, dripped a drop of tomato ketchup into the mixture. Didn't look at him. He leaned against the wall watching her. When at last she did meet his eye, her gaze was fraught with guilt and longing. 'Sorry,' she said, voice low.

'For what?'

'Dumping on you. Crying like that. Letting go.'

'Don't apologise.' Stepping closer to her. 'Next time it's my turn to dump on you.'

She looked at him. He touched her arm. She'd look forward to that.

CHAPTER TWENTY-ONE

Connie's life was on the up. She had taken over the editor's desk.
She was busy. For the first time in years, there were letters from
readers about the Beseleys. A surprise for everyone. Nobody
thought anyone read them. In fact, despite the regular sales figures,
nobody really thought anybody read the magazine. There was a
feeling in the office that it had been going for such a long time that
people got it delivered and threw it to one side, meaning to cancel
their order, but never got round to it. The new shift in the life of
the Beseleys, and the response to it, had brought hope to the staff.
Roz had a new credibility. There was a growing buzz about her,
though she didn't know it. Connie thought it best not to tell her
lest she went to work for someone else.

Recent telephone calls to Roz at home fascinated Connie. First
there had been a male voice. Her son. He sounded interesting.
Quietly jokey. Then there had been a woman, a soft, husky voice.
Her daughter. Yesterday there had been another man. A gentle
voice. Who was he? There had been sounds of a child in the
background. Connie had always found Roz intriguing. A woman
who had left her children and come to London. Made her way.
Bought a flat.

Roz was famously messy. She had friends who didn't like to
visit, preferred to meet for coffee or a drink in a bar. It was that
bad. Connie had heard rumours. A cupboard full of biscuit packets,
each with one biscuit, softened with age, left in. A fridge over-
flowing with mushy things. Cups everywhere, all with a murky
ring of hardened coffee at the bottom. Sink stuffed with dishes.
Clothes left lying. A heap of dirty laundry by the washing machine,
another multicoloured tangle spilling from the tumble-drier.

...away wrappers jammed into the carrier bag hanging on the kitchen door that she used as a rubbish bin. Someone reported finding knickers in her fridge. Someone else said there had been a beetroot left on the draining board so long it had turned into something resembling a pickled walnut. The mould in her bread bin had gone beyond interesting. It had turned from green to a strange powdery colour that steamed up when touched. If anyone could bring themselves to touch it. Connie longed to visit and check the flat out. She was obsessively tidy. But recently, with her rise in importance, she was beginning to find messiness alluring. Not that she could take it up personally. She couldn't relax if there was even the tiniest thing out of place. Had been known to get up from bed on a chill winter's night to sort the towels in the bathroom and to place her shoes neatly side by side when one was lying askew. But people who had no urge to clean up fascinated her. She thought they must be artistic. Depression, guilt, self-loathing were not part of her emotional repertoire.

Since there was no chance of Roz ever inviting her home, Connie decided to drop by one evening. She'd find an excuse, she was sure.

Meantime, the Beseleys were coming along nicely.

Frank thundered into the kitchen. 'Where's the TV remote? Have you hidden it?'

'No,' said Pam. 'Of course not.'

Frank thundered out again. 'Who's hidden the TV remote?'

Pam patted her pocket. The remote was in there. It was war. She wasn't going to sit watching Frank surf the channels evening after evening.

Frank thundered back in again. 'And another thing. I don't like you buying yourself a bike and going breezing off every morning.'

'Well, I like it. It keeps me trim.'

'Then there's your job thing. Why can't you find yourself a nice little part-time job? Like Mary next door in the chemist's.'

'Because I want a full-time job. Full-time pay. Independence.'

'Huh. Independence. I work full time. Do I have independence?'

'Yes,' said Pam. She threw the tea towel at him. 'Here, you finish the dishes. I'm off to watch *EastEnders*.' She didn't thunder out. She skipped. Ha, ha, she had the remote.

Roz was neither skipping nor thundering. She and the other occupants of her flat had moved easily into a kind of emotional choreography. She resisted the temptation to be alone with Will. Zoe made sure *she* was never alone with him either. He would only pressurise her to make a decision about Toby. She knew what that would have to be. Toby would have to return to Edinburgh with Will. He had to go back to school. She also avoided Roz, for the same reason – a decision. Jamie went to the pub. He was making some headway with the barmaid in the Nietzsche T-shirt.

Toby was doing a deal of thumb-sucking and genital-twiddling. He sensed the confusion between Zoe and Will, and clung to Roz. He'd sit under her work table with a pile of little cars, zooming them up and down the lines in her Indian rug, making car noises, screechings of brakes, roaring of engines, whinings of speedy reversing. Every now and then Roz would loom down, looking at him. 'You all right down there?'

'Yes.' Little voice. 'When will you come and play with me?'

'Soon.'

Sometimes he'd climb on her knee and type the words she was writing. Letter by painful letter as she pointed them out to him. Whispering them in his ear. 'B, now E. There it is. T. Two of them. And another E. Now an R. *Better*. That's the way.' Innocent cheek against hers. Worried face frowning in concentration. He found comfort in the closeness of her body. She loved the feel of him against her. She'd watch his lips move as he searched the keyboard. She'd touch his hair. He was hers, she thought. Her kin. A fresh generation. She wondered if it would go on. Her genes. Wave after wave of muddled people.

Friday night and sleepless. They'd eaten late – a takeaway ordered after eleven. Roz, plagued by indigestion, slipped into the kitchen to make tea. The pigeons on the ledge outside her window were cooing up a storm. Moved to distraction, Roz thought, by the full moon. Full moons did that to pigeons, and people.

The house was quiet. Full of people snoring, breathing, gathering strength for tomorrow's round of moving carefully round each other. Talking and never saying any of the things that needed saying.

She put the kettle on. Found a tea bag and a cleanish cup. Stood listening to a dog in the yard below baying. And the people below fighting. The moon did that to them, too.

Will came in, wakened by her absurd stealthiness as she tiptoed past him. He'd been scrunged on the edge of the folded down sofa, as far from Jamie as he could manage. Jamie was a graceless sleeper. He pulled the duvet over his head. Dreamed and moaned. Cried out to unknown adversaries. Twitched. And struggled with midnight demons.

'Can't sleep?' he asked.

'No.' Not wanting to admit to suffering the pain of pizza eaten after eleven. 'It's the moon. It's unsettling.'

'I know.'

He wore only boxers and a T-shirt. She thought he looked . . . vulnerable. Still sleepy. She tried not to gaze at him. At his shoulders. His eyelashes. Such long lashes. What are you thinking? she chastised herself. Teenage rubbish. She let her gaze slip to his crotch. Stop it, she told herself. Kept on gazing. Longing.

'What are you staring at?'

Shamed. 'Nothing,' she said. 'I was thinking. Was I staring? Sorry.'

'What were you thinking?'

'Oh, nothing. Besides, it's your turn to dump on me.'

'I could tell you about my guardian angel.'

'You have a guardian angel?'

'Oh yes. Marianne. I don't think she knows she's my guardian angel, though.'

Roz smiled. 'What did she do to merit the position?'

'Basically she told me to stop beating myself up. She asked which I would rather – to have written an exquisite piece of music, or to be making love one perfect balmy night, beside a lake, with nightjars singing in trees nearby.'

'What did you choose?'

'The love. The lake. The nightjars.'

'That's for me, too. I like your guardian angel. I hope I meet her. She sounds beautiful.'

'It's on the inside only, I'm afraid. Externally she looks a bit lived-in. Drink, cigarettes.'

'If Zoe carries on like she is at the moment, she'll end up like that. I fear she's heading for a tumble.'

'She's tumbling. She just hasn't fully realised it.'

Roz made tea. Handed him a cup. 'I can't help, can I?'

'Nope. She has to make the gulp on her own. Like you said.'

She smiled. Excused herself. 'I think I'll take this tea back to bed.'

'Um,' he said. 'Can I ask you something?'

Her heart jumped. What? Can I kiss you? Do you love me?

'Would you mind,' he said, 'if I cleaned out your kitchen cupboards? And the fridge? Only you seem too busy, and I thought I might do it.' He didn't say that the lack of hygiene was worrying.

'Go ahead,' she said. 'That would be fine.' She felt like she was doing him a favour. Then she supposed that he'd worked it that way.

She sat propped against the pillows, listening to the pigeons giving each other hell. She thought about Will. Wished she could touch him. His face. Wished she would stop going gooey when love songs were played on the radio. 'The First Time Ever I Saw Your Face'. She'd find herself staring into the middle distance. Smiling.

'What's up with you?' Jamie had asked.

'I like that song.'

'It's mushy.'

'I like mushy.'

'Yumph,' he'd said. Or some such disapproving sound. 'Wimmen.'

She cursed herself. She was stupid. Old and stupid. Too old, she thought, to be eating pizza at midnight. Too old for this stupid job I do. Too old to find myself thinking about this man all the time. Too old for all this sighing and swooning and longing. Too old, too old, too old.

Will left his tea. He lay in bed keeping as far from Jamie as he could. Drifted into a deep and disturbing sleep. He dreamed he was in a shell of a ruined house, walking round a giant, gleaming grand piano. When he lifted the lid, there were no keys. Only sea. Blue and unfathomably deep. He tried to plunge in. But the sea was set like jelly. With, he noticed, crumblings of some sort of reddish chocolate on top. When he plunged, he rebounded off on to grubby rock.

He woke, sweating and mumbling. Lay till dawn working out meanings for his dream. Afraid to sleep again lest he dreamed some more.

The next evening, Connie turned up. She could contain her curiosity no longer. Roz had been Beseleying most of the afternoon. Will had scrubbed the cupboards and defrosted the fridge. It was humming in the corner, sounding, Roz thought, domestic and somehow sane for the first time in years. After cleaning out the fridge, Will had vacuumed, dusted and tidied.

Zoe and Toby had spent the afternoon at the park. Jamie had been in the pub, squandering money borrowed from Roz, drinking beer and seeking illumination. Every time Roz left her desk to come to the kitchen for tea, she watched Will. He'd stand beside her, giving her a rundown on the junk he'd found in her cupboards and the softened fruit and veg he'd removed from her fridge. 'It was a baby turnip, I think. Hard to tell. There were almost forty empty biscuit packets. Don't you ever eat the last one?'

'No. Seems greedy. Or rude. To finish them all by myself. I feel virtuous if I leave one.'

She thought he was standing too close to her. Touching her more often than usual. And he touched a lot.

'You're a slut,' he said. Arm round her shoulder. 'What are you?'

'A slut. A disgrace.' She rested her head on him. 'Sorry.'

'Don't apologise. It's . . .' He searched for what it was. Something tactful. 'Refreshing. You're so engrossed in your work you forget about everything round you.'

'Well put,' not removing her head from his chest. 'You should go into politics. Such diplomacy.' She did not want to leave this place. So close to him. But she took her tea and returned to the Beseleys, who were squabbling nicely.

Connie arrived after eight. She looked round eagerly. The mess she'd hoped for was not here. The artistic filth she sought had been cleaned up.

'I brought you some more letters to answer. If you don't mind,' said Connie. 'Only we feel you can do it so much more imaginatively than us. You can get into the Mrs Beseley role. It is going well, isn't it?'

Roz nodded. Slim excuse, you just want to see the famous dirt, she thought. Well ha, ha, it's gone. She offered Connie a glass of wine.

'Lovely,' said Connie. She followed Roz into the kitchen. She had to see this. But oh, disappointment, it was sparkling. Connie watched as Roz took her corkscrew from the drawer. She loomed over, hoping for a glimpse of some mess. The drawer was horribly tidy. Roz opened the fridge, took out a bottle of Chilean white. The fridge was bright and full of healthy, eatable things. Connie was bitterly disappointed.

She followed Roz back to the living room and sat dutifully on the chair she was offered. The best chair. The one that didn't complain and wheeze when sat upon. She smiled graciously when introduced to everybody. And tried to hide how awestruck she was by Zoe. Exquisitely beautiful and poised. Perfect lips, polished nails. Black jeans, white Superga shoes and fabulously expensive grey cashmere tunic. God, Connie thought, if I looked like that.

Zoe smiled slightly, lit a Marlboro Light and stared at the window. Indifference, her favourite defence. As Connie spoke to Roz about work, Zoe stole sneaky looks across at her. She was, Zoe decided, a woman in transition. She was moving from what she was to what she thought she ought to be. Zoe was expert at sussing people's attitude to themselves. She could gaze round a room and spot the egotists, the self-deprecating, the downright humble, and the shivering emotional cowards. And always knew who to home in on. She judged haircuts and clothes. The way people stood, held their drinks, laughed or didn't laugh. The way they looked at other people in the room, or idly turned to consider the wall, the floor or the ceiling.

This Connie person, Zoe noted, was wearing new shoes. Higher heels than she was used to. She teetered on them. Her top was new, showing more cleavage than she was comfortable with. The skirt was shorter than her normal skirts; she tugged at it. Worried about her fat knees, Zoe thought. Though her knees weren't as fat as she thought they were. The hair needed fixing. And nobody had taught her to do make-up.

That was the big giveaway. You learnt about make-up in nightclub loos with your mates. In their bedrooms, smoking secretly, exhaling out the window. Drinking Grant's vodka and Coke, lots of it, cheap but lethal. Fabulously effective when you were sixteen and hungry for life. This woman Zoe was sizing up had been drunk, but never out-of-her-brains plastered. She's got her wildness to come, Zoe decided. It was one of Zoe's many theories, that everybody had to go daft at some time in their lives. Best to make it when you were sixteen and excusable. Leave it till past thirty and you'd make an arse of yourself.

She got bored listening to Connie talk about work and this person called Ronnie who seemed to have had a bit of a breakdown, locking himself in the cupboard. There you go, thought Zoe. He should have gone off his head when he was a lad. Running, bawling, through the streets, getting in punch-ups in bars, getting thrown out of clubs, taking illegal substances. Then he'd be fine. She kept this thought to herself.

She drifted off, reminiscing to herself about her own wild times. Her and her mates running four abreast down West Bow, screaming. The party in someone's house where they'd got so wild they'd smashed all the gilt-framed mirrors in the hall, broken the stair banisters, and the wall between the kitchen and the living room had caved in. Sleeping with three blokes in a bed in some flat off the West End. Tequila challenges. She'd been champ. A record sixteen before she passed out. Her mates would carry her home, dump her on the doorstep, ring the bell and run away before Matthew answered. (Some mates, she snorted inwardly.) He'd bring her into the living room, and before his lecture could begin, Zoe would smile, look expertly innocent. 'I only had two sherries. I didn't know it'd make me drunk. Honest.'

Matthew would send her to bed. When he was sleeping, she'd climb out the window and start her wildness all over again. It was the night did it to her, she thought. Something about the dark that made you want to drink and drink and escape from the dreadful business of being you.

She nodded. That was it. Lit another Marlboro. Revisited her fractured youth. It came to her in a series of moments. Wild things. And other things in between. Lying things. Sitting at the kitchen table with Matthew and Jamie, eating the instant food Matthew threw together. Stilted conversation. 'You were late last night, Zoe.'

'I missed the bus.' A lie. She'd been snogging somebody and had let the bus go. A good kiss was too sweet to lose to a tenpenny ride taking her home in time. Not when there were good lies for the telling.

'Any homework?'

'No.' Lie. Lie. Why stay in with Chaucer when you could be out snogging Richard Riley in between cheap ciggies, Lambert and Butler (Lammy Bammies, Zoe wrinkled her nose, how gross), and swigs of cider?

Matthew again, slowly chewing a slice of Milanda and marge. 'Where did you get to last night, Jamie?'

'Study night with Dominic.' Lie. Lie. He'd been joyriding in Dominic's dad's car. Sunroof open, despite the sub-zero temperature. Hanging out the open windows, thumping the car door, howling at girls on the pavement. NWA, 'Straight Outta Compton', thumping on the stereo.

Jamie, slapping the bottom of the ketchup bottle. 'You were out last night, Dad.'

'A quiet drink at the golf club.' Lie. Lie. He'd been seeing the new lady in his life, Claire. They were discussing how to tell Zoe and Jamie about their marriage next summer.

Tea time with Zoe, Jamie and Matthew. Linda McCartney burgers, oven chips, peas and lies, lies, lies.

There were gigs Zoe went to where they'd thrown food – jam doughnuts, was it? she couldn't remember – at the band. And spat at them. Bit naff, she scolded herself. Then there was a club somewhere off Tollcross where a bunch of people – all in black – had tried to form a human pyramid. They'd fallen on top of the crowd and someone had broken his arm. Crazy. Drink. God, the drink. The Burns Night somewhere in Leith where there had been so much whisky they'd all got paralytic. She'd shagged some man she'd been eying, under the table, whilst someone at the top table was belting out 'Tam o'Shanter'. Resurfaced to see people reeling and groping, swigging from the bottle and talking rubbish. Sank below for another shag. Not very nice.

Connie started talking office politics. She was hoping Ronnie would get some sort of sideways promotion. She didn't want to give up her new position. She'd applied for a few other jobs. Couldn't work under him again, oh no. Shook her head.

For two crazed years Zoe had run wild. Weekend after weekend. Some of them lost. She didn't know what she'd got up to. Then she'd met Will.

'I have ambitions,' Connie was saying. 'I'm not going to get a chance to fulfil them there.'

Zoe finished her wine. Will had saved her. Will had nursed her through a million hangovers, picked her up from dubious clubs and bars all times of the night, whenever she phoned. Will had never scolded her, never disapproved. He'd waited. Waited till the wildness abated. Then he'd been there for her and Toby. Toby wasn't his. She didn't know if he knew that. They'd never talked about it. She knew he suspected it.

After Toby, she'd calmed down. Stayed in nights. Only small

bouts of wildness. At parties, trying to shock people when she got bored. Or when she thought they were being pompous. Nothing too outrageous. Except she'd lost her best friend, Lisa.

Lisa was ambitious, like Connie. She'd gone off on some outdoor team-bonding thing, romping across the Highlands with people she was to form working relationships with. Got sick. Came home early. Into her flat. Found Zoe on the sofa with her husband, Geoff. They'd both been stark naked, too busy bonking to hear Lisa come in.

'Well,' said Lisa, 'I'm fucking out of the house for a day . . . and . . . look at you . . .'

'I can explain,' said Zoe.

'I'll just bet you can come up with the most amazing explanation,' said Lisa. 'I don't want to hear it. Ever. Get out.'

They'd never spoken again. Zoe lit up another Marlboro. Memories were painful. She shrugged. Will looked at her. He knew she was off in her own world.

Zoe wondered what she'd do if she found someone with Will. Be angry? She searched inside herself. Jealous? Yes, she'd be jealous. She imagined the scene. She arrived home late one night to find Will naked and feverishly shagging this Connie person. She looked at Connie.

'You can only stay in one place for so long,' Connie was saying. Jamie was sitting, leg draped over the end of the sofa, feigning interest. Will was nodding. Roz was on the floor, sipping wine and agreeing with everything Connie said.

Zoe sucked on her Marlboro, thought of Connie and Will sweating and heaving on this squeaky sofa of Roz's. 'Uuuuh. Uuh. Uuuuh.' Grunting and groaning. Connie's nails, which Zoe noticed could do with a bit of varnish, digging into Will's bum. They'd look round, see her, Zoe, standing in the doorway, watching. What would she do? She snorted. Flushed. Splurted. Coughed. Got up, excused herself. Into her bedroom to stuff her mouth with the sheet, stifling illicit giggles. The more she tried to compose herself, the worse she got. Tears in her eyes. Helpless. She held her arms across her stomach. Aching with laughter. Deep breath. She went into the loo. Flushed. Slapped some foundation on her face and returned to the living room.

'Sorry. The wine went down the wrong way.'

'Any chance of some food?' asked Jamie.

'My goodness,' said Connie. 'I'm keeping you back. I didn't realise the time.'

'Stay,' said Roz. 'Have some food with us.'

Connie beamed. 'Is that all right? I'd love to.'

'No problem,' said Roz. She headed for the kitchen.

Will followed. 'I'll give you a hand.'

Zoe looked at Connie. Here was a woman with some untapped wildness in her. Zoe considered herself just the person to set it free. She moved over to sit next to her. 'So, Connie . . .' she said.

In the kitchen, Roz put on a big pot of water for pasta. Fished a packet of herb salad from the shiny fridge. Will stood next to her, chopping tomatoes and red onions. Their hands touched. They both moved away. Swiftly. 'Sorry.' They looked at one another. Gazes lingered. Stop it, Roz told herself. This is wrong.

CHAPTER TWENTY-TWO

Sunday lunchtime, Jamie took Toby to the British Museum, then on for a burger.

Toby pondered the restaurant, savouring his thumb whilst waiting for his chocolate shake. Jamie decided it was time they talked man to man. He thought it his duty as an uncle.

'Want to know something, Tobes?'

Toby nodded. Jamie always told him interesting things. Pagers for dogs. See-thru toasters.

'There's this girl down the pub. And, well, you know . . .'

Toby nodded. He didn't know. But knew this was not the moment to mention it. His shake arrived. Thick. It required a deal of sucking. Cheeks hollowed with effort, he waited for more from Jamie.

'She's gorgeous. And I think this is it. The One. I've only just met her, but, you know, you can tell.'

Toby nodded again.

'Thing is,' Jamie sipped his coffee, 'she's really bossy.'

Toby removed his straw from his mouth. 'Maybe you need a bossy woman. Maybe you need bossing around. Like me.'

This was a new thought to Jamie. 'You think?' he asked.

Toby nodded. Straw back in mouth.

'This could be big,' said Jamie.

'The Big Idea is a woman?' asked Toby.

'Christ, Tobes. You're right. Are you going to get married when you're big?'

Toby nodded. 'I don't mind if my wife's bossy. Just as long as she doesn't cook lentils.'

Jamie gave him the thumbs-up. 'My man.'

It was after four when they emerged into Leicester Square. Dark. A siren sounding somewhere, streets away. They cut through Soho to Oxford Street to look at the lights. Toby held on to Jamie's hand. All these people. All this twinkling around him. It called for a deal of thumb-sucking. When Jamie spoke to him, he answered using the side of his mouth, keeping the sodden, slightly wrinkled digit in place. They sat on a bench, sharing a packet of M&Ms, watching cars and people. Jamie thought now was uncle time.

'Tobes, I have to speak to you man to man,' he said. 'You've got to start behaving like a bloke. It's painful. But there you go.'

Toby stared at him.

'This fiddling with yourself in public has to stop.'

'But I like it.'

'I know. Who doesn't? But not in public.'

'When then?'

'When you're alone. In the middle of the night. It's OK then, don't let anyone tell you otherwise.'

Toby continued to stare.

'Then there's the thumb-sucking. Blokes don't do that. We hitch up our trousers, walk round our cars and make deals.'

'But I haven't got a car. Neither have you.'

'No. But that's the theory of it. That's the language of it. I don't have a car, but I have trousers to hitch.' Jamie wasn't backing down on the trouser-hitching and deal-making. 'OK, this bench is the car. We have a deal to make. We walk round it. We adjust the trousers. We talk.' Jamie rose. 'We kick the car tyres.' He slowly walked round the bench. Dunting it now and then with the side of his foot. A manly strut, he congratulated himself. Halfway round his circumnavigation, he paused. Looked Toby in the eye and, without losing contact, gave his trousers a swift hitch upwards. 'We look each other in the eye. We are not prepared to back down.'

Toby watched. 'Will this work on my mother? What if I'm not talking about cars? What if I'm talking about supper? If I do this, will I get proper food?'

'Guaranteed,' Jamie assured him. Though he wasn't sure. With Zoe, you never knew. Zoe had wiles and had no pity when using them. 'In the case of refusing lentils, you strut the kitchen. Don't forget the trouser-hitch. And you say, "This lentil business has to stop. It's OK for you to eat them. I've no problem with that. But they're not for me."'

'Will that work?'

'Christ, Toby. With Zoe? Who knows with Zoe? But it's a lot less tiring than lying on the floor drumming your heels.'

Toby pulled his thumb from his mouth. Slow steam rose from it in the chill air.

'You're not a baby any more,' said Jamie. 'And you've got to stop doing baby things.'

Toby looked glumly at his thumb. He seemed to be bidding it goodbye. He looked Jamie in the eye. Said nothing.

They took the tube home. It was after six when they arrived. Zoe was in the kitchen, preparing supper. She wanted to eat early. Last night, as Connie left, Zoe had asked if she'd like to go for a drink. They were meeting at eight. She had made a salad of lentils with olives and some steamed vegetables to go with the smoked mackerel she'd bought yesterday. Toby crossed the room to look at it. He did not like what he saw.

'Lovely supper coming up, Toby,' Zoe assured him cheerily.

Toby turned to Jamie, who gave him a swift trouser-hitch.

Roz came into the room. There was something going on. She could feel it in the air. A certain frisson between Toby and Jamie that seemed, for the moment, to have escaped Zoe.

Toby hooked his thumbs into his jeans. Yanked at them. Frowned. 'This lentil business,' he said, squeakily. He breathed, little anxious pants. 'It's not for me.'

Zoe turned. 'What?'

Toby couldn't look at her. 'It's not for me. Lentils. I don't like them. They're horrible.'

'No they're not. They're good for you.'

Toby was weakening. The thumb came out. Jamie punched his shoulder.

'Other things are good for me. Apples. Bananas. I eat them. But I hate lentils.'

Zoe said nothing.

Toby remembered Jamie's speech. 'If you want them, I've no problem with that. But they're not for me.'

Zoe looked astounded. 'I don't like the sound of this.'

'Well, there you go,' said Toby. 'That's the deal.'

'Does the deal include salad?' asked Zoe.

Toby wanted to say no, no salad. But instinct told him not to. 'Lettuce,' he told her.

'You want that with your mackerel?'

'Lettuce. No mackerel.'

'What then?' Zoe asked.

'Fish fingers. With chips.'

Zoe snorted, but didn't feel like making an issue of this. She wanted to go out and couldn't face a fight. 'Fine,' she said, stiff-lipped.

'And another thing,' said Toby, too young to realise that one victory at a time was the diplomatic way to go. 'I want to go home.'

'With Will?' said Zoe.

'Yes,' nodded Toby. 'I want to go back to school. I don't want to miss the trip to the panto.'

'Right,' said Zoe, defeated. 'Home with Will it is.' She turned back to her lentil and olive salad. Swallowing, gulping. Will had won. Roz watched her.

Toby walked from the room, eyes brimming. The strain of polite defiance took the thrill from his triumph. Jamie came after him. Did a little boxer's glory knee-dip. Fists clenched. Toby turned on him. Wiped his eyes on the back of his hand. But he could not stop the grin that spread across his pale little face. He made to punch Jamie, who reeled in mock defeat. Toby hurled himself on him, fists flailing. Jamie fell on the ground, wrestled him. 'There you go.'

Roz came through. She watched Jamie with Toby. Sparring with him, a fake boxing match. Faking agony whenever a flimsy blow struck him. Her son, the uncle. She remembered she'd had uncles like that. Maybe men were happier being uncles than they were being fathers. Were uncles across the globe like this? Affable, easy, friendly. Universal uncles.

Zoe gulped. And gulped. And gave up. She abandoned her lentil and olive salad and rushed from the kitchen. She burst into her bedroom, threw herself on the bed and wept.

Roz left her to it. Twenty minutes she gave her. Then she went to her.

'Are you all right?' Roz asked.

Zoe was sitting on the bed in the dark, wiping her nose with a tissue. 'No,' she said. 'I'm not. Toby doesn't want me.'

'Don't be silly,' said Roz. She fetched a fresh tissue, dabbed Zoe's eyes. 'He does want you. Very much. But he wants to be in his own house. He wants to see his friends. He's little. He likes his little routine. He wants to go home. But home would be better if you were there too.'

Zoe sniffed. 'He doesn't love me. Nobody loves me.'

'He loves you,' said Roz. 'We all love you. Why else would we put up with you?' She wiped Zoe's nose. 'And your smoked mackerel.'

Despite herself, Zoe smiled.

'Oh, Zoe . . .' said Roz.

'Oh, Zoe . . . what?'

'Just oh, Zoe,' said Roz. She held her. Stroked her hair. 'Everything will be fine. You'll see.'

Zoe clung to her. When at last she pulled away, she said, 'I have to get ready. I'm meeting Connie for a drink.'

'Well get ready,' said Roz. 'Wash your face. Make yourself look ravishing and go out. It'll do you good. Have a wonderful time.'

'I will,' said Zoe, giving her nose a blasting blow into her crumpled tissue. As Roz crossed the room to leave, Zoe muttered, 'Thanks.'

Roz stepped into the hall. Looked up. There you go, Nan. How about that?

CHAPTER TWENTY-THREE

Sunday night, half past eight. Matthew fretted. He stood by the phone. Stroking his chin. Dipping his hands in and out of his pockets. 'I don't want to phone.'

'You just said you did,' said Claire. She had no time for him in this mood.

'I know. But now it comes to it, I don't know. I don't like to.'

'You want to know what's going on. There's only one way. Phone.'

He hovered. 'What if Roz answers?'

'Speak to her.'

'I don't want to speak to her.'

'I know that. You never want to speak to anybody.'

'I do. I talk to you.' He looked huffy.

'You speak. How are you? What sort of day did you have? That's not talking. I have the feeling that if you had talked, none of this would have happened.'

'Rubbish. I speak. I spoke to Roz. It was her left. Just left. No warning. One day she was there. Next day gone. That was it. Don't talk to me about talking. She's the one didn't talk.'

Claire had heard this a million times. She couldn't quite recall when she'd stopped believing it. But it had been years ago. 'Just phone,' she said. And left him to it.

She went into the living room and plumped the cushions. Sometimes Matthew was the most irritating man alive. Talk? He didn't know the meaning.

Then there was golf. He'd taken it up not long before he met her. It had been a mild little hobby then. But now it had become an obsession. He disappeared most evenings during the summer,

221

afternoons at the weekends. The bad weather didn't stop him when the year rolled round past autumn. Howling gales, rain, snow, he still went. He played against himself. When he came home, often soaked, freezing, Claire would ask if he'd enjoyed himself. 'How did it go?'

'Good.'

'Who won?' A joke.

'Me.' Matthew didn't understand jokes.

'By much?' Still joking.

'No. I was two strokes over par, the winning me. The other me was six over. Not bad for either of us. Or both of us. Whichever.'

Claire would walk away, making faces. Life with such an isolated man as Matthew could be unnerving.

Not that she minded, really. In fact, if he suddenly changed and started wanting to do things together, she didn't know what she'd do. Her life was neatly arranged, and she liked it. Friends and gossip at the office. Badminton on Mondays. Her mother on Tuesdays. Night out Wednesdays. Painting class Thursdays. Wine group Fridays. Saturdays shopping and round to her mother's, nights she stayed in with a video, a bottle of wine and a pack of Pringles. Sundays a bit of a clean-up and ironing clothes for work. There were people to phone. Chums dropping round. She loved her life. She was even planning a trip to Italy. Without Matthew. And she was a Mrs, which was a bonus. When the gossip got round to husbands, she was not left out.

Matthew picked up the phone and dialled. He heard his breath, heavy against the receiver. One ring, two, three, four, nobody was in. He should put down. Five. Six.

'Hello.'

Damn, it was Roz.

'Hello. It's Matthew. Is Zoe there?'

'No. 'Fraid not.'

Zoe was out with Connie.

'Jamie?' asked Matthew.

'Nope. He's gone to the pub. Again.'

Over the past few days Jamie had spent a deal of time in the pub. Roz wondered about that.

'Will?'

'He's popped out. He'll be back soon.'

Will had gone for a video and a bottle of wine. But choosing something that Roz would like was a problem. It wasn't just a matter of picking a video she'd enjoy. He wanted to select something that would impress her with his sensitivity. Then again, he didn't want to sit watching something overly womanly. It was tough.

'I'll just have to talk to you, then,' Matthew said. He couldn't hide his disappointment.

'Looks like it.'

'What's going on down there? When are they coming home?'

'Nothing's going on. Seriously nothing. They're meant to be sorting things out. But as far as I can tell they're just making a show of hardly talking to each other. Will's going home on Monday night. He has work next day.'

'How's Jamie?'

'Fine. No change there. Though he seems to have abandoned the Big Idea and gone in search of his inner self and sudden illumination.'

'What?'

'Don't ask. Jamie's just being Jamie. He'll come to himself.'

'He's a waster.'

'Oh, probably. But he's a nice waster.'

Matthew was appalled. How dare she like him? How dare she defend him? She'd no right.

'Will they be home for Christmas?'

'Christmas?' Roz looked alarmed. Christmas? She hadn't given it a thought, till now. It was only weeks away. Of course there were signs of it everywhere. A certain gleaminess in shop windows. Lights. Adverts on television. Tinkling tannoy carols. But it hadn't registered.

'I don't know. I expect so,' she said.

They couldn't stay till then, surely. She imagined it. Turkey, silly hats, a tree. Here in this flat. No. She didn't think so. 'They'll definitely be home. Definitely. Toby'll want to be in his own house to play with his toys.'

'How is Toby?'

'Fine,' said Roz. 'How are you?'

'Me?' Matthew couldn't think. 'Me? I'm fine.'

'Good. So am I. I'll get Zoe to call you tomorrow.'

'Right.' He made to replace the receiver, then remembered he ought to say goodbye. Put it back to his ear. 'Goodbye.' He rang off.

Roz went back to the living room and slumped. 'Christ.' She hid her face in her hands. 'Christ.'

Will found her head in hands and moaning. 'What are you Christing at?' He sat next to her, putting down his wine (a bottle of Sancerre that cost his twice his usual wine money – he was a £4.99 man) and *The Opposite of Sex* (an excellent choice, he thought, rude, non-PC, yet with a strong female interest, though not so womanish that he wouldn't enjoy it. It had taken him three quarters of an hour to decide upon it). He wanted praise.

'It's Matthew. He phoned.'

'Was he rude to you?'

'Not really. He was just his usual distant, grumpy self.'

'So?'

'He said Christmas,' Roz said.

'Is that all?'

'It's enough. There are two things depress me. Christmas and Matthew. Hearing Matthew actually say the word is just too much. It'd be too much for anyone.'

Will supposed she was right. 'I always have trouble with Matthew and Christmas. I never know what to get him.'

'Neither did I,' Roz agreed. She snickered and sniffed. Reached for a tissue. Raspingly blew her nose. 'I lived with a stranger for years. Silence. It was all silence. Silence when he was out. Even worse silence when he was in. The house rang with it. It was awful.'

'I expect it was.' Will put his arm round her.

She leaned on him. 'It was.'

It was a reaction. He touched her hair. She looked up at him. They kissed. Neither of them meant to. They pulled apart. Apologised to one another. Kissed again. And she sank into it. Eyes shut. Only the softness of lips, and the pleasant warmth, moistness of mouth. She felt his tongue move through her lips. And wanted more of him.

Roz put an end to it, pulled away. 'This is wrong. This is the wrongest thing I've ever done. And I've done some wrong things in my time.'

'Feels right to me,' Will said.

'You're Zoe's.'

'I'm my own.'

He reached for her. The front door opened. Zoe's voice, calling, 'Hello. It's me.'

They leapt apart. Roz pulled her hair into place, listening to Zoe hang up her coat. They smiled at her as she came into the room.

'Ooh, guilty faces.' She grinned. 'You've been talking about me.'

'We've got better things to talk about,' said Roz. 'Thought you were out with Connie.'

Zoe flopped on to a chair. 'I was. But she had to go home. She's going to take a bit of leading astray. It's a challenge. But I'm up to it. Actually, she's not as innocent as she looks. Bit of a dark horse. Quite raunchy after a couple of gins.' Zoe nodded. 'Yeah. Time we had some naughtiness around here.'

Will and Roz exchanged looks. Zoe picked up the video. 'Excellent. Just what I'm in the mood for.' She put it on and started fast-forwarding past the certificate guidance messages and the bloke in the lime jersey selling dodgy black-market copies.

Roz excused herself. She could not, post-kiss, sit and be polite to Zoe and Will. 'I think I'll go to bed.'

'Not staying to see the film?' Zoe was being horribly bright.

Roz shook her head. 'Seen it.' How odd, she thought, that someone with such wide experience in adulterous doings didn't seem to have a clue when her own partner was cheating on her. 'Your father phoned,' she said. 'He wants to know if you're coming home for Christmas.'

'Christmas?' said Zoe. 'Is that soon?'

'A few weeks,' Roz told her.

'What are you doing for Christmas?' Zoe asked Will.

'Spending it with my son. At home.'

Zoe shot him an oh-no-you're-not look. Leaned back and stared at the film. 'Isn't anybody going to open the wine?'

Roz stood by the window of her bedroom. The little over-crowded spare room. Abandoned things – old resolutions, hopes, the exercise bike, guitar – shapes in the dark behind her. No heating on in here. She chittered. It was cold, but that was good. She didn't deserve to be warm. Somewhere a police helicopter thundered and juddered the air overhead. She pressed against the pane, peering up. Couldn't see it. Sunday night. The weekend ends here.

She remembered weekends years ago. They were filled with vibrant expectation. She hoped too much. Dreaded rejection in clubs. That hideous, tactless and cruel curl of young male lips, 'Nah. Don't fancy that.' She drank too much. Held her breath. And prayed for something wonderful to happen. It rarely had. And somewhere, at some distant stop on the road between sixteen and now, she had stopped hoping, dreaming, expecting wonderful things to come to her. She just took what she got, and didn't complain She hadn't even griped to Matthew about the state their lives were in, hadn't properly reproached him about his silence and the comfort he took in counting. She had just left.

Leaving was glorious. A glistening couple of hours. She walked down the garden path carrying her suitcase. Arrived at the bus station. She was on her way. She was headed for new pastures, dreamtime. Climbing on the bus to London. Here we go. No stopping me now.

Sitting on that long journey south, the guilt and dread had set in. What if she couldn't find work? A home? Friends? Penniless, she'd be. She'd walk bitter streets asking for a spare coin or two to buy a cup of tea. She shook her head. Silly, silly, stop it. The movement of the bus lulled her dread into a deep twisting and yanking of the gut. A mood, a feeling. No thoughts to sustain it. The sounds of the bus – the sizzle of a Walkman across the aisle, the riff of indecipherable conversations, rumbling voices, paperback pages turning, the rustling of sandwiches being unwrapped – became a hollowed echo. Strange muted bellows, like at the swimming baths when she resurfaced after swimming underwater. This'll be me for the rest of my life, she thought. No real feelings, no real sounds, just the loneliness, and a slight fear of swimming underwater. I'm selfish. I'm guilty. Heartless. She still thought that. Years on. She never allowed herself forgiveness.

Yet tonight, something wonderful had happened. Will had kissed her. The thrill of it. She was sixteen again. She wished she had someone to phone. To giggle with. To share her thrill. But here was something she couldn't even have discussed with Nan.

'I know. I know,' she said to the ghost of Nan. Her conscience. 'It's wrong.'

'It's more than wrong,' Nan said in Roz's head. 'It'll lead to terrible trouble.'

'Don't tell me,' said Roz.

'Then there's my ashes,' nagged Nan.

'I'm doing them. At Christmas. Mull, remember? I'll do it. I'll do it.'

Zoe, visiting the loo after several gins with Connie and a glass of Will's wine, stopped outside the door of Roz's room to listen. She smiled drunkenly. Knocked on Roz's door. 'Are you all right in there?'

'I'm fine,' said Roz.

'Who are you talking to?'

Roz wondered which sounded more absurd. Should she confess she was talking to herself, or own up to having a discussion with Nan, dead Nan?

'I'm talking to me,' she shouted through the closed door.

Zoe sniggered.

227

'Can't I have a reasonable conversation with myself without being interrupted?' said Roz.

'If you must,' said Zoe. And left her to it.

Roz undressed. Crawled into bed. She thought of Will. Her longing. Was this love? She didn't know. This was new to her. The ache. The yearning. Him on her mind all the time. In the supermarket, stopping by the dairy section, thinking of him and sighing. In the street. Driving her car. Staring sadly at her face in the mirror. He couldn't possibly want that assemblage of cheeks, nose, puckered forehead and lips. Oh, Will. The pain of all this longing. She pulled the duvet over her head and thought that things couldn't possibly get more confused. Could they? Sometimes she wished she was a Beseley.

CHAPTER TWENTY-FOUR

Monday morning Matthew phoned again. Since breakfast, Roz and Will had been sending shooting, burning, guilty looks at one another behind Zoe's back. In the night Roz had slipped into the kitchen to make tea. Will had come to her. Pulled her to him. Kissed her. Kissed her whilst Zoe, Toby and Jamie were dreaming in other parts of the flat. He slipped his hand under her dressing gown and touched her breast. The heat and yearning of it. She gave in to it, pulled him to her. She was in the midst of a full kiss, losing herself to him, when Nan spoke.

'Roz! What the hell are you doing?'

It was a scolding from the conscience. But it was so clear. She turned. Nobody there. It was in my head, she told herself. It must have been. Nan is with me. Nan is looming. She jumped back from Will. 'Don't,' she said.

'Why not? You like it. I can tell.'

'I may have no control over my nipples. But I can control the rest of me. This is wrong. I don't want to go too far.'

He grinned at her. 'I haven't heard that since I was seventeen.'

She felt foolish. Patronised. And blushed. She hadn't done that since *she* was seventeen. She'd gone back to bed. Lain shaking her head on the pillow. 'Wrong. Wrong. Wrong.'

Zoe busily discussed Connie, and how she was going to free her from her inner self. This was bravado. She didn't want to admit that last evening, the drink with Connie had scared her. She had felt out of her depth.

They had gone with Connie's colleagues to a pub. Zoe trotted beside Connie through strange streets, watching passers-by. Thinking how cosmopolitan they looked. She imagined that every single one of them led a more glamorous life than she did. If closely questioned she wouldn't have been able to exactly define what that more glamorous life might be. It came to her in a series of small visions. A curtain blowing in a soft morning breeze. Fresh coffee. Wandering around Sunday mornings in an exotic robe. Manicured toes on a gleaming hardwood floor. Gentle laughter.

Connie went to the bar. Stood waiting for drinks joking with some people. They looked across at Zoe sitting, elbows leaning on the table in front of her. Chin cupped in palms. 'Who's that?' The lips were easily read. She watched Connie and the people she was with. They were all drinking and laughing. Talking, Zoe imagined, about careers, second homes, luxury holidays in distant sun-soaked places. They smiled across at her when Connie told them who she was. Zoe smiled back, till her face ached. They were all thinking, God, she's gorgeous. If I looked like that, I could do anything, go anywhere. Zoe was thinking, God, look at them. They're all so sure of themselves. She imagined that when people looked at her, they could see all her insecurities. So she smiled. And smiled. Hiding.

She made her excuses early and went home cursing herself. Vowing to sort herself out. Get some sort of life together.

Jamie ate his cornflakes and asked Roz about writing a CV.

'What will I put?' he asked. 'I know about afternoon telly. I'm an expert on *Quincy* and *Murder She Wrote*. I have a good knowledge of the flavours of crisps.'

'Who are you trying to impress?' asked Roz.

Matthew's call was almost a relief. Zoe answered it.

'I have to speak to Roz,' he said.

Zoe handed her the phone.

'What do you want? It's dawn.'

'It's never dawn,' said Matthew. What sort of bohemian was she? 'It's nine o'clock.'

'Different people have dawn at different times,' Roz explained.

'It's Nan's house,' he told her. 'I want to sell it.'

'Well sell it,' said Roz.

'It's still full of her furniture.'

'Empty it, then. I can't believe you haven't done that.'

'I can't. I can't go in there. It's just too much. I can't go through her things. I don't know what I'll find.'

'She's dead. She won't know you've found her secrets.'

'You do it.' He was blatant. 'I can't. She'd like you to do it. She was fond of you.'

'She was your mother.'

'I know. But I don't want to. I won't do it. I won't go in there.' Long pause, then, 'Please.'

'What?'

'Please.'

Now he says it, she thought. Please. He never said he loved me. I said I loved him. But it was a lie. I didn't. She wondered if she could go for another please before she agreed to do it. But perhaps best leave it at two. 'OK. I'll come up. Why didn't you mention this last night?'

'One thing at a time,' he said. 'When will you come?'

'Next week. I have to get some work finished first.'

'A fortnight before Christmas.'

'Thank you for reminding me.'

Long, thoughtful silence. 'Sorry. And thank you.' He rang off. Roz thought he might have given her another thank you. But that would've been too much.

She put the phone down. The others were gathered round, waiting to hear what Matthew wanted. Zoe looked fabulous in an old T-shirt and knickers, hair gathered roughly, casually on top of her head, held with an elastic band. No make-up. Nobody should look that good first thing in the morning, Roz thought. It's not fair.

Jamie stared into the distance, hair on end, thinking about his CV. Sleep still with him. He had not joined the human race yet. Never did till approaching noon. Will was feigning disinterest. Toby was standing, fists clenched by his sides. He was working at not sucking his thumb.

'What was that all about?' asked Zoe.

'Nan's house. Matthew wants me to clear it out.'

'Are you going to?'

231

'You heard,' said Roz. 'Yes, I am.'

She went to run a bath. Turned on the taps. Then re-emerged. 'What's all this about *Quincy* and crisps and CVs?' she asked Jamie.

Jamie shrugged. 'I need a job.'

'You've found sudden illumination?' Roz asked.

'Perhaps,' said Jamie. 'You could say that.'

Roz looked at him. Narrowed eyes. He'd found sudden illumination. And sudden illumination was a woman.

Roz was not the type of person to weigh things up. Her approach to life was not a series of balanced, calculated steps toward a desired goal. She lived, head down, shuffling towards whatever was her destiny. There were moments of rushing forward, eyes shut, fingers crossed. She rarely planned ahead. Each day brought whatever each day brought. She never sought enlightenment. Avoided self-analysis. When she indulged in it, she didn't like what she found. On the odd occasion when enlightenment did strike her, it came, as now, when she wasn't seeking it. When her mind was running on empty, busy with the banal doings of the day – filling the kettle, dunking a tea bag in boiling water, watching the clear liquid in her cup turn brown. Or staring at the swirl of foam seething where the gush tumbled from the tap.

The truth struck with such sudden force that she turned, looked behind, checking where it had come from. *Boing*, a light going on in her head. She knew why her children had come back to her. So that they might leave of their own accord, in the natural way of things. Of course, they didn't understand this. They were following their noses. Such foolish noses, too.

It was all about parting. She remembered when Jamie was a baby. Leaving him alone in a room was almost beyond her. She'd rush to the loo, hurtle back to loom over him, checking he was still breathing. The worry of it. He might die. Might slip from life, as mysteriously, incomprehensibly as he'd slipped into it.

Time passed, and tiny partings grew into less tiny partings. Ten minutes, an hour could go by before she'd return to peer at the new beloved in her life. Days stretched into weeks, months, years. The partings grew longer. An entire afternoon with Nan. Evenings out. Then whole days without him when he went to school. The hell she went through when he insisted on going alone. She'd wanted to disguise herself in a long black coat and follow him, peering round corners, making sure he'd arrived safely.

That had been the start of the big parting. He'd started out on his own life, making his own friends. Surviving the playground pecking order. Life according to the children's code: you do not tell on your friends, you do not involve adults. He'd made his way. As had Zoe.

Roz lowered herself into her bath. Held her breath as the heat of it spread upwards from her bum. Roasting over her. 'I buggered the whole process up,' she scolded herself. 'I left them. I should've let them leave me. That's the way of things.'

She held her leg up. Gazed at it. Not a bad leg, considering the time it had been in use as a leg, wear and tear. She smeared it with shaving foam. Reached for Jamie's razor, drew it over her calf. She had to take a stand. A matriarchal show of strength. She should do what mothers do, pretend they know what they're doing. Give them someone to leave. Then one day they'd come back again. Hopefully. That was the theory, anyway.

She stood up, dripping. 'OK, OK. I'll be a mum.' She reached for a towel. It was damp. 'I'll nag. I'll fuss. Make sure they wrap up before they go out. I'll make cocoa. Nourish them with vegetables. Insist they eat their greens. I'll bake little cakes. With pink icing on. I'll be Mrs Beseley.' Thought about this. 'Fuck that. That's going too far.'

She wiped her arms and legs, scrubbed vainly at her tummy. Held out the towel. It was more than damp; it was sopping wet. The floor was pooled with tiny puddles. Soggy size ten footprints between them. 'Jamie,' she muttered. 'No idea of sharing a bathroom. What would a real mother do?' Nag, she decided.

She pulled her clothes stiffly over her steamy body. Threw the soaking towel into the laundry basket, replaced it with two fluffy dry ones. Hosed down the bath. And renewed, full of the mumsy spirit, went to sort everybody out.

Zoe and Will were sitting at opposite ends of the sofa.

'We've decided,' said Zoe, 'that Will and Toby will go home, then I'll follow later to spend Christmas with Toby. When you drive up to clean out Nan's house, I'll go with you.'

'Drive?' said Roz, new resolve crumbling. 'You know I hate driving.'

'You'll be fine,' said Zoe. She came over to Roz, remembering the kindly soul who had comforted her last night, wiped her nose, dried her tears, wrapped her in her arms. 'You'll be with me. I'll look after you.'

Roz felt her palms sweaty with fear. She more than hated driving. Motorways terrified her. The speed of passing cars, the nearness of them shooting past her, coming up behind her. Being sucked against her will into a frenzied hurtle. The fear she felt was verging on phobia. Yet she could not admit to any of this in front of Will.

'Fine,' she said. And swallowed. She turned, looked around. 'Where's Jamie? I want to nag him about the state of the bathroom.'

'He went out,' said Will.

'Where to?' asked Roz.

'Dunno,' said Will. 'But he ironed a shirt before he left.'

'Sounds like he's gone to see some female, then. Ironed shirt, it must be serious. Bloody hell, I was all set to give him a proper maternal talking-to. It's my new plan, be decisive.' She sank on to the sofa, her resolve scuppered. She wanted to phone Nan. Every day she wanted to phone Nan. There was a hole in her life. Soon she'd have to face her fear of driving. And after that, she'd have to take Nan's ashes to Mull and finally say goodbye. She looked at Zoe, who seemed to have taken momentary command. 'Now that I've decided to be decisive, what do you think I should decide to do?'

Zoe smiled. Damned if she knew.

CHAPTER TWENTY-FIVE

Zoe had a vision she kept in her head. A daydream. A fantasy. A secret. It had come to her for the first time years ago on the bus home from school. Bored by the hum of the tired engine, and by the bland faces of her fellow travellers, her mind had gone into neutral. That was when the vision had come to her. It puzzled her. But there it was. It kept coming back, again and again. When she was sitting in the kitchen drinking coffee, or lying in bed waiting for sleep, or just when she wasn't doing anything in particular with her brain. She seemed to have no control over it, or when it would visit her. It had a will of its own.

She was skating exquisitely in some spotlit arena before an enthralled crowd. She twirled, leapt and danced. She did triple axles, whatever they were. She didn't know. Quadruple spins. Landing perfectly, sailing into toe loops. Gliding, head dipped, one leg raised. Sped backwards, cruised upwards, hovering, whirling. Then she sailed to centre rink and moved into a long whirl, round and round, till she was a spinning blur, as the music crescendoed. Flowers rained down on her to enraptured applause. The cheering was deafening. She bowed humbly. Skated to the edge.

This was the triumphal daydream. She liked this fantasy. There was another. In this one, she danced to centre rink, twirled fabulously. Stopped. And the tiers and tiers of people continued to hurtle round her, so fast she couldn't make them out. A reeling confusion of colours. She turned to skate to the side. The exit. But she couldn't locate it. It was moving too fast. Arms reached before her as she fumbled giddily forward, stumbling towards something she couldn't find. Till her wobbly legs crumpled under her and she crawled achingly to the edge. She hated this ending. Tried to scrub it out of her thoughts when it appeared. But it appeared, and, despite her efforts, kept on reappearing.

Thing was, she hated skating. Never watched it on TV and had only done it once, when her mother had taken her and a few chums to the ice rink. She had inched gingerly forward. Shakily let go the barrier and landed on her bum. She hadn't attempted any further venturings into the swirl of accomplished people skimming to and fro.

An old Dean Martin tune had played over and over – *When the moon . . . an old pizza pie*. Since that day she never liked that song, but supposed it was an excellent piece to fall on your bum to.

It seemed to her that her mind just did whatever it wanted with her dreams and fantasies, waking or sleeping. She felt the first fantasy proved that she had the will and mindset to succeed at whatever it was she wanted to succeed at. She didn't really know. But the second, absurd one, with the giddying, confused ending, showed what she secretly dreaded. That she could get within grasping point of success, then fall on her face.

Will and Toby went home. The weather changed. Crisp, chill early December turned raw and wet. It rained. A bitter wind rattled and hissed round the building. Roz, Jamie and Zoe stared out at the world through rivers of water streaking the windows, listened to the groan of relentless swirling air shoving against ill-fitting frames. They dressed against draughts. Turned the heating to full blast. Evenings Jamie disappeared to the pub. And if Connie didn't phone Zoe, she would phone Connie, and they would go together to one of many clubs Connie belonged to. Roz watched her daughter. She was changing.

When she wasn't looking mournfully at the street below, daydreaming about ice skating, fighting the nonsensical ending, becoming so sucked in by wild whirlings she had to put her hand on a nearby chair to stop herself toppling over, Zoe phoned Toby. She talked to him every evening, desperately trying to hang on to him, keep him chatting when he wanted to hang up and get back to whatever he was watching on television, or his Playstation scores. She carefully avoided the subject of food.

Zoe was withdrawn. That her daughter seemed to have lost the will to snipe at her bothered Roz. She had grown accustomed to combating Zoe's barbs. Swift, stinging remarks about Roz's choice of hair mousse, or fabric conditioner. Any chance Zoe got to have a swipe, she'd take. The badgering had been distressing, but the sudden lack of it was worse. Roz wanted to hold out her cheap marmalade: 'Look. Naff. Scorn me.'

Zoe sighed, wrapped herself in her pale grey cashmere sweater, and moved from bed to sofa, to window, to sofa, then, at night, back to bed. Sometimes Roz noticed her reaching out to steady herself, on the chair by the window. 'Are you all right?' she asked Zoe.

'Course. Why?'

'I thought you seemed dizzy.'

'Oh no. Just missed my footing.' Zoe could not confess she'd been skating in her head. And twirling absurdly, showing off, had met her comeuppance. She could not say she was trying not to land on her arse.

Zoe and Connie became friends. Connie confused Zoe. She was not what she seemed. Zoe had thought she'd come across someone she could manipulate. Introduce to a bit of wild living. She was wrong. Strip away Connie's outward politeness, her seemingly almost old-fashioned gentility, and underneath there was a woman more daring than Zoe would ever be.

Zoe watched Connie as she let a gin and tonic slide over her throat. 'Needed that.' Watched as Connie slumped, slipped off her shoes, pulled the chair opposite close and put her feet on it, wriggling tired toes. 'Crap day.' Her mobile rang, a polite murmur somewhere in the depths of her handbag. 'Shit.' She yanked the thing out, cursing. Pressed the button. Put it to her ear and twinkled. 'Hi. How *are* you? It's great to talk to you.'

Zoe marvelled. She thought she was a good twinkler. But this woman could out-twinkle anyone.

'How do you do that?' Zoe asked. 'Sound so up when you're

knackered and pissed off. How doesn't it show?'

'It's a gift,' Connie said. Then, 'It's how it is.' She broke, mildly drunk, into early Bessie Smith. *'Nobody knows ya, when you're down and out.'* She grinned. 'You'll get the hang of it.'

If Zoe had started out wanting to take Connie under her wicked wing, the opposite had happened. It was Connie's wicked wing she was tumbling under. And so willingly. Take me, she thought. Show me how to be you.

Connie existed on several levels. There was the good daughter. She shopped for her mum. Chatted blandly about the weather or what Mrs Next-Door had said, and yes, she'd get the curtains dry-cleaned next week.

There was the working woman. She turned up on time. Took her calls. Went to meetings. Made contacts. Plotted her next move – upwards.

Connie the socialiser, who drank with mates after work, who laughed at old jokes, bantered. Stayed discreetly sober.

Connie the insecure, who counted calories, fretted by the silent phone, sent her mind forward twenty years and saw a lonely middle-aged woman, slightly the worse for gin and Kettles crisps, childless and on her way down from a relatively successful career, making way for younger, hungrier people who all thought they knew more about 'now' than she did. This Connie cried alone in the night.

Connie the wild, who had affairs, one-night stands, who went to clubs where waiters turned their heads and deliberately did not see what was going on. Connie the wild, who gave herself to the moment. Who laughed and drank and said, 'Stuff everything.' Only the moment mattered.

Zoe wanted to be all of them. She even wanted to be the good daughter. Recently, she had found it comforting to have a mother. 'My mum . . .' she had said when out with a group of Connie's friends. 'I'm staying with my mother . . .' 'My mother and I . . .' 'My mother said . . .' It made her feel . . . she found it hard to define. Whole?

She found she did not care for her wildness any more. She no longer thought to reel people in. Love them. Shock them. Let them go.

Her wild side, now waning, was nothing compared to Connie's. She was the opposite of Connie. Scrape away Zoe's brash exterior and the trembling child, fearing rejection, was revealed. Scrape away Connie's shy exterior, and the wild child was waving. Still, she could not understand why Connie was so friendly. Why Connie phoned to invite her out. She did not realise the importance, the intrigue, of being seen about with a new, fascinating and utterly, utterly beautiful person.

Connie's got it all, Zoe thought. Connie always knows what to do, whatever happens to her. She knows how to smile, and when to smile.

Zoe turned from the rain-streaked window to Roz. 'Do you remember, you asked me what was the meaning of life? I was three, for Chrissakes.' A sudden flash of her infancy.

'Did I?' said Roz. 'Oh God, yes,' she said, going gooey, 'I remember. We were at the kitchen table. You had on your corduroy dungarees and your little T-shirt with a teddy on the front.' She went misty-eyed. 'I loved you in that. Whatever happened to it?'

'It's too small for me now,' said Zoe. 'And I'm not into wearing T-shirts with teddies on them any more. Anyway, you asked me the meaning of life and I was three.'

'Yes, I know. I just wondered what you would say. I mean, you were so much nearer to the beginning of things. You were just new yourself. And I'd never had the chance to ask someone so close to birth what they thought of life before.'

'Remember what I said?'

'You said the meaning of life was you didn't cry if you lost at animal dominoes.'

'Good one,' said Zoe. 'I was pretty astute, even then. I think I got it right.'

Roz nodded.

'You just don't let everything show. All these people,' Zoe said, piecing her thoughts together as she spoke, 'Connie and the like.' People who hung about with Connie, who turned up with her, whose names Zoe could hardly remember. 'They have their lives sussed. When they lose at animal dominoes, they don't cry.'

'That's the trick of it,' said Roz.

'I thought I was cool. Then I met Connie. And I'm not cool at all. I got miles to go before I get to cool.'

'Everybody's squirming inside. Remember that when you're with Connie.'

'No,' said Zoe. 'I've just got to stop crying out loud. In public. *That's* the trick of it.'

Jamie was out at the pub in his ironed shirt. It had been over a week since he'd talked to Roz about the Big Idea, or sudden illumination. There was a new calm about him. Not that he wasn't calm before. His calmness had been near-to-dammit irritating. But now, he was resolute. Sure of himself. Roz was sure there was a woman in Jamie's life. She suddenly missed the person who avoided issues, dreamed of sudden riches, and the highlight of whose day was to go round the corner for a copy of the *Sun* and a Biscuit Boost. She felt she hadn't known him long.

Zoe was going through some sort of catharsis. A more reasonable person was emerging. Roz missed the unpredictable, overdramatic being who flounced from room to room, not speaking, just making outrageous comments.

Wasn't that the way of things? Now that Zoe and Jamie were making signs of going, growing up, Roz wanted to keep them with her. Just the way they were.

Half past midnight. Zoe was sleeping, Jamie was out in his ironed shirt. Roz phoned Fred. She got his answering machine. Remembering the last time they were together – how she, in a moment of near ecstasy, shouted out the wrong name – Roz felt awkward, embarrassed, and replaced the receiver without saying a word.

She imagined Fred to be out somewhere, with the woman she'd dreamed up for him. In fact Fred was driving his daughter home from university for Christmas. His jacket, with his letter to her in the pocket, was buried beneath a pile of dirty laundry, CDs, books, a moth-eaten teddy bear and an ivy plant that were also coming home for Christmas.

They were... He then ...

CHAPTER TWENTY-SIX

Toby liked being back home. There was comfort in the familiar. He had his toys. His special Bart Simpson mug. He could sit in front of the telly after school and watch whatever he wanted. But nights were tricky. He was alone upstairs and had to strain to hear sounds of Will moving about on the lower floor. And it was dark. Shapes, familiar by daylight, became monsters. Madmen and beasts from movie trailers seeking his blood.

It hadn't been so in Roz's flat. He liked the smallness of it. Light from the hallway seeped under his door, and his dressing gown hanging on the back of the door remained his dressing gown. Nothing to fear. Then there was the constant, distant hum of adult voices, shifting tones, that came to him, reminding him of the closeness of grown-up people. Nothing to fear. Later, when night was black, if he woke there was his mother breathing beside him. The relief. Nobody would come and harm him while she was there. He loved his mummy when she was sleeping. He loved her when she played with him, silly games. I-spy in the car. Charades sometimes in the evening when he'd done his homework. Or they'd do jigsaws, heads close, puzzling over the pieces. Twisting them, turning them round and round to see where they'd fit. But sometimes she spoke about what he'd be when he grew up – a musician, a doctor, a lawyer. He didn't want to do these things. They were hard. He didn't understand them. They scared him. He didn't want to grow up. He wanted things to stay like they were. He wanted to stay in this house with Will and for Zoe to come home. Then they could stay like this for ever.

Once, when Zoe had some friends in, they were laughing downstairs and he got up to find out what the noise was. What the jokes were. They sounded like good ones. Fun. He came into the living room, and six women turned to gaze at him. The room smelled of smoke and booze. They swooned. 'Is this Toby?' 'He's lovely.' 'You're so lucky, Zoe.' 'Oooh,' one woman said, 'I want one of those.'

Zoe had introduced him. 'Toby,' quiet, patronising voice, 'this is Lisa. And Marie. And Joanna.' They had smiled. Said, 'Hi, Toby.' He stared at them, thumb in mouth. Their faces, as he turned to them, lined up with his knuckles. One woman came to him, squatted to his level. 'What do you want to do when you're grown up, Toby?'

He could smell tobacco on her breath. She had bright red lips and sparkly stuff on her eyelids. She was scented.

'I don't want to grow up,' he told her. 'I want to be a little boy when I grow up.'

How they'd laughed. Clapped their hands in joy. 'Ha, ha.'

The red-lipped woman stood, ruffled his hair. He hated that. 'That's honest. Don't worry, you will be. All men are.'

And they'd all fallen about.

Toby had gone to the kitchen to pour himself a glass of Evian. He'd have preferred Pepsi, but Zoe wouldn't let him have that at night on account of his teeth. He took the drink upstairs to bed. He was puzzled. But no more than usual. Adults were funny people. They liked to eat olives, which were horrible. And anchovies, which were worse. They spoke about cars, how fast they went and how many miles they could go on a gallon of petrol. Tax discs. He'd never understand all that. Inland Revenue. When to water a plant. So-and-so's new sofa. When they were eating, they'd talk about recipes. They spent ages discussing what somebody had said to somebody else and how hurtful or silly it had been. And this woman was sleeping with that man, and it wasn't right. How did they know that? Then there were things they couldn't get their heads round. They were always saying that. They said words he wasn't allowed to say. *Fuck*. When he said it, Zoe looked at him. That look that stung him worse than hailstones. Made him want to cover his head with his arms and run away. Yet she could say it. Sometimes she said it three or four times in one sentence. He counted.

He saved the word, and the worse one, *cunt*, for the middle of the night. When the demons and evil people came for him. He'd sit up in bed, fists clenched, and say them. Say them in his deepest whisper till his throat hurt, and the cords in his tiny thin neck stuck out. His face went red with saying it. 'Fuck. Fuck. Fuck,' he'd say. And 'Cunt. Cunt.' Then the laughing man with the claw hand, and the toothless, cackling hag with stringy hair, beaky nose, beady eyes, who did not speak, but hissed, would go away.

Toby couldn't understand it. One thing he knew: if all these things were what grown-ups did, spoke about, ate, he definitely did not want to be one. He'd never know about plants, or car discs or pay slips. Roz was always looking at hers. It was all too hard.

Another thing. Grown-up people did funny things. They kissed on the mouth. For ages. Mouths open, too. He'd seen it in films. And he'd seen Zoe and Will doing it. Once, when he was in London, he'd been wakened by voices. They'd come in a slow trickle from the kitchen. Whispering. He'd climbed from bed to investigate. There in the corner, only one small light on, he'd seen Will kissing Roz. Zoe's mum, his gran. She had her hand on his head. He had his arms round her. And one hand was on her bum. They made noises. 'Oh,' she said. They didn't see him. When they pulled apart – and it seemed ages before they did, as Toby sucked his thumb and watched – Roz said, 'This is wrong.'

If it was wrong, why were they doing it? Though Zoe did it too. Kissed men who weren't Will. Toby had seen her. He supposed Roz and Will and Zoe could do wrong things because nobody would tell them not to. Nobody would shout at them or send them to their rooms or stop them seeing their favourite television programmes.

He had thought to ask Zoe about this kiss he'd witnessed. But when the time came the next morning, when Zoe had fetched him fresh underwear from the tumble-drier, and was fussing round him, trying to comb his hair, he changed his mind. He'd sucked his thumb, looked up at her, and some tiny intuition told him to keep it to himself.

Will went back to work. It was a relief to be back amidst rows and rows of books. On his small journeys from home to shop and back again, he looked for Marianne, his guardian angel. He had a lot to tell her.

He wanted to confess to somebody that he was attracted to his partner's mother. And that he couldn't understand it. Because she was so much older than him. Not his scene at all. But there was something easy about her, a quiet humour, her soft voice. And he liked her face. The way she'd turn and smile at him. He loved being with someone who seemed to know what she wanted, and who, unlike Zoe, made no demands of him. He wanted to lie next to her, put his head on her. And sleep. This wasn't like him at all, he wanted to tell Marianne. What was happening to him? Was he, perhaps, God forbid, getting old?

But he didn't see Marianne. He didn't see anybody. Evenings he stayed in. He worried about drinking too much. So, after he'd eaten, and after Toby had gone to bed, he laid out three glasses, poured three gins, filled them with tonic, ice and a slice of lemon and carried them to the living room. Lined them up on the coffee table in front of him. He'd drink them slowly. Television on, for company, voices. He'd read newspapers. Do crosswords. Play patience. Anything to stop himself thinking. Now that he was away from Zoe, all the things he should have said to her when they were together flooded his mind. Not that it mattered. Were she here, they'd all flood out again. There was something about her, about looking at her, that took his words, his very breath away.

CHAPTER TWENTY-SEVEN

It was bitter on the day Roz and Zoe chose to drive north to clean out Nan's house. At eight in the morning, they stepped out into the thin morning air clasping their coats round them, gasping at the chill. The sky was frozen pale. A mean, almost spiritless wind nipped and rattled the branches of the trees in gardens across the road.

'Black ice,' said Roz. 'I don't fancy this.'

'Rubbish,' said Zoe the optimist. 'We'll be fine.'

They filled the boot and back seat of the car with cases, and Christmas gifts wrapped in gleamy paper, adorned with bows, for Toby and Will. Placed Nan's ashes in a place of honour beside them, and apologised to her for putting her in the boot, but felt the journey was going to be arduous enough without her ghost nagging in the back seat. She was still a presence.

Roz decided to take the back road across the border, coming off the motorway as soon as possible. Wide and busy three-or four-laned roads were, she thought, wretched places filled with wretched drivers in wretched cars. Lorries with flapping tarpaulins and grinning front grilles, with hissing air brakes that rode the highway inches from her tail bumper. She hated them all.

The car started first turn of the key in the ignition. 'Good sign,' said Zoe. 'See. It's going to be a grand journey.'

Roz thought that the travel gods were offering her false hope. But didn't say so. Still, by the time they were slouching out of London, nose to tail with other motorists, objects of Roz's loathing and derision, her spirits lifted. If the road they were on, the landscape they were passing through seemed loveless and grim, inside the car they were snug. Heater blasting. Dixie Chicks on the tape deck and Polo mints to suck. It wasn't bad. Wasn't bad at all.

By the time they reached Newcastle it was raining. The wipers squeaked against the windscreen. They'd replaced the Dixie Chicks with Nina Simone, sung along with 'Sunday in Savannah'. Finished the Polos and started on their bars of marzipan Rittersport. They'd discussed Connie, Toby, Matthew (briefly, not much to say there), Will and were analysing Jamie, who had just this morning received word of his driving test shortly before Christmas.

'I'll fail,' he'd protested. 'Those bastards have got it in for me.'

'No they haven't.'

'Have, too.'

'Have not.' Then, before the whole discussion disintegrated into a have-too, have-not sparring match, Roz took his arm and pleaded, 'Just once. Just for an hour. Do what they say. Obey the rules. Smile. Be polite. Signal. Position yourself correctly. Look in your mirror. Don't overtake. Don't honk the horn at people going slower than you. Don't reverse-park at sixty miles an hour. Just don't. Remember that. Don't. And you'll pass. And never have to see an examiner again as long as you live.'

Jamie said, 'You're asking me to corrupt myself. Become a yes-man. This is not an honourable thing.'

'OK.' Roz was fed up. Anxious to get going. 'Be an honourable learner. Or a corrupt yes-man with a driving licence. You choose. I'm off. Goodbye. Don't make a mess.' She wanted to say, 'When you get your girlfriend in here, don't use my bed,' but didn't. That last bit of nagging was enough. She thought her nagging was getting better. Not quite four-star, but on her way. She was becoming Mrs Beseley.

About twenty miles out of Newcastle, the rain thickened. Icy droplets hit the windscreen, spread and melted. 'Is that snow?' asked Roz.

'No way,' said Zoe the optimist.

They stopped at a roadside café for lasagne, hot chocolate and carrot cake. It was the weather for calories. Huddled by a giant heater, they watched a small company of hens peck the ground, squabble and kowtow to Mrs Hen, who rushed after any upstart, head forward, wings flapping, clucking insanely. She was obeyed. Lesser hens kept clear.

'That's how I want to be,' said Roz.

'Like that hen?' said Zoe. 'She's insufferable.'

'She gets her way. When her chicks grow up they'll leave home. Mature beings.'

'Bollocks. They'll be drug addicts before they get to the end of the street.'

'You know nothing. She struts and clucks, pecks and nags. Then her kids feel secure. They think she knows what she's doing. She leaves the little ones for a bit. Then checks them. Leaves them for longer. Then one day, after they've gone through the school trips, the late nights, the first drinks, the sex, the lies, they leave her.'

'You think?' said Zoe.

'I know. That's us.' She hadn't meant to tell Zoe her new theory. The Big Parting notion. But here it was, coming out. 'That's what you and Jamie are doing. Coming to me so you can abandon me in the proper way of things. It's a sort of adolescence we're going through.'

'Crap,' said Zoe, putting her feet up on the seat opposite, slowly picking the icing off her cake. Sticking a small piece on the tip of each of her fingers before dipping them one at a careful time into her mouth. She lifted her mug of chocolate to her face and licked the frothy leavings. 'That's a shite theory. Anyway, what's this with the *we*? You're not going through any adolescence. You're old. Past it.'

'Am not,' said Roz, leaning close. Holding out a proud chin. Pointing – not without triumph – at a spot, glowing, erupting. 'See. A spot. How's that for hormones? I'm not past it.' I can be adolescent if I want, she didn't say. I've got such a crush on your partner, I ache and yearn for him at night. I dream of him. I sigh. I've stolen one of his socks and take it out and fondle it. I'm a complete idiot. I claim my right to be an adolescent. I didn't get the chance when I was sixteen.

Zoe loomed in to examine the shiny red mark on her mother's chin. 'That's not a proper spot. Not the sort to make you cringe with embarrassment. That's a middle-aged pimple. The sort of tiny thing you get in between the proper spots.' She stuck her hands in her pockets and scowled at a couple two tables away who were eating tuna salad washed down with Evian. Wankers, eating healthy shite, she thought. Weather like this you need stodge. Adolescence. What drivel her mother came up with. Listen to her philosophising about hens, boasting about a pimple. Christ, you couldn't take her anywhere.

The weather was driving in cruelly as they made their way across the car park. Horizontal sleet. The car wouldn't start. Three, four times Roz gunned the engine before it roared. 'It's trying to tell us something,' said Roz. 'We shouldn't go on. A car knows.'

'Crap,' said Zoe. 'It's just a little sleet. If we get a move on down the road, we'll be in Edinburgh before the weather turns.'

'Suppose,' said Roz. She turned into the road. Empty now. There was nobody else travelling. Four miles on, the snow started. It came in small flurries that spread and danced, scattering over the tarmac.

'It's not lying,' said Zoe the optimist.

They headed for the border. Climbing. Hills and forests about them now. Distant peaks disappearing into heavy and grey cloud. Roz switched on the lights. They cut a small wedge into the swirling weather, spotlighting the white-out. Wipers creaked. The snow turned nasty. Stopped swirling and came sheeting in. Merciless. Thick, hard flakes dropped on the windscreen, gathered at the sides, pushed by the wipers. They could hear the groan of snow crushed under tyre as they crawled forwards, fifteen miles an hour. Then ten. Zoe craned ahead, watching the road. 'Couple of miles down the road we'll come out of this.'

Roz doubted that. She could see nothing but blizzard. Hear nothing but wind. There was nobody else about. She no longer knew where the road was, but kept moving anyway. As long as she could, she'd move. Half an hour they took to cover two miles.

Creeping and anxious. More than anxious; downright scared. The wheels slid, whined on the heaping snow.

'I think we're going to die,' said Roz.

'You think?' said Zoe. 'Oh, shit. Oh, Christ. I haven't been to Florence. And I might want to have another baby.'

'Who with?' asked Roz, white-knuckling the wheel.

'Jesus,' said Zoe. 'Who with?' She looked about. Snow. 'There's nobody about. Anybody.'

There was nothing around them but weather. Vicious weather.

'I'm not going to die,' said Zoe. 'You can die, but I'm not finished yet.'

'Finished what?' Roz noticed with horror that they were not moving. The wheels were howling and screaming but not doing anything, taking them anywhere.

'Whatever the fuck it is I've started.' Zoe's voice went up an octave. She was scared.

'I think we've stopped,' said Roz, her voice a hush. 'We're stuck.' Yes, definitely. They were going to die. Freeze to death. Out here in the wastes of nowhere.

'I'm sorry,' said Roz.

'What for?' Zoe was an optimist no longer.

'For being such a crap mother.'

'Bugger that. Can you get out and push?'

'You push. I'm the one who's driving.'

'I'll ruin my shoes.'

'Fuck your shoes. What are you thinking of? Shoes like that in this weather. "Wear sensible shoes," I said.'

'I don't have sensible shoes. I refuse to have sensible shoes. I'm too young for that. I don't dress for this sort of weather.'

'Well you should,' screamed Roz. 'It's December. We're in the north. Sensible shoes are the thing.'

'Like you've got on sensible shoes. Fuck you,' countered Zoe, looking down at Roz's feet. 'This is your fault. You won't take the motorway. You're scared of proper roads. Scared of other, bigger cars. Scared of everything. Look at you.'

'What the hell do you mean by that?'

'What do you think I mean?' Zoe looked away. Out the window. She could see nothing but snow. She shivered. 'I'm freezing. You don't have a blanket, do you?'

'No,' said Roz.

'I suppose it'd be too much to expect you to have a spade to dig us out.'

'It would,' Roz agreed.

'A driver shouldn't leave home without these things.'

'In London?' said Roz. 'In London all you need to drive about is change for meters, an A to Z and a brass neck.'

'And you haven't got any of those things. You're chicken. This is all your fault. Taking the back road 'cos you hate motorways. Chicken.'

'All my fault? Mine? Oh, everything's my fault,' said Roz.

'Yes, it is.' They were climbing past hissing hostility at each other. Voices were getting shriller. 'Look at this shit you've got us into. You and your chicken crap driving. You're crap at everything. Crap cook. Crap writer. Crap housewife. Crap mother.'

'Me? A crap mother? Unlike you. Look at Toby. Sucking his thumb, fiddling with himself. At his age. Jesus Christ.'

'My son is a lot better balanced,' Zoe shouted, voice battering round the stuffy car interior, 'than any child you produced.'

Silence. They both let the words slide round their heads. Glaring at one another.

'What do we make of that remark?' said Roz.

The wind shifted round the car. Whipped under it. Rocking it.

'Whatever you like,' said Zoe.

'That you're a mess, and it's my fault?' asked Roz.

'I'd go for that.'

'It wouldn't be, it couldn't be,' Roz frothed, 'that you are just a mess. That you manipulate people. That you sleep around because you seek constant reassurance that you're wanted. You shag your friends' partners so you can get one over on them. You always were a scheming little minx.'

'You never loved me. You never cuddled me,' complained Zoe.

'Did too. All the time when you were little. You didn't want anyone to touch you later. Any time anyone went near you, you told them to leave you alone. You didn't want me. There was nothing in it for you.'

Zoe whacked Roz across the cheek.

A long, long, horrified silence. Roz nursing her injury. Zoe hands to mouth. Shocked at what she'd done.

'It's been a shit day,' said Roz. 'Well,' she pursed her lips, 'any sort of physical contact is better than no physical contact.' Her cheek smarted, cruelly. 'I suppose.'

'Fuck you,' said Zoe. 'Look at you.'

'What the hell do you mean by that?'

'Sitting there feeling righteous 'cos I whacked you and you didn't whack me back. So like you. You're a do-nothing. You don't branch out. You hardly know anyone. You should network. You're a coward.'

'I am not.'

'Are too. My mother, the runaway and coward.'

'How dare you say that to me?' said Roz.

The wind shuddered round them, the car shook. There was white. Only white. Piling up on the windscreen. They glared. Eyeball to eyeball. A full three minutes passed. The glare was turning stale.

'OK, OK,' said Roz. 'I'll look away. You win.' The air was damp. Windows steamed.

'Win what?' Zoe asked.

'This glaring contest. You're the superior animal now. Top cat. King of the herd.'

'Queen,' said Zoe.

'Whatever,' said Roz. She yanked down her jersey collar. Jabbed insanely at her neck. 'There you go. I offer you my jugular, a sign of submission.' She'd seen this in a wildlife film about wolves, once, when visiting Nan.

'What do I do with that? I don't want that.' Zoe shook her hands in protest.

'You make to bite it. To let me know you could kill me.' The wind shrilled and howled. 'If you wanted,' added Roz. 'But you won't. That'd be bad manners.'

Zoe pulled Roz's collar back. Exposed her neck. To Roz's alarm, she moved in on her, teeth bared. This girl really wanted to hurt her. Roz looked panic-stricken. Zoe looked insane. Somewhere on that short journey to the jugular, Zoe's resolve collapsed. She was a child again. She put her head on Roz's shoulder. Wept.

'Not tears,' said Roz. She felt weak. Weak and slightly stupid. Seconds ago they'd both been hysterical. 'Please not tears. Anything but that. Your rage I can take. Sorrow is so much harder. The guilt.' She lifted Zoe's face. Kissed the tears. 'Please don't.'

'Sorry,' said Zoe.

'You're not really.' Roz looked at her. Unaccountably, she wanted to burst out laughing. 'Have you got a cigarette?'

'You don't smoke.' Zoe rummaged in her handbag for her Marlboro Lights. Handed one to Roz, lit one herself. They sat blowing out smoke. Shivering. Sorry for each other. Sorry for themselves.

'How long have we been stuck out here?' asked Roz.

'Twenty minutes.'

'Didn't take us long to lose it. Panic. We'd better not go on a polar expedition together.'

They sniggered.

An hour later, it stopped snowing. Roz got out of the car to look round. The whiteness astounded her. It had been years since she'd seen a world reshaped and bounded by snow. Not since the back garden of her childhood. And then it had been safe. Comfort, hot cocoa and toast only a step away. The gale had shoved and steeped the snow into a giant wall at the other side of the road, and heaped up on the passenger side of the car. The wheels were lodged in deep. Snow was slapped against tree trunks, huge branches drooping with the weight of it. The sky was curdled grey. Great swagging clouds rolled in. More snow coming. The wind howled, shrill, over the icy surfaces, the only noise in this shimmering place. Except, of course, for Dolly Parton crooning on the radio. 'I will always love you'. Well, that was nice. Roz got back into the car. 'We are seriously stuck.'

'What are we going to do?'

'Dunno,' said Roz. 'One of us could go for help.'

'You,' said Zoe. 'Your shoes are more up to it than mine.' She lifted a scantily clad foot.

Roz sighed. Leaned in the back for a jumper, yanked it on. Pulled her coat over it. Told Zoe to switch on the engine and the heater at intervals, to keep warm. And not to panic. She'd be back soon enough. She started back the way they'd come. She could at least follow the tyre marks. If they weren't too badly covered up.

Ten minutes she walked. Listening to her grim breathing. The crunch of snow underfoot. The wind and the odd tree groaning. The weather started up again. Giant flakes coming at her. Coating her till she was so thickly covered it looked like it was baked on. Head down, she just walked. 'This is stupid. This is stupid. Should've stayed put. I'm going to die out here.'

Zoe smoked. She listened to Roz's tapes. The car steamed and fugged. She got hungry and searched in the glove box for Polo mints. Nothing. 'Jesus, I could starve.' Then she remembered the Christmas selection box Roz had bought for Toby. She took the keys from the ignition, heaved open the door, pushing the snow aside. Climbed out, and felt her way round to the back of the car. Iced water seeped over the edges of her shoes. She found the sweets and made her way back to her seat. She tore open the wrapping, opened the box and selected a Wispa. Unwrapped it and took a huge bite, ramming it into her mouth. She lit another cigarette. Found a Dolly Parton tape and shoved it on. *Nine to five*, sang Dolly. Roz was never coming back. She knew it. She was alone out here in the middle of nowhere. She was going to freeze to death. She finished the Wispa and opened a Flake.

The music was blaring from the car. The windows were steamed up. Zoe neither heard nor saw the Land Rover coming up behind her. She'd eaten the bar of Dairy Milk and was starting on the chocolate buttons. A brown rim round her mouth. Dolly Parton sang 'Tennessee homesick blues'. Zoe couldn't help herself. She sobbed. Not the quiet weep of a woman alone at the roadside in a stranded car. But hands over her face, indiscreet sobbing of a woman abandoned by the ones she loves. I've lost my Will, my Toby and my mother.

Roz opened the car door. 'You all right?'

Zoe looked up mid howl. 'Yes.'

Dolly started to sing 'Save the Last Dance For Me'. It was too much. Zoe gave herself up to her lonesomeness and the weather and her fear and her horror at the huge number of calories she'd eaten, and wept. 'I thought you weren't coming back.'

'I've hardly been away half an hour. I got picked up down the road by a bloke in a Land Rover.' She leaned into the car and coughed. 'The fug in here. How much have you smoked?'

'About ten cigarettes.' Sob. 'It seemed longer than half an hour.'

Roz had been heading, head down, into the storm, feet soaked and numb with cold, face red and stung by sweeping snow, when the Land Rover stopped. 'What the hell are you doing out here?' A face, reddened by weather, unshaven, leaned out.

'Getting help,' said Roz.

He looked at her. Skirt up past her knees. High heels and a woollen coat, sodden. Hair iced and flecked liberally with snow. Mascara running. City woman. 'Oh aye. Well, lassie, you're in luck.'

Roz climbed in, stiffly. Her legs were raw, chafed and numb. She pulled her hands from her pockets, though they were refusing to come out. They seemed wedged in. 'Thank you.' She started chittering.

'You should stay put if yer car gets stuck in this weather.'

'I know. I was worried about my daughter.'

'Aye. Well. What're you doing out this weather?'

'Wasn't like this when we started out.'

Roz sat in the passenger seat. Felt the wave of warmth and started to shiver and thaw. Little pools of water dripped to the floor to puddle amongst the tools and rusting tractor bits. The cab smelled of pig dung and fertiliser and pipe smoke. Her rescuer snorted. Just what he needed. Some daft woman dripping wet. He noticed her high heels. Nice legs.

'Where're you from?'

'London.'

'Thought so. You won't get weather there.' He sounded like he never spoke more than four words at a time.

'No,' said Roz. 'Not like this.'

They rumbled on. Minutes it took them to cover the distance Roz had trudged and stumbled. They stopped at the car and Roz clambered out. To find Zoe, the wrecked optimist, chocolate-caked and weeping. The reek of smoke was overpowering.

'Is this your daughter?' Their rescuer was surprised. Didn't hide it. 'Way you spoke, I thought she was about ten.'

'No,' said Roz.

He looked at her. 'You don't look old enough to have a daughter that age.'

'Thank you,' Roz grinned. And flirted. She was never too cold, wet or downright scared to flirt.

They roped up the car, and the Land Rover hauled it out of the drift and pulled it, lights flashing, ten miles to where the snow petered out, roads turned black again. Their rescuer secretly cursing. Miles out of his way. Hours past dinner time. These folks ought to stick to their sushi bars. There ought to be ramparts and wire fences to keep them out. Daft women. Good-looking, especially that daughter, but he'd have the mother, older, well preserved and good-mannered. He'd have her. Daft or not. And it'd be a good tale to tell in the pub. Coming across her, caked with snow, bundled up, trudging in little strappy shoes, wringing wet, shivering. Alone, with the worst December in fifteen years whirling round her. He was a hero. Already he was telling it, elaborating it. Him carrying her to safety. Her half conscious. It was well worth a whisky or three.

Roz and Zoe drove the last part of the journey in silence Windows open to ease the smell coming from Roz, pig dung, fertiliser and sopping wool. And because Zoe felt nauseous from a surfeit of chocolate, shock and nicotine. Roz nauseous from cold, lack of food and worry about the drive back to London. Every now and then they thought about the horror they had just lived through, sighed and thanked whatever gods were up there.

'I'm rubbish in a crisis,' said Zoe.

'Yep,' said Roz.

'Thank you,' said Zoe.

'For what?'

'For saving my life.'

'Jesus, Zoe. You were alone for less than half an hour. You were never going to die. Besides, that Land Rover would've come along anyway.'

'I know that now. But at the time . . . And you went off, alone into the storm, to get help.'

'Stupid thing to do. You can freeze to death in four minutes going out in weather like that. Or is that at sea? I dunno. Oh God, I need a bath. A cup of tea. A plate of something hot, and at least twelve hours' sleep.'

They arrived at Nan's house after eight. The night was chill, and the skies clear. Roz stopped halfway up the path to the front door, looked up. A million stars. 'Star light,' she said.

Zoe joined her, neck cricked, craning. 'Star bright,' she said.

'First star I see tonight,' said Roz.

'Wish I may, wish I might,' said Zoe. 'Yeah, I remember all that stuff.'

They went indoors.

CHAPTER TWENTY-EIGHT

Nan's house was cold. The air inside felt thick. Nothing had shifted through it, breathed it, since her death. It felt as still, untouched and dusty as the heavy brown furniture that pressed against the floral walls. Roz reluctantly opened a window and lit the gas fire. They stood side by side: Roz, palms spread, warming her face and aching body; Zoe, back to it, letting the heat at her bum, which was numb after fourteen hours sitting down. They discussed where to sleep. Neither fancied Nan's bed, for fear she had died in it.

'It isn't catching,' argued Roz. 'Death.'

'I know.' Zoe was defensive. 'So you sleep in it, then.'

Roz sighed. She knew there was no point in bickering. She'd be the one to give in eventually. Her foolhardy excursion into the blizzard had made its mark on their relationship. She was the one to take risks. Zoe would hang back, egg her on, and criticise. She went upstairs to find fresh sheets, left Zoe to cook the bacon and eggs they'd brought with them.

'I don't want to cook,' said Zoe. 'I'm too cold. I feel sick.'

'Cook,' demanded Roz. 'I didn't want to go out into the snow. I don't want to make up beds. I don't want to empty out this house. I don't want to be here. You cook, or . . .' She paused. Or what? She couldn't think. What did you threaten Zoe with?

'Or what?' Zoe strutted. She could strut standing still.

'Else,' said Roz. And stamped out. Before her ineffectual threat was challenged.

Next morning Zoe disappeared early to catch up with chums, and to see if there was any chance of getting her old job in the design shop back.

Roz filled black bin bags. Nan's larder was stuffed with sugar.

Her wartime habits. Jars of jam, marked *Blackcurrant 1964. Gooseberry 1967. Rhubarb 1970*. Ancient pots with a good layering of penicillin formed on top. Tins of corned beef and ham, peas and fruit salad. Soft biscuits.

She went upstairs to Nan's bedroom. Opened the wardrobe. Nan's collection of winter coats. Mostly dark green or beige. She wondered if anyone would want them. The smell of mothballs was overpowering. Nobody would want them. She shoved them guiltily into a bag. In went a lifetime's shoes – from stilettos to the wide, comfortable, flat heels she'd worn in her last years. Pencil-thin skirts from fifteen years ago, tweed skirts into the bag with them. The red dress she'd worn six New Years running. Goodbye, Nan. She went through Nan's drawers: a thousand pairs of wrinkled tights, laundered. Nan's girdles and longline bras, huge cups. A small leather jewel box, stiff hinge. Inside, a brooch with tiny pearls inlaid in silver, gathered round the white outlined head of a woman.

She opened the drawers of Nan's bedside cabinet. Her watch. A new Swatch Zoe had given her. Sleeping pills. Some photographs. Nan with her grandchildren in the back garden. Nan as a young woman, holding baby Matthew, smiling. Roz had forgotten what a beauty she'd been all those years ago. Nan in some strange place. India? Surely not, thought Roz. She peered at the photo. No, it must be some illusion.

Nan with a man Roz had never seen before. A big man, in jeans and a checked shirt. They were standing hand in hand beside a gleaming Bentley. Who was he? Some friend from long ago? She supposed Nan had known all sorts of people through the years. People she'd known before she met Matthew's father. People they'd teamed up with on holiday. Vowed to keep in touch. Never had. She'd done that.

There were more pictures of the man. Sitting in a bistro, looked like Paris. And him again with Nan, standing arms round each other, grinning wildly at the camera. Roz held the snap up to her face, peering. She could swear that was Amsterdam. Nan? She'd never mentioned it. Thing was – Roz scrutinised the photo – Nan was wearing her New Year special red dress. Roz could remember when she'd bought it. This photo had been taken since she'd known Nan. Roz shrugged, oh well. You never knew everything about a person, no matter how often you saw them. She could not bring herself to throw the photos out. They were creased. Much handled. She put them in her pocket.

Roz stood up. She'd spent the last three hours bent double. Her back ached. She put her hand on the pain, leaned against it, groaning. Behind her the silence. She turned. Feeling Nan was watching. She felt like a voyeur, riffling through the old lady's life. A stranger, prying. She hated this. She listened to the house, the stillness. Only slight creaks and a clock ticking in the hall downstairs. It was oddly silent without Nan's television playing.

Roz went downstairs to switch on the radio. Find some loud, rubbishy rock'n'roll. The new huge-screen television and video had been removed. Matthew had taken them, along with Nan's hi-fi system that she used to play her Peggy Lee, Perry Como and Mario Lanza CDs. In the back of the hall cupboard Roz found an old wooden radio with large, comforting bakelite knobs. She plugged it in. Twiddled and found what she wanted. Booming out, deep bass. Playing old John Lennon hits. Perfect. Just what she wanted.

A rolling piano. *Imagine* . . . She looked at the sideboard. Opened it. Old shoe boxes crammed with letters, cards, notes. A lifetime of them. She fetched a new bag. There were Christmas cards stretching back to 1957. Seasons greetings from Mavis and Fran? The friends Nan wouldn't let her meet. She found cards to Nan from herself and Matthew. *Love and Christmases from Roz, Matthew, Jamie and Zoe. Though not necessarily in that order.* Roz remembered how witty and pithy she'd thought that at the time. Laid it aside. Couldn't quite throw it out.

There were postcards to Nan from New York, Amsterdam, Dublin, Moscow. She'd stayed still, in her pink chair, but her friends got around.

. . . *All the people* . . . Roz opened the another door on the sideboard. Nan's bills and receipts, in tight elastic-banded bundles.

Gas bills, phone bills, electric bills from ten years ago till the last quarter, carefully preserved. Kept lest the gasman came to cut her off. She'd show him proof. Roz flicked through them. Receipts for a mattress bought eight years ago, a coat from twelve years ago, a toaster three years ago. Kept because Nan seemed incapable of throwing anything away. (Roz had already found and disposed of three sets of false teeth, a pack of condoms and several squeezed-empty tubes of haemorrhoid cream, and felt she now knew more about Nan than she wanted to.)

Propped against the back of the sideboard, Roz found a fat envelope, sealed, and on the front, *To Roz*, written in Nan's recent wavering hand. She turned it over, considering it, before carefully lifting the glued flap. Inside was a letter and a ring. A beautiful thing, dark blue sapphires and diamonds. She slipped it on her finger, held her hand in front of her, admiring it. Then read the letter. Pages of it.

Dear Roz,

I'm hiding this behind my old bills. Matthew will never look there. And I know it'll be you empties my house. You'll see I've given you my ring. It's a lovely thing. A secret thing. It's from my Billy. And none of you knows nothing about him.

I have to tell you I've had my day. You think you were bad, walking out. I was worse. Billy saved me. God knows what would've become of me if he hadn't come along. I was past forty when we met again. And I fell in love with him. Past forty and in love for the first time in my life. Sad, really.

I was seventeen when I discovered sex. Oh my. What a discovery! I thought I was the only one doing it. I thought about it all the time. I was seeing Billy then. We'd sneak off to the park. The excitement of it. I could hardly function for thinking about the next time I'd see him. My father didn't like him. He probably guessed. No probably about it – he guessed. You can always tell when your kids start having sex. Their skin clears up. Mine started to glow.

We went out for two years, me and Billy. Going steady,

though I don't think we called it that then. We weren't engaged, but everyone thought we'd get married. Only Billy went off. He joined the Merchant Navy, and that was that.

If it bothered me, it must have hit some spot deep inside that I didn't acknowledge. Soon as he left, I was out dancing. My life was a jig, then.

Dances I did. Long ago. When I was young. When I believed in thrills and sought them out. Strip the Willow, Dashing White Sergeant, things like that. We did them in the gym, pre-Christmas under the critical scrutiny of teachers. Begowned bullies who sought to teach young souls to socialise, and doing so, spoiled the dance.

But there I was, all those years ago, alone amidst the musical hurtle. Thrust forward, twirling with strangers. Arm in arm and round and round. Then on to the next one. The rage, the rage of Celtic tunes. Dancing, and breathless. Then it all would stop. And there was me. Alone again and headed for the corner. You'd think that after that, soon as I could, I'd give up the dance. But I didn't. Couldn't. Those painful school dance rehearsals had just been a practice for what lay ahead for me. My life was like that.

After Billy left I had affairs. I sit here in my living room with the sparrows out the window, bickering over the crumbs I've spread, and afternoon rubbish on telly, and I try to remember all the men. Thirteen I get to, fourteen. But there were more. I know there were.

It was the night. I loved the night. City night. Calls in the street. The smell of drinking. The lights. The feeling when you were out in the night, part of the night, and something was about to happen. Never did. But just the anticipation that it might was enough. A tingle it was. I was mad for it. Mad for sex. The touch of men. The feel of their skin. I got myself a reputation.

One day my daddy came at me with his belt. He hit me and hit me. He was so ashamed of me. It went on and on. I thought it'd never stop. It hurt. And he was shouting, 'Hoor, hoor.' The buckle curled round me each blow, and cut into me. I've the marks yet. He kept on till he was all angered out. Then he stood, breathing. And spat at me. And kicked me. Broke a rib.

Women then didn't sleep around. You were a virgin when you married and were expected to never stray. Though lots did. Kept it secret.

But I couldn't help it. I just loved men. The feel of them. Their voices in my ear. The roughness of their cheeks. And sex, it was lovely. Just lovely. I tell you, Roz, and I hate to say this, it's rude, and I wasn't brought up to be rude, but I was wet constantly for about five years.

Then I met Alec, Matthew's dad. Actually I'd met him before the beating from my daddy. But I didn't think nothing of him. He was boring. Didn't dance. We met at a Conservative Party do. Not that I was a member nor nothing. I just went along because folks did. It was the in thing to do. Actually, we were all poor with no prospects. I think it just made us feel like we were rubbing shoulders with the gentry.

Anyway, after my beating, I was covered with welts, sore red weals on my back, over my bum. I bled. And my eyes were black. My lips swollen. Couldn't hardly speak. It hurt to speak, to cry, to smile – though I wasn't doing that much. Everything hurt. Lying down. Sitting still. Walking. Every movement, every breath I was reminded of the whore I was.

I was so angry at him. God, I raged. I raged and I felt humiliated, dirty. I didn't want nobody to know. I didn't want to see anybody. The surprise and horror when I looked at myself in the mirror. 'Is that me?' A beat-up, mournful person looking back at me. Haunted eyes. And, 'Jesus Christ, is that me?' The shock of it. Horrible, I looked. I stayed in for weeks.

I miscarried a baby. Don't know whose it was. I didn't tell anybody. I just dealt with it. I had cramps that bent me double. And I bled and bled. I sat in that bathroom of ours. Cold place, dirty yellow walls, and squares of newspaper to wipe your bum, listening to my own crying. I wasn't crying for me. But the baby. I thought it was my fault. I'd done it with my sleeping around. Funny thing was, I imagined it was a boy. And it'd look like Billy.

Of course it was just libido. And young energy. If it was now I'd have somewhere to put it all. A career. I'd probably work so hard I'd have nothing left for sex. But back then there wasn't the education, especially for girls. Roz, I left school at fourteen. Went to work in the dairy. In the creamery. Four of us. Wasn't much call for cream back then. Rich folks bought it. We put evaporated milk on our strawberries. If we had strawberries. I was past thirty when I first ate one. I couldn't believe it. All that pinky sweetness pouring into my mouth.

Well, Alec came to find me on account of I hadn't been around for a time. I went to the door, bruises yellow now, lip still swole up. He took one look at me, and said, 'Come away with me. Now.' I packed my bags (not that I had much worth packing) and went. Never saw my father or my mother – she stood back and let him beat me – again. Never went to either of their funerals. Nothing. I married Alec.

We bought this house. Fifty years I've lived here. Poky wee house. Never liked it much.

I settled down. Did the thing. Baked fruit cakes for tea. Polished the lino Wednesdays. Mondays were for the washing. Tuesday ironing. Thursdays I did the bedroom and scrubbed the loo. Fridays I shopped. I hoovered the carpets, starched collars, weeded the garden. I was bored stiff. Well, no, the garden, I never minded that. Except Alec always mowed the lawn Sundays. Said I never made a proper job of it.

Then came the war. I loved the war. I know I shouldn't say that, folks dying. But it was a lovely time for me. I worked in London for a while. Following Alec before he got sent abroad. After he'd gone I stayed there. There was a bonding. Folks spoke. Don't do that now. Lost the knack of chatting in queues. It's them tabloids. All that stuff about psychos knifing you.

Really, Roz, if you put a hundred people in a room, how many people would be nutty? Three, maybe. Only folks don't speak 'cos they always think that it's them that's next to the loony. Even when I go to the hospital for my check-ups, I'm sitting in the waiting room next to another old biddy and we hardly say a word. We're both looking at each other, thinking, My God, do I look like that?

Age takes you by surprise. You look at yourself in the mirror and think, Is that me? What happened? When you're away from the mirror you don't imagine yourself like that. You stick in your mind as somewhere about thirty-nine. Anyway, I loved the war. Parties. Singing. I think I drank a lot of gin. And yes, there were men. Some of them died.

Then Alec came home. We came back here. I got pregnant. And miscarried. I cried for weeks. Pregnant again. Miscarried again. More crying. I dreamed of babies floating away down the Forth. I thought I was paying for my sins. My wild times. I was a wicked woman. I deserved this. I miscarried again.

I think I slipped into some sort of terrible despond. Everything seemed hollow. Empty. I had the feeling everyone in the world knew how useless I was, letting Alec down. He so wanted a child. I felt there was a stigma about me. People were whispering behind my back. And sympathy. I hated that. Sympathy saps your will, makes you weep openly. I think back to that time and I remember staying still for hours and hours. Staring. There were tunes I couldn't stand because they'd been on the wireless when I was bleeding. Guy Mitchell, 'She Wore Red Feathers'. Daft song.

I got so's I hated going to the loo. Always looking for blood. And nobody to talk to. My mother and father would just have said I'd had it coming.

Depressed? I don't think I smiled for two years. I could hear the depression in my head. A hum, a hollow, empty, loveless place I was in. Just me. I was a failure. A failed woman. I was letting everyone down. I let myself go. Didn't care how I looked. Ate too many biscuits. Sat about the house. Hated seeing babies. I got so I wanted one so bad, I didn't know if I wanted a child or just to know that I could actually produce one. I was in awful pain.

In them days they just shipped you into hospital, gave you a swift D and C and shipped you home again. Slap on the back and 'Better luck next time.' There was no counselling nor nothing. If you were just bleeding they'd make you lie in bed till the dangerous time was over. Doctors coming round once a day to loom over you and talk in loud voices about your problems and the shape of your womb. Made you blush. Shame. Shame. Shame. It was all shame. And guilt.

Seemed like every other month the ambulance came, wheeled me away. Ambulancemen complaining about the weight of me as they stretchered me up the path. Once they went off and had a cup of tea whilst I lay bleeding in the back. They forgot about me. And me too ashamed of myself and guilty to complain. Nasty buggers. Wouldn't do that these days.

Then I got pregnant. And they took me into hospital. Months I had to lie. Just lie. Bedded. Not even getting up for a pee. Bedpans. I hate them. And bed baths. No privacy. Folk poking at your secret bits. Twice a day this midget nurse came by to listen to Matthew (for that was him) inside me with that long earphone thing. Pressed into me. Her on a box on account of how wee she was.

Bored. God, you don't know how bored. I feel for folks in prison. That institutional life. You live for the sound of tea trolleys. Me and the woman next to me used to play skimming the digestive biscuit out of the window. Till mine skimmed out and hit Matron in the eye. Six months gone, they let me home. I remember being surprised to see carpets. Hospitals were all shiny lino.

Then Matthew was born. I loved him. Carried him everywhere with me. Him hanging on to my hair, me clutching him close for fear he would die on me. I waited daily for death. Loomed over his cot, listening to him breathe. We bought him the best of everything. Clothes, toys. He never wanted for nothing. I insisted his pram came from Jenners. Nothing too much for my boy.

I think he was about five, gone to school, when the wildness came on me again. I longed to be out at midnight. On the streets and singing. Gin inside me. A man on my arm. I told Alec I'd joined a dance class – ballroom – and off I went carousing. Shameful, me. The rest of the week I did the housewife thing. Polishing. Shoving stuff down the loo. Baking Swiss rolls and scones. Fridays I was me. I lived for Fridays. Nobody knew.

Roz looked up. 'Imagine' had long stopped. They were playing some more oldies. 'The Sound of Silence'. 'My God,' she said. 'Nan.' Then again, 'Nan?' She returned to the letter.

Funny how things happen. I tell you, girl, I was on my way down. When you're knocking on, wildness doesn't suit you. It was the sixties. The Beatles were on the radio, we'd stopped calling it the wireless. We were all modern now. I had a fridge. Fitted carpets. No more lino-polishing. Alec had a car, a red Mini, standing gleaming in the driveway. I was making chips. Fat sizzling in the pan. Potatoes chopped and waiting to be dipped in, fat sparking. I'd spread out the *Scotsman* to wrap the peelings before putting them in the bin. And there he was, smiling at me. Billy. Big businessman now. Owned a haulage firm. Lived in Morningside, big house. Him, only twenty minutes on the bus and twenty years away.

I wrote to him.

Is this letter too long? I just seem to have started writing and I can't stop. My life.

Two days later he phoned me. We arranged to meet at the North British Hotel, as it was called then. Posh. I was late. It didn't do for a woman to be sitting alone in a bar. Though, heaven knows, I'd done it often enough. I saw him across the room and something happened to me. Boom. Something inside. It was like the room stopped, everything stopped, except my heart. And my stomach. They were whirring inside me. Love it was. And me past forty.

That was that. I never saw another man after Billy. We booked a room and made love. Not sex. Love. I felt the very room was pouring with it. Through the dark.

Talking about never seeing another man, I think of all the men I went with, and you know, I wonder what made me do it. I think it was power. I found I could make men writhe and pant, and shout out. I could control them. There's things you can do to them and they just come. Yelling.

'What?' said Roz. 'Tell me.'

And I'd do it. They'd be on top of me, and I'd be laughing at them. I don't think, till Billy, I liked men. I think I was taking revenge on account of what my father did. Of course I liked Alec. He was boring, but kind. Very kind. Too kind.

I told Billy everything. He saw the marks on my back and my belly and I had to say how I got them. Old scars, white now. He kissed them.

I saw Billy Tuesdays when I told Alec I was going to ballroom dancing, and Sundays when I told him I was seeing Fran and Mavis. No such people. I invented them. It was our joke; he even sent me Christmas cards from them. And birthday cards, and little notes. I sent him cards from all the gang at The Sweet Hollow Trucking Company.

Twice a year I went off with Mavis and Fran. Billy really. We went to Amsterdam, Paris, Rome, Florence. We even went to India once. I had a hell of a job explaining my tan, since I said Fran and Mavis lived in Paisley. They hadn't a phone. Oh, Roz, me and Billy went all over the world. I had a secret passport hidden in a Tampax box in my bedside dresser. One place Alec would never look. He hated women's things, troubles. Stuff like that. Shut it out.

Once a year, September time, we went to Mull. Lovely place. White beaches. Dolphins sloping by, in green seas. And down the south end, huge rock faces, all layered, lines. It's like standing looking at the centuries they've seen. Tiny roads. Dragonflies you've never seen the like of in your life. Eagles.

We always saw an eagle. It's like they rise up, five o'clock, shrieking, announcing their place in the sky. We were happy there. Scatter me there. I can't lie beside Billy, but I can forever be where we loved most.

Dammit, thought Roz. Now I'll have to go. She had been going to cheat. Scatter Nan on Portobello beach, or off the Forth Bridge. But now, knowing this, she had to let the old lady lie where she longed to be.

Alec and Matthew were close. Going off to football matches every Saturday. Making model aeroplanes. Talking about cars. They shut me out. Matthew always preferred him to me. A man's man.

And I saw Billy. I was happy. We'd lock ourselves in a hotel room, and the things we did. I'd dress as a French maid for him. Positions, oh yes. But I don't expect that's what you want to hear from an old lady.

Roz nodded. 'No, I don't.'

Things he did for me – I'm not telling. But I was in heaven. After forty, I had a wonderful sex life. Folks said I glowed. I never told nobody why.

'Nan,' Roz said again. 'Nan?' She was still sitting scrunged beside the sideboard. When she stood, her leg had gone to sleep. She stamped till the blood fizzed back through it. She hobbled to the kitchen, made tea. Brought it back to the living room, to sit in Nan's chair and finish the letter. The scrawly epistle from beyond the grave. Nan's life.

Then I made the Big Mistake. Well, I would. Sinners, liars always do. Alec was ill. Prostate. He was taken into hospital. Never came out. He was sixty-six. I'd been seeing Billy for twenty years. If Alec knew, and I think he did, I know he did, he never said. Not till the end. Last words he said to me, 'Well, you've been happy. You've had it all your own way.' Then he died.

I was sixty-five. For the first time, Billy came to see me. He parked his Bentley (oh yes, he was rich) two streets away. I was sitting in the living room having a wee cry for Alec. I felt bad about all I'd done. Well, Billy pulled me to my feet and cuddled me. He was a big man. 'Come on, Nan,' he says, 'cheer up. What's done's done. And don't tell me you'd change any of it.' He was right, I wouldn't.

One thing led to another, and we went up to the bedroom. We were, as they say, going at it. Very noisy. There's something about sex as a comfort for grief. You let go in a different way. A deeper howl. Something made me stop. I don't know. That something when you know someone's watching you. I looked over Billy's shoulder. Matthew was standing in the doorway watching us. Me and Billy starkers and screaming ecstasy.

Matthew looked drained. A face stricken with shock. I'll never forget that. When I got up to go to him, he just looked at me, 'You whore,' he said.

Don't blame him. Turns out he'd come over to see if I was all right. If I needed company. He wanted to talk about his dad. He loved his dad. He hardly spoke to me again. It was my fault. But I was only taking a bit of comfort. Matthew wouldn't understand that.

I still saw Billy. Nothing would stop me. Tuesdays and Sundays. No telling lies now. He wouldn't leave his wife and daughter. Said he loved me. Owed them.

Then one day I went to the North British and he didn't come up. I waited and waited. Heart black with worry. Billy didn't come. Couple of days later I looked in the obituaries (you do when you get on a bit) and there he was. William McKormak Robertson, peacefully at home on 15 September, beloved husband of Mary, father of Sophie and friend of many. Service at Warriston on 20th. Donations to the British Heart Foundation.

His poor old heart, great big heart, had given out on him.

I went to the crematorium but didn't go in. I just watched the folks gather and come out again after. I sent a single red rose, no name. I'll never know what his Mary made of it.

That was me. Twenty-odd years of foolishness. Twenty or so of happiness. Then another fifteen thinking back, being alone. I have my memories. I've been happy.

But that's how I know it'll be you cleans out my house. Matthew won't come near. Scared what he'll find. And that Claire doesn't care. Feels it's nothing to do with her. Neither is it.

See, I think what you did was honest. You didn't lie. Shame about Matthew. Uptight. Never lets go. Trusts nobody. My fault. Me and my libido. And my love. I bet he never told you about finding me and Billy.

And I bet that's why he counts. Sort of holding on to things. Keeping everything in its place. No more shocks. You know what they say. There's safety in numbers. Pathetic, guilty old woman's joke.

But here's Billy's ring. He gave it me on our first night away. In Amsterdam. Wear it. It's lucky.

And that's that. Keep well. Follow your heart. And do what's right. You'll know when the time comes. When we first met I had a soft spot for you. And later, when I knew you, I loved you. And see, everything isn't your fault. It's my fault. I started the whole family turmoil. Me and my libido.

Nan. xxx

Roz put the letter down. Her tea had gone cold. 'My God, Nan,' was all she could say. She was stunned. Stared at the wall. 'Nan. My God, Nan.' She turned the last page over. A swift PS.

Don't worry about coming across the French maid's outfit when you clean out my bedroom. It's long gone.

Yes, she had been vaguely worrying about that. Nan knew everything.

CHAPTER TWENTY-NINE

Next day Roz phoned Connie to tell her the Beseleys would be coming from Edinburgh on a disk and she'd be back as soon as she could.

'How long are you going to be away?' Connie wanted to know. 'Only, I mightn't be here.'

'Two weeks. More. Maybe. I don't know. Where are you going?'

'I'll tell you when I see you. Can't you just stuff things into bags and throw them out for the bin men?'

'That's what I thought I'd do. That's how I thought it'd take a couple of days. But now I've got to look at everything. It's more complicated than I thought.'

She set up her work on a table by the window. Cleaned out rooms till late afternoon. Made tea and a sandwich. Worked from five till late.

Zoe came and went. Didn't help. 'It's too painful.'

Over the days, Roz uncovered Nan's life. News cuttings – Matthew winning a prize with the school chess team. Alec's obituary. Matthew's birth announcement. She kept them all. Old birthday cards, postcards from friends – into the bin with them. Hand-written recipes in a fat-spattered, stained notebook – kept. A Chalmers dictionary with wild flowers pressed in between the pages – kept. A couple of insurance policies – set aside for Matthew. Alec's death certificate – for Matthew. On and on. Things. A life. Roz sifted through every piece of paper, every postcard, every old bill.

Apart from the odd photograph and cards from Mavis and Fran, she found little of the truth. It took a week to go through the living room, dining room and kitchen. To pack everything in boxes and take what was worthy to the Oxfam shop.

Meantime the Beseleys bickered and fought. The air round them strained. Pam and Frank were facing difficult times. Pam stared out the kitchen window and longed for something. She didn't know what. Excitement? Fulfilment? Tenderness? One of those. All of those.

In her second week, Christmas days away, Roz started on the bedrooms. First the spare room, where Zoe was sleeping. Nothing much there. A few cracked ornaments. Some clothes so old they'd come out of fashion, into fashion, out again, time after time. But they were faded. And cheap. Relics of Nan's carousing days. Wondering what naughtiness these frocks and skirts had known, Roz lifted them to her nose, inhaled. She could smell Nan's gardenia perfume, with a slight after-waft of gin. Into the bin with them.

Slowly the house changed from the home that Nan had lived in to a place filled with boxes and overstuffed black bin bags. It got sparser and sparser. Zoe liked it. 'A certain minimalism,' she claimed. 'We could lift the carpets, polish the wooden floors, paint it all white.'

'It's going up for sale,' said Roz. She was feeling grubby and worn out from all the heaving and packing and discarding useless things – a waffle iron, a greasy sandwich toaster, an ancient electric frying pan.

'The new décor would up the price by thousands. I have a feel for decorating. Connie said so.'

'Connie?'

'Yes. She offered me work doing interiors for her new magazine.'

'Connie? New magazine?' Roz felt a stab of jealousy. And fear. If Connie was moving on, what would happen to her?

'Yes,' said Zoe mildly, unaware of the chaos she had caused in Roz's head, her stomach. 'Don't you just love wood?' She stroked Nan's sideboard, empty now. A huge thing, mirror atop. 'We could strip this and lime it. It'd be wonderful.'

'It's going to the sale room,' Roz told her flatly. She wanted to pursue the Connie conversation.

'Still,' said Zoe, 'I think I'll do it. It's the wood. And the craftsmanship. It's wonderful.' She got her coat. 'I'm off to get the stuff. Can I take the car?'

Roz threw her the keys, gladly. With Zoe out of the way she could nurse her resentment in peace. And consider the new Connie. Somewhere, at some time, Connie had ceased to be the young woman hiding in middle-aged outfits, waltzing the corridors on shy tiptoes, using charmingly outdated language, 'Pardon me for interceding at this juncture.' She had become assertive, modern, bought shorter skirts, jackets, had her hair bobbed and knew how to handle people. It was necessary, Roz supposed. But the old Connie had a certain quaintness. Roz missed her.

After lunch Matthew phoned. He wanted to know how Roz was getting on. 'Nearly done?' he asked.

'A bit to do,' said Roz. 'But we're getting there.' We? she thought. Why am I saying that? I'm doing this on my own.

'Did you find anything interesting?' he asked.

Roz told him no.

Zoe returned. She'd bought paint-stripper. A hot-air gun. Wire wool.

'Where did you get the money for all that?' Roz wanted to know.

'I've still got a secret credit card Will hasn't stopped.' She waved it. Gleefully.

'Right,' said Roz. 'Do it. But not in here. Move the thing into the dining room. I don't want the smell of that stripping stuff.'

Together they heaved the old sideboard down the hall, tiny shuffling steps. Wheezing and each complaining the other wasn't doing her bit. They bickered, but their bickering had become affable.

'Christ, this is heavy,' said Roz.

'It isn't really,' Zoe panted. 'It's you. You're getting old.'

Sideboard in place, Zoe started work. As the afternoon drifted into evening, she and Roz traded friendly insults whenever they came across one another. They had stopped bickering, started to banter.

The home they were in was being dismantled. No longer welcoming. Heaps of papers, black bags and cardboard boxes in the hall. It wasn't cold, really. It just felt like it was.

Roz emptied the last of Nan's drawers. Cosy floral nightdresses. A couple of discarded pairs of spectacles. An empty bottle of Chanel No. 5. Sets of beads, a string of pearls. She left the old Tampax box in the bedside cabinet. Somehow, looking into it seemed nosy.

Four o'clock. Lights on throughout the house. Zoe busy downstairs, music booming up. Oasis on the radio. Roz lay on Nan's bed. Stared at the ceiling. She could not face clearing out Matthew's room. Outside in the garden birds were squabbling, a small frenzy of sparrows. Noises. Other people's lives. Children arriving home from school. Car doors slamming. Young voices calling. Pull the curtains, switch on the telly, raid the biscuit tin and make a mug of coffee. Home life.

Years ago, thirty years younger, she had gone home on the bus, upstairs so she could catch swift glimpses of passing living rooms. People moving about, living their lives. Things folk got up to in their living rooms fascinated her. Her best friend practised her piano for two hours every day. The fumbling scales moved, in time, to perfect tunes – Mozart, Chopin. The neighbours next door used to collect beer mats. Often they'd fetch them out, thumb through them, reminiscing about bars across the globe they'd visited. Mr and Mrs Morgan round the corner danced. Nights they'd roll back the carpet, put Mantovani on their old gramophone and waltz. Her in an elaborate sequined gown – each sparkling coloured speck hand-sewn – him in tails. At the time she'd thought them daft. Now, thinking about it, she decided it was lovely. Here, in this house, Nan had made soup in her big pot – ham bone, lentils – pressed shirts, watered her garden, fed the sparrows and dreamed of her secret love.

CHAPTER THIRTY

'I have to see you,' said Roz.

'Why?' said Matthew.

'It's time we spoke, exchanged words. I'm going up town to shop. I'll see you in Princes Street gardens. West End, two o'clock.'

'I'm working.'

'Take time off.' She hung up.

She took the bus into town; parking was hell. She bought Zoe a book on furniture restoration, and some Aveda toiletries to make up for the downmarket bath foam in her flat. A shirt and some Mozart for Will. A couple of games for Toby's Playstation, some chocolate, a kite that she sensed she liked more than he would, and a microscope with slides. She figured a child that intense might find some wonderment in gazing down at bits of butterfly, spider and honey bee.

Matthew was sitting on a bench looking on to the fountain. Somewhere a brass band was playing carols. 'Once in Royal David's City'. 'Hark the Herald Angels Sing'. She always liked that one. She thought the best bit of Christmas was the lead-in. The days before the Big Day. Shopping. Buying little treats. Walking, collar up against the cold, through thronging streets. She worked alone in her tiny flat. News from other parts of the planet boomed in at her on the hour every hour. She often felt things were happening everywhere, the world was hurtling round her, as she sat still hoping the phone would ring. This contact with other beings going about the same business as she was was always comforting.

She sat on the bench with Matthew.

'Been shopping?' he asked.

'Just a few things for Zoe and Will, and Toby.'

He nodded.

She shivered. 'God, when Edinburgh gets cold, it gets cold. Still, it's pretty. It's a city that can't help being pretty.' She looked round at the castle, at the church.

He shrugged.

'I found a letter from Nan,' Roz said. 'She told me about you finding her in bed with another man a few days after your father died.'

'Right,' said Matthew. Painfully.

'Is that it?' Roz asked. 'Please don't tell me that's why you went all silent. Disappeared into yourself.'

'She was having sex. I'd never seen the bloke before. It was disgusting. She was old.'

'So?' said Roz. 'What's wrong with old?'

'They were making a noise.'

'And you don't? No, you don't. I remember. He was her first love. They'd met again after you were born. They'd been seeing each other for years.'

'She was being unfaithful to my father. He was a good man.'

'I know. I know. But somehow, the way Nan tells it – it's lovely. Did you talk to her about it?'

He shook his head.

'Did she talk to you?'

'She tried. I wouldn't listen. She kept on seeing her fancy man, though.'

'Listen to you,' said Roz. 'Fancy man. Matthew, forgive her. She was lovely.'

It started to drizzle. She thought drizzle was like non-rain. You hardly noticed it till you were soaked. It seeped through your clothes, plastered your hair to your head. They sat, staring ahead. Silent and nervy. The band started 'The Holly and The Ivy'. Even the carol sounded damp.

He was turned away. Not looking at her.

'Matthew,' she said. 'There was Nan sitting in that living room of hers on her chair watching soaps, and us all fussing round her.

And her watching us, ticking us off, dispensing advice. Us all thinking she was a sweet old lady. And she had a million secrets. Some of them painful. All of them naughty. Matthew,' she reached out to touch his arm, 'it's funny.'

'I don't find it funny.'

'It is,' she assured him. 'It really, really is.'

He moved his arm from her touch.

'Oh, Matthew,' she said gently. 'What are we going to do with you?'

'I don't know.'

'What happened to us, Matthew?' Roz asked.

'We got married too young. We weren't ready. We grew up. Grew out of each other.'

An office party, city suits, tinsel-draped, carrying champagne and balloons, moved down the slope towards them. Their slightly drunken afternoon merriment echoed through the sweeping wetness.

'On a sourer note,' Roz said, gathering her bags, 'why didn't you give Zoe and Jamie the presents I sent them?'

The giggling gaggle reached the bottom of the path. Started across the gardens, passing them.

'Why should I have given them your gifts? You were away having a fine time. Why should you get to send them things? I was looking after them. I was paying the bills.'

'I sent money. More than I could afford.'

He snorted.

The passing gigglers turned to look at him. And her.

'I loved them,' Matthew said, louder than he'd meant to. 'My children. I didn't want them to love you.'

The gigglers looked interested.

'If I'd given them the things you sent, they'd have wanted you. They'd have started preferring you to me. It was always the same. People liked you best. Even Nan. Even my own mother,' Matthew near-as-dammit shouted. He was not a person given to shouting. The gigglers stopped, turned and watched.

Roz got up. 'She had a soft spot for me,' she said. 'That was all.

She told me.' She did not tell him that Nan had told her she loved her. She walked away. Didn't look back.

The gigglers lost interest. Walked on. Matthew sat alone, looking at the fountain.

Back on Princes Street, she pushed and jostled through the crowds, making her way towards Will's bookshop. She was just homing in on someone she could talk to, a friendly ear.

The shop was crowded. Will was behind the counter totting up the price of a pile of Christmas gift paperbacks. Roz stood in front of him. Shoving his customer to one side. Dripping. Mascara running, 'Sorry,' she said.

'Sorry?' to Roz. 'Thirty-five pounds ninety-four, please,' to his customer.

'Yes,' said Roz. 'You're busy. I shouldn't have come. I just wanted to see you.'

'That's nice.' He took the proffered credit card. Swiped it. Waited for it to register. Smiling at her. 'You seem in a bit of a state.'

'It's raining,' she said. Looking down at herself. Her sopping coat. Soggy shoes. 'Sorry,' she said again.

'Stop apologising,' Will told her.

The receipt started to rattle through. Will handed it over to be signed. Packed the books. Came round to the front of the counter and ushered Roz through to the stockroom. Piles of books. Cardboard boxes full of more books. A desk with a flickering computer and piles of invoices. A kettle, tea-stained mugs. And a beaten-up armchair before a blasting electric fire, where Will made himself comfortable, reading, in late January and February when sales dropped off and the shop was empty. He helped her off with her coat. 'State of you.'

'I've been talking to Matthew,' she told him.

'Talking to Matthew? That's a first.'

She shivered. 'You know how you go through life and inside yourself you think you're a mess. Lurking in the depths of your head is a bubbling broth of insecurities, emotions, unaddressed fears. And you look out from yourself and you think everyone you see is fine. And you think you're the only one who's screwed up.'

Will nodded. Begrudgingly. 'Uh-huh.'

'Well, when you talk to Matthew you feel like you're the one who is fine. And he's the one with the emotional broth.'

He put his hand under her chin. 'You're soaked,' he told her. Kissed her lightly. A peck.

She clung to him. Arms round him. Holding on. 'Say something nice to me.'

He could think of nothing nice. He held her at arm's length. Thinking, something nice? Something nice? 'You look shitty.' Handing her a hankie.

She took it, blew her nose. 'That'll do.'

Marcia, his part-time assistant, working full-time during the school holidays, came through to fetch him. 'It's hell out there. Are you coming?'

'Yes,' said Will. 'In a minute.'

'In a minute won't do. I can't cope.'

Will kissed Roz lightly once more. Told her to make herself comfortable. Have a cup of tea. He'd be with her soon.

'Who's that?' Marcia asked when he joined her behind the counter.

'Zoe's mother,' said Will.

'Her mother!' said Marcia, looking at him. 'Christ, families.' Taking books from a customer. 'And to think I thought you were boring.'

'Thank you for that,' said Will. 'You've made my day.'

It was almost eight before Will closed up the shop. Roz had been in the stockroom since half past three. She liked it there. She dried out. Fixed her hair and make-up. Then sat reading, waiting for Will to finish work.

They went down into Stockbridge to find somewhere to eat. Zoe had picked up Toby and taken him back to Nan's to show him her handiwork.

They ordered pasta and a bottle of red. Fiddled with the cutlery as they waited for their food.

'So what did Matthew say when he was actually talking?' Will wanted to know.

Roz sighed. Made a face. Wondered if she should tell him. 'He said,' she decided she would, 'that he didn't give Zoe and Jamie the presents I sent them because that would make them love me more than they did him. He said people loved me more than him. Even Nan.' She tried hard not to look smug about this.

'Well,' said Will. He couldn't think of anything else. He thought that Matthew was right.

'And,' said Roz, slowly, 'he said he'd never forgive Nan. Because not long after his dad died he came into the house unexpectedly and found her in bed with another man.'

Will leaned forward. 'Nan?'

Roz nodded. 'Nan.' She grinned. 'Our Nan. Turns out she was having a long-term affair with a bloke from her past.' She leaned towards him. Faces close. 'It was love. They went all over the world together.'

Will responded as she had when she read the letter. 'Nan?' he said. 'Nan?' Then he leaned back. Clapped his hands. 'I love it.' He filled their glasses. Raised his. 'Nan,' he said.

'Nan,' Roz joined the toast. 'Our Nan.' She drank. 'Before she got together with this Billy who was the love of her life, she had all sorts of affairs. She was a real goer. One-night stands.'

'So,' said Will, 'that's where Zoe gets it.'

'I'd love to agree with that. It'd let me off the hook. But I think my leaving has a lot to do with this rejecting people before they reject her.' She hiccupped. 'Sorry. I haven't eaten today.'

'Why not?'

'I forgot.'

Wasn't it always the way? Will thought, looking up. You look for someone every day for ages, then just when you don't really want to see them, there they are coming across the room towards you, smiling, rosily friendly with drink. It was Marianne. His guardian angel.

'I thought it was you. Haven't seen you for months. Where have you been?'

'Here,' said Will. 'In London for a while.'

'Ah, right.' She looked at Roz.

'This is Roz,' said Will. 'Roz, Marianne.' He wondered if he should tell Marianne who Roz was. Decided not to.

Roz smiled hello. Marianne smiled it back. They considered one another, trying to figure out where they'd met before.

Scrutinising Marianne, Roz said, 'Don't I know you? Haven't we met?'

'Strange you should say that. I was just thinking the very same thing.'

Marianne took off her coat, slung it over a chair.

'Won't you join us?' asked Roz. Not necessary. Marianne was joining them.

'Christmas, eh?' said Marianne. 'Who needs it? A fuck of a thing. I never know what to get folk. Then, this year everyone's coming to me.'

Will imagined a bunch of bohemian, slightly elderly people in velvet jackets sipping sherry and discussing opera. Though plainly the woman was a tad more vulgar than that.

'I've ordered a turkey. Got in the sprouts. Though I hate them. Put up a tree. All the trimmings. But it's not the same. We used to go to my mother's. But she died a few months back. I just don't feel Christmassy.'

Roz flushed. She remembered where she'd seen this woman. At that funeral. The one that she went to by mistake. The fabulous one where people cried and sang. This woman had been weeping floods as everyone joined in 'Knockin' On Heaven's Door'.

Marianne noticed the sudden rush of colour to Roz's cheeks. 'Something the matter?'

'No, no,' said Roz. 'I just remembered something, that's all.'

'Ah, right,' said Marianne. 'Brains are like that. Always bringing up stuff you want to forget.'

The food arrived. Rather than look at the menu, Marianne ordered the same as Roz and another bottle of wine. Through dinner she carried the conversation. Books, music, her family, Christmas. Roz and Will spent the evening saying yes, and hmm, and I know. It wasn't the intimacy they'd both secretly hoped for.

As they waited for coffee, Will excused himself and went to the loo.

'Do you like funerals, then?' Marianne leaned over the table to Roz as soon as he'd gone. 'I remembered where I saw you.'

'No,' said Roz. 'Not really. But your mother's was a cracker.'

'Was that.'

'I came to it by mistake. Nan, my mother-in-law, was the one after. I got the time wrong.'

'They get you like that.'

'She must've been loved. Your mother.'

'Aye. She was. It was easy to love her. She made it easy. Loved everyone. Criticised nobody. Never raised her voice. Left that to me. Behind every lovable person is a bully screaming, "You be nice to my beloved." '

'Probably,' Roz agreed. She put her elbows on the table. Rubbed her face. 'Oh God.'

'Been a day, has it?'

Roz nodded. 'I had words with my ex. He would appear to have been jealous of me. He thought people preferred me to him.'

'Ah,' said Marianne. 'Bit mixed up when your marriage turns into some sort of sibling rivalry. I hope you smacked him on the jaw and told him to stop being silly.'

'No,' said Roz, shocked. 'I've never smacked anyone in my life. Is that what you do?'

'Nah,' said Marianne. 'In my dreams. The number of moments I've relived in my head where I just whack someone. Never done it. Sometimes all this liberal, understanding-folk stuff just gets on my tits, though. And I'd like to let go and strike out for political incorrectness. Never done it. Still,' she added, 'it's a lovely bloke you've got.'

'No,' said Roz. 'He's not . . .'

'But you want him to be. That's plain. And he wants you to be. Written all over your faces.'

It was after ten when they left the restaurant. Marianne said goodbye. Went on her way. Roz and Will watched her go.

'I love your friend,' said Roz. 'Even if she talks bollocks. She said I ought to whack Matthew.'

'My guardian angel,' Will took her arm, 'does talk bollocks. But it's good bollocks.'

'Ah,' said Roz. 'The dispenser of advice you haven't got the guts to take. I should get back. I have to work in the morning. Then I'll be done with Nan's place.'

'Going back home for Christmas?'

'I'm going to Mull to scatter Nan's ashes.'

'You're going to Mull for Christmas?'

'Yes.'

'Can I come?'

'Aren't you going to be with Toby?'

'He's going to Matthew's with Zoe. It's best I'm not there. Zoe and me aren't . . .' His voice trailed off. He didn't know how to put it. 'You know.'

'I know,' said Roz, touching his arm. 'But you can't come with me. What would people think?'

'People wouldn't know. I don't want to be alone.'

She shrugged. Thought to act nonchalant, though her stomach was churning, heart racing. She was having trouble breathing. 'Well, come, then.'

They stood looking up the road. Waiting for a taxi. A distant light was coming towards them. Will raised his arm, hailing it. Turned to her, held her. The drizzle continued. Insidious sneaky rain. Soaking them, and them not noticing.

'What if I kissed you?' he said.

'That'd do the trick,' she said, surprising herself. 'That'd be the thing,' she said. 'That'd hit the spot.'

They kissed. Lips. Taste of drizzle and wine and garlic. Pulling each other closer. Losing themselves in each other. Till the taxi stopped beside them. Engine rattling. Roz climbed in. 'I'll phone you,' she said.

The cab rustled along suburban streets. Muted lights, drawn curtains. It was all going on in there. All the stuff nobody talked about. Deceits and betrayals, passions and longings. She wondered if the couple round the corner from her childhood house still danced. Secrets of the living room.

CHAPTER THIRTY-ONE

Once, coming home early evening, Roz had met the woman downstairs whose muffled fights with her partner sounded through the floorboards like a foreign language. Her name was Rosie Dewhurst. Her eye was puffed and bruised purple and yellow.

She caught Roz looking at it, and at her lip, which was split, crusty with healing. 'I fell,' she said. Saw the disbelief spread over Roz's face. 'No, really.' It all spilled out. Her mother had just died. Her father hadn't taken it well and had started to drink. He'd blacked out. It would have been understandable, but when she found him, he'd been lying on the floor wearing his wife's clothes. 'People have their own ways of coping with grief,' she said. 'I can't cope with his.' Then her partner had lost his job, and they were fighting about that. And, oh, her brother had been in a car crash and lost his left arm. 'It never rains,' she said. 'Then I go and do this. I slipped in the bath and hit my face on the cold tap. It could have been worse,' she said, touching her wounds. 'It could've been the hot tap, then I'd've been burned as well.'

'Goodness,' said Roz. It was all she could think of. 'So what are you doing now?'

'I've just been to buy some bananas,' Rosie Dewhurst told her.

Considering all that had happened to her recently, Roz thought she might be lying on the floor screaming. Or taking it easy in bed, forehead swathed in a soothing poultice. But no, she'd been to buy bananas. Life went on. People went to and fro, and nobody knew the turmoil within.

Roz took stock of herself. On the plus side, her daughter was talking about becoming a carpenter or a furniture restorer, her son had definitely found a girlfriend, her grandson had stopped wetting the bed. Against that, her mother-in-law, now deceased, had led a secret wanton life, her ex had found his mother in bed in the throes of ecstasy with a strange man and would never forgive her. She, meantime, was embarking on an affair with her daughter's ex-partner. She really hoped that couple round the corner, old though they might be now, were still dancing. It pleased her to imagine something nice was happening, somewhere.

She made a cup of coffee and phoned Connie. 'You're leaving,' she said.

'Uh-huh,' said Connie.

'What about the Beseleys?' Which meant, what about me?

'What about them?' Which meant, what *about* you?

'Well. They've been bickering and falling out. And Mrs B. isn't happy.' I'm not happy.

'You haven't been doing anything definite with them. Definite things have to happen. People make decisions about their lives.' I've moved on, Roz, why don't you?

'You're saying I can do what I like with them?' I can move on. I can do that.

'Yes.' Move on, then.

'What will Ronnie say when he gets back?' I'm scared.

'I don't care. I won't be here,' Connie said. Meaning, neither should you be.

'So. You're saying I should just go for it. Kill them all off in a bloody road crash. Give Frank syphilis, put Pam on the streets, make Simon a junkie, Susan shoplifting to get money for cocaine – type thing.' I can do it. I can move on. Just watch me.

'Don't be silly, Roz.' There's moving on and there's professional suicide.

'Just joking. Um. Is there work for me on your new magazine?'

'Could be.' Just what are you going to do with the Beseleys? Move on, babe. Take the leap.

'Only, I've got the next few episodes worked out. They're cool. You'll love them.'

'I hope.' Leap, girl, leap.

'You'll see.' I can leap. I don't need to be pushed. 'When's Ronnie coming back anyway?'

'Late January.' About six episodes away.

Pam pressed the off button on the television remote.

'Hey,' shouted Frank. 'I was watching that.'

'No you weren't. You were sleeping.'

'Was not.'

'You were snoring.'

'Was not. Was I? Well, switch it back on again. I'm not snoring now.'

'No. We should talk. We don't talk any more.'

'Don't we? OK. Let's talk. You start.'

She could tell he wasn't enthused. He was indulging her. They stared at the carpet. In the hall, the clock ticked. Water gurgled in the central heating.

Pam pulled her legs up under her. The sound of her tights brushing against the soft velour of the sofa filled the room. 'What were we thinking of?' she said.

It took Roz three hours to finish the piece. She ran it through the spell-check. Clicked on Save. Then before she could change her mind, she ejected the disk, put it in an envelope and took it down to the postbox. First move, she thought. Then onwards. For the Beseleys and me. She went home, started another episode. By midnight she had three done. This was easy writing. The following day, the day before her planned trip with Will, she wrote another three. She collapsed on her bed after posting the disks. Back aching. Nothing in her mind. She thought she'd used up all the language she had.

Christmas Eve, Roz packed the car. She put Nan's ashes in the boot beside her case. Then went indoors to phone Jamie.

'Hi,' said Jamie.

'It's me,' said Roz.

'I know,' said Jamie. 'How are you?'

'Fine. I'm phoning to say I'll be in Mull. I've left the number of the hotel beside the phone if you need me.'

'I know. It's here.'

'What are you doing for Christmas?'

'I'm spending it with a friend.'

'What's her name?'

'Angela.'

'Well, have a good time. And don't make a mess.'

'I won't. Angela won't let me.'

'Excellent,' said Roz. She liked Angela. 'See you when I get back.'

She hung up. Phoned Fred. She got his answering machine. 'I'm off to scatter Nan's ashes over Christmas,' she told him. 'I'll ring you when I get back.' She made to replace the receiver, lifted it to her ear again. 'Um . . . merry Christmas,' she said.

Zoe was working on Nan's sideboard when Roz came to say goodbye to her, guiltily. This is wrong, she told herself, very wrong.

'What's up with you?' asked Zoe.

'Nothing. Just anxious to get going.'

'Time is it?'

'Nine.'

'Time's the ferry?'

'Four.'

Zoe looked vacant for a few seconds, whilst she counted. 'Seven hours you've got to get there.'

'I worry about missing it.'

'You could walk and not miss it.'

'I don't like driving fast.'

'I know. I noticed. Time you started driving like a grown-up. On grown-up roads.'

'I'll see you on the twenty-seventh,' said Roz. 'Here. Merry Christmas.' She handed Zoe her presents. 'Don't open them till tomorrow.'

Zoe shook the ornately wrapped gift, holding it to her ear. Smiling. 'I've got something for you.' She took a parcel from inside her meticulously stripped sideboard, gave it to Roz, who repeated the holding-to-ear, shaking process. Smiling. Their first exchange of gifts in years.

Roz walked through the house. It looked naked. Walls stripped of pictures, bright squares against faded walls. Photographs, trinkets, knick-knacks removed from shelves and surfaces. Drawers emptied. No newspapers. Nan's collections of thrillers and video musicals. All gone.

'Look what we've done,' she said. 'I feel like a vandal. I've de-Naned the place. She's gone. No trace of her left.'

'We've got memories. I still love Nan. I want to be like her. I want to be loved by everybody. To walk,' Zoe was getting carried away with this love notion, 'through the realms of love. Soaking it all up. I am loved. I am loved. Nothing else matters.'

'You better mend your ways,' said Roz sharply. 'And have a bath. You smell of paint-stripper and sweat.'

'I know.' Repentant Zoe. Slightly repentant Zoe.

'You'll need a bully. Someone told me the other day that totally loved people need a backup to do the nasty for them.'

'You can do that,' suggested Zoe. 'Nobody likes you anyway.' Gleeful. Never pass up a chance for a nifty insult. A jokey jibe at her errant mother.

'Thank you for that,' said Roz. 'On that note, I'll leave you. Goodbye and merry Christmas.'

Roz drove into town to pick up Will.

Toby was with his new best friend. A big day ahead. Serious television viewing till it was time to go to a panto. Then back to Matthew and Claire's to spend Christmas Eve with them and Zoe. He'd been high. Jumping about. Anxious to get going. He'd fussed about what he'd wear, refused to eat any breakfast and asked if it was time to go yet fifteen times between half past eight and nine o'clock. Will was wrecked.

They drove to Glasgow in the inside lane, forty-five miles an hour. Will fidgeted. He wanted to keep asking, 'Are we there yet?' This pensioner's pace was killing him. 'You're allowed to go faster,' he told Roz.

'I know. But we'll get there. Plenty of time.' She gripped the wheel. Stared ahead.

Will felt his jaw tighten; he scraped his nails on his thigh. Car like this, they ought to be flying along. Roof down despite the cold. Hair breezing out behind them. Huge expensive mufflers round their necks, superior expressions on their faces.

They reached Oban after two. Killed the time before the ferry left drinking coffee in a steamy café. The last half-hour they spent sitting in the car, Will gazing out to sea, Roz staring at the docking bay, where the ramp would come down.

'Isn't it gorgeous?' said Will. 'The air. The anticipation of travelling across the water.'

'Uh-huh,' said Roz, chewing gum furiously. She was worrying about driving on to the ferry. She feared she'd skid, fall over the edge and into the bay. And die. Trapped in her car. She planned how to get out as water gurgled and poured round her. It started to rain.

The ferry arrived. Bleeping, the ramp clanged on to the dock. Cars drove audaciously on. Roz inched forward. Bumped on to the ramp. A hot sweat dampening her forehead, neck and down between her breasts. Damn you, Nan. She made it into the belly of the boat. Breathed again.

They stood on the deck, leaning on the rails. Watching the spume of water trailing behind the boat. A single seagull, braving the storm, followed them as they moved out into the open channel. The boat heaved from side to side. Rain lashed their faces. Roz stared over to distant mountains, purpling peaks, shrouded with cloud. She worried. This was wrong.

'I think,' said Will, pulling his coat round him, 'that we should go inside.'

The inner deck was packed with rucksacks and cases. People going home for Christmas. A single sheepdog lay, head between paws, staring mournfully ahead. Dogs weren't allowed beyond this point. He looked worried. Roz sympathised.

They went to the bar. Will bought them both a malt. 'Seems the thing to have. Day like this. Place like this.'

They sat clutching their drinks. Said little. Will looked at the other passengers. Barbour-clad, ruddy-faced. Laughing. This time of year, tourist season over, the ferries to the isles became local again. It seemed like everyone knew everyone. They laughed, gossiped. He felt like a gatecrasher in a movable party.

Roz hardly spoke. She worried. This thing she was doing, sneaking off for a dirty Christmas with her daughter's partner, was wrong. She worried about Jamie. What was he up to without her nagging him? She worried about Zoe, who wanted to be loved. This new longing was all her fault. If she hadn't walked out, Zoe would have her act together by now. If anybody ever got their act together. She worried about the Beseleys. What had she done? What would Ronnie say? Would she ever work again? She worried about driving off the boat. She decided she was a good worrier. Perhaps there was an opening somewhere for a full-time, professional agoniser.

She crawled off the boat. Drove along the road towards Tobermory. This was fine. A wide, relatively empty road. She could do this. Herons stooped, hunched small by the shore. Mountains loomed. The air was soft. Rain beat against the window.

'My God,' said Will. 'All that time I stand in the bookshop, or walking to and from work, all this is out here, waiting for me. I didn't know. Didn't know.'

Roz peered over the wheel. The road narrowed to a single track and started to climb. She worried. What if she met a car coming towards her, and there was no passing place? She'd have to reverse. She hated reversing. 'I don't like going backwards,' she said.

Will looked puzzled. Roz slowed to thirty-five miles an hour. Several miles before Tobermory, the road widened again. Roz breathed relief. It took them two hours to do the forty-minute drive to Tobermory. They arrived at their hotel looking pale, worn, soaked and worried.

Their room looked out over the bay. Will enjoyed the view. Roz eyed the double bed. He moved towards her. She backed away. 'Later. Let's have a look round before dinner.'

They wandered along the street. Houses painted, blues, pinks, glinting in the street lights. They looked into the bookshop and chandler's. In the sweet shop. The butcher's. The jewellery shop. Then walked back along the shore side of the street, tree-lined. Speculated about the yachts moored in the bay. And what it would be like to live there.

They've got a bookshop. There's a market. I could specialise in Scottish history, Will thought.

'I would work by e-mail,' Roz said.

They nodded. It was possible. They could escape. They sighed. Imagining a life together. Growing old in peace. An idyll.

Watched the mountains across the water. Breathed the air. The stillness engulfed them. Roz relaxed. 'Doesn't feel like Christmas,' she said.

He put his arm round her. 'It will.'

They dined in the hotel, sitting by the window. Slowly chewing their venison in red wine. Not speaking much.

'I can't believe it,' said Will.

'What?' asked Roz.

'Us. Here. For Christmas. It's romantic.'

'Is it?' She knew it was. If he wasn't who he was, she'd be thrilled. Her heart was tumbling. She could hardly believe her luck. He likes me. She felt teenage again. She told herself not to forget to breathe. It's love, she thought. But. But. But. Always a but.

They drank an Islay malt by the fire in the bar and looked at the decorations. Spoke about Christmas trees they'd known.

'It's funny,' said Roz. 'This time of year and I haven't bought a tree. Or a turkey. Or any tasty little things to eat. Filled the wine rack. I haven't even sent any cards.'

'Enjoy yourself,' he told her. 'Feel guilty later.'

And she thought, How do you do that? Teach me to do that.

In the bedroom, she bathed and slipped into a pale blue silk nightdress. Will thought she looked lovely. He didn't usually wear anything in bed. But for her he put on a fresh pair of boxers and a T-shirt. They slid between the sheets. Turned to each other. Kissed. Deep and passionate. Roz held him to her, thrilled at this.

It was wonderful. Wonderful – but. Damnable old *but* again. She turned away from him.

'What's wrong?' he asked.

'Nothing. I'm just tired. And a little drunk. I'll be fine in the morning. It'll be better in the morning.' She knew she wouldn't be there in the morning.

She slept. Dreamed she was carrying Zoe – Zoe the baby – in her arms. They were walking down a corridor and a tribe of wild women with painted faces, robed in flowing red, charged towards them, chanting. Not stopping. They howled past her, pressing her to the wall.

At five in the morning she woke. Slipped from bed. Dressed in jeans and a thick jersey. Put on her walking boots and sneaked from the room, pausing only to look at Will. Head on the pillow, eyes shut. She thought how lucky Zoe was. And left.

In the hall she picked up a map of the island. Went out to the car. Drove along the main street up the steep brae, past the distillery and turned left. Headed for Calgary Bay. Time to bid Nan farewell.

By the time she got there, driving along tiny twisting roads, day had broken. Sunny and chill. It was a perfect place. A long grassy bank leading to the shore, white sands, and sea, clean and icy clear. Nobody else but her. A wind blowing, shoving waves forwards, lifting their foamy tops, little sparks of spume dancing. On each side of the bay, a line of rocks, gleaming black in the steely light. A seal's head dipped up from below the surface, then down again. Watching Roz. Birds skimmed the surface of the water, calling. Apart from the tide, and the cries of the birds – silence. This was a perfect place for sorrow and joy.

Once, centuries ago, during the Clearances, crofters had been herded on the huge galleons anchored here and transported to Nova Scotia. In the summer picnickers would sit, children running, squealing, into the water. Otters swam here. And seals. Nan and Billy had walked here. Arm in arm. Pressing close. Smiling. Singing favourite songs – 'Some Enchanted Evening', 'I Could Have Danced All Night', 'Every Time We Say Goodbye'. Nan's scalding, smoky voice cruising out, filling the bay. They might have danced here. Kissed here. An old-fashioned love affair.

Roz walked down to the sea. She opened the urn, tipped the contents out. A tumble of ash. The wind took the dust, spread it inland. Over her. She was caked. Coughed. Feverishly brushed herself down. 'Thanks for that, Nan. Christ.' She held her jumper from her, flapped it, loosening the ash. She watched it lie in tender drops on the wet sand, before the tide flooded over it, pulling it back into the deep. 'Goodbye, Nan. Be happy.'

The words spun out and joined the day, the sparkle on the water, the crystalline air. Where, Roz imagined, Nan was. Well, not Nan. Her soul. Roz couldn't think where Nan was really. It was hard to come to terms with such a vibrant spirit suddenly ceasing to exist. Snuffed out, forever silent. She looked round. She felt Nan was with her, watching.

She stood staring at the horizon till her eyes ached. Christmas Day, the sea was empty. If she walked into the water and started swimming, next stop would be America. That glisten was tempting. No more worries. It had been months since she cried for Nan. Thought the old lady deserved a few tears now. And she got them. At her feet, Roz noticed a tiny pink and perfect shell. She picked it up, put it in her pocket, then walked back up the beach to her car.

It was after nine now, bright and sunny. Steely cold. She stopped and put the roof down. Shoved on a woolly hat. Hey, it was Christmas. She was meant to have a good time. She played Nina Simone. 'I'm feeling fine.' Drove the tiny roads. Up through Dervaig, stopped at the top of the hill to take one last look at the view. Then away and on to Tobermory, and Will. The only living things about today were sheep, who gazed at her blankly as she passed. Nothing in their heads. She envied them.

Will was waiting outside the hotel when she got back. Hands in pockets, leaning huffily against the rail on the shore side of the street. He hardly smiled when she drove up.

'Where've you been?'

'I told you. I came to scatter Nan's ashes.'

'I could have come with you.'

She shook her head. 'This was between Nan and me.'

'Private?'

'Sort of. And messy.' She gave her jumper a dusting-down. 'She flew back in at me. I got covered. Do you think she was trying to tell me something?'

'What?'

That this is wrong. That between us we'll break Zoe's heart. She'll hate me forever, just when she was letting go, allowing herself to like me, Roz thought.

'Us,' she said. 'This.'

'It isn't wrong. We want this.'

Roz joined him, leaning on the rail.

'Don't we?' he said.

She nodded. 'Of course I do. You'll never know how much. I've wanted this, and wanted this.' She was about to tell him how much she cared. How she dreamed of him, lay awake nights sighing for him. And suddenly it was all too much. Farewell to Nan, then heavy relationship talk with Will. To hell with it all.

Will put his hand on hers. 'What are we going to do?'

'What about?' asked Roz.

'About us. For Chrissakes, about us.'

'Oh, something,' said Roz, turning away from him. 'Let's not talk about that now.'

'But we have to, sometime. We have to tell Zoe.'

'Please.' Roz turned back to him. Stroked his cheek. Kissed his lips, a little kiss. A soothing, be-quiet, let's-not-speak-about-this kiss. 'Please. Please. Please not now. Let's go get some breakfast. I'm starving. It's Christmas. We should have buck's fizz. We should be happy. I've got a present for you.'

Will looked at her. God, he thought. Sometimes this woman was wonderful, she was so unlike Zoe. A relief. And sometimes, like now, he thought, was this woman like Zoe, or what?

'Also,' said Roz, 'I have to put on another jumper. And I have to phone Jamie and Zoe to wish them merry Christmas.' Though she didn't actually want to speak to Zoe. Not with Will hanging around in the same room.

They ate porridge, poached eggs, kippers and bacon. Drank orange juice and champagne and dark coffee. Will wanted to go upstairs. Roz wanted to walk off the huge amount of food she'd just eaten. 'We could go along past the garage at the end of the street. Take the coastal walk to the lighthouse. See what we can see. Maybe a whale passing. Or an eagle rising. Or seals. Or something. You never know.'

They walked. But the wildlife didn't perform for them. 'Christmas,' said Roz. 'It's their day off too.' She felt cheery. Nothing to do with the champagne, she told herself. Her spirits were lifting. The day, the sunlight. Duty done, she was free. And she was with the one she loved. She should enjoy herself. She deserved it. This could be a romance, an old-fashioned affair. Like Nan and Billy.

What would Nan do? Sing. '*Some enchanted evening,*' Roz sang. Then stopped. She only knew three words.

'*Tum, tum, te, tum, tum, tum,*' sang Will.

'Tum, tum, tum, tum, te, tum,' sang Roz.

Arms round each other, they walked on. Stopped, kissed. Walked some more. Sang snatches of songs neither of them quite knew. But Nan would have known. They kissed again. His arms round her, inside her coat, pulling her close.

'Your nose is cold,' she said, kissing it. On tiptoes. 'But then,' small seductive laugh, 'it's not your nose I'm interested in.'

'Ooh, dirty mind,' he said. 'I like that in a woman.'

They kissed again.

An old-fashioned love affair, thought Roz. I want this.

Back at the hotel, they bathed and, at last, exchanged presents. Roz found this swapping of gifts late in the day very cool. Usually she ripped open her parcels first thing, still in her dressing gown, hair uncombed. Face still slack from sleeping.

He gave her a couple of scented candles, beautifully boxed. A little metal model of her car, found in a box at the antique shop where he'd also bought her an old portable typewriter, a thirties thing. Stiff-keyed, but still working.

'It'll take pride of place on my bookshelves,' she told him.

'And never get dusted,' he said.

'I don't know. I might change. I've been considering it. Deciding to clean up your act takes time. It's a big thing.'

At seven they went down for dinner. Which felt odd to Roz. Usually by this time, on this day, she was stuffed with food, slumped on the sofa watching nonsense of the season on television and wondering what to eat next.

They pulled crackers, read the silly jokes and wore the paper hats. For a full two minutes they wore them, looked at one another. His red, hers yellow. She hated yellow. Tore it off. They ate the traditional fare. Turkey with everything Christmas demanded. It was a funny meal, Roz thought. She'd never serve it on any other day. Chipolata sausages, gravy, cranberry sauce, roast potatoes, sprouts. No, she'd never eat it on an ordinary day. So, she thought, she should enjoy it now.

She looked at her glass. Empty. When had that happened? She sure as hell couldn't remember emptying it. But there it was. Wineless. And she must've done it. Will was certainly not the sort of person who would wantonly drain someone else's glass. She did, she had to admit, feel a little woozy. Pleasantly woozy. And this wooziness was worth pursuing. She held up the empty glass. 'Fill me up,' she said.

'This is lovely,' said Will. 'Best Christmas ever.'

'I know,' agreed Roz. Rather over-enthusiastically, she thought. The champagne. 'We should do this every Christmas. Have a secret love affair. Like Nan and Billy. Send each other secret notes. *To Will, love and kisses from The Sweet Hollow Trucking Company. To Roz, glad tidings and cuddles from Mavis and Fran.*'

'I don't want a secret love affair,' Will, flushed with wine, exclaimed. 'I want everyone to know. I want to climb to a mountaintop and shout it out. "I love Roz." ' It was the booze talking. Who cared?

'Oh,' swooned Roz, 'I love that. Let's have more champagne.'

When they went upstairs to their room, they held hands. Lingered going along the hall, looking at the paintings. He put his arm round her. Smelled the top of her head. Warmth, and coconut shampoo and turkey. He liked it. She was heady on champagne. Very drunk, wilful and reckless.

In the room they kissed. Slid from their clothes and, in bed, turned to each other. This is me, thought Roz. Me and Will, and I love him. Outside the night was still. The water moved gently and seagulls laughed in the dark. Skin, she thought. So much skin. His lips on her. It was just like Nan said. The room was pouring love.

She ran her hands down him. Touching him. She'd dreamed of this. Put her mouth on his. Pulled his tongue into her. His hands. The hands she had dreamed of, yearned for whilst she watched him make coffee, hold a book, were on her breasts. Between her legs.

He had done this to Zoe. These hands had touched Zoe's breasts. Between Zoe's legs. This tongue had pushed into Zoe's mouth. This body had lain on top of Zoe's. This . . . oh my God, she couldn't allow her mind to go further. It was too much. She was discovering that just as children don't want to think about their parents having sex, parents don't want to think of their children's deepest intimacies.

'I'm terribly sorry. I can't do this,' she said.

'What?'

'I'm sorry. I can't. You're Zoe's.'

'You said that before. I'm mine. I can do what I want.'

'Yes, you can. But not with me. Sorry.'

'Why? You go this far? Are you teasing me?'

'No. No, really. I want to. I really, really want to. But. You know . . . I keep thinking about Zoe. You've done all this with her. It's wrong. It's almost . . .' She wanted to say *incestuous*. But couldn't bring herself to.

'I've done all this with a lot more women than Zoe.'

'Zoe's the one that bothers me. There are places Zoe's been,' indicating the lower parts of Will, 'that I find I do not want to go to too. And there are bits of you that have been with Zoe, and I find that I can't quite accept it in me too.' She turned to him, explaining. 'I've just, after all these years, started to make friends with my daughter. I don't think she'd ever forgive this.'

'I don't believe this.'

'Actually, now you mention it, neither do I. I never wanted anyone so much in my life. I've never felt like this before. This feeling for you – it's more than me. It's overwhelming. It's everything to me. I've wanted you ever since I first saw you. I think of you all the time.' She was saying too much.

Will sat up. 'For God's sake, you're not going to say you love me, are you?'

'You said at dinner that you loved me.' She defended what she had been about to admit.

'I know, but . . .'

'I know,' she said. 'It wasn't you talking. It was the champagne. It's OK. I wasn't.'

But, yes, she had been about to say that. Thank Christ she hadn't. 'I was just going to say I'd love it. Love it with you. That's all. Love you? How could I? I hardly know you. I couldn't possibly love you. I've hardly ever seen you laugh. Never seen you cry. Do you cry? I don't know what colour you like best. Or what your favourite television programme is. Or the music that moves you. Or what your childhood was like. We haven't had a fight. You can't love someone properly till you've fallen out with them. I haven't forgiven you for anything. Or you me. I haven't seen you in any sort of state. Like first thing in the morning when you arrive in the kitchen, hair on end, face crumpled from sleep, eyes crusty, yawning, sweaty, mumbling, too knackered to make a proper sentence. That's when you truly love somebody. When you see them alone, dishevelled, rumpled, slightly smelly, and you think, Ah, that's my Will.'

She finished. She'd been spouting out her truth. Fuck, thought Roz. I've said too much. Fuck. Fuck. Fuck.

'Right,' said Will. 'I see.' He nodded. He didn't love her. She was a comfort. She was nice. She said the right things – usually –

she was easy to be with. He liked her. But no, definitely, he did not love her. Not now he was sober.

'You only wanted a shag, didn't you?' she said.

'And you didn't?'

'Yes.' She said it reluctantly. As if it was all right for her, but not him. She had a crush. She guessed he wanted comfort. And so did she. But more than that. She was lonely. Deeply lonely. An isolation nobody could touch, that she carried with her all the time, wherever she went, whoever she was with. She wanted it to stop. She reached out to anyone who nodded or smiled to her. Eager to love. She wanted someone to love her. To say it to her. No man ever had.

She lay down. She felt proud of herself. Incredibly horny. Unsatisfied. Frustrated. But proud. She could hold her champagne-head high. Though right now, it was on the pillow, headachy with it. 'Don't you ever tell Zoe about this,' she warned.

'You think I would? Never. She'd kill me.'

'Good for her. Well, there you go. We've got a secret.'

In the early morning Roz rose. She crept around the room, packing her bag. Before she left the room, she bent down to brush her lips against Will's sleeping cheek. She went downstairs, paid the bill, then drove off to catch the early ferry. On her way, moving through high places, before the road dipped back to the shore, she looked across the rolling moorlands, heather and distant hills. She saw an eagle sloping lazy in the early sky. And she thought about Nan.

Without even bothering about how Will would get home, she'd left him. But he'd get home. She knew he would. And she knew he would know why she had gone without him. There was nothing more to say. This fling of theirs would never work. They'd only hurt people they both loved. And now she was sure they both loved Zoe.

She ate a hideous breakfast on the boat. Bacon, eggs and beans. I'll have indigestion for a week, she thought. Then she walked out on the deck. Felt the icy air on her face. The chill. The day was clear, water smooth. I have done the right thing, she said. For

302

once, I have done the right thing. I will go to heaven. Though I don't believe in it. I'll go. I made a decision. I have stopped stumbling forwards. I think I even almost, well sort of, like myself.

'What do you think of me, Nan?'

'Well,' old voice from the past, 'well, on the one hand I don't blame you. There've been times when I could happily have done what you've done. You're brave. Then again, I think you're daft. But you're no longer selfish. Not that.'

She leaned over the rail, watching mountains. Thinking of Nan. Nan was beautiful. For the rest of her life, Roz thought, she would be haunted by Nan.

CHAPTER THIRTY-TWO

Pam Beseley dumped the shopping on the kitchen table then switched on the kettle. A swift cup of coffee before she put the groceries away. She turned on the radio, retuned it away from the incessant pop music Simon and Susan played to a chat station. These days the sound of human voices, especially opinionated ones, cheered her. She felt nobody talked to her any more. She just exchanged words. 'Where's my socks?' 'In the tumble-drier.' 'Did you get any biscuits?' 'Yes. In the kitchen cupboard.' It was all words. No conversation.

She'd tried to have a conversation with Frank last night. But their failure had sunk from not being able to talk, to not talking. They still weren't talking this morning. Hadn't spoken in bed, not even to say goodnight. Once bed had been lovely. Now they only used it for sleep. Once they'd chatted, laughed, told jokes, giggled, tickled, pulled the duvet over them, hiding from the world, made love and spooned into one another. Now – nothing. Just the odd bicker about who was hogging the covers. Something must be done, Pam decided. Something drastic. She was not one to consider anything less. It was drastic or nothing.

Zoe stood holding Toby's hand, looking skywards.

'What are you doing?' Toby asked.

'Watching for shooting stars,' said Zoe. 'If you see one, you get a wish.'

Toby joined her staring up. 'If we see one, do we both get a wish? Does one star do two people? Or do we have to see one each?'

'I don't know, Toby. I expect we both get a wish.'

'What about all the other people seeing the star? Do they get their wishes?'

'What other people?'

'All the other people in the world looking up. There's miles of sky. There's bound to be hundreds of other people see the star.'

'Right,' said Zoe.

'So do they get their wish?'

'Yes.'

Recently, Zoe had noticed that Toby rarely stopped talking. For years, it seemed, he'd hardly spoken at all. Now it was as if he was making up for all the time he'd missed. All the words he'd hoarded up, all the thoughts he'd secreted away, were now pouring out.

'And,' said Toby, 'what about all the stars we've missed? Does the wish shoot away with the star? Or does it stay around for you to have?'

This was a new thought to Zoe. 'I think the wish only lasts as long as the star is shooting.'

They were standing in Matthew's front garden. Necks cricked.

'I wish . . .' said Toby.

'Did you see one?' Zoe was jealous. She scanned the heavens.

'Not exactly,' said Toby. 'But there's sky everywhere. All over the world. There's bound to be a star shooting somewhere. And I'm wishing on it.'

'Good one,' said Zoe. 'Can I wish on it too?'

'It'll be gone now.' Toby wasn't sharing his star.

'What did you wish for?' asked Zoe.

'I'm not telling. You don't get it if you tell.'

He shivered.

'You want to go inside?' asked Zoe.

Toby shook his head. 'I want to see the taxi coming.'

They were going home. Back to the flat Zoe had once shared with Will. She was to stay there with Toby till Will returned from wherever he'd been for Christmas. Zoe didn't know.

'You're cold,' said Zoe. She put her arm round him. Rubbed him. Warming him.

'Don't care. I like it out here.'

Zoe opened her coat, wrapped Toby into it, close to her. 'It would make a lot more sense to go inside.'

'No.' Toby stood his ground. 'I don't like it in there.'

'Grandad's always a bit on edge.'

'On what edge?'

'He's tense.' Life's edge.

Matthew had spent Christmas dropping things and sighing. Once Zoe had looked across the table at him and could have sworn the man was about to start weeping.

Roz had guessed right, Toby did find the world he discovered down the microscope enchanting. He'd spent the morning gathering things to examine, exclaiming loudly at what he saw. A tiny frond of chrysanthemum, curled and wondrous. The pollen from a lily was a golden gathering of minuscule seeds, like saffron rice. His hair looked like rope. Zoe decided that he wasn't a musician after all. Thank God she hadn't invested in a violin. She'd buy him slides when the shops opened again.

She and Toby had stayed overnight with Matthew and Claire. But now, early evening on Boxing Day, she was glad to escape. She wished she'd gone to Mull with Roz. She'd wanted to. Suggested it. But Roz had thought Matthew would be hurt if they didn't go to him.

'Claire will have shopped. She'll have cupboards full of salted peanuts and crisps and chocolate things. Cakes and mince pies. You have to go.'

Now Zoe thought about it, Roz had seemed nervous too. And, thinking about it even more, Will had been a bit twitchy and very evasive about where he was going. It seemed to Zoe that she was the only sane member of her family. That was a first.

The flat, when they got back to it, was two-days-empty cold. Zoe switched on the heating and made them both hot chocolate. They sat curled on the sofa together till Toby was almost sleeping. Zoe put him to bed, then went to bed herself. Will would be home tomorrow, and she would return to Nan's. When Nan's house was sold, she'd worry. She'd have nowhere to live. But for the moment, she didn't give a damn. And not giving a damn was lovely.

She woke after twelve. The front door slammed. She got up and went downstairs, wrapping Will's towelling robe round her. Will was standing in the hall looking forlorn.

'What are you doing here?' asked Zoe.

'I came home early. Things didn't work out.'

'What things?'

'Christmas things. I wanted to get back.'

Zoe sat on the stairs. 'Didn't you have a good time?'

Will shook his head. 'It was OK. Then not OK. What about you?'

'I don't know what's up with Matthew. He's all weepy.'

Will hung up his coat and went into the kitchen.

Zoe followed him. 'Toby had a good time. Roz gave him a microscope. He's thrilled with it. Been looking at things all day. Perhaps he's going to be a botanist. Or a microbiologist.'

Will nodded. 'Great.' Dourly. Nothing enthused him tonight.

'He could win the Nobel Prize,' said Zoe.

'Zoe,' said Will, 'pack it in. Let him just be a boy with a microscope.'

'We should encourage him.'

'Zoe,' Will snapped. 'Leave him be.'

Zoe shrugged. 'OK,' she relented. 'I'll let him be. Anyway, I wouldn't know what to wear to the ceremony.'

Will smiled. 'You never stop.'

'I know. I'll try. I'll concentrate on me getting the Nobel Prize. For plotting other people's lives.'

Will put on the kettle. It had been a dreadful day. He'd wakened and discovered he was alone. Roz had abandoned him. The journey home had taken all day. A taxi, hired at huge expense, to Craignure to catch the ferry. A whisky-soaked ferry ride, spent in the bar. A train to Glasgow. More whisky in the station bar, sitting staring at the other passengers. People in anoraks, carrying cases. Blank travellers' expressions on their faces. Then, finally, a late train back to Edinburgh. He felt grubby. Had moved straight into hangover without getting drunk. Gritty-eyed, and sweaty and headachy. Travelling baffled him. All he did was sit. Transported. Yet it was exhausting. He couldn't understand it.

Zoe felt sorry for him. He looked confused. Will often looked confused. But tonight he looked really confused. The kettle boiled and she made him coffee. 'You don't look as if you had a very good time.'

'It was OK. Fine. Not exactly what I'd planned.'

'What had you planned?'

'More thrills and spills than I got.'

'I didn't know you were a one for thrills and spills.' Zoe looked troubled. She hadn't realised Will was planning to enjoy himself. She liked to imagine him sitting alone, pining for her. 'Where are you going to sleep?' she asked. 'I'm in our bed.'

'My bed now.'

'You're not getting into it tonight.'

'No?' Hopeful Will. Though he didn't know why. All he wanted to do was sleep.

'No.' Adamant Zoe. Though she didn't know why. She'd been sexless for months and thought it was beginning to show. She was fidgety and eating too much.

Will gathered sheets and spare duvet to make up the sofa. Zoe went upstairs.

In the morning, after a lingering hug with Toby, she left for Nan's house. Will walked her to the bus stop. 'We have to talk,' he said.

'We have talked.'

'Properly. We have to decide what to do.'

Zoe stood gazing up the road, willing the bus to come.

'We have to face up to things,' Will insisted.

Zoe supposed they did. Though facing up to things never appealed to her. She nodded. 'We'll go somewhere. Neutral territory. A pub where we don't know anybody.' She fancied the allure of it. She'd wear her velvet coat, and black high heels. Paint her lips red. It was like some sort of illicit date. And she'd come out of it with custody of Toby. And the flat.

When her bus arrived, she leaned over and kissed Will on the cheek. Her nose was cold. Will, briefly, painfully, remembered what Roz had said about cold noses. 'It's not the bit I'm interested in.'

'Phone me,' Zoe said.

When she got back to Nan's, Roz was sitting in the living room drinking coffee and listening to the radio. She was wearing the Celtic necklace Zoe had given her.

'Nice,' she said. 'Thank you.'

'And thank you for all the stuff you gave me. When did you get here?'

'Yesterday. Late afternoon.'

'You could have come to Matthew's,' said Zoe.

'I don't think so,' said Roz.

She had gone home. Made tea. Wandered about Nan's empty house thinking about Will. Saying goodbye to him in her head. And gone to bed early. Turning down the lust of your life was tiring.

'I was just waiting to say goodbye to you,' said Roz. 'I'm going home today.'

'All that long way, on your own? Better leave soon. The way you drive it'll take till next week.'

'Yeah, well, maybe I'll become accustomed to the roads.'

'The world. Life,' said Zoe.

'You never know,' said Roz.

Zoe made coffee and joined her. They sat, listening to the quiet hiss of the gas fire.

'Did you have a good time?' Zoe asked.

'It was fine. Said goodbye to Nan. And she blew back on me. I got covered.'

'Typical Nan.'

They nodded.

'What happened when I left?' asked Roz. 'When I went away?'

'Nothing, said Zoe. 'We hardly spoke about it. It was all bottled up. Matthew never said your name. It was always my wife, my ex or your mother. We fell into a silent routine. Cooking. Laundry.

Eating. Homework. Then going bananas weekends when we were out of the house.'

'I shouldn't have gone,' said Roz. 'I should've stayed and worked things out.'

Zoe nodded. 'Probably. But if it were me, now, I'd go.'

'Thank you for saying that,' said Roz. 'I didn't think you'd miss me. I didn't think anyone cared.'

'Oh, don't say that.' Zoe looked troubled. 'Don't.'

Roz smiled.

'Course, we didn't care. We only missed your tuna sarnies.' Zoe swigged her coffee, enjoying the little bit of wickedness. It pleased her to tease her mother.

'Cheek,' said Roz. Then, heaving herself from her chair, groaned. 'Stop it,' she told herself.

'Stop what?' asked Zoe.

'Groaning when I get up. I just recently noticed I was doing that. It's such a sign of middle age.'

'Soon you'll be another Nan.'

Roz shook her head. 'Nah. That's your job. You're the one with the colourful past. I have to go.'

She went upstairs to pick up her case. Then opened the bedside cabinet and took out the old Tampax box. Inside were postcards from across the world, and Nan's passport. Roz put them in her handbag. She opened the passport to look at Nan's photograph. Inside, she found a cheque for ten thousand pounds made out to her, and a note. *For you,* Nan had written, *a wee something for all your trouble. Matthew won't give you anything. But that's the way he is. Forgive him. And thanks for Mull. Keep well. Look after yourself. I'll be watching you. Love always, Nan.*

Roz put the cheque in her bag. Christmas and bills for feeding Jamie, she was more than a thousand pounds overdrawn at the bank.

Zoe was waiting in the hall.

'How are you for money?' asked Roz.

'Financially this is not my finest hour,' said Zoe.

Roz wrote her a cheque for three thousand pounds. 'This'll

keep you going. For a couple of weeks at least, the way you throw it around! But you'll have to wait for a couple of weeks before you cash it.'

Zoe looked at it. 'Where did you get this?'

'Nan left me it. I just found a cheque in the bedside cabinet upstairs.'

Zoe handed it back. 'Keep it. Nan left me and Jamie a share in the house when it's sold.'

Roz took her hand, tucked the cheque into it. 'No. You have it to tide you over. It'll make up for all the presents you didn't get.'

'There's something going on,' sensed Zoe. 'Something about Nan.' Her eyes narrowed. 'Have you uncovered a secret murky past?'

'Colourful,' Roz told her. 'I'll tell you about it some day. Promise. Right now, I have to go see Matthew and Claire, then get off down the road to London.'

'Why are you going to see them?'

'Just to wave,' said Roz. 'Maybe more than that. Settle a score. Don't ask.'

Zoe walked Roz to her car. 'Will and me are meeting somewhere neutral. We want to sort things out. We're going to play at being civilised human beings.'

'Good. You need sorting out. As for civilised human beings, you can but try.'

The garden was frosted. No sun today to thaw it. Their breath hung in front of them. Words, dallying in the air.

Roz unlocked her car. Threw in her case.

'You've got a lovely son and a bloke you should try to hang on to.'

'Hmm,' said Zoe. 'The son I'll have. The bloke I'm thinking about.'

'Will's fine,' said Roz. 'I like him.'

'I didn't say I didn't like him. I said I'm considering him. You should find yourself a good bloke.'

'Easier said than done. Anyway, I don't know if I want a good bloke. I like being on my own. Good blokes are tying.'

'It was just a suggestion,' said Zoe. 'It's not written in tablets of stone. Like the four commandments.'

'Ten,' said Roz. 'There're ten commandments.'

Zoe kicked at a stone. 'I know. But I only do four.'

Roz laughed. Hugged her daughter. Kissed her. 'Take care. And try to work your commandment total up to ten. Be good.'

Zoe kissed her back. 'I will. I'll phone.'

Pam Beseley put a casserole in the oven. Switched it on low. Her stomach griped and fluttered. Today was the day. She had it planned. She was leaving. She had a job in Brighton, working in an estate agent's. She'd thought about taking another name. Disappearing for ever. A new person, new life.

She propped a note on the kitchen table, leaning against the milk jug. *I'm going away. I have to find out who I am. If I stay here I will drown. I'll phone tonight. Love Pam.*

She could not think of anything else to say.

She picked up her case. Walked out the door. She was wearing her red silk shirt and new black suit. Skirt a couple of inches shorter than normal. It was the first time in ten years she'd shown the world her knees. She shut the door. Down the path and out of the gate. The air was soft. She felt as if she was smelling it for the first time. Tears in her eyes. She'd miss them all. Little Sammy, who was at nursery and was spending the rest of the day with her friends Fran and Mavis. Frank and Susan and Simon, who'd all get in after five. Susan was going to her best pal Lorna's for tea. Simon had football practice. What would they do without her? Get by.

Pam sniffed. But she was going to a new life. And going away was wonderful.

Roz drew up at Matthew's gate. Slammed the car door. Didn't lock it. She wasn't staying long. And she definitely wasn't going inside. She walked up the path, rang the bell. Matthew answered.

'What do you want?'

'To see you for a moment.'

'Why?'

'I want to smack your face,' Roz said. And she did. She felt the shock of the blow, singing up her arm.

'That's for not forgiving Nan. And,' she socked him again, 'that's for not giving Jamie and Zoe any of my presents.'

Matthew reeled. Stunned. He heard ringing in his ears. A moment's numbness before the pain set in. His cheek flamed up. Matthew nursed it.

Claire came to the door, saw what had happened, looked up and down the street checking that no neighbours were spying. 'What are you doing?' she asked Roz, horror in her voice.

'Whacking Matthew,' said Roz. She was on an adrenalin rush.

'What for?' Claire squared up to her. How dare someone hit her Matthew. That was her job, now she thought of it.

'He'll tell you,' said Roz, glaring. 'Won't you, Matthew?' Poking him. She fixed Claire with a look. Did she want a fight? Right now, Roz was up for it. Knew she'd win. Though battling with another woman in a prim little front garden had no appeal. Also, she thought, at such moments, what does a person do with her handbag? She opted for the sympathy vote. 'Do you know, he never passed on any of the presents I sent my children?'

'Matthew, that's awful,' said Claire.

Roz grinned. She'd won the sympathy vote.

'Anyway, Marianne said a good whack did the trick. Though she's never done it herself. She put the notion in my mind.'

'Who is Marianne?' asked Claire.

'To be honest,' said Roz, 'I don't really know. But there it is, a whack on the jaw from Marianne and me.' She turned and walked jubilantly back to her car.

Roz drove home. Sixty miles an hour, all the way down the grown-up motorway. Hood down, laughing at the freeze. Though after an hour, the freeze got too much, and she stopped and put the hood up. But she motored on, swirling into the fast lane, overtaking. And it was wonderful.

CHAPTER THIRTY-THREE

The flat was strangely quiet. Messy and silent. Roz dropped her bag in the hall and went through to the living room, calling, 'Jamie. Jamie.'

A muffled rustle of movement in her bedroom. Roz knew well the sound of sheets. Voices. Hushed voices. Jamie appeared at the door in boxers. Hair rumpled. He looked pale and sleepy and confused. Ah, that's my Jamie.

Such a flood of love, Roz even smiled hugely at the woman who appeared behind him. She looked abashed. A little afraid, guilty. Aah, that's my . . .

'Who are you?' Roz asked.

'Angela,' Angela said.

'Right. Hello, Angela.' Roz held out an icy hand.

Angela took it. Astonished at the frozen, if friendly, grip. 'Hello.'

They all stood looking at each other.

'Well,' said Roz. 'What I really want is a cup of tea.'

'I'll make it,' Angela offered, heading for the kitchen. She plainly knew her way around.

'Perhaps you should put a little more on first,' Roz suggested.

Angela disappeared. Reappeared wrapping a white towelling dressing gown round her.

'That's Angela,' said Jamie.

'I know,' said Roz.

Jamie walked into the living room, sat on the sofa. 'She's been here since you went away.'

'Guessed that.'

'I said she could move in.'

Roz leaned back. 'You what?'

'Well,' said Jamie. He sat opposite her. Absently scratched his leg. 'See . . .'

Roz watched him scratch. God, his legs were hairy. Funny how that happens. How people grow. She remembered those legs when they were tiny and chubby and baby-soft. She'd played with them when she was changing his nappy. An ankle in each hand, making gentle running movements, before leaning down to give him a raspberry on his fat little tummy. She pulled herself from the memory. Stop it. If he knew what she was thinking, he'd cringe.

'See . . .' repeated Jamie. 'She was in a flat with a couple of other girls, but one's leaving to live with her bloke. And the other has given up her course and is going home. It's too late in the term to find other people, and . . .'

'She's at university?' asked Roz.

'She's studying law.'

'Law? How clever. What's she doing with you?'

Jamie stopped scratching. Let the insult soak in. 'She's clever,' he told her. 'Anyway, she can't afford her flat any more. So I said, "Stay here. With us." I told her you wouldn't mind.'

'Oh, did you?'

'Yes.'

Roz let this new information roll round her head. 'This means you're staying. You're not going back to Edinburgh.'

'No. I'm staying here. With Angela.'

'And me?'

'Uh-huh.'

'Right. And where are you going to sleep? You and Angela?'

Jamie had been planning to sleep in Roz's bed. But thought now was not the time to mention it. 'We could buy a bed. Me and Angela. Put it in the other bedroom.'

'With what will you buy a bed?'

'Money. I've got a job. In a bar. Where I met Angela. She works there after uni, and weekends.'

'She works. Earns money. She's putting herself through university.' She liked Angela.

Jamie nodded.

'OK.' Roz gave in. 'Why not. I'm getting used to crowds in my living room. It'd be lonely without you.'

Jamie smiled. Came over to give her a hug and a blokey punch on the shoulder. Roz thought a kiss on the cheek would've been nicer. But she supposed grown-ups who drove at absurd speeds down the grown-up motorway had to take whatever affection they were offered. Angela appeared with tea in a pot, on a tray with three cups and some toast. What a civilised person, Roz thought. Will she take us up? Or will we bring her down? Angela poured tea. And Jamie told her it was cool, she could stay.

On the evening of her second day away, Pam Beseley phoned home. Frank sounded more than frosty; he was furious.

'I wondered how you were all managing,' said Pam.

'We are not managing,' Frank told her. 'It is not up to us to manage. You manage.'

'I'm not prepared to do that any more, Frank. I want more out of life.'

'What do you mean, more?'

'I've got a job. I'm earning money. I'm finding myself. I'm Pam now.'

'Goodness' sake, woman. Stop all this rubbish and come home where you're needed.'

'I won't do that, Frank. Not now. Not yet.'

'When, then?'

'One day.' Long pause. 'Maybe.'

'And you imagine I'll be here waiting for you? Don't fool yourself.'

'That's a chance I'll have to take. Make sure Sammy cleans his teeth. And Simon has a dentist's appointment tomorrow. And Susan will need her gym kit washed for Thursday. I'm sure she can manage to put it through the machine.' She hung up. Sat alone in her little bedsit and cried.

A week after Angela moved in, a new bed arrived. She and Jamie cleared out the spare room, putting the disassembled exercise machine and other stuff into the cupboard in the hall. They painted their room dark red. Jamie hung white pictures in thin black frames round the walls. Angela set up her computer and brought round her piles of books, CDs, clothes, and that was her. Ensconced.

Roz liked her. She was quiet, humorous, considerate, intelligent. Roz wanted to ask, 'What's a nice girl like you doing with my son?' She had the vague feeling that Angela was too good for him. But then, Angela would know more about Jamie than she did.

At last Roz got her own room, her own bed back. She set up her computer on a table by the window, but didn't work. She sat and stared. She worried. She did crosswords. Listened to favourite CDs. It wouldn't be long before Ronnie returned to work. And then, what? She didn't know. She didn't think she even cared.

A month after leaving home, Pam felt useless. She enjoyed her work. Loved it. She was Pam. She had new chums. They gossiped. They spoke about work, clients. But all the girls and Mr Bingham, the boss, went home nights. To their families. She went to the bedsit. She read. She listened to the radio. She phoned home.

Susan had mastered the washing machine. Simon had learned to cook a mean plate of poached eggs and beans and little Sammy could, at last, tie his own shoelaces. His front tooth was loose. Pam reminded Frank to leave money under his pillow. 'You're on tooth fairy duty now.'

'You think I'd forget?' said Frank. 'I'm as good a tooth fairy as the next man.'

Pam was disheartened. Nobody said they missed her. Though she told them every time she phoned that she missed them.

A freezing night, mid January. Jamie and Angela were going to the cinema. And did Roz want to come with them?

'You sit here alone every night. You should get out more.'

'No,' said Roz automatically. 'I can't come.' Then she thought about this. 'Yes, why not?' It'd do her good. A trip to the cinema. Popcorn. Sitting in the dark. A film, a story. Music. Films were lovely. They rolled before you. All you had to do was breathe. She got her coat and went with them.

Outside they gathered by the car.

'I'll drive,' said Jamie.

Roz pointed out that the L-plates weren't on.

'Don't need them. I passed my test. Angela took me out in her dad's car. And I passed.'

'No shit,' said Roz. 'Why didn't you tell me?'

Jamie shrugged. 'I'm telling you now.' He took the keys from Roz, opened the car. Let her get in the back, whilst he and Angela sat up front. Roz felt like a child. Ushered to the cinema. Not even given the chance to help choose the film. I'm turning into an old lady, she thought. Wheeled out into a world I've left behind.

'I've applied for a course,' Jamie said. He was driving too fast, Roz thought. Brake, brake.

'A course?' she said.

'Yeah. I want to work with disturbed children. It's a three-year thing. But I can do it. I did a great job on Toby.'

'You did, too,' Roz agreed. 'Though Toby isn't disturbed. He's just confused, like the rest of us.'

'True,' said Jamie.

Angela told him to signal left.

'Angela suggested it. She thought I'd got a deal of satisfaction from dealing with Toby. A sense of self.'

'Right,' said Roz. Angela was an organised, disciplined woman. She studied. She worked. She never ate anything that wasn't good for her. Looked dismayed when she caught Roz nibbling crisps between meals. Angela was assertive. Breezed positively through life. Last week Angela had bought shoes, decided she didn't like them. Returned them. Decided the new pair didn't fit properly Returned them. Then returned the new pair and got her money back. Angela could do that. Roz couldn't have been bothered. Roz's cupboards were full of things she didn't want, clothes that didn't fit properly, because she could never face taking them back.

'Take the inside lane,' Angela told Jamie.

Jamie obliged. Smiling.

Roz saw their life ahead. Angela would rise and rise. She'd dress in snappy, expensive suits. Jamie would always be a scruff. Angela would work long hours. Jamie would come home to an empty flat. They'd have an appropriate number of children, at a time convenient to Angela. Jamie would care for them. After the divorce they'd stay with Jamie. They'd live in a run-down, ramshackle flat, children milling about, noisy and needing their hair cut. They'd be happy.

'The lights are turning red,' Angela told Jamie. He moved down through the gears. Pressed the brake.

Angela would come by, tidy a bit and tell Jamie to do something about himself. Jamie would fret over the disturbed children he'd set out to work with. His own children would clamber over him, making endless demands. Jamie, ever amiable, would give in to them. They'd love him. Angela would pursue her career. Only sometimes, alone in her perfect flat after a date or a late drink with colleagues, would she sit and wonder if unambitious, relatively happy Jamie had got it right after all. But she'd never admit it. Not out loud.

Roz saw it all. 'Don't do it,' she said.

Jamie stopped braking. Stalled. The car behind tooted angrily.

'Why did you say that?' Jamie was angry too.

'He has to brake,' Angela turned to explain. 'The lights are against him.'

'Yes,' said Roz. 'Sorry. I was dreaming.'

Eventually Angela would remarry someone more like herself. They'd be an upwardly mobile professional couple. Have a second home. A couple of smart cars. Trips abroad. A wide circle of like-minded friends. Dinner parties. But she'd always have a soft spot for Jamie. Like everybody whose life touched his.

'You shouldn't dream out loud,' said Angela. 'You could cause an accident.'

Then, at last, probably through his work, Jamie would find a gentle, charming soul with a wonderful sense of humour. She would quietly nag him. Cuddle him. And having been through a series of disastrous affairs, thank her lucky stars for finding him. She'd love him. Utterly. They'd have more children. Rumpled, tousled, chatty children who went to music lessons and gym classes. They'd be adorable, every single one of them. And she, Roz, would visit often. Babysit. Fuss. Christmas she'd arrive laden with gifts. They'd squeal round her. Sit on her knee. Tell her their little lives.

'I'd like that,' said Roz. Out loud.

Angela turned. Looked disapproving.

There was a soft knock on Pam's door. A gentle, almost tentative tapping. She put down her coffee and the banana that was her evening meal. She never could be bothered cooking for herself. This leaving home had been good for her weight. She'd lost ten pounds.

It was Frank. 'I've come to get you,' he said.

Pam could not help the movement of emotion coursing through her when she saw him. But she said, 'I don't know if I want to be got.'

'We all miss you terribly,' said Frank. 'Please come home.'

Roz had looked up sadly when she wrote this. She wished Matthew had come for her. She wished someone had told her they missed her.

'I'm not coming home to the same old routine. I want things changed.'

'What things?' asked Frank.

'Us. Our life. We should do things. Before it's too late for us. Go out together. Have midnight picnics. Climb mountains. I don't know, Frank. Just things.'

Frank looked round her little room. 'Is this where you've been staying?'

'Yes.'

'You prefer this to home?'

'No. But I can do what I like. You know. No demands.'

'I know,' said Frank. 'You think I don't feel the same?'

'How do I know how you feel? We never talk.'

Frank held out his arms. 'Come here.'

'You come here,' said Pam. 'If you want me, come all the way to me. From our house to this place, then right across the room. This is where I am.'

'I'm on my way,' said Frank. He took the last few steps to where Pam was. Put his arms round her and whispered that he'd missed her and that he loved her.

At this point Roz had started to cry.

Zoe had found her sitting at Nan's table, sniffing and, tissueless as always, wiping her tears on her sleeve cuff. 'What's up with you?' she'd asked.

'Nobody has ever told me they loved me,' said Roz. 'When I left, nobody said they wanted me back.'

'Didn't we?' said Zoe. 'I thought you knew that. Didn't Matthew tell you?'

'No,' said Roz. 'I'd have come if someone said they wanted me. I just thought you all got on without me. You had your life. Jamie his. And, in his funny way, Matthew his.' She wiped her cheeks again. The screen in front of her was blurred. 'Do you know,' she confessed, 'my whole life, nobody has ever said they loved me. Except Nan.'

'Oh,' Zoe wailed. 'That's tragic. You're likeable enough. Lovable.' She paused. 'I love you.'

'Don't say that because you're sorry for me. Not if you don't mean it.'

'I do. Well, maybe I don't.' Zoe wasn't sure. 'Yes. I think I do, deep down. In a daughterly sort of way. The way you do love your mother. I could get to love you more.' A pause. She wasn't sure of what this entailed. 'If you want.'

'I want,' said Roz. She looked embarrassed at being found weeping. Shamed by her confession. 'I think. Probably.' Then, what the hell, admit it. 'Yes. I want.'

❋ ❋ ❋

'What do you want?' asked Frank. 'Don't tell me you don't know. You do. I know you do.'

'I want,' said Pam, 'to go across America in a camper van. I want to see the Arizona desert. And sleep in motels. And drink coffee in the morning with the sun shining on the road ahead. I want to see the Grand Canyon and the Rocky Mountains and Venice Beach and stand with my feet in the ocean. I want to eat apple pie and . . . everything. I want everything.'

Frank rubbed her back. 'We can't do that. What about the children?'

'We'll take them with us, of course. I'm not going without them.'

'What about school?'

'We can take books with us. Get them from their teachers. They can skip a year. We can do this.'

'We can't afford it.'

'We can sell the house. Put what money we don't need in the bank. When we come back we can buy a business. A bed and breakfast. A market garden. Breed camels. Something we can do together.'

'What if it fails? What if we fail?'

'Frank,' Pam almost yelled. 'It doesn't matter if we fail. As long as we fail together.'

At this, Roz had put her head on Nan's table and sobbed.

Zoe watched, not knowing what to do. 'I said I love you. Really I do. I've come to love you to bits. You're just the same sort of mess as me.'

But Roz just cried. 'I know what I should've done. It's just come to me.'

Zoe had hung back. She should go to Roz. Touch her. Tell her everything was all right. But she couldn't quite bring herself to do it. She wrung her hands in dismay, shrugged, almost hopped. A balletic bewilderment. 'What? What should you have done?'

'Made demands. It's what feasible people do. I just never thought of it till a second ago.'

CHAPTER THIRTY-FOUR

'I think,' said Zoe, 'that I have led a charmed life.'

Will sipped his pint, rolled his eyes. 'A few weeks ago you were complaining that your life had been ruined.' Zoe. You never knew what was coming next.

'I didn't see things clearly,' said Zoe. 'Now I know it's charmed.'

She had decided this only ten minutes ago, walking alone along the dark street leading to this neutral meeting place Will had selected. Listening to the click of her heels against damp winter pavement, and the sound of her own breathing, she had stilled the fear within her that silent dark streets always brought by reminding herself of happy times.

She'd been at it all day. It had been advised in her horoscope. *Try to think well of people you have fallen out with. Remember the good times. This is a day that should be spent building hope.* Zoe had taken this advice on board with her usual enthusiasm. Good times, she mused, rummaging through her past, her childhood. At first it was a blank.

Then she remembered. Herself at three in red wellies, cracking icy puddles in the park. Hacking at them with her heel. Holding Roz's hand. And Roz joining in. Jumping on thin ice. Chill on their faces. Then, at eight, ploughing through the water in the swimming pool, water up her nose, in her eyes, face screwed with effort, limbs flailing. Roz holding her chin. Then not holding her chin, shouting, 'You're away. On your own. You're swimming.' She remembered that. A glorious ten seconds before she sank. Gasping.

The floodgates opened and other times came back. Picnics. Birthday parties, where Roz had put plastic spiders through the jelly. Bath times. Pillow fights. Hide and seek in the garden. Sand pies at the beach. Turning over huge stones in rock pools, looking for crabs. Squealing when they found them. Her mother, wrapping her into her coat waiting for the bus on chilly days. Taking her tiny frozen hand and putting in into her pocket, entwined with hers. Keeping it cosy. Zoe's childhood. Full of very ordinary delights. But it hadn't been that bad.

Then, scurrying along the street, mind a blank, listening for following footsteps, she was a child again, bold and free, riding the wind on her new mountain bike. A lovely thing, gleaming and new. It filled her heart to come downstairs and see it. She loved that bike. First time she'd taken it out, it rained. Oh, the bike would get wet. Poor bike. It wouldn't know about rain yet. Just out of the shop. It was hard enough learning to live with a new family. It'd be missing the other bikes it had left behind. Zoe had taken off her anorak and draped it over the handle bars to keep it dry and cosy. Wheeled it home, patting it. Telling it they'd soon be there. Not to worry, she'd rub it dry with a towel, soon as they arrived.

She remembered arriving home, bike dry. She was soaked to the skin. 'But it's a bike,' Roz exclaimed. 'It's meant to get wet. That's its job.'

Zoe had sobbed that it was still young, and didn't know about rain. It needed drying right away. Whilst Jamie mocked, Roz had dumped her in a hot bath. Made her hot chocolate, and given the bike a rub-down.

Zoe stopped. Her mother, she wasn't a bad old bat, she thought. As mums go, she'd do. There were worse.

Now, after making her usual dramatic entrance, sweeping in, velvet coat floating round her, not looking at any of the dozen or so men who sat at the bar, looking at her, she sat in the pub next to Will. 'Funny place to pick,' she said.

'Used to hang out here in my youth. They never asked my age.'

'Wish I'd known about it.' Zoe looked round. It was seedy, but unthreateningly so. Worn wooden floor, beer-stained. It had seen a bit of life, that floor. A pockmarked darts board. Pictures of

Gene Vincent and Chuck Berry on the wall. Seats caved in, bum-shaped. She took a sip of the gin and tonic Will had waiting for her. No ice, no lemon. Not in a bar like this.

'I was drinking myself senseless here whilst you were having your charmed life.'

'Yes,' agreed Zoe. 'Charmed.'

Across the bar a fat man walked to the piano. Ancient thing with two brass chandeliers each side of the front. He opened it. Gave a swift boogie riff before thumping into some old Jerry Lewis.

'Charmed.' Zoe raised her voice above the music. 'I mean, look at me.' She turned to smile at Will.

His heart did things he didn't want it to. 'I see you. You are beautiful. Though I wish you weren't.'

'Why not?'

'I think life's always easier for beautiful people.'

'We suffer,' said Zoe. 'I have suffered. And survived. That's what I mean – charmed. Think what could have happened to me. Those wild days. Moving from pub to pub, drinking vodka and cider mix. Smoking dope. Picking up boys. I could've been raped. But I wasn't. I took E and anything I could get my hands on. I could have become addicted. But I'm not. I could've ended up goodness knows where. But I ended up with you. I could've got pregnant . . .'

'You did get pregnant,' Will pointed out. Zoe was always on the cusp of female lunacy. But he'd been weeks without it. He missed it.

This blunt fact did not stop Zoe. She'd had a charmed life for sure. 'But it was with you. And we had Toby. And he's lovely. See, charmed.'

'But you didn't have Toby with me,' said Will.

Zoe stopped enthusing. 'You know that?'

'Yeah. I guessed it. Doesn't stop me loving him. I still want him. I've changed his nappies. Helped him to walk and talk. Held his hand in the park. Taken him to school. I won't give him up without a fight.'

'I don't want a fight,' said Zoe.

'Neither do I.'

'I just want the flat and Toby.'

'Looks like we got a fight.' Will drank his beer and did not look at her. It pained him to look at her. He loved her. And he had betrayed her with her mother. He appeased his guilt, telling himself he'd been lonely. And so was she. He'd only wanted some comfort. And so did she. A shag. And so did she. It had come to nothing. But the thought, the willingness had been there. He took another drink of his beer. He was already three pints up. Was filled with a strange and disturbing melancholy. It didn't upset him. He almost enjoyed it.

The shag with Roz that he hadn't had would have been fabulous. Knowing that it would have been fabulous was almost as good as, if not even better than, having it. But he didn't want to look at Zoe. The three pints up were pressing on his bladder. Looking at Zoe would mean composing his face. Not letting the need for a pee and his love for her show. Life for three quarters of an hour, the beer, the just sitting, waiting for Zoe, had been relaxing. Uncomplicated. Now there was this. The complex femaleness of her. And he would not look at her face. He loved that face. Every inch of it. It was his world.

'I need another,' Zoe said, waving her empty glass at him.

He fetched her a double.

Zoe drank and stared. And sucked on a Marlboro. The booze mellowed her. This is who I am, she thought. Where I am. Here. I should've done my nails. They're all chipped. Will, she thought. I will find nobody better. He loves me. Cares for me. I haven't eaten today. Listen to the gin talking. Do I care for anything? Do I even care for me? She was drunk.

The fat man, threadbare sweatshirt barely covering his belly, intriguing crack of bum and waistband of somewhat overly laundered underpants showing as he sat on the piano stool, launched into a thunderous version of 'Feelings'. Stopped halfway through and announced he needed a slash. He'd be back.

Will sipped his beer and watched. He didn't know what got into him. He stood up, crossed to the piano. Sat down. Played 'Feelings'. A song he loathed. But he played with all his heart. Everything he had. There were only about fifteen people in the bar, but they stopped. Everything stopped. Will played. And the fat man came back.

'Fuck are you doing at my piano?'

'Just playing,' said Will.

'That's my piano. I play it. Nobody else.'

Will stopped. He looked down at the keys. At his fingers.

'Bugger off,' said the man. 'Get the fuck out of here. Who the fuck d'you think you are? That's my song.'

'Don't you think you're overreacting?' asked Will, mildly. He was beer-mellow, and losing the one he loved.

'I'm not overreacting. I'm telling you to fuck off. Get off the stool. Get your fingers off my piano.'

'OK, OK,' said Will. Standing up. 'But listen,' and he meant this kindly. And he'd been wishing for a moment like this since that day in the bookshop when Marianne had offered him life options. 'Just because someone played a tune better than you, there's no need to behave like this. Your whole life isn't falling apart.'

'Are you talking to me? You taking the piss?' The fat piano-player took a step nearer Will.

'No,' said Will. 'No. Listen to me. Music belongs to everybody. But there's more to life.' He launched into Marianne's words of wisdom. 'Which would you rather? To have written "Feelings"? Or to make love to this fabulous person? You have one night. Outside, by a lonely lake, with the water whispering nearby, and the sound of a nightjar singing in the trees overhead.'

'Cheeky shite,' said the fat man. He stepped closer. Head back. One swift movement. He nutted Will.

Will slumped forward. Grunting. Holding his nose. Blood pouring on to his hands. He made noises of agony. He thought he was going to be sick. He looked up. The room was swimming and moving. The pain was everywhere. In his head, his nose, thrumming in his ears. Jaw slack, blood searing down his jacket and shirt. He looked round. Where was Zoe? She was moving in on Will's attacker. Handbag poised. 'You bastard. You shite.' She hit the man, and hit him again and again. Handbag flailing. Stilettoed feet kicking. 'How dare you? Fucking bully.'

Will lurched to the loo. He washed his face. Water, running bloody, rushing round the sink, down the plug. He was still making noises. 'Uuuh, aaaahh, urgh . . . fuck. Oh God almighty fuck . . .'

He peed. Groaning. Then, mustering his courage, lurched from the loo. Across the bar. He was not to escape easily. The piano-player caught his arm as he stumbled towards the door.

'You must fuckin' think I'm stupid.'

'No,' said Will. Nasally.

'I'm not king of the bar quiz for nuthin'. I know things. A nightjar doesn't sing, you cunt. They croak. Stupid sound.' He croaked. A rasping demonstration. It sounded not unlike Marianne's voice. A throat-scouring attempt at song.

Will could only say, 'Uuh. Is that so?' And stumbled on. Christ, he thought. Marianne. Bloody hell. She was taking the piss. Some fucking guardian angel. She knew.

Into the night, at last, the stagger and sway from bar to door seemed endless. The chill and the dark. So soothing. 'Don't come back, you poncy shite,' someone called.

Zoe was waiting. She cradled his head. Kissed him. 'That was wonderful. That was so wonderful. A whispering lake. A nightjar singing. That's beautiful.'

Will did not tell her about the croak. Nor did he confess that the words weren't his. Marianne owed him.

She led him back up the street. He leaned on her. 'Let's go home,' she said.

'I got nutted,' Will said.

'I don't care. It was wonderful.'

Will knew it. Just *knew* it. They'd go home. To bed. Make love, and it would be rapturous. Best shag ever. Zoe's legs wrapped round him. They'd be one. He'd become her. She him. One. Moving. They'd come together. The swoon of it. Passion. Fall back, exhausted. Dripping sweat. He'd have a bandage on his nose. It would throb now he'd rejoined the living. Zoe would spread herself. Arms, legs. 'Will,' she'd sigh, voice husky with sex, eyes orgasmic. 'I told you I'd had a charmed life.'

Fuck it. He'd do it. Who could resist it?

CHAPTER THIRTY-FIVE

'I'm back,' called Pam. She dropped her case in her hall and went into the living room. Frank followed, jingling the car keys. Pam's breath smelled slightly of the white wine she'd had when they stopped at a pub on the way home. She was smiling.

Sammy rushed to her, leapt into her arms. She held him. Smelled his hair and his neck. He smelled of being Sammy. Simon gave her a shy, uncomfortable smile. Susan walked out of the room. Ran upstairs, slammed her bedroom door.

'Oh dear,' said Pam. 'Someone's not speaking to me.' Still holding Sammy, she turned to Simon. 'Am I to be forgiven? I still love you, you know.'

Simon still smiled, the shy, uncomfortable smile.

Susan stayed in her room for two hours. Then Pam went up to her. She tapped gently on the door. 'Susan?'

Silence.

'Susan?'

'Go away. I hate you,' snapped Susan.

Pam opened the door. Slowly slid her head round into the room. 'I'm sure that's not true.'

'It is. It is.' Susan shook with spite and rage. 'I hate you. You abandoned me. I needed you. Where were you when I took my swimming certificate? Where were you when I nearly had pneumonia?'

'You had pneumonia?' Pam was shocked. Guilty.

'Nearly. A bad flu. It could've developed into pneumonia.'

'I see,' said Pam. Still guilty. She would not gain forgiveness easily. If at all. 'Well, thank goodness you're all right.'

'I could've died and you wouldn't care.'

'Oh, I would. I'd care very much.'

'I'd've been lying dead. Stretched out. And nobody would even have noticed.' Tears now. Susan was dying a tragic death.

'They would. They would,' Pam assured her. Tears from her eyes, too.

'I'd miss the school dance. I wouldn't ever meet Posh Spice. Sammy would have my room.'

'No. No,' said Pam. She sank on to the bed. This forgiveness business was wearing.

'Nobody would miss me,' wailed Susan.

'They would,' said Pam. 'Really. I know how you feel. Nobody noticed me. Nobody knew I was here. I felt just like you.'

Susan stopped crying. Dabbed her eyes. Face shiny, lips trembling. 'You? You felt that? But of course nobody would notice you. You're the mother.'

Time, thought Pam. Give it time. She'll be there one day. 'Guess what,' she said. 'We're all going off to America. In a camper van. See the sights. New York. San Francisco.'

Ronnie returned to work. He'd lost weight. He'd worried about first entering the office. The looks. Everyone knew. He'd lost the plot for a while. Tipped over the edge. Gone bananas. He turned up early, at half past seven. It was best he was sitting behind his desk when everyone else arrived. That way he wouldn't have to cross the room with everyone looking at him.

He flicked through copies of the magazine he'd missed. Then caught up with the Beseleys. The bickering. Pam had gone all stroppy. This wasn't good. Where was the cosiness? The family fun? Pam had left home. He looked up. Thought about this. Noticed the letters page. Frank had gone after Pam. That was nice. He liked that. That Roz had a touch. Of course, he'd always known that. Wasn't it him who'd suggested her for the Beseleys?

It was overcast when the Beseleys shut the door and walked down the path to the taxi.

'America or bust,' said Simon.

'You bet,' said Pam.

Ronnie nodded. Fresh start. Lovely. Of course Roz would know all about things like that. He'd known her for years. But, reading this, he felt he hardly knew her at all. There was so much more to her. Why hadn't he seen that? She was a woman of the world. Been around, seen a thing or three. She'd probably been one of those free-thinking hippy types when she was younger. There was a Scottish lilt in her voice. A Celt, mystic, imaginative.

He'd never visited her at home, but now imagined her living in an ornate flat. Persian rugs hanging on the walls. Plants, lush and nurtured, on the shelves. The room she worked in would be painted a rich plum colour, white cornices. She'd sip espresso and mineral water whilst she worked. And she'd work all hours. She'd have opinions, but wouldn't force them on others. Her opinions would all have been born out of experience. She'd have had lovers, many, many lovers. There was a wicked warmth about her. Knowing, she was knowing. Humorous. A rich, throaty laugh. Dark, deep eyes. Stare into them and you'd see the pain, the ache this woman had known. Yes, that was the sort of person the Beseleys needed. A woman of the world. That Willa who'd written them before had no idea about the trials and troubles of modern living. She'd tucked herself away in that terrible cottage. But Roz – Roz was wonderful. A real woman. He sighed. He could adore a woman like Roz. Why hadn't he noticed her before?

He phoned her. 'Ah, Roz. Lovely to hear you.'

'Ronnie,' she said. 'How are you?'

'Well. And getting better since I've read what you've done with the Beseleys.'

Roz smiled.

'I trust,' said Ronnie, 'that you are racing on with new adventures for them.'

'Oh, I am,' said Roz. She wasn't.

'We wouldn't want to lose the momentum, as it were,' said Ronnie.

'No,' said Roz.

'I can look forward to lots more episodes, then?' asked Ronnie.

'Um,' said Roz.

'We will, of course, negotiate a new rate.'

'Well,' said Roz.

'We're not going to have to put the fate of the Beseleys into fresh hands, are we? I don't think they'd like that,' said Ronnie. 'They like you.'

Roz let out a slow breath. It wasn't that she wanted to continue writing the Beseleys; more she didn't want them to fall into someone else's hands. She found she cared about them. They'd grown on her. 'No,' she said. 'You won't have to put them into fresh hands. I'll carry on with them.' Little pause. 'I don't suppose there's any chance of me going to America? You know, with them? Research?'

Long pause from Ronnie. 'I don't think so. Budgets, you know. We will, naturally, send you holiday brochures at no expense to yourself.' He smiled.

'Well,' said Roz. 'Thanks for that.'

'Good,' said Ronnie. Can't wait for the next episode.' He rang off.

Claire removed Matthew's tie. She carefully undid the knot, pushed his collar up, draped the tie back round his neck and tied a proper knot. 'There, that's better.' She fixed his collar, tidied his jacket and declared him ready to meet the world. 'Smile.'

He didn't.

Claire put a finger on each corner of his mouth and pushed it up. 'That's how you do it. Smile, damn you.'

He grimaced.

'I don't know. I don't understand you. You cop a glimpse of your mother in bed with another man just after your dad dies. And you go into yourself.'

'Well,' he said, defensively.

'And are you going to continue with this isolation? Or are you going to start communicating?'

'Probably.' He wasn't committing himself to anything.

'Nan,' she said. 'Nan?' She clapped her hands, as Will had done. 'It's lovely. I love it. She had secrets. It's wonderful.'

'It is?' asked Matthew.

'It is,' said Claire. 'You had a wonderful mother.'

'I did?'

'Yes.'

'You're so lucky,' said Claire. 'I just love Nan.'

'You do?' said Matthew.

'I do,' Claire told him. 'But this business of not passing on Roz's gifts, that wasn't good.' She wagged her finger.

'Suppose not,' said Matthew. 'But I thought she had it all. I thought she was living some wild life.' He looked at his hands. 'I was jealous.'

'I know,' said Claire. 'No need. She was miserable and guilty. So,' smiling slightly, 'that's fine. The woman's a vandal. Now we are going to the golf club dance. And you will smile. You will take other men's wives to the floor. Dance with them. You'll buy drinks. And you will chat amiably with people.'

'What about?' Matthew was worried about this.

'About the weather. Your game. Our holidays next year. The price of gas. What was on telly. Anything.' She gripped his shoulders, shoved them down. 'Loosen up. Relax. This is meant to be fun. We are meant to be enjoying ourselves.'

'I can't do that.'

Claire lightly smacked his cheek. 'You can and you will.'

It was a grey day when the Beseleys got on the plane. Average British weather, thought Pam. Susan was whining. But whining with panache, Pam thought.

'You are ruining my life. I'll never recover from this. I'll be a year behind my friends at school. You don't know what you are doing to me.'

'Yes I do,' said Pam.

'Patricia's having a sleepover party and I'll miss it. And *ER*, I won't see that.'

'You wouldn't anyway,' said Pam. 'It's after your bedtime.'

'I want the window seat,' Susan whined again.

Simon sheepishly got up and moved over. Susan plonked into it.

'Now,' said Pam, 'we are going to America and we're going to enjoy it. Do you hear me? Enjoy, or answer to me.'

She put Sammy in his seat. Strapped him in. Sat down next to Frank and took his hand.

Zoe moved back into the flat with Will. Mornings Toby would come to her, climb into bed beside her. Lie, putting off the moment he'd have to get into his school uniform and wrestle with his laces. He didn't understand laces. Why did things have to tie?

Zoe would pull the duvet over his head and say, 'Where's Toby? We've lost Toby.' Then she'd whisk the duvet back and cry, 'Oh, there he is.' Toby would giggle. Silly game; they'd played it when he was little. But he still loved it. He had a beautiful smile, Zoe thought. He was lovely. He was going to be handsome. She could see that. Handsome and slightly shy, endearingly awkward. But what a sense of humour. Perhaps he'd be a great comic actor. She should find out about drama schools.

After Will had left for work, and Toby for school, Zoe would sit in the living room drinking coffee, contemplating her future. She might phone Connie. That was something. She might start her own furniture-renovating firm. She might go to university. Study . . . what? Anthropology? English literature? Drama? She could do anything.

A few nights ago, coming home from the pub, filled with enthusiasm and gin, Zoe, in her six-inch heels, had run the length of the street shouting, 'I can do anything!' Velvet coat flying out behind her.

Will followed. Zoe's gusto delighted and depressed him. It swept him along. And it made him feel inadequate. The sex since she came back had been excellent. Make-up sex. Best sex. Soon they'd be at it again. Her legs wrapped round him. Unless, of course, she wanted to go on top. Which she did often. Or maybe she'd want him to take her from behind. Which he quite liked. There were other positions. Zoe had bought a magazine, which they consulted. He got grumpy. She giggled.

Still, the bruising around his nose was going down. He could breathe again.

CHAPTER THIRTY-SIX

A week after New Year, Fred came to see Roz. It was evening. Jamie and Angela were out.

'How long have you been back?' he asked.

'A week. More,' she told him.

'And you didn't phone?'

'No.'

'Why not?'

'I didn't like to.'

'Why ever not?'

'You know. I shouted "Will" at the wrong moment. Quite decidedly the wrong moment. A wronger moment you couldn't imagine.'

'I noticed. How is Will, by the way?'

'Fine,' Roz told him. 'He and Zoe are getting back together.'

'Ah,' said Fred. 'That's good?'

'Good for Toby. Good for Zoe. I don't know about Will. He's in for a time of drama and dreams. Zoe's a dreamer. Except she dreams other people's dreams.'

'Leave them to it,' advised Fred.

'I will,' said Roz.

She fetched a bottle of wine. They drank by the fire, exchanged news. She told him about Mull. Edited highlights. She did not tell him about Will.

'I imagined you had someone else,' she admitted.

'Why?'

'It sort of got into my head. She was lovely, though. She was tall, witty, young. I'm sure you would have liked her.'

'Excellent,' he said. 'Did she have a name?'

'Mel, I decided.'

'Ah. I quite like Mel. Though not really my type.' He reached out, touched her cheek. 'I got it into my head you had a crush on this Will person.'

'Really.' She drank. 'He's Zoe's.'

'So there's nothing between you?'

'Nothing,' she said. Did not look at him. Like Nan, she would have her secrets. She looked across at him, smiled.

He smiled back. 'Good,' he said.

He was such a nice man. She wondered what had got into her. Some sort of delayed adolescence, she supposed. Zoe and Jamie had worked out the remnants of their youth with her; maybe it was catching. He reached for her. They sat entwined, saying little, till Jamie and Angela returned, and Fred decided it was time to go.

She walked him to his car. Shivered.

'You should have put on a coat,' he told her. Took off his jacket and slipped it round her. Held her hand. Looked at it. 'Nice hand.' He squeezed it. 'Resilient. I hope you will be calling me soon in the middle of the night demanding a cuddle.'

'I could do that,' Roz said.

Leaving home was wonderful. That moment of freedom. It was like running along the street, arms spread, jumping in the air, clicking your heels. None of which Roz had ever actually done. Though she had in her heart. Emotional heel-clicking. Then there was getting back together again. The warmth, the smiles, the spurt of newsy conversation. And for her, after years, the forgiveness. Of sorts. From Zoe.

Wonderful.

There were, Roz thought, all sorts of wonderful. But for now, two would be fine to be getting along with.

They reached Fred's car. She dipped her hands into his pockets. Found an envelope and pulled it out. It was addressed to her.

'A letter to me,' she told him.

'My God.' He looked at it. It was his note, drawn weeks ago, that had lain forgotten in his jacket. 'I thought I'd posted that.' *To Roz*, it said, *who I adore*.

'What is it?' she wanted to know.

He got into his car. Rolled down the window. Started the engine. Drove off. Stopped. Stuck his head out to shout at Roz.

'Open it and see.'

ISLA DEWAR

Giving Up on Ordinary

When Megs became a cleaner, she didn't realise that
if people looked at her a cleaner would be all they
saw. Megs has as full a life as the people she does for,
Mrs Terribly Clean Pearson or Mrs Oh-Just-Keep-It-
Above-The Dysentery-Line McGhee. She's the mother
of three children and still mourning the death of a
son; she enjoys a constant sparring match with her
mother; she drinks away her troubles with Lorraine,
her friend since Primary One; and she sings the blues
in a local club.

Megs has been getting by. But somehow that's not
enough any more. It's time Megs gave up on being
ordinary . . .

'Explosively funny and chokingly poignant . . .
extraordinary' *Scotland on Sunday*

'Observant and needle sharp . . . entertainment with
energy and attack' *The Times*

'A remarkably uplifting novel, sharp and funny'
Edinburgh Evening News

0 7472 5550 4

review

ISLA DEWAR

It Could Happen To You

Rowan has always cherished an ambition to travel. She didn't just leave the small Scottish town where she grew up; she fled from it as fast as she could. Now she's become expert at metropolitan living; she could walk by a million faces and not notice any of them. And her dream is almost within her grasp.

When Rowan does start packing her bags, she has to find room for one very unexpected item. And she's headed not for exotic distant shores but back to Scotland. There, she feels at first like nothing more than a source of good gossip. But as she discovers that no one is quite who she thought they were, Rowan begins to see that home could be where she'll find what she was looking for after all . . .

'Enchanting' *Options*

'Few writers are so good at making the reader empathise . . . Rowan is a delight' *Scotland on Sunday*

0 7472 5551 2

review